I0608674

The Collected Papers of Sherlock Holmes

Volume VIII – Documents

(16 Holmes Adventures and a Poem)

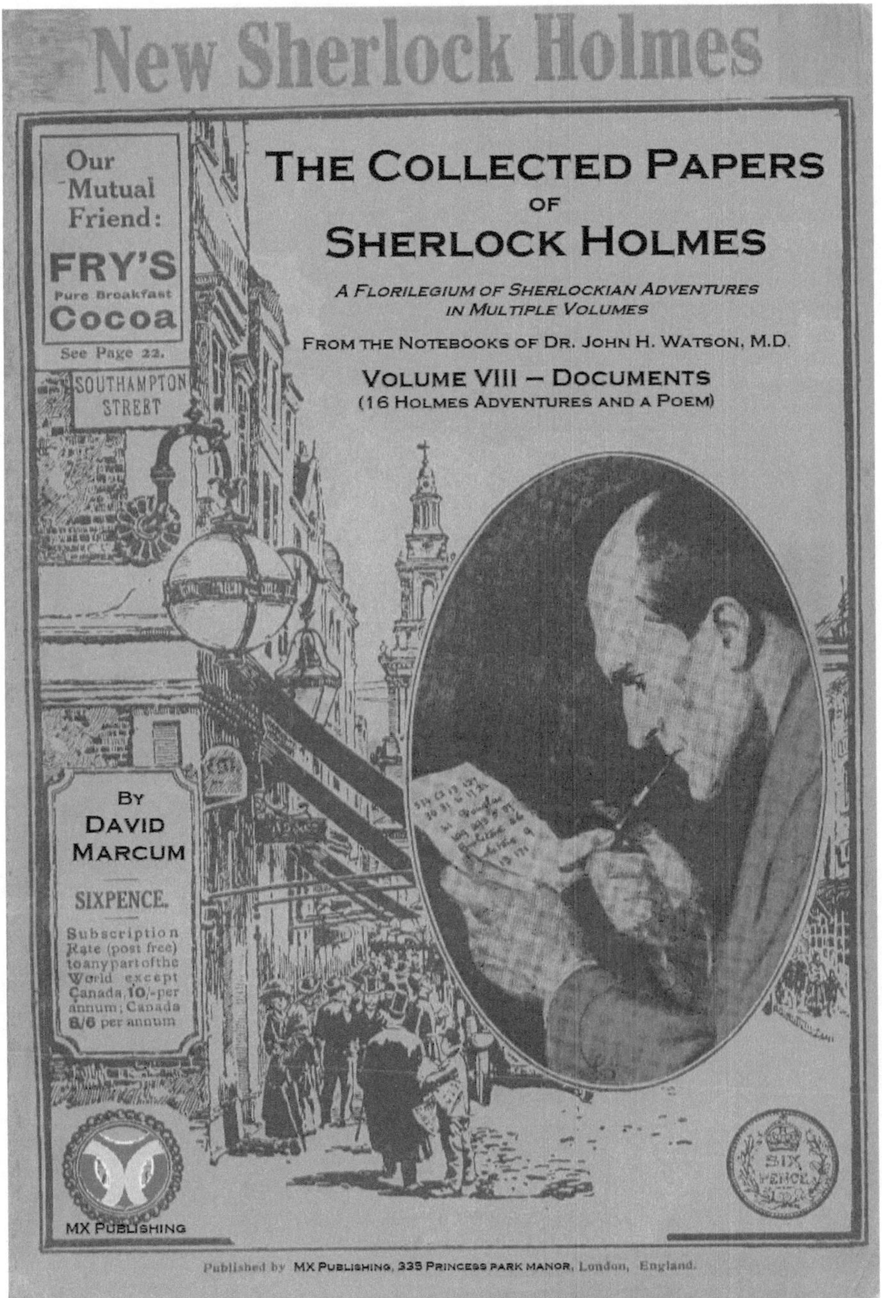
New Sherlock Holmes
Our Mutual Friend: FRY'S Pure Breakfast Cocoa
See Page 22.
SOUTHAMPTON STREET
THE COLLECTED PAPERS OF SHERLOCK HOLMES
A FLORILEGIUM OF SHERLOCKIAN ADVENTURES IN MULTIPLE VOLUMES
FROM THE NOTEBOOKS OF DR. JOHN H. WATSON, M.D.
VOLUME VIII – DOCUMENTS
(16 HOLMES ADVENTURES AND A POEM)
BY DAVID MARCUM
SIXPENCE.
Subscription Rate (post free) to any part of the World except Canada, 10/- per annum; Canada 8/6 per annum
MX PUBLISHING
SIX PENCE
Published by MX PUBLISHING, 335 PRINCESS PARK MANOR, London, England.

Copyright David Marcum 2025
ALL RIGHTS RESERVED

The right of the individuals listed on the Copyright Information page to be identified as the authors of this work has been asserted by them in accordance with the Copyright, Designs, and Patents Act 1998.

All rights reserved. No reproduction, copy, or transmission of this publication may be made without express prior written permission. No paragraph of this publication may be reproduced, copied, or transmitted except with express prior written permission or in accordance with the provisions of the Copyright Act 1956 (as amended). Any person who commits any unauthorised act in relation to this publication may be liable to criminal prosecution and civil claims for damage.

All characters appearing in this work are fictitious or used fictitiously. Except for certain historical personages, any resemblance to real persons, living or dead, is purely coincidental. The opinions expressed herein are those of the authors and not of MX Publishing.

"Watson's Descendants" ©2021 by Nicholas Meyer. All Rights Reserved.
First publication, original to this collection. Printed by permission of the author.

Illustrations for "The Bellmaker's Boon" and "The Crofter's Curious Demise"
by Thaddeus Tuffentesamer ©2025 – All Rights Reserved

ISBN Hardback 978-1-80424-775-4
ISBN Paperback 978-1-80424-776-1
AUK ePub ISBN 978-1-80424-777-8
AUK PDF ISBN 978-1-80424-778-5

Published by
MX Publishing
335 Princess Park Manor, Royal Drive,
London, N11 3GX
www.mxpublishing.co.uk

David Marcum can be reached at:
thepapersofsherlockholmes@gmail.com

Cover design by Brian Belanger
www.belangerbooks.com and *www.redbubble.com/people/zhahadun*

Internal illustrations by Sidney Paget

CONTENTS

Forewords

Documents

Sources

- "Mission (Some Sort of Sonnet) – *A Poem*" *The MX Book of New Sherlock Holmes Stories – Part XLVII: Occupants of the Canonical Realm (1890-1898)*
- "The Indiscriminate Paragraph" *The MX Book of New Sherlock Holmes Stories – Part L: The True Mr. Sherlock Holmes – England's Greatest Hero (1889-1996)*
- "The Bellmaker's Boon" *The Denarian Adventures of Sherlock Holmes – Volume II*
- "The Swapped Names of the Savior" *The MX Book of New Sherlock Holmes Stories – Part XLVIII: Occupants of the Canonical Realm (1899-1924)*
- "The Debt to Jabez Wilson" *The MX Book of New Sherlock Holmes Stories – Part XLVII: Occupants of the Canonical Realm (1890-1898)*
- "The X-Marked Boxes" *The MX Book of New Sherlock Holmes Stories – Part XLVI: Occupants of the Canonical Realm (1861-1889)*
- "The Clue of the Undamaged Stones" *The MX Book of New Sherlock Holmes Stories – Part LII: The True Mr. Sherlock Holmes – England's Greatest Hero (1902-1923)*
- "Soiled Doves" *Sherlock Holmes and the Great Lady Detectives*
- "The Uncle's Cryptic Clues" *The MX Book of New Sherlock Holmes Stories – Part LI: The True Mr. Sherlock Holmes – England's Greatest Hero (1897-1901)*
- "The Adventure of the Flagitious Sire" *The MX Book of New Sherlock Holmes Stories – Part XLIX: The True Mr. Sherlock Holmes – England's Greatest Hero (1880-1888)*
- "The Morning Encounter with the Velocipede Racer" *The Denarian Adventures of Sherlock Holmes – Volume I*
- "The Man with the Stolen Luck" *Steel True, Blade Straight – 2024-2025 Annual*
- "The Clue of the Crested Ring" *Sherlock Holmes: A Year of Mystery 1887*
- "The Bishop's Painful Path" *Sherlock Holmes: A Year of Mystery 1888*
- "The Crofter's Curious Demise" *The Denarian Adventures of Sherlock Holmes – Volume I*
- "The Curious Business at the Princess's Theatre" *Sherlock Holmes Takes the Stage – Volume II*
- "The Old Tin Dispatch Box" *The MX Book of New Sherlock Holmes Stories – Part LII: The True Mr. Sherlock Holmes – England's Greatest Hero (1902-1923)*

These additional adventures are contained in

The Collected Papers of Sherlock Holmes

Volume I – Tales

(9 Short Stories and a Novel)

The Papers of Sherlock Holmes (9 Short Stories)

The Adventure of the Least Winning Woman
The Adventure of the Treacherous Tea
The Singular Affair at Sissinghurst Castle
The Adventure of the Second Chance
The Haunting of Sutton House
The Adventure of the Missing Missing Link
The Affair of The Brother's Request
The Adventure of the Madman's Ceremony
The Adventure of the Other Brother

and

Sherlock Holmes and A Quantity of Debt (A Novel)

Volume II – Records

(5 Short Stories and a Novel)

Sherlock Holmes – Tangled Skeins

The Mystery at Kerrett's Rood
The Curious Incident of the Goat-Cart Man
The Matter of Boz's Last Letter
The Tangled Skein at Birling Gap
The Gower Street Murder

and

Sherlock Holmes and The Eye of Heka (A Novel)

Volume III – Accounts

(22 Holmes Adventures)

The Adventure of the Pawnbroker's Daughter
The Problem of the Holy Oil
The Trusted Advisor
An Actor and a Rare One
The Unnerved Estate Agent
The Cat's Meat Lady of Cavendish Square

(Continued on the next page . . . .)

The Hammerford Will Business
The Farraway Street Lodger
November, 1888
Some Notes Upon the Matter of John Douglas
The Adventure of the Old Brownstone
The Doctor's Tale
The Treasures of the Gog Magog Hills
The Inner Temple Intruder
The Cambridge Codes
The Adventure of the Retired Beekeeper
An Actual Treasure
The Manipulative Messages
The Civil Engineer's Discovery
The Girl at the Northumberland Hotel (A Simple Solution)
The Austrian Certificates
The Adventure of the Home Office Baby

Volume IV – Narratives
(19 Holmes Adventures)

The London Wheel
The Two Different Women
The Coffee House Girl
The Affair of the Regressive Man
The Gordon Square Discovery
The Secret in Lowndes Court
The Sunderland Tragedies
No Good Deed
The Dorset Square Business
The Brook Street Mystery
The Colchester Experiment
The Keeper's Tale
The Village on the Cliff
The Tuefel Murders
The Unpleasant Affair in Clipstone Street
The Lincoln Street Minister
The Tea Merchant's Dilemma
The Dowser's Discovery
The Triangle of Death

(Continued on the next page . . . .)

Volume V – Chronicles
(20 Holmes Adventures)

The Stolen Relic
The Helverton Inheritance
The Carroun Document
The Reappearance of Mr. James Phillimore
The Keadby Cross
The Rhayader Affair
The Cliddesden Questions
The Affair of the Mother's Return
The Painting in the Parlour
The Two Bullets
The Coombs Contrivance
The True Account of the Bushell Street Killing
The Polmayne Puzzles
The Curious Cardboard Boxes
The Bizarre Affair of the Octagon House
The Peculiar Persecution of Mr. Druitt
The Service for the American Colonel
The Rescue at Ypres
The Problem of the Hindhead Minister
The Edinburgh Bankers

Volume VI – Muniments
(21 Holmes Adventures)

The Fashionably Dressed Girl
The Christmas Ghost of Crailloch Taigh
The Curious Affair of the Temporal Traveler
The Father Christmas Brigade
Some Additional Notes Regarding Mr. Melas
The Vodou Drum
The Tragic Affair at the Millennium Manor
The Canterbury Manifesto
The Noel Street Oracle
The Well-Lit Séance
The Templarian Tattoo
The Betrayer Moon
The Distasteful Affair of the Minatory Messages
The First Spivey Encounter

(Continued on the next page . . . .)

Volume VII – Annals
(19 Holmes Adventures,
3 Scripts, and a Poem)

Three Sherlockian Scripts

ALSO BY DAVID MARCUM

As author. . . .

- ☐ *The Papers of Sherlock Holmes* (Volumes I and II)
- ☐ *Sherlock Holmes and A Quantity of Debt*
- ☐ *Sherlock Holmes – Tangled Skeins*
- ☐ *Sherlock Holmes and The Eye of Heka*
- ☐ *The Complete Papers of Solar Pons* (Volumes I-VIII - More forthcoming)
- ☐ *The Papers of Solar Pons*
- ☐ *The Further Papers of Solar Pons*
- ☐ *The Singular Papers of Solar Ponds*

As editor . . . .

- ☐ *The MX Book of New Sherlock Holmes Stories* (Volumes I-LII)
- ☐ *Sherlock Holmes: Before Baker Street*
- ☐ *Holmes Away From Home: Adventures from The Great Hiatus* (Volumes I and II)
- ☐ *Sherlock Holmes and Doctor Watson: The Early Adventures* (Volumes I, II, and III)
- ☐ *Sherlock Holmes: Adventures Beyond the Canon* (Volumes I, II, and III)
- ☐ *After the East Wind Blows: World War I and Roaring Twenties Adventures of Sherlock Holmes* (Volumes I, II, and III)
- ☐ *The Nefarious Villains of Sherlock Holmes* (Volumes I and II)
- ☐ *The Detective and the Clergyman: The Adventures of Sherlock Holmes and Father Brown*
- ☐ *The Complete Solar Pons* (by August Derleth – Volumes I-VIII)
- ☐ *The New Adventures of Solar Pons*
- ☐ *The Meeting of the Minds: The Cases of Sherlock Holmes and Solar Pons* (Volumes I and II)
- ☐ *The American Adventures of Solar Pons*
- ☐ *Solar Pons – A Year of Mystery: 1919* (Forthcoming)
- ☐ *Sherlock Holmes in Montague Street* (by Arthur Morrison – Volumes I, II, and III: The Complete Martin Hewitt stories retold as early Sherlock Holmes Adventures)
- ☐ *The Complete Dr. Thorndyke* (by R. Austin Freeman – Volumes I-IX)
- ☐ *The Complete Max Carrados* (by Ernest Bramah – Volumes I and II)
- ☐ *A Proofreader's Adventures of Sherlock Holmes* (by Nick Dunn-Meynell)
- ☐ *The Rediscovered Annals of Sherlock Holmes* (by Terry Golledge)
- ☐ *Tales of Light, Tales of Shadow*, and *Tales of Darkness* (by Tracy J. Revels – Volumes I-III)
- ☐ *Sherlock Holmes and the Scotland Yarders* (by Marcia Wilson – Volumes I-IX)
- ☐ *Sherlock Holmes is Everywhere!* (co-edited with Sonia Fetherston and Derrick Belanger)

• • • •

□

As always, this is for Rebecca and Dan, with all my love

"It's all one case."
by David Marcum

It's all about playing *The Game*.

That's the bottom-line reason behind these stories. And what is *The Game*? For those who don't know, it's reading the Sherlock Holmes stories with the firm belief that he and Watson were *real historical figures*. That Dr. Watson *wrote* the stories, and Sir Arthur Conan Doyle was his *Literary Agent*. That Our Heroes actually *lived* in Baker Street (for a couple of decades, off and on, and *not* forever) and solved real cases for real people, even if names and places and dates were changed and obfuscated to protect the innocent, or maybe because Watson's handwriting was bad, or because of some hidden agenda that the Literary Agent needed to fulfill.

By acknowledging that Holmes and Watson were real, living, breathing, functioning people, then it's a given that were born, lived, and died. (No magic immortal detectives need apply!) And if they were born and lived and died, then these lives occurred across a fixed period. These men aren't Time Lords who can be picked up and dropped into other eras, or supernaturally gifted monster hunters in a world where such things exist, and they cannot be remade into a plethora of completely different people to fit whatever agenda some current reader needs to project upon them.

No, the stories in these books are about the same Sherlock Holmes and Dr. Watson that one finds in the original Canon – those pitifully few sixty stories that were published from 1887 to 1927.

I've enjoyed the notion that Mr. Sherlock Holmes was real from nearly the same time that I discovered him – as a boy of ten in 1975. Before I'd even read many of the Canonical adventures, I found two other books that reinforced this idea: William S. Baring-Gould's biography *Sherlock Holmes of Baker Street* (1962), with its chronology of the events in Holmes's long and amazing life (1854-1957), and also Nicholas Meyer's *The Seven-Per-Cent Solution* (1974), in which Holmes meets historical figures such as Sigmund Freud. How could one read those books, especially at that age, and not be convinced that Holmes was real?

In the decades that have passed since then, my interest in Mr. Holmes has only grown. While I read and collect a great many volumes about my other "book friends", as my son called them when he was small – and there are a great lot of them besides Holmes – I've always had a special interest in the consulting detective in Baker Street and his Boswell. Since obtaining my first Holmes book in 1975, I've managed to collect and read (and create a massively dense chronology for) literally thousands of traditional Canonical adventures. I've worn a deerstalker as my only hat, all year long and everywhere since age nineteen. I've been able to make five extensive Holmes Pilgrimages to England and Scotland (so far), wherein I pretty much visited only Holmes-related sites. So it was probably inevitable that, in 2008, I started writing Holmes adventures.

I'd always wanted to write, all the way back to when I was eight years old and intensely reading about The Three Investigators and The Hardy Boys. Not satisfied with just the official publications, I wanted more new stories too. I spent quite a few Saturdays of my young boyhood tapping away on my dad's typewriter to create new "books".

As I grew, I dabbled with writing little short pieces, mostly humorous, just intended to make family members laugh, because I loved to write, and it always came easily to me. By the late 1980's, I was a U.S. Federal Investigator employed by an obscure government agency, often sent away from home for long periods, conducting investigations that lasted anywhere from five weeks to three months. Once, when I was sent to Albuquerque for several months to conduct extensive field investigations, I impulsively stopped at a local Walmart and bought a hundred-dollar typewriter and a big pack of paper with some of my *per diem* money. (This was the early 1990's – a long time before personal computers or laptops.)

It was there that I sat down for my first real effort at being a writer – and before I departed I'd finished most of a 600-plus page Ludlumesque novel. (One can get a lot of writing done night after night in a bleak hotel room.) The book was coincidentally about a heroic federal investigator – not unlike myself – who stumbled into a vast Russian-led conspiracy in the American southeast where I'm from. I still have that book – *Civil Servants* – stored in my old federal investigator briefcase, pushed underneath my bed. Its plot is mired in the early 1990's when it was written, locked to the aftermath of the Cold War, but it isn't half bad, and it taught me the valuable lesson that other writers also know: *The secret to writing is to put your butt in the chair and do it.*

After that particular trip, I went back home, finished up what was left of my epic adventure novel, and then settled back into writing the occasional short piece for our private amusement – but it was inevitable that at some point I would write a Holmes adventure.

In the mid-1990's, the federal agency where I'd been employed was abruptly eliminated, a victim of the end of the Cold War and a move to reduce the size of government. (After all, the higher-up wise men thought, who needs security now? We won!) Over the next few years, I went back to school and obtained a second degree in Civil Engineering. Then, in 2008 at the start of the Great Recession, I was unexpectedly laid off from my engineering job. With time on my hands, and a desire to try my hand at Sherlockian pastichery, I began writing each morning after the daily job searching was finished.

I ended up with nine Holmes pastiches, written over several weeks, and then . . . I did nothing with them. That's right. Simply satisfied that I'd written them and that they existed, I put them in a binder labeled *The Papers of Sherlock Holmes* and shelved them with the rest of my Holmes Collection, happy with my secret collector's item.

But eventually I began to wish for other Sherlockians to see them. I shared one with a Sherlockian friend here and another one there, and the response was very positive. Finally I became bolder and wanted more people to see them, asking myself: *Why not put them in a real book of my own?*

I communicated about it with a Sherlockian publisher from whom I'd bought books in the past. He immediately offered to publish *The Papers*, and after a great deal of back-and-forth, my first book eventually appeared. For those who have had that experience – Opening the newly delivered carton to see *your book!* – there is nothing like it. It's a satisfaction that cannot easily be described.

That was in 2011. Over the next couple of years, I became aware of MX Publishing. I saw that an acquaintance of mine who'd also had his first book published with the same original publisher as mine had switched to MX, and I reached out to him. He informed me that he was happy to have switched to MX. With that in mind, I sent an email to Steve Emecz, Sherlockian Publisher Extraordinaire – and that was truly life-changing and improving decision.

In 2013, Steve republished my first book, *The Papers of Sherlock Holmes*, and he made the whole experience so painless that I set about writing a Holmes novel, *Sherlock Holmes and A Quantity of Debt.* That same fall, I was making my long-planned first Holmes Pilgrimage to London, and Steve arranged for me to have a book-signing in The Sherlock Holmes Hotel in Baker Street, where I was staying (when not traveling about to Dartmoor, the Sussex Coast, Edinburgh, and other locations). I was able to meet Steve for the first time on that trip, and found him to be one of the nicest, most supportive, and most thoughtful people around – and that hasn't changed a bit.

Jump ahead a little bit: In early 2015, I woke up early from a dream in which I'd edited a Holmes anthology. Instead of rolling over and forgetting the idea, I arose and started thinking about authors whom I admired and that I might want to invite to write stories. I ran the idea by Steve, and he was willing to publish it, so I began sending invitations. I hoped that I might get a dozen stories (at best) for a modest paperback volume. Fearing a lack of response, I kept sending invitations to everyone that I could think of – and then, amazingly, people started signing up. New Sherlock Holmes stories started to arrive in my email in-box – which quickly becomes addictive. More and more authors heard about it – some that I didn't even know about yet – and before we knew it, the little idea had grown into a three-volume hardcover behemoth of over 60 new Holmes stories – *Parts I, II*, and *III* of *The MX Book of New Sherlock Holmes Stories*, the largest collection of its kind ever produced to that point.

Early on, Steve and I had decided that the royalties from the project would go to support the Stepping Stones School for special needs children, located at Undershaw, one of Sir Arthur Conan Doyle's former homes. The books were a smashing success and received a lot of attention, and I was able to go to London in the fall of 2015 for the release party – what turned out to be Holmes Pilgrimage No. 2. There I was able to meet a number of the contributing authors in person – and to my everlasting regret, I was so thrilled that I barely remembered to take any photos!

After I returned home, I began to receive more emails, now asking when the next book was planned – *Good grief! A next book?!?* – and also stating that many authors (both returning and new) wanted to contribute.

I'd had no plans to do any more books, thinking that the first three were lightning in a bottle that couldn't be recaptured . . . but then I realized that the heavy-lifting in terms of decision-making and set-up and formatting and process-building had already occurred, so Steve and I decided to keep going. (I think I said to him "Let's do one more . . . .")

Part IV came out in the spring of 2016 – and after that, more people kept sending stories for *the next books* and wanting to join the party. We came up with the plan to have yearly books. But we received so many stories that it grew to twice a year. We had an un-themed spring collection – the yearly *Annual* – and also a fall collection with a specific theme, such as Christmas adventures, seemingly impossible crimes, Untold Cases, etc. As more and more stories kept rolling in, it became necessary for each season's particular set to grow to multiple simultaneously published volumes. That's how, in just a few short years, we reached 52 volumes.

I decided to finish up the series in Spring 2025. Ten years seemed gook, with 52 volumes and over 1,000 stories from over 200 contributors worldwide. And I turned sixty that year – another milestone.

So far, the books have raised over $165,000 for Undershaw – That's *0.165-Million Dollars*, as I like to point out! – and that will just keep going up!

As part of editing these books, I couldn't let them pass by without adding my own stories – editor's prerogative. Thus, that helped to motivate me to sit my butt in the chair and write more about Mr. Holmes. By way of these books, I've met some really incredible people, including the incomparable Belanger Brothers, Derrick and Brian. Derrick initially contributed short stories, while Brian – a truly gifted artist – became the MX cover artist after the original artist passed away.

At one point, the two Belangers wrote a series of Holmes books for children. Eventually they formed Belanger Books – another amazing Sherlockian publishing venture. Between MX and Belanger Books – both of which cooperate beautifully with one another – the Sherlockian publishing field is amazingly well covered, providing an opportunity for so many people to be Sherlockian pasticheurs when they would otherwise be excluded by those who happily and aggressively seek to squash that aspect of the Sherlockian experience.

In 2016, the Belangers asked me to assemble and edit a Holmes story collection for them. I did, and as it also consisted of traditional and Canonical adventures, and had many of the same authors as in the MX anthologies, I formatted it the same way. After that, I edited another one for them, and another, and those also grew to simultaneously published multiple volumes. This extra editing also served to motivate me to write more Holmes stories for each of those collections as well – because I didn't want those trains leaving without me being on them.

From there, I began to receive invitations to write still more stories for other editors' anthologies and magazines. Along the way I published a couple more of my own books – *Sherlock Holmes – Tangled Skeins* (2015) and *Sherlock Holmes and The Eye of Heka* (2021) – but most of my stories that I wrote over those years remained uncollected within the various anthologies and magazines in which they had originally appeared. All along, I stayed too busy with real life and family and my dream job (as a civil engineer working for my home town's public works department), along with writing more stories and editing various books, to take the time to properly collect them all into my own books.

At some point, I ended up writing my 100th pastiche, (along with over forty pastiches about Solar Pons, "The Sherlock Holmes of Baker Street" – but that's another story and another hero.) In 2021, I had the idea of collecting my uncollected Holmes stories.

The initial five books of *The Complete Papers*, published in 2021, contained 77 of those stories. Volumes VI and VII had 21 and 19 stories respectively. This book has 16 more, and there are still in the pipeline to be published elsewhere. I have a number of other pastiched planned and promised for 2026, so Volume 9 of *The Complete Papers* will hopefully appear in the next year or so . . . *Fingers crossed!*

Many people have sports figures or musicians or actors or (curiously) politicians as heroes. My heroes have always been my book friends and authors – all the way back to when I was eight or nine and wondering about why I couldn't track down satisfying biographical information concerning the brilliant and prolific and mysterious author, Franklin W. Dixon. I've always admired writers for what they accomplish and create while spending great chunks of their lives self-imposed isolation – something which I now understand. And at least if I had to set aside all that time to put my butt in the chair, I've been very fortunate that all of these stories almost told themselves. I almost never outline or plan. Instead, when I write – when I find that it's time for another story – I simply open a blank Word document on the computer and then wait for Watson to begin whispering to me. It's scary, but I trust the process now, and when it works – and it always has so far – there's no feeling quite like it.

Through these stories, I've achieved two important personal goals: In my own small way, I've become a writer, and I've also added to *The Great Holmes Tapestry*, a phrase I coined several years ago to describe the massive collection of narratives about the *true* Holmes and Watson – novels, short stories, radio and television episodes, movies and scripts, comics and fan-fiction, and unpublished manuscripts – that tell the complete and entire course of their lives from beginning to end. The Canon serves as the supporting structure – the wire core of the rope, the heavy steel girders of the skyscraper – but the thousands of traditional post-Canonical pastiches provide essential depth and color, filling in all the spaces around The Canon, and adding important information about The Whole Lives of Our Heroes.

I've long described myself as a missionary for The Church of the Traditional Canonical Holmes, preaching that the bigger picture of both Canon and the traditional pastiches should be seen and supported. This means giving respect and value to additional Holmes adventures, and not just those original sixty because they were the ones that came across the first Literary Agent's desk.

Ross MacDonald – (Real Name: Kenneth Millar, another of my authorial heroes because of his incredible private eye, Lew Archer) – said "*It's all one case.*" In other words, a *Great Tapestry*. He meant that even though he'd written eighteen Archer novels and a number of short stories from the 1940's to the 1970's, they were never meant to stand alone. They were all part of one overall arching story – Lew Archer's story – spanning across multiple narratives.

It's the same with the Holmes adventures – *all* of them, Canon and traditional pastiche, mine and everyone else's. They fit together to tell the *entire* story of Sherlock Holmes, and with the stories in this collection, I'm incredibly proud to have added my own contribution.

* * * * *

"Of course, I could only stammer out my thanks."
– The unhappy John Hector McFarlane, "The Norwood Builder"

At some point during the foreword-writing for the various MX anthologies, I began to use the quote shown above from Mr. McFarlane in regard to *Thank You*'s. It's fitting – I can only stammer out thanks, and never adequately express how grateful I am for all the help and encouragement I've received over the years in all aspects of my life – not just the writing and editing of Sherlock Holmes stories.

First and foremost, I am always overwhelmed at how incredibly fortunate I am to have my wife and son in my life. In all aspects, my wife – nearly 38 years as I write this – is the kindest and wisest and most beautiful person inside and out I know, and she has been there throughout with complete support and encouragement when we went through such things as some terrible jobs and the grind of my returning to school to be an engineer. We have pushed through together, and anything that I can ever accomplish I owe to her. And equally amazing is our son, so incredibly funny and smart, and truly a wonderful person in every way. I enjoy every minute spent with him, and it only gets better. I love you both, and you are everything to me!

Then there are my parents and sister, who put up with me during those first couple of decades – I probably don't even realize how bad that was for them. My parents did everything to encourage me – music lessons leading to a piano scholarship in college, all the books that I could read, and generally anything to help me grow as a person, so that it never occurred to me that I couldn't do whatever I wanted. And my sister was my best friend then, patiently listening as I rambled about whatever interested me. Even then, she probably heard more about Sherlock Holmes than she'd ever bargained for!

Next, I wish to send several huge *Thank You*'s to the following:

- *Steve Emecz* – When I first emailed Steve from out of the blue back in 2013, I was interested in MX re-publishing my first book. Even then, as a guy who works to accumulate *all* traditional Sherlockian pastiches, I could see that MX (under Steve's leadership) was *the* fast-rising superstar of the Sherlockian publishing world.

The re-publication of my first book with MX was an amazing life-changing event for me, leading to writing many more stories and then editing books, along with unexpected additional Holmes Pilgrimages to England. By way of that first email with Steve, I've had the chance to make some incredible Sherlockian friends and play in the Holmesian Sandbox in ways that I'd never before dreamed possible.

Through all of it, Steve has been one of the most positive and supportive people that I've ever known. He works far more than a full-time week at his day job, and he still finds time to take care of all aspects of MX Publishing, with the help of his wife Sharon Emecz, and sister-in-law, Timi Emecz. (That's right – MX is just the three of them who get all of this done!)

Many who just buy books and have a vague idea of how the publishing industry works now might not realize that MX, a non-profit which supports several important charities, consists of simply these three people. Between them, they take care of running the entire business, including the production, marketing, and shipping – all in their precious spare time, in and around their real lives.

With incredible hard work, they have made MX into a world-wide Sherlockian publishing phenomenon, providing opportunities for authors who would never have them otherwise. There are some like me who return more than once to Watson's Tin Dispatch Box, and there are others who only find one or two stories there – but they get the chance to publish their books, and then they can point with pride at this accomplishment, and how they too have added to The Great Holmes Tapestry.

From the beginning, Steve has let me explore various Sherlockian projects and open up my own personal possibilities in ways that otherwise would have never happened. Thank you, Steve, for every opportunity!

- *Derrick Belanger* and *Brian Belanger* – I first "met" Derrick Belanger when he graciously reviewed one of my early books, and we quickly became friends. Then he interviewed me several times for his online blog, and when I had the idea for the first MX Holmes anthology in 2015, he quickly joined the party and contributed a fine pastiche. From there he's written a number of others, and then he formed Belanger Books with his brother, Brian. It's turned into a Sherlockian powerhouse, working in tandem with MX Publishing, supporting each other to produce more and more wonderful Holmes adventures. I've very grateful to have had this additional opportunity to further contribute to The Great Holmes Tapestry by editing and writing stories for their different anthologies. Derrick continues to write, but he also stays quite busy as a noted aware-winning teacher, husband, and father, as well as running Belanger Books with Brian.

Over the last few years, my amazement at Brian Belanger's ever-increasing talent has only grown. I initially became acquainted with him when he took over the duties of creating the covers for MX Books following the untimely death of their previous graphic artist. I found Brian to be a great collaborator, very easy-going and stress-free in his approach and willingness to work with authors, and wonderfully creative and positive too. His skills became most apparent to me when he created the cover for my 2017 book, *The Papers of Solar Pons*, which was one of the most striking covers that I've ever seen. Later, when the Belangers and I began reissuing the original Pons books in new editions, and then new Pons anthologies, Brian's similarly themed covers continued to astound me. He truly deserves an award for these.

In the meantime, he has become busier and busier, continuing to provide covers for MX Books, and now for Belanger Books as well, along with editing and occasionally writing.

I finally met both Brian and Derrick in person in early (pre-pandemic) 2020 at the annual Sherlock Holmes Birthday Celebration in New York City, and they're just as great in person as they were by way of email. I immediately felt like I'd known them both forever. I cannot express to either one of you just how grateful I am.

- *Roger Johnson* – I had known of Roger for quite a while, having seen his name connected with the "District Messenger" newsletter of *The Sherlock Holmes Society of London Journal.* I could tell, even then, that he represented the finest kind of Sherlockian. When I wrote my first Holmes book, I sent him a copy – out of the blue, as he had no idea who I was – as a thank you, and with the timid and dim spark of a hope that he would review it, because having him do so would mean (to me) that what I had written was legitimized. He did write a great review, and we began to correspond. When I was able to get to England for my first Holmes Pilgrimage in 2013, I made arrangements to meet with Roger and his wonderful wife, Jean Upton, in person, and I discovered that what I'd already known by email was true: They are both the very best people!

  Later, in 2015 on Holmes Pilgrimage No. 2, they invited me to stay with them for several days in their home, and that was one of the best parts of all the trips. They gave me tours, they showed me their incredible collection, they let me see life in a real British household and not just from a hotel room, and we had some wonderful conversations along the way. I was able to see them again in 2016, Holmes Pilgrimage No. 3, when we attended the Grand Opening of the Stepping Stones School (as it was called then) at Undershaw.

  I'm more grateful than I can say that I know Roger. His Sherlockian knowledge is exceptional, as is the work that he does to further the cause of The Master. But even more than that, both Roger and his wonderful wife, Jean, are simply the finest and best, and I'm very lucky to know both of them – even though I don't get to see them nearly as often as I'd like, and especially in these crazy days! In so many ways, Roger, I can't thank you enough, and I can't imagine these books without you.
- *Thaddeus Tuffentsamer* – Special thanks to Thad – Sherlockian author, editor, and artist – for allowing me to contribute three stories and the foreword to his 2025 two-volume anthology, *The Denarian Adventures of Sherlock Holmes*, and for allowing me to include his illustrations for two of those stories in this volume. It is very much appreciated!

- *Nicholas Meyer* – I started reading Nick Meyer's Holmes books before I'd even read all of The Canon, and for that I'm eternally grateful. It was through his first two books, *The Seven-Per-Cent Solution* and *The West End Horror* (the latter of which is still one of my favorite pastiches to this very day) that I firmly understood that The Canon wasn't the be-all end-all of Sherlockian story-telling. I obtained Nick's first book as part of a free book give-away at school, and I found the second not long after when my mother took my sister and me to buy school clothes and I spotted it in the mall bookstore. (I sat cross-legged along an out-of-the-way wall in a Sears while my mother and sister shopped and started reading *The West End Horror* straight out of the bag.)

  After those first two books, Nick went on to have a very successful career in film. (More about that in a minute.) But he has continued to dip in an out of Sherlockian pastichery with several further volumes. He is a Sherlockian legend, and it's an indisputable fact that the publication in 1974 of *The Seven-Per-Cent Solution* – a *pastiche*, mind you! – was the beginning of the Sherlockian Golden Age when has grown and grown, and has never stopped, all the way to today.

  If it was just that, Sherlockians – and especially pasticheurs – would owe him an unpayable debt. But then there's *Star Trek*, which he also saved. As mentioned above, I have lots of interests besides Mr. Holmes, although he does demand more and more attention as my years pass. But I've been a Trekkie (or Trekker, or whatever the correct term is) since I was a wee lad in the late 1960's, when my babysitter happened to watch one of the original prime-time episodes. After that, I grew up seeing the original series in re-reruns, and then I was among those who saw the first Star Trek film in 1979 (and truthfully felt mightily disappointed. I do like it better now.) But it was Nick Meyer's *Star Trek: The Wrath of Khan* (1982) which electrified the Trek Universe, jump-starting it into motion in a way that – like the Holmes Golden Age – has only grown. And how it's grown! Hundreds and hundreds of Star Trek novels and comic books, multiple films and television shows, with more in planning and production all the time, and fan interest around the world at an all-time high. As a nearly life-long Star Trek fan, who loves it nearly as much as The World of Sherlock Holmes, I credit the origin of this original escalation entirely to Nick Meyer.

I generally despise social media, but it's a very useful way for Sherlockians to connect. Imagine my thrill when I began to see occasional online posts from Nick Meyer – and when I dared to respond, sometimes he would respond back! I've learned that if you don't ask, you'll never know, so I connected with him a bit more often, and eventually I boldly asked him to write a foreword to one of the MX anthologies that I edit, and he most-generously agreed. After that, we've stayed in touch off-and-on, and that still never ceases to amaze me.

I met him in person at the 2011 *From Gillette to Brett* conference in Bloomington, Indiana, where he was the featured guest. I took my copies of his Holmes books, asked him to autograph them, and asked – like everyone does – when he'd write his next Holmes book. He certainly doesn't remember that, but he was the main reason I chose to attend that event.

One of my greatest regrets is that, while attending the 2020 Sherlock Holmes Birthday Celebration in New York, I was almost able to meet him in person again – and this time he'd know who I was – but I didn't get to speak with him, and it was my own fault. We had emailed ahead of time, planning to meet, and that day I entered the famed dealer's room and saw him seated at a table near the door, surrounded by many fans. I wandered away, intending to return in a just a very few minutes and dive into the crowd, hoping that it might have thinned a bit. But when I got back over there, he'd already left! Hopefully I'll get another chance, sooner rather than later, where I can thank him in person for so many things . . .

. . . including generously writing a foreword for this ongoing series of volumes. When I was considering who could write a foreword, I couldn't think of anyone more fitting. Through Nicholas Meyer I found pastiches, which have been so important to me over the years. Nick, thanks from the bottom of my heart for taking the time to be part of these books!

And finally, last but certainly *not* least, thanks to **Sir Arthur Conan Doyle**: Author, doctor, adventurer, and the Founder of the Sherlockian Feast. Honored, and present in spirit.

As I always note when putting together a collection of Holmes stories, the effort has been a labor of love. This time the labor and love have been mine. These adventures are more tiny threads woven into the ongoing *Great Holmes Tapestry*, continuing to grow and grow, for there can *never* be enough stories about the man whom Watson described as "*the best and wisest . . . whom I have ever known.*"

David Marcum
Originally written September 8th, 2021
Revised September 8th,, 2025

Questions, comments, or story submissions may be addressed to David Marcum at

thepapersofsherlockholmes@gmail.com

Watson's Descendants
by Nicholas Meyer

It is generally felt that the short story was Sherlock Holmes's best venue. The novellas, by contrast, are judged to be . . . lesser. Even the fabled *The Hound of the Baskervilles* suffers from the detective's absence for many pages. Though *A Study in Scarlet*, *The Sign of the Four*, and *The Valley of Fear* remain deliciously absorbing, it is in the short stories that Holmes and Watson truly flourish.

As Michael Chabon has observed, all fiction is fan fiction. Almost from the beginning, Sherlock Holmes has prompted imitators of his creator's creation. Arthur Conan Doyle wrote sixty Holmes cases in all – fifty-six short stories and four novellas. When they ended, boys and girls, men and women of all ages mourned Watson's silence and the series' cessation. But it wasn't long before others took up – or attempted to take up – Sir Arthur's pen.

Writing a full-length Holmes novel has always posed a challenge, even for Doyle himself, to say nothing of generations of later writers and filmmakers. Short stories, on the other hand, pose problems of their own. A good short story must compress action and character. It must – obviously – be short. The gift of writing compelling short fiction remains in a class by itself. Poe, Doyle of course, Twain, Saki, and Hawthorne are among the masters of the form from the Victorian and Edwardian eras, but over the years, the short story has produced many masters.

I alas am not among them. Even as a kid in art class, my paintings were so huge the murals I attempted had to be unfurled in the hall, not the studio. And so it comes as no surprise that writing a short Holmes story does not come easily to me. In fact, it does not come at all.

I retain nothing but admiration for those writers who *can* create short fiction, and a special respect for those who can bring off simulacra of Doyle's charming and distinctive Holmes tales. There many practitioners, including some whose efforts, unfortunately, resemble nothing so much as taxidermy. But among the best I must number David Marcum, who, by this point has written more Holmes stories than Doyle himself. Characterized by unflagging imagination and ceaseless ingenuity, along with felicitous prose, these tales continue to provide what we all crave: More Sherlock.

All Sherlock Holmes stories, (except Doyle's), are of course forgeries. And it's the rare forger who can resist signing his own work. See if you can spot David Marcum's fine Italian hand.

Enjoy.

Nicholas Meyer
Los Angeles, 2021

A Note on the Modern Publishing Paradigm

For the longest time, publishing something was mostly impossible for most people. The Great Publishing Houses – which sounds like something from *Dune* – are giant machines, with carefully calculated formulas to know just how many books they need to sell to make a profit. It's no different than selling cereal: Many of the boxes of cereal on grocery store shelves won't be sold, and they were never meant to be sold, and the manufacturers are okay with that, because they've calculated the amount that they do need to actually sell in order to stay profitable while figuring in just how much can be discarded.

It used to be the same with books. Publishers would create a print run of a certain number of copies, sending out so many of them to bookstores across the country. Some would be sold – enough, hopefully, to cover costs – while many copies would just sit there, unsold, forever. Then, after a certain amount of time, they would be removed – either destroyed, or "remaindered", to be sold at rock-bottom prices in bargain bins.

It's an investment by the publishers to go to the trouble and expense to create all of those physical books, hoping to make their money back on enough of them to justify the waste of the others. That's why they're so restrictive about what they publish: They must meet the razor-thin edge of profit. But that makes the path to being published a very narrow needle's eye.

Several years ago, the paradigm began to shift. Online sales began to disrupt the physical bookstore model. And as people ordered online, some publishers figured out that they didn't have to have back rooms and warehouses jammed full of physical books sitting around waiting for a physical customer to enter a store or a dealer's room, examine it, and possibly buy it. Instead, when an online order arrived, the manufacturing of the book could commence right then, only as needed, and not months or years earlier.

This print-on-demand idea had been around for a while. (When I was going back to school for my second degree in civil engineering, the campus print shop did the same thing for certain locally produced text-books, printing them as they were purchased on fancy copying machines.) Publishers and authors began to take advantage of technological advances to produce their own books – straight from author to reader, happily eliminating the giant publishing middlemen.

Steve Emecz of MX Publishing brilliantly took advantage of this, building his business and allowing authors who would have never had a chance otherwise – like me – to create and connect.

But there are certain legitimate complaints.

In the olden days, the giant publishers slow-walked books through the process, so that it sometimes took literally years for a book to actually be published. Authors could actually die before ever seeing their work excreted at the far end of the giant publisher's process. The print-on-demand process, by comparison, is nearly immediate. As part of the large publishers' slow walk, there were battalions of editors who went through books forwards, backwards, and upside down. With the new technology, where a file can be loaded with the book manufacturer with very little effort and time spent, there is clearly less editing . . . and mistakes slip through.

Some readers continue to expect flawless and perfect works, as if legions of editors were behind the curtain as in days of old, still involved in the process. For this type of reader/consumer, the new format of publishing will always be pain they just can't ease. That's why, with this set of my stories, I want to apologize up front to those who will find typos – *because in spite of every effort, there will be some typos.*

In my own case, I love to write and edit, and I spend a sizeable amount of time doing both, but I also have a very busy and rich life doing other things. I spend time with my family, and I work more-than-full time as a civil engineer, fitting in these Sherlockian writing and editing projects during lunch hours, evenings, and weekends. It's a high wire act with no safety net. I'm the writer and sole editor of the stories in this collection. My wife, with a Bachelor's Degree in Journalism and two Master's Degrees in English Literature and Library Science, and with a first job as a copy editor, used to go through my stories and catch what I missed – because you never *ever* see your own mistakes – but she works way more than full time at her own job, and she just doesn't have any extra time to spare for playing uncredited editor on these projects. So they're all on me.

It's the same with the anthologies that I edit – any mistake that slips through in the end is my fault, because there are no other editors. When assembling a Holmes anthology, I receive the stories, format them to the "house style", print them on 8½ x 11-inch paper, edit and revise with a red pen, go back and forth with emails to the author – sometimes a lot of emails – and then plug them into a giant Word document for more editing and revision. But from the time I get the story until I send the final file to the publisher, there isn't anyone else to do additional editing or proofreading, and no time to work someone into the process. It's the new publishing paradigm.

As a print-on-demand publisher, MX does not have squadrons of editors. The business consists of three part-time people who also have busy lives elsewhere – so the editing effort largely falls on the contributors. Some readers and consumers out there in the world absolutely despise this – They foam at the mouth in rage, apparently forgetting about all those self-produced Holmes stories and volumes from decades ago with awkward self-published formatting and loads of errors that are now prized as collector's items.

These critics should recall that every one of these new volumes by various authors – even those that have typographic and formatting errors – are the very best efforts that can be produced by very sincere people who don't have professional full-time editors to help, and who would never ever have had the opportunity to publish otherwise, and because of these authors, there is thankfully more Sherlockian content in the world.

I'm personally mortified when errors slip through – ironically, there will probably be errors in this essay – and I apologize now, but without a regiment of editors looking over my shoulder, this is as good as it gets. Real life is more important than writing and editing, and only so much time can be spent preparing these books before they are released into the wild. I hope that you can look past any errors, small or huge, and simply enjoy these stories, and appreciate the effort involved, and the sincere desire to add to The Great Holmes Tapestry.

And in spite of any errors here, there are more Sherlock Holmes stories than there were before, and that's a good thing.

David Marcum

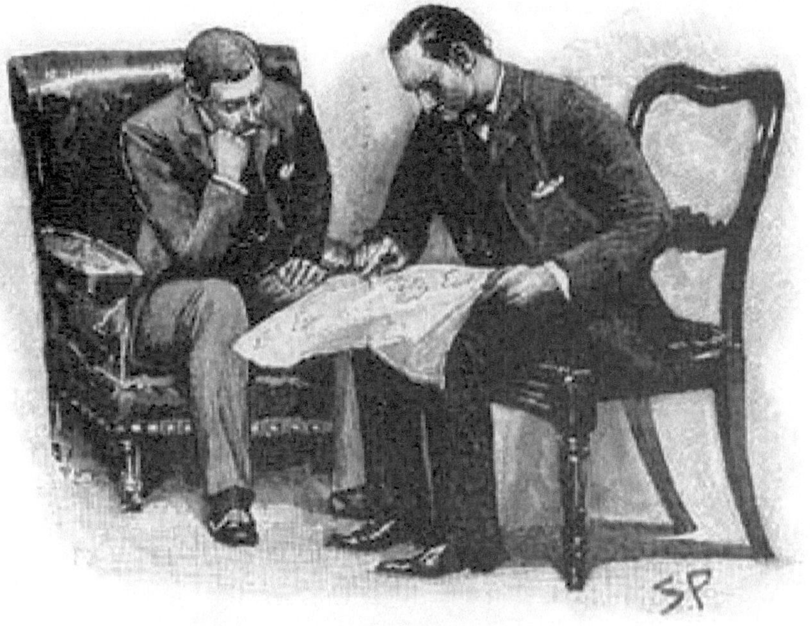
SP

Sherlock Holmes (1854-1957) was born in Yorkshire, England, on 6 January, 1854. In the mid-1870's, he moved to 24 Montague Street, London, where he established himself as the world's first Consulting Detective. After meeting Dr. John H. Watson in early 1881, he and Watson moved to rooms at 221b Baker Street, where his reputation as the world's greatest detective grew for several decades. He was presumed to have died battling noted criminal Professor James Moriarty on 4 May, 1891, but he returned to London on 5 April, 1894, resuming his consulting practice in Baker Street. Retiring to the Sussex coast near Beachy Head in October 1903, he continued to be associated in various private and government investigations while giving the impression of being a reclusive apiarist. He was very involved in the events encompassing World War I, and to a lesser degree those of World War II. He passed away peacefully upon the cliffs above his Sussex home on his 103rd birthday, 6 January, 1957.

Dr. John Hamish Watson (1852-1929) was born in Stranraer, Scotland on 7 August, 1852. In 1878, he took his Doctor of Medicine Degree from the University of London, and later joined the army as a surgeon. Wounded at the Battle of Maiwand in Afghanistan (27 July, 1880), he returned to London late that same year. On New Year's Day, 1881, he was introduced to Sherlock Holmes in the chemical laboratory at Barts. Agreeing to share rooms with Holmes in Baker Street, Watson became invaluable to Holmes's consulting detective practice. Watson was married and widowed three times, and from the late 1880's onward, in addition to his participation in Holmes's investigations and his medical practice, he chronicled Holmes's adventures, with the assistance of his literary agent, Sir Arthur Conan Doyle, in a series of popular narratives, most of which were first published in *The Strand* magazine. Watson's later years were spent preparing a vast number of his notes of Holmes's cases for future publication. Following a final important investigation with Holmes, Watson contracted pneumonia and passed away on 24 July, 1929.

Photos of Sherlock Holmes and Dr. John H. Watson courtesy of Roger Johnson

The Collected Papers of Sherlock Holmes

Volume VIII – Documents

(16 Holmes Adventures and a Poem)

Mission
(Some Sort of Sonnet)

Observe what those around you do not see.
Assist the folk who climb the stairs to plea.
At times the case can be solved from your chair,
but you like best to move around out there.

Opine when Scotland Yard misses a fact.
Your role is fixed to make up what they lack.
Over time they learn what you have long shown,
Watson smiles – before the rest he has known.

Index random facts that seem quite *outrè*.
Plain and dull then, shining with light today.
It's your mission to see what they all miss.
Finding the truth has always been your liss.

Since a lad you have known your direction:
Mastering *The Whole Art of Detection*.

The Indiscriminate Paragraph

Paddington was quiet that Sunday morning when I stepped down from the hansom, threw up a wave of farewell, and stepped to my door. The brisk late-October air was bracing, and after being up all night it should have felt refreshing, but I felt a rawness in my throat that might be a new head-cold, or possibly just the need for a strong cup of coffee. It was far too early to rouse my wife or the maid, so I would make it myself. Truth be told, my former years of military service had given me great insight into the style of coffee-making that I most appreciated, and such a strong cup would be welcome.

I turned my key in the lock and was surprised when the door opened quickly, before I could make the effort myself and jerking the knob from my grip. But my surprise was even greater when I was confronted by the tall scowling Sikh, holding a gun . . . .

Less than twenty-four hours before, I had called upon my friend, Mr. Sherlock Holmes, not long after our recent trip to Vienna [1] and found him in deep conversation with an elderly gentleman displaying fiery red hair. Although it was a Saturday, it wasn't very unusual by then to find Holmes's services being sought on a daily basis, and weekends were no barrier to those in trouble. When I'd first began to share rooms with Holmes, nearly a decade before, his investigations consisted largely of consultations in our joint sitting room, wherein people of all walks and professions would climb the steps and take a seat, describing this or that situation. Holmes would listen, ask a few pointed questions, offer his opinion based on already-vast experience – "If you have all the details of a thousand at your finger ends," he would say, "it is odd if you can't unravel the thousand and first." – and pocket his fee.

Rarely in those early days did he have to get up and "move around", as he put it. Only in the last year or so, after meeting Holmes's older brother and seeing how he performed the same sort of armchair consultations on a much vaster scale, did I understand that when he was younger, Holmes was – perhaps without realizing it – trying to emulate the same format. But as his cases became more complex, and his fame more wide-spread, he often needed to personally examine the locations of crimes, or go out and question witnesses, or follow a person of interest, or don a disguise and insert himself into the narrative. And he much preferred movement around the web to sitting in the middle of it.

Such had been the requirement the previous day after Holmes's new client explained his difficulty: He had been lured to a run-down building for two months, paid a more-than-respectable fee by an odd organization for insignificant work, and then turned up that morning as usual to find the rooms locked and his employers vanished. Holmes's curiosity had been aroused, and after the client was shooed out of the sitting room – with a stern warning not to mention anything of his visit to engage Holmes's services – my friend and I set off for Aldersgate, and the client's small shop on the southeastern corner of adjacent Charterhouse Square. Although he didn't intimate so at the time, Holmes recognized the unusual clerk who was manning the business, marked by an acid splash and holes for earrings, as a significant agent of Professor Moriarty. This fellow's presence meant that something illegal was certainly going on, and Holmes soon established to his own satisfaction that a robbery on an ambitious scale of the nearby local branch of the City and Suburban Bank was afoot.

That night, we met late in Baker Street, crossed London to the bank, and hid ourselves in the dank lower vaults, sitting in darkness for a number of hours, constantly fearful that the gregarious and cranky bank officer who accompanied us would suddenly bawl out some question or lose patience and do something to alert robbers, whom Holmes was certain would make their play that night, leaving the rest of the weekend for their escape, undiscovered. But the hunt was successful, and soon we had the entire gang in custody – including the Professor's man, who claimed to have Royal blood in his veins. What followed were several more long hours at Scotland Yard as Holmes and I, along with Inspector Peter Jones (who had made the official arrest) and a number of other ever-increasing personalities carried out the man's interrogation.

Early morning had arrived, and with it enough of the wily criminal's story had been pulled from him to get a sense of the larger scheme. I could see that the young man, one John Clay (with no apparent connection to the Leen Valley mining magnate whose kidnapped sister Holmes had recovered), had started to realize that his arrogant bragging might have been just a little too forthright, possibly incommoding and inconveniencing his master, the Professor. We departed as he was shifting his tune from haughty demands to rather fearful suggestions that he be placed under protective guard, as his life might very well be in peril.

Outside, Holmes and I found a hansom – not unusual, even that early, as cabs are always to be found in the vicinity of the Yard, day or night – and set out to the northwest, first to drop me in Paddington, and then continuing with Holmes to Marylebone and Baker Street.

I was weary, and only half-responding to Holmes's conversation. He was quite alert, as often was the case after a particular success, but I knew that within a few hours he would display a certain marked exhaustion until the next affair to pique his imagination climbed the steps to his first-floor sitting room.

"He is the fourth-smartest man in London," Holmes repeated, having first said it the previous day after initially laying eyes on John Clay. I was mildly curious as to the identities of the first three, deciding that he certainly meant himself, his brother Mycroft, and Professor Moriarty. Holmes would place his brother above him in the hierarchy – had had no patience with false modesty – but I wondered just where the Professor fell. I hoped that Holmes didn't rank him at the top of that narrow pyramid, as I was certain that both of the Holmes Brothers placed higher than the Professor, and that with the two brothers working together, he would be no match for them. I thought about our last view of the prisoner, a glint of personal fear in his eyes as we departed the interrogation room. If John Clay was the fourth-smartest man in London, and presumably the second-smartest in the Professor's organization after the leader himiself, it boded well for the eventual defeat of the sinister academic.

The street was quiet when the hansom stopped, and I told Holmes that I would check in with him in a day or so. Then with a wave, I crossed the damp pavement to my own door, whereupon I encountered the threatening Sikh and his gun, looming large in the dim pre-dawn illumination of the nearby gas lamps.

"Dr. Watson," he said, with that curious accented English that had been so familiar during my long-ago days in India and Afghanistan. "It is good that you have returned. Your wife had no idea when to expect you, and my foster brother is becoming impatient. I must say that I, too, am more anxious that I'd like, here at the end, after waiting for so long. Come inside." And he stepped back into the shadowed hallway to allow me to enter.

When he mentioned Mary, I felt a flush of heat run all over me, and my initial thought was to charge the man, weapon be damned. Such had worked for me on more than one occasion, including the affair when I had overrun Desmond Wagenaar, [2] but I reined in my flaring emotions and stood my ground silently – possibly one of the most difficult things I've been forced to do.

I had no thought of turning to run away. When I had departed the previous evening, a little after nine-thirty to be in Baker Street by ten, I had kissed Mary good night and made sure that the door was locked behind me, leaving my wife and our maid secure – or so I thought. Now, nine or so hours later, I found that our defenses had been breached, and there were at least two intruders inside – this tall fierce man and his still-unseen foster brother.

And this one *was* fierce, there was no mistaking that. He was probably in his fifties, although I was uncertain. His already darkened features had been permanently burned by a lifetime spent in hot sun, and his skin was wrinkled and cured like very old and worn leather. The creases across his face were deep, and those around his eyes were particularly numerous – not from smiling, but rather from squinting, as if he had spent nearly all of his time outdoors in every sort of weather. The schlera of his eyes was a muddy yellow, offering further confirmation of his hard outdoor life.

In spite of his rugged appearance, he had contrived to garb himself in the required Sikh adornments. I observed the *kesh*, his untrimmed beard and unshorn hair, the latter of which was wrapped in a *pagari*, or turban, a wooden *kangha* or comb for his *kesh*, an iron bracelet called a *kara*, and a *kirpan*, a small curved iron knife tucked into the band wrapped round his waste. These were four of what was called "The Five *K*'s", and I was sure that the fifth, an undergarment called a *kachhera*, was beneath his outer clothing.

"Take off your coat and hat, Doctor Watson," said my captor, his voice a deep and damaged rasp. "We have much to discuss." I did so slowly, aware that my service revolver was resting in my right overcoat pocket that I was hanging it on the peg, abandoning it in the front hallway. Clearly the older man hadn't seen it, and it didn't occur to him to search for it, but he would certainly be aware if I made any movement to retrieve it, either to raise it against him, or to slip it surreptitiously into my suit pocket. I placed my hat on an adjacent peg and, with an internal curse at being forced to do so, walked away from my weapon and toward the parlour, as directed by a wave of the Sikh's own outsized revolver.

It was a curious sensation to walk through my own modest home as a prisoner, directed at gunpoint and uncertain as to what I would find in the next room. This was a location where I ought to feel safe – and more importantly where my *wife* should expect to feel safe – with the world safely shut outside whenever we should choose to lock the doors. Instead, there were intruders here, and even the scents that I associated with home were masked by the odor of the armed stranger directing me deeper into the house.

And as we walked, I had time to identify the odor emanating from the man – that peculiar smell when someone is starving. I tried to remember what else I had noticed about him in the few seconds before he'd ordered me inside and moved behind me, out of sight, but I could recall very little – his height and weathered skin, his native clothing and accoutrements, and the menacing and brutal expression upon his angry features.

I was five paces from the back parlour, where the lamplight was spilling into the narrow hall. What would I find? My wife, also held at gunpoint by the unseen foster brother, her features constricted with terror. Or worse, would some violation have already been perpetrated against her? (I confess that for a moment, any consideration for our poor maid didn't cross my mind as I worried for Mary.) Would I find, instead of her fearful gaze meeting my own, her lifeless body, staring into eternity, her eyes already glazed with that flat sheen signifying death –

No! I cried to myself. I would not believe it. I would know in seconds – and should I find her so grievously taken from me, I swore that neither intruder would live, and that they would depart in agony, even if my own death – my very soul – was the price.

And then I entered the room –

– to find Mary sitting in her usual chair, a concerned and solicitous expression upon her face, while a man beside her in my customary seat, also dressed in quite-worn foreign costume, huddled and folded forward, grimacing as if in pain.

She glanced at me, betraying only mild annoyance, and then beyond and behind me to the doorway where the Sikh was holding the gun. "John," she said with no quaver in her voice, "this poor man is ill."

Even as she spoke, the man in the chair shuddered. He was focused on the floor a yard or so in front of his feet, and if he was supposed to be acting as Mary's guard, he had abandoned his post for internal contemplation of his illness. At a glance, I could see that he was also a visitor to our shores, likely the same place as the Sikh, and he appeared feverish. I could only hope that, sitting so close to my wife, he carried nothing contagious.

Beside Mary was our poor maid, Ivy, [3] sitting absolutely still, wide-eyed but calm, watching in every direction at once. I was proud of her – it took a special kind of brave girl to live in that house, which was often affected to varying levels by involvement with Sherlock Holmes.

Behind me, the Sikh whispered, "How long has he been like this?" I was puzzled – To whom was he speaking? Mary? She ignored the question, and then, to my surprise, a third man, whom I had not previously seen, stepped forward, behind me and at my left, replying in a harsh rasp.

"Five or ten minutes." His manner of speech, like the man holding the gun, was clearly from a foreign land, and I turned to my left, where I spotted the third intruder. "Just after you went to wait by the front door. He became dizzy and sat down."

The speaker was smaller than the others, his bones heavier and his stature wide at the shoulders. But like his companions, he was lean, as if something essential had been burned out of him long ago, leaving only tendons and gristle and sun-darkened leathery skin. He was also dressed as a Sikh, but seemed much more lax about the requirements. The second man, indifferent to our conversation as he tightened his ill grip upon himself, was simply dressed in foreign clothing, with no signs of apparent religious affectation.

At least the question was answered as to who had been guarding Mary while the man in the chair fell ill.

"John," Mary stated, more firmly this time, "can you do something for this poor man?"

My tone remained level as I turned to the Sikh who had met me at my own door with a gun. "Who are you, and why are you here? What do you want?"

"Ah, Doctor, we mean you no harm."

I nodded toward the weapon in his hand. "They why – ?

He glanced down as well, but did not lower the gun. "Perhaps I should say we don't wish to cause you any harm – but I cannot promise that we won't, if our questions are not answered satisfactorily. Killing is against our beliefs, but we have done it before, in pursuit of what we have bought with the years of our lives. Surely you have anticipated this moment – when we would arrive at your door. Feared it, perhaps? We knew that you would expect us. Any man who has the treasure, and knows its history, would surely know that someday we would come for it. It was inevitable. From what I've read of you – unless you have exaggerated your own qualities, and I do not think you are that sort of man – you would not be so innocent as to believe you were safe forever. Thus, we took the precaution of obtaining a weapon."

I shook my head. "I have no clue what you're raving about. Look around. This is a modest house and practice, and we're grateful for it, but if we had a treasure, would we be living in Paddington? Would we not be on a countryside estate, out of the smoke and fogs of London?"

The man to my left began to whisper rather harshly in his own tongue, and the first with the gun listened for a moment before waving his free hand, causing the other to fall silent.

"Mahomet Singh does not believe you. He reminds me that we have been lied to by British military officers before – and you were one of them once – and that you all lie very convincingly. Your wife's father lied to us. Major Sholto lied. It would be nothing for you to violate your supposed 'honor' and tell lies to protect the treasure. Men have killed for it. *We* have killed for it.

"From what we read," he continued, "you are not the type who would live an ostentatious life, flaunting the treasure. Rather, you are instead hoarding it for troubled times, taking from it only when necessary – a jewel here, a jewel here. Perhaps two when the house needs a repair or your lady wishes for a holiday. I cannot say that I blame you, Doctor Watson, for taking it when you had the chance. It was within your grasp, and you were canny enough to seize the opportunity. That is what we did, so many years ago. Perhaps you had to pay a share to the inspector who knew you had it, although as you have related the events, he never knew. You must have an excellent reputation for honesty, sir, to have pulled it off so neatly."

I was beginning to have a brighter idea to what he referred – and I was also starting to agree with Sherlock Holmes when he'd lamented that my tentative steps into publishing narratives of his adventures could only lead to trouble.

"Mahomet Singh," I said, glancing toward the second Sikh and repeating the name I'd just heard. The man took a deep breath and drew himself taller. Waves of hostility rolled from his angry features. I looked back at the Sikh with the gun. "Then you would be . . . Abdullah Khan?"

The man's eyes narrowed, and a smile pulled at the corner of his lips. He nodded, a glint in his eyes. "You *do* know us, then, Doctor. It was of never of any use to pretend otherwise."

I glanced toward the sick man in my chair. "And this would be your foster-brother, Dost Akbar."

"He is." The sick man chose that moment to give a small wet-sounding cough. "Unfortunately, his health suffered greatly during the long years of our unfortunate captivity, and his condition has only worsened by the London smoke and fogs you mentioned, and also the terrible cold."

"Captivity?" I said. "Is that how you define it to yourself? You were all jailed for murder. You were given penal servitude for life for the brutal death of the servant of a northern rajah, and the theft of the Agra treasure which had been entrusted to him. How is it that you are here – now, in my home?"

Khan smile widened – but there was no warmth in it. "Ah, Doctor, that is a tale, and after living it for so many years, I have no patience to sit here before your fire and relate it. Suffice it to say that, after many years, we escaped – together. Individually, we'd all had the chance many times over, but we waited until such time as all three of us could go. We had made a vow to one another, as you know. Such things mean something to men like us. We traveled – at first with urgency, and then, as the distance grew from our captivity, with greater confidence. Always we have kept to our vow that each will protect the interest of the others. Possibly a man such as yourself – another lying British officer – cannot understand such a thing as honor, where sworn obligations, sealed in blood, cannot be ignored."

"My husband is a man of honor," Mary interrupted. "As I've already told you, he does not lie, and we do not have the treasure. It lies on the bottom of the Thames, scattered for all time by your friend between Westminster Pier and the Plumstead Marshes."

The fierce Sikh shook his head. "You will forgive me, Miss Morstan – or should I say 'Mrs. Watson'? – if I choose to doubt you too. Your father lied to us, and you are married to a liar. You think to convince us with your charm, but it will not work, for you see, we have the doctor's own written account of what occurred and – as you British say – 'reading between the lines' reveals the truth.

With his free hand, he reached into his tunic and tugged forth a tattered periodical. Shifting his hand, he turned it so that I could see the cover. It was a copy of *Lippincott's Monthly Magazine*. Without leaning closer, I was certain that I knew which issue he held. Published the previous February, it contained a copy of my second written narrative describing one of Sherlock Holmes's investigations – and more specifically, a tale that included, in one way or another, every person there in that room, save Ivy the maid.

When the investigation recounted in the magazine had commenced, during those busy months in early September 1888, I had thought it no different than any other which regularly challenged Holmes. Little did I know what life-changing events were about to spiral from the initial visit to our Baker Street sitting room by a lovely orphaned governess, the recipient of six years' worth of particularly fine pearls – one every year, large and lustrous and with no explanation – and more recently a most-strange message requesting that she and two friends present themselves that night in front of the Lyceum Theatre.

The young lady was Miss Mary Morstan – now my wife for over a year. Her mother was long dead, and her father had been an officer in an Indian regiment who sent her home to Edinburgh when she was but a child. She remained there in a boarding establishment until she was seventeen, in 1878, when her father returned to England, requesting that Mary join him in London, at the Langham. She hurried south but just missed him, as he'd departed the night before on a mysterious errand from which he never returned, and no word was ever heard. A retired friend of her father's who had served in the same regiment, Major Sholto, was also living in London, and he could provide no information – though Holmes's investigation later established that Sholto had been involved in Morstan's death – possibly by accident, although I suspected a more intentional act on Sholto's part – and that he had subsequently hidden the body, the location of which ever after remained a mystery, even when the rest of the case was concluded.

Mary made do as best she could for the next four years, and just after obtaining a position as a governess in the spring of 1882, she answered a newspaper advertisement from someone trying to contact her. Upon replying, she received a single magnificent pearl, delivered anonymously and without explanation. Such had been the case on each of the subsequent five years. Finally, on that September night in 1888, she'd received another letter stating that she was a "*wronged woman*", with an invitation for that night to "*have justice*". From this curious beginning, Holmes and I had found ourselves involved in an *outrè* murder, a search across London to pick up some indication of a trail, and a desperate boat chase down the Thames, trying to catch the killers and recover the fabled Agra treasure.

Although we caught the surviving killer, a rough and dangerous man named Jonathan Small, the jewels were lost as he poured them over the side of the boat while being pursued down the Thames, vowing that if he and the other members of "The Four" couldn't have them, than no one would. But I found the actual treasure when Mary Morstan agreed to be my wife. [4] We married the following spring and settled into our Paddington house, with my practice taking up a portion of the ground floor. Then, in the following August, I had been invited to meet with an American publisher – Joseph Marshall Stoddart of the aforementioned *Lippincott's*, for dinner at the Langham.

I was unable to attend the small gathering – and frankly rather uninterested in allowing another of Holmes's adventures into print after the disappointing experience of late 1887 when *A Study in Scarlet* was published to resounding indifference, and with my name mistakenly left off the cover [5] – but at the last minute, I arranged for the some-time amateur literary agent who was connected with the first project to attend in my stead. He made a deal with Stoddart to publish another of Holmes's cases and, with my domestic joy still forefront in my mind, I chose to tell the story of how I met my wife, and the mysterious events related to the Sholto deaths, the elusive treasure, Jonathan Small and his curious companion who had perished during the Thames pursuit, and the band of killers who had given all that they had for the cursed jewels – Small and three others who had bonded themselves under the name "The Sign of the Four". Small was currently breaking rocks and digging ditches in Dartmoor, but the other three were now in my parlour, demanding the return of a treasure that was lost forever.

When Khan pulled out the magazine, I groaned to myself, although I didn't share any change of expression. I knew what he had read – for Sherlock Holmes had spotted the same thing when he looked over the manuscript and had commented upon my choice of description.

"*This may cause you some Merry Hell,*" he'd commented after I urged him to read the publication.

"*I cannot help it,*" was my reply. "*That's the way that events played out.*"

He *tsk*'d twice and shook his head. "*You've left yourself open to some misinterpretation. Mark my words – this may come back to haunt you some day.*"

And now it had.

Khan was flipping through the well-worn magazine until he found the page he sought. Holding it up to his eyes – and displaying a weakened vision that didn't need someone with Sherlock Holmes's gifts to observe – he read:

> *They landed me at Vauxhall, with my heavy iron box, and with a bluff, genial inspector as my companion. A quarter-of-an-hour's drive brought us to Mrs. Cecil Forrester's. The servant seemed surprised at so late a visitor. Mrs. Cecil Forrester was out for the evening, she explained, and likely to be very late. Miss Morstan, however, was in the drawing-room: so to the drawing-room I went, box in hand, leaving the obliging inspector in the cab.*

He lowered the magazine, looked at Mary with a knowing sneer – "*Your husband is a liar,*" he seemed to say without words – and then at me. "'*Leaving the obliging inspector in the cab.*' Really, Doctor – do you take us for fools? You recovered the chest from Jonathan Small, who swore along with us to protect the interests of The Four throughout the rest of our lives. You were sent with it *alone*, except for a police inspector, to Miss Morstan's house, and then you took it inside – *again, alone* – to where this lady waited – *alone* – and opened it to find that it was *empty*?"

His tone darkened. "Do you think we are *gullible dullards*?" he snarled. "The two of you, all alone and without witnesses, opened that chest and found the Agra treasure, and between the two of you, an arrangement was made to hide it – to *steal* it! I can only assume that you must really love the lady, Doctor, to have bothered to go all the way to see her and share anything with her at all. Or possibly you lied to the lady as well, and stopped to remove the treasure and hid it somewhere before you ever arrived at her lodgings to show her an empty chest."

"That is not true!" I said with heat. "There was an inspector with me – Youghal. He knows that I went straight from being put ashore in Vauxhall to the Forrester's house."

"If this inspector really exists," snapped Khan, "what does he really know? He didn't go inside with you. You carelessly revealed the events. *Alone* you carried in the chest. Only you and the lady were present when the box was opened. If this inspector exists, then all that he can confirm –

as based on your own narrative – is that you carried the sealed chest inside, and then told everyone that the box was empty!"

I took a deep breath. "You are deliberately choosing to misunderstand. If you focus so sharply on those few words – that I had charge of the box and opened it with only Mary present – and if you give that statement such weight, why do you then ignore what is written just after that segment? I clearly describe about how Inspector Youghal and I took the empty box back to Baker Street and showed it to Athelney Jones, the officer in charge, and how we then questioned Jonathan Small, who confirmed to us that he had poured the jewels over the side of the boat during the chase along the Thames, preferring that no man should have it if you four couldn't."

"That is the final proof of your lie, Doctor, for Jonathan Small would have never simply thrown away the treasure. You kept the treasure and hid it – possibly in a bank vault, or more likely here in this house – and then you convinced the police that there was no treasure at all, adding the additional charge of putting it in the river on Small's already burdened back. You must have quite the reputation for honesty, Doctor, for them to have believed you so easily. Or more likely, you played upon the prejudice against Small, so that his denials were immediately taken to be lies. Then, when Small was safely tucked away in prison, you wrote your fictional account to further give weight to your version of what happened. History is always written by the winners. But you never expected that we three would cross the world to find you, and now you understand the mistake you made by writing the book – for if we hadn't found and read it after landing in London, on the trail of our old companion, we would have never known that you were the man who stole the treasure."

He took a step closer. "I have no wish to harm either you or your wife, or this little girl – but my friends and I traded our lives for that treasure, possibly before you were born, and we shall have it."

I had no idea how to respond to such dogmatic idiocy. When I'd arrived home, I had been weary from far too many hours without sleep, and the excitement of catching the men tunneling into the City and Suburban Bank. At that moment, I'd already been awake for slightly over twenty-four hours, and even though being taken prisoner at my own front door had given me a rush of excited energy, I could tell that my thinking was slow.

"John," said Mary, now holding out her hand to invite me over beside her, "I think that you should take care of this sick man, and then we can discuss the location of the treasure."

Her gaze held mine with extra emphasis, and as slow as my mind was, I could see that she was trying to relay something unsaid, if I was only able to grasp it. Apparently joining her was necessary, as she gave a small shake to her hand, finally setting me in motion toward her.

I took her hand and it was warm – not cold with fear as I might have expected. But then, my wife was no wilting flower. She might be small, and her body was not as strong as we would hope, but she had great strength. When she had been taken prisoner by the Rippers in the terrible autumn of '88, as leverage in an attempt to control Holmes's investigation, she had displayed none of the weaknesses that one might expect when found in such a situation. And it was her presence of mind that calmed me when we rescued her, and kept me from blotting my own soul with the righteous and surely-earned deaths then and there of her captors. They had deserved no mercy, but received it from me anyway, solely at the behest of my dear wife.

Reaching her, I looked into her eyes, again sensing that she was trying to tell me something. Not knowing what, but understanding that there was something to be learned, I gave a small nod and turned back to face Khan and Singh.

Together, they radiated menace. I hadn't realized from my brief glance just how wicked a figure was Mahomet Singh. His barely suppressed rage made Abdullah Khan seem almost avuncular by comparison.

But seeing the two of them together, one with a gun trained upon me and the other flexing his fingers as if he'd like to crush my throat, was suddenly irrelevant when I understood what Mary had been trying to tell me –

– For standing in the door behind the two killers, just barely visible as he leaned forward from the concealment of the dark hallway, and with a finger to his lips letting me know that I should betray no reaction to his presence, was Sherlock Holmes.

When he knew that I'd seen him, he nodded, gestured with a finger toward the darkened hallway behind him, and slipped silently back into the shadows. Before I could consider the implications of his presence, or how it might contribute to a plan to defeat the men who had invaded my home, Dost Akbar fell into a timely paroxysm of terribly racking coughs.

I glanced his way, noting that from where he was seated and the floorward angle of his gaze, he wouldn't have been able to observe Holmes in the hall. Ivy was to one side. Only Mary would have known that my friend was in the house. I didn't yet know how he'd entered, or what have given him to understand that his presence was necessary, but I was grateful.

"John . . ." Mary said, concern in her voice, and I nodded, suddenly understanding a way forward. I stepped to the sick man, raising my hand toward his head. He was bent forward, looking down and unaware of my approach. Singh growled behind me, but I continued, reaching forward and touching Akbar's forehead with the back of my hand. He was burning with fever. I turned and directed an accusatory look toward Khan.

"You say he's been like this since you arrived in London?" I asked. "When was that?"

"Three weeks ago," replied Khan. For such a cruel looking fellow, he looked momentarily abashed, as if confessing a sin. "We worked our passage from North Africa," he explained, "and were released at the West India Dock. We found help from an important Oriental man we were told to seek, in Limehouse. His name is not important, but his influence is great. We sought word of Jonathan Small, as we had in other ports across the world since regaining our freedom. We learned that our search was nearing completion – Small was in England, as we'd thought. But then our joy immediately turned to bitter ashes upon our tongues when we learned that he was in prison for murder. When we asked for further information, our local friend provided us with your account of Small's arrest. It was an easy matter to find where you live.

"By then, Dost Akbar had grown more and more ill, but we felt that we had no time to waste. Despite our attempts to be discreet, our interest in Small has generated speculation in certain quarters that we seek the lost treasure. It is unavoidable. As it becomes known that we are looking for you, others will follow. So we came here this morning, waiting until the hour when the house appeared to be awake. Then, believing that it was late enough for your office hours to begin, we knocked upon the door, planning to gain entry by seeking treatment for our sick friend's condition. We gained admittance, only to learn that you were away on a professional call. So we waited for you to return."

"And you've held my wife and poor Ivy hostage the entire time, while your foster brother becomes sicker by the minute," I said. "Before we discuss anything else, he must be treated." I looked at Singh. "You – bring him across to my consulting room."

I said it with authority, a combination of the stern gravitas cultivated by all physicians, and also as the military officer I'd been a decade earlier when speaking to fearful or recalcitrant patients who needed treatment in spite of their reluctance.

Singh looked back and forth from me to Khan, waiting for some confirmation. Finally, realizing that he still had the upper hand by way of his hostages, Khan nodded.

"Take him through to the consulting room. I will remain here with the ladies." He lifted the gun to remind me that he still held all the power. "I searched the consulting room when we arrived," he added, speaking to the more dangerous man beside him. "He has nothing there that can be used as a weapon." Singh grumbled something too low to understand, and Khan replied, "You won't need the gun. The doctor knows that while he's gone, it will be trained upon his wife. That will prevent him from doing anything foolish, and you are strong enough to prevent him from attempting to flee."

I stepped to Dost Akbar and touched him on the shoulder, telling him to come with me. He raised his rheumy eyes to me, displaying little comprehension of what was required.

"Does he understand English?" I asked. Khan shook his head.

"Not very well. Enough to follow simple commands – but he seems to have lost some of the ability since he became ill." Then he rattled off a string of syllables that I roughly thought to be, "Go with the doctor." The fellow rose and shakily found his balance. I gestured toward the hallway. Then I gave Mary a confident nod, smiled encouragingly at Ivy, and followed, Singh at my back.

I didn't know what to expect from Holmes, or even if I was doing the right thing. He had gestured toward the hallway. Did he mean that he would be out there and that I should join him? Mary had suggested treating Dost Akbar, and that served the purpose of separating the men – *Divide and conquer* – but had I misunderstood? *Was I doing something that would make things worse instead of better?*

There was no way that I could not be fearful at leaving my wife and our maid under the watch of a killer with a gun. I tried to tell myself that Khan didn't *want* to hurt us, and that as a Sikh, he was essentially a man of honor, believing in honesty, humility, hard work, and service. But this was the same man who had schemed with the others of "The Four" to murder a misled servant, brutally killed to steal his master's cursed jewels. Khan, Singh, Akbar, and Jonathan Small had all participated in the killing and subsequent hiding of the corpse, and then they had spent the next years – decades – in prison. Small had escaped by killing a prison guard – hitting him over the head with his wooden leg. He was complicit when his bizarre companion, Tonga the Andaman Islander, had killed Bartholomew Sholto. Who knew how many others Small and Tonga killed in their wanderings, and how many others had died at the hands of the rest of The Four during their escape and travels? Anything of the honorable man that might have once lived in Khan was likely burned out ages ago, and such a one, obsessed with a treasure to the point that he would sacrifice his whole life to obtain it, would not care one jot about murdering two innocent women.

As I directed Dost Akbar into my consulting room, I hardened my heart for whatever must be done.

I'm not sure what I expected – for Sherlock Holmes to be waiting to one side, ready to affect a capture and arrest, perhaps, but there was no sign of him. The house was silent, and might have been empty save for the shuffling sound of Dost Akbar's shoes as he wearily dragged himself toward the treatment room. I considered quickly pivoting toward the front door to retrieve my gun, but it was never something I'd truly attempt. Vigilant Singh would cry out at my first movement, or attack me with the least provocation, and even if I managed to elude him and retrieve the gun, what would I do? Shoot both Singh and Akbar? Take them as my own hostages to trade for my wife and Ivy, whom Khan was still holding? It could only end badly. I would need to do something different, and no plan was springing to mind, other than to trust in the fact that Sherlock Holmes was somewhere nearby.

I directed Akbar to sit on the examining table, and then proceeded to give him a cursory medical examination. His fever was high, and if it climbed a few degrees more, he would likely pass out. With my stethoscope, I listened to his breathing, hearing the congestion that filled him. I poked and prodded, but he didn't have any unusual reactions. His heart was racing, but that was likely due to the fever and his impeded clogged breathing.

I continued my examination, aware that any minute my various maneuverings would be identified as simple attempts to waste time. All the while, Singh stood in the door, his back to the hall, watching carefully, tense and suspicious. I was becoming more uncertain as to what I might be able to accomplish.

During my movements around the patient, here and there, side to side, picking up the thermometer and then the stethoscope, I had shifted my reflex hammer where it could be easily grabbed – although I knew that finding just the right place to stand behind Singh and strike the narrow precise spot to knock him unconscious would likely be impossible. I had managed to palm a scalpel, slipping it into my pocket unseen, but I wasn't anywhere near the point where I'd consider brutally and preemptively killing Singh, slicing his throat before he could understand what had happened – although I had no doubt that he'd kill me at the slightest provocation.

Thinking of something else to delay further, I turned to a glass-fronted cabinet and pulled out a brownish bottle. Showing it to Singh, I said, "Medicine. To help him breathe."

I held out the bottle for him to examine. Likely the label meant nothing to him, and when he opened it, the bitter odor caused no suspicions. But then he shook his head. "No, no. *Poison*. You try to poison him."

I raised an eyebrow, looking as if I were talking to a child ranting nonsense. "It is medicine – to help him." I gestured toward a nearby tabletop, where a glass was sitting. "I'll take a sip first if you'd like."

In truth, I had no intention of doing any such thing. The bottle contained chloral hydrate, as my latest idea was to drug Dost Akbar – if Singh would let me get away with it – and then figure out what to do from there. My taking a drink, even a small one, would blunt my reactions. The various available drugs that I might have used to render either or both of them unconscious, despite the public perception to the contrary, were slow-acting, and useless in my situation. Chloral hydrate, chloroform, ether – all required several minutes to take effect. Various melodramas had convinced ignorant audiences that such drugs caused an instantaneous and long-lasting comatose state. In fact, I would have to soak a pad in chloroform and hold it over Singh's nose for several minutes until he finally dropped insensate at my feet – and as sick as Akbar was, he would certainly notice what was going on and rally himself to his comrade's defense.

I was aware that time was passing, and soon Khan would become suspicious. I was widely casting my mind, trying to see my next best option, when the matter became moot. Slipping behind Mahomet Singh was Sherlock Holmes. He made not a sound as he approached. As he was almost directly behind Singh, I made no inadvertent cutting of my eyes in a different direction, so there was nothing to betray Holmes's approach, his right arm raised. Just in case some indication might give away what was happening – the tiniest slip of shoe upon linoleum – I spoke anyway.

"Your friend is becoming more ill as we speak. If he isn't treated – " And then, Holmes's arm dropped quickly, the life preserver in his hand connecting surgically with the back of Singh's head. With nothing but a sigh, the villain dropped at my feet.

Holmes didn't wait, or bother to speak. He pivoted around me and the unconscious man to the examination table, where Akbar was just raising his glazed eyes toward us, little comprehension in them as everything he witnessed was certainly nothing but a fevered dream. Holmes, who had long before made a scientific study of such things, delivered another precise blow, this time to Akbar, and then eased the inert man to a reclining position.

Holmes held up the cosh, turned it to catch the light, and smiled. I recognized it – one of his favorite trophies, taken from Sir George Burnwell in early '88, when he was on the trail of some stolen Royal jewels.

He slipped the weapon into his pocket and raised a finger to his lips, stifling any of my questions. Then, to my puzzlement, he stepped to the window, opening the latch and raising it slowly and quietly.

To my astonishment, a pair of faces appeared at the window – young Peake, one of his Irregulars (as he called them), and Inspector Bradstreet of Scotland Yard. The latter had an inquiring look on his face, but he too exchanged no words. Holmes nodded, and then turned back toward me, gesturing with his head toward Singh.

"*Out the window,*" he whispered, in a tone so low as to barely be perceived.

Not bothering to question my orders, I took Singh's shoulders while Holmes grabbed his feet. We lifted him, and I was surprised to find him lighter than I'd expected. Underneath his filthy garments, he was more lean and bony than his frame suggested, and I suspected that, in spite of working his way to London, he'd been on a starvation diet more often than not.

Holmes and I shifted until Singh was passed out headfirst to the waiting policeman and street lad. Even as they were lowering him out of our sight, Holmes and I were retrieving Dost Akbar for similar disposal. When he was passed through, Bradstreet nodded and vanished out of sight. Holmes quietly lowered the window and turned back to me. "*Do you have your gun?*" he mouthed.

I shook my head. "*In my coat pocket,*" I similarly replied. "*By the front door.*"

"*Get it, and then go back with the others. Stand ready.*" Then he gestured toward the hallway. He followed me out, turning right, deeper into the house, while I quietly retrieved my weapon. Then, slipping it into my coat pocket, I took a deep breath, stretched and sighed, and returned with a false relaxed confidence to the sitting room, where Khan was standing between the two women and the parlour. The end of his gun was pressed against Mary's temple.

"Where is Dost Akbar?" Singh asked. "Where is Mahomet Singh?"

I clenched my fists, ready to charge the man, and yet fearful that he would have time to fire – or that the gun would accidentally discharge during my attempt.

"He's resting comfortably," I managed ot say, trying to sound as if I were simply reporting a patient's condition to a family member in the waiting room. "His fever is high, and he has an infection of the lungs, but with proper treatment. There is no need – "

"Singh?" he interrupted, looking past me toward the door. "Singh!" he called out, louder, and then he added something in Punjabi.

In a moment, from the depths of the house, there was a faint growling response. I couldn't understand it, but whatever was said, just a few terse words, seemed to slightly calm Khan. I knew that Holmes had some understanding of a number of languages. Apparently Punjabi was one of them.

Khan then turned back to me. "Now, Doctor, let us continue our discussion. You have our treasure, and we have paid heavily and then crossed the world to find it. If you want to avoid any injuries to your wife or this girl, you will tell me now where you've hidden it."

I was facing Khan and the women, and had no idea what happened. Apparently Holmes had returned, thinking that what had worked before would work again. He had approached the doorway and leaned just enough to see into the room. But this time he wasn't so lucky, as Ivy, finally surprised beyond restraint, gasped and cut her eyes in Holmes's direction. Khan immediately sensed that something was up, and with a snarl, he turned toward his gaze to the doorway – and Sherlock Holmes.

"So," Khan snarled. "More lies." He looked more closely at my friend, now fully entered into the room. "You would be Sherlock Holmes. I should not be surprised. I was warned, you see." Then he shifted the gun, pressing it more firmly against Mary's temple.

"I expect you have my friends in custody," he said, his voice low and menacing. "I only have this woman's life to trade for the treasure and my freedom, and such a bargain seems very unlikely to work out well for any of us. I will surrender – for in the end I must – but I have one demand before I do so."

"And what is that?" asked Holmes, a terrible expression of suppressed anger upon his face.

"I would speak with Jonathan Small."

Holmes was allowed to depart in order to make arrangements, and Khan let Ivy accompany him. With a grieved look back at her mistress, and assured by Mary's instructions for her to go, they departed, and I was left in the parlour with the weathered and wasted Sikh and his prisoner – my wife.

I found a seat across from them, and after a while, Khan lowered the gun, but he kept his wife by my side, and more importantly, he never seemed to lose focus on his purpose. From where they sat, he could see the door to the hall, so there would be no more unexpected observations. The house was deadly quiet, with only the usual noises drifting in from the street as the morning passed and more and more people moved about on their usual errands, unaware of the little drama that was being enacted so close, behind the plain door marked only by my professional plate.

It occurred to me that the police must have the area cordoned off, as there were no knocks at the door from patients. I attempted several times to engage Khan in conversation, possibly with some notion of lulling him into complacency. I asked questions about his time as a prisoner, and what else he had done during the Mutiny, and specifics of his travels to reach England, but he was having none of it, and while he didn't threaten either of us to make me be quiet, he did frown and express his disinterest by a complete refusal to engage with me.

Even as Khan never seemed to lose focus, neither did I. It was not my plan to find a way to charge him, or fight him for the gun, being unwilling to take any chances that Mary might be inadvertently injured. While Khan's companions had been rather wasted from their experiences, I couldn't say for certain whether my captor was in the same shape, and he might best me in combat. In any case, I was trusting that Sherlock Holmes was taking care of things beyond the walls of my house.

I don't how he did it, and he was never willing to provide specifics after the fact, but he used his influence to have Jonathan Small brought to London as fast as could be arranged. I did understand that upon departing, he and Bradstreet immediately arranged to have Small brought to the local station and put on a train – no small thing, this. Next, Holmes arranged for his brother Mycroft to pull all the strings required to clear the tracks so that the newly designated special train made a straight and flying trip to the capital. It was a journey of over two-hundred miles, and shortly after the time when I would have normally been eating my lunch before returning to my medical duties, there was a ring at the doorbell. The door opened and closed, and there were footsteps in the hall. Then, in walked Sherlock Holmes and beside him, in his prison uniform and chains, and still soiled from whatever labors he'd already begun that morning when yanked toward London, was Jonathan Small. I could see that his health was shattered after just a couple of years laboring in Dartmoor, and that he wasn't long for this world. (And after that morning, he died within a month.)

Khan rose, the gun hanging by his side. I think that just then, I could have walked to him and taken it, so surprised was his expression. He looked and looked at his old comrade, and Small met his gaze, but there was something broken about him, with none of the fierceness he'd displayed upon being arrested two years earlier.

"Khan," said the prisoner, his voice broken and weak. "It was an evil day when my path crossed yours. Curse you! I should have let you kill me."

The Sikh did not speak, though his mouth tightened.

"You told me that I must be with you, or that I must be silenced forever," continued Small. "I swore myself to you and the others, and little did I know just how that oath would bind me. I became a murderer – even if my only involvement was tripping that poor little man so that you could butcher him. I should have testified against you right then, but my damned honor held me to a promise that destroyed the rest of my life."

Small then looked toward Mary, who gazed upon him with a mixture of curiosity and pity and horror. "Apologies for the language, ma'am. You would be Major Moran's daughter, I expect. He treated us decent – as best he could. Not like that Sholto – may he be burning in Hell. I expect you feel the same, considering that he likely killed your father."

Mary's eyes widened. We'd both suspected as much, and talked about it before, but this was a bit more confirmation – although we'd never know for sure.

It was then that Khan decided to speak. "Moran was a liar, the same as Sholto. And now this doctor lies as well. He stole the treasure on the night he took it from you, Small, and he hid it, and then made everyone believe his story. They have all gone along with him and placed the blame upon you, but you know the truth – that you would never allow the treasure to be lost. That you would do all that you could preserve it for us – for The Four! You swore it!"

Small shook his head and gave a bitter laugh, saying something in Punjabi that made Khan growl. Then Small added, "I called him a fool, and something else that was worse. I did my best, Khan. I kept to my oath. When I escaped, I spent years working my way closer and closer to the treasure. Sholto had it, and I could find no way to get it back. Then he died, and I had to bide my time, watching while his fool sons searched for it. Then, they found it, and I managed to get it back – before these two – " He jerked his head toward Holmes and me. " – got on my trail. What you heard is the exact truth: I poured it over the side of the boat when I knew there was no escape. Better that none of them should have it than we four who wasted our lives over it.

"Until I met you, Khan, I'd never done an evil thing. I'd always tried my best to do what was right. But you gave me a choice, and I was weak. And having done one evil thing, others came more easily. I killed the guard to escape. I've killed since then – lives that should not have been taken. Those men had done nothing to deserve death. Their only misfortune was crossing my path. And I can see that my path – every step of it – led back to that night outside the Great Fort at Agra and *you.* You're a devil, Khan, and two things I know: In spite of it all, I kept my oath, even though it wasted my life doing so, and also I'm glad – damned glad – that the loss of the treasure to Old Man Thames will make you grind your teeth in frustration and rage to the end of your days, and likely in your forgotten grave as well."

He turned to Holmes. "I've said my peace. Send me back to Dartmoor."

At that, Khan gave a cry that seemed to rip his soul, and he raised his gun toward the shackled and broken prisoner.

The single shot caused devastating damage, and the sound was deafening in the small room. I stepped forward, surprised at just how quickly it had occurred, even though the conclusion was inevitable.

The smell of smoke from the discharged gun was raw, and it caused a haze in the lamp-lit room. Before I could step forward or say anything, thundering footsteps clattered through the house, drawn by the gunshot. Inspector Bradstreet, followed by a pair of constables, appeared in the doorway, instantly perceiving what had occurred.

Abdullah Khan looked from the policeman to me, his expression was a mixture of shock, anger, and disappointment. His quest for the treasure had ended. As the policemen took him into custody, he glanced at the blood puddling at his feet, symbolizing all of the violence that had attached itself to the jewels over the centuries.

Then he slowly lowered his ruined hand, where my bullet had ripped a path when he had tried to fire at Jonathan Small. Meanwhile, Holmes stepped forward and picked up Khan's fallen weapon.

"I doubt that this would have even fired. It's in terrible condition." He looked at Khan. "Did you buy it from Evans, in the Commercial Road? As a newcomer to London, you wouldn't have known any better."

Khan started to nod before catching himself. Then he stumbled as he became dizzy, going into shock from blood loss. I had Bradstreet and the constables take him across the hallway to the consulting room, where I would fix him up before he was transported to Scotland Yard, where a police surgeon would carry on from there. But first, I went to my wife, who leaned into my embrace with a sigh of release.

Khan and Akbar received proper treatment, and were soon returned to the best possible health, although Khan's hand was permanently ruined. I was told that Khan continued to rage that I had stolen the treasure, even to Inspector Youghal, who made the pointless effort to meet with the prisoner and explain the true facts of the matter.

Small returned to Dartmoor, while the other members of The Four were each sent to different prisons, so that their association could never be rekindled, and I received no knowledge of them henceforth, except for the notifications when each one died of natural causes over the next three or four years.

After the prisoners were removed from my home and into police custody, Holmes and I settled into the consulting room, taking the first welcome sips of hot bitter coffee. Mary had put Ivy to work, realizing that the distraction of familiar tasks would calm her more than being allowed to dwell on their recent experience.

"How did you happen to be in the house?" I asked, and then, rephrasing to what I really wished to know, I added, "How did you know that we needed help?"

He paused for a moment, as if considering how to share his answer. "A mixture of chance and planning," he replied. "By merest chance, I happened to look back as the hansom drove away, and I had an instantaneous glimpse of what looked like a gun barrel projecting from your doorway, while you paused there, instead of stepping immediately inside. It was enough to alarm me, and on the next street I had the driver stop."

"And planning?" I asked. "How could you have planned for any of this?"

I thought that he would answer directly, but instead he played for time by taking a sip of coffee, and then another. That uneasy delay was rather unlike Sherlock Holmes, and my curiosity as to his answer was magnified. Finally, he sighed and answered the question.

"For some months, I've had your house watched."

That surprised me, and unexpectedly irritated me, but I held my tongue for an instant before immediately replying. Then, "You fear for our safety?"

Holmes sighed and nodded. "I do. My investigations into Professor Moriarty's affairs have been progressively more successful of late, with each crack giving me a finger-hold to open two others. He is aware, of course, and making counter-moves. And always he is seeking leverage to prevent my efforts."

"And Mary and I are that leverage," I added.

"I'm afraid so." He frowned. "Several years ago, the Professor was simply a consultant, happy to sit far back in the shadows, aware of each pluck and tug on the strands of his web, but willing to let his agents carry out his public actions. But when he was first publicly exposed – the Lorait killing, and the trial where he contrived his alibi by manipulating the Royal Society, and then, when he was injured at The Tower while trying to steal the Crown Jewels, [6] he changed. He stopped trying to hide, and he became more vindictive. Dangerous. Unhinged."

"How long have you had us watched?"

"Since that flying trip to Germany and Switzerland last February, when we arranged for his assets to be seized, and simultaneously spoiled his attempt to disrupt the peace conference. [7] Upon our return, I knew that the danger had escalated exponentially."

"And when you returned this morning, you found your watchers and learned what was happening."

"I did. Peake was on duty, and was thrilled that I appeared so fortuitously. Just moments before, Khan and the others had knocked on the front door, ostensibly seeking treatment. Peake overheard as they were told you weren't home, and then he saw how they forced their way inside. He had just sent Mannering in one direction, to seek a constable, and Willett in the other, to notify me in Baker Street, when I arrived. I waited long enough for the constable to join us. Then I quickly briefed him, and had him summon an inspector. Then I picked the lock to enter your cellar, where I slipped through the house until I had a sense of what was going on, and who was involved.

"I was as surprised as you must have been when I figured out who the three men were – but at the same time, it wasn't entirely unexpected – nor should it be unexpected if something like this happens again. I recall warning you at the time I read your manuscript that your description of the order of events would doubtless lead some perspicacious but misguided reader to believe you'd had time to squirrel away the treasure during that period when you and Mary were out of official observation. One can only imagine what other clues and contradictions have appeared in your two published narratives that might lead to even-worse confusion. You'll recall the fiasco when we tracked down that supposed-woman who came calling for Jefferson Hope's wedding ring?"

I did recall, and I had to agree that he'd put his finger on the perfect example to make his point. That had turned into quite a farce – and the mess was revived upon the publication of that narrative in late '87. Yet I was not willing to concede that he was entirely correct.

"I really must advise you," Holmes continued, "yet again, not to put any more of my cases to paper."

"And I must disagree," I countered. "Let alone that my writing has served as a form of therapy for me. I have believed from the time I first understood your work that you should be publicly recognized, and that you should receive the proper credit for what you do." I kept my tone level, although the temptation was there to raise the discussion to a more heated level – as it had been on many past occasions when the same topic lay between us.

Holmes responded as expected. I contended upon a different but well-traveled track. Move and counter-move, the discussion continued through the rest of the coffee, now cold, my office hours fully neglected for the morning. Neither side had capitulated by the time lunch was served, and we tabled the discussion for more agreeable topics.

I had walked Holmes to the front door, conferring on when we would next meet, when there was a knock. Opening it, I found both Inspectors Lestrade and Gregson, uncharacteristically side-by-side, as they were noted rivals. Without explanation, Gregson held out a sheet of paper. Holmes studied it carefully, while I looked more quickly over his shoulder. I stepped inside to retrieve my hat and coat and tell Mary that I would send word when I knew what time I'd return. Then I joined Holmes and the inspectors in a waiting growler, headed to Hampstead at a fast trot. It would be many more hours before I obtained any sleep, but at the end of that new affair, another crack in Moriarty's edifice had been opened.

Looking back as we drove away, I was glad to see young Peake keeping watch nearby. He nodded, and I returned it, happy to know that my friend had taken precautions against whatever rising dangers were gathering around us.

NOTES

1. Research has indicated that the basic events of *The Seven-Per-Cent Solution* (as discovered by Nicholas Meyer in 1974) – Holmes's trip to Vienna to meet Dr. Sigmund Freud and attempt to master his cocaine addiction, and the mad chase across Europe – occurred in Autumn 1890 (and not the spring of 1891). However, Watson's original manuscript was horribly butchered by someone – likely a relative of the Moriarty family – in an attempt to rehabilitate the Professor's foul reputation by implying that he was simply an innocent academic, persecuted by a drug-crazed Holmes, and that The Great Hiatus never actually occurred, and was instead simply Holmes's journey about the Continent while his recovery continued. All nonsense, of course. Moriarty was evil, and the Hiatus – as described in The Canon and a number of other post-Canonical adventures – did occur.
2. For more about the encounter with Desmond Wagenaar, see "The Tracking and Arrest of a Cold-Blooded Soundrel" in *The Collected Papers of Sherock Holmes: Volume VII – Annals* and *The MX Book of New Sherlock Holmes Stories – Part XLII: Further Untold Cases (1894-1922)*
3. The identification of Ivy as the Watsons' maid during the Paddington years is attributed to Marcia Wilson, as explained in her *Sherlock Holmes and the Scotland Yarders* series – particularly in *A Sword for Defense.*
4. For more about what really happened to the Agra Treasure, see "An Actual Treasure" in *The Collected Papers of Sherock Holmes: Volume III – Accounts* and *The Strand Magazine* Issue LIII, 2017
5. See "The Unintended Offenses" in *The Collected Papers of Sherock Holmes: Volume VII – Annals* and *Steel True, Blade Straight – 2022 Annual*
6. Details of Professor Moriarty's disastrous attempt to steal the Crown Jewels were later somewhat fictionalized and presented in the 1939 film *The Adventures of Sherlock Holmes* starring Basil Rathbone.
7. Perhaps this trip to Switzerland served as the basis for the highly fictionalized events of *Sherlock Holmes: Game of Shadows* (2011), which unfortunately had a great deal of incorrect information (from the imagination of Hollywood film adapters) stacked on top of whatever real events were originally recorded in Watson's notes.

The Bellmaker's Boon

Outside the attorney's office, the day was warm and the sun high overhead, but the young doctor facing me was rather chill. During our past encounters, I had never found him otherwise.

He and I shook hands, formally, our business concluded. Inside the building, the door now closed behind us, my lawyer, Marchmont, had facilitated the sale of my now-former Kensington medical practice to young Dr. Verner, who hadn't bothered to bargain at all when I set the highest price that I dared to ask. Verner, with all questions answered, papers signed, and funds transferred, was now in possession of the practice, the lease to the building, such possessions as I cared to leave behind, and the keys. There was nothing left to exchange but the handshake. I suppose that I should have invited him to join Holmes and me for lunch, but I was ready to be shed of the whole business – and in truth, the young man as well.

I had known Verner for several years, by way of Holmes, but he had never seemed very friendly, and as their irregular conversations did not involve me whenever Verner came to call, I'd made no effort to make him a better acquaintance. The last time that I remembered seeing him was in mid-May of '91, at a memorial service organized in Holmes's honor during that period when all but Mycroft Holmes had believed him to be dead. Verner had stood along a back wall, and I remember his presence because he looked more angry than grief-stricken. Often he glared at me for no reason that I could discern.

I stood for a moment, Holmes beside me, watching as Verner turned and walked east along the Holborn before being lost in the crowds.

"Rather taciturn fellow," I remarked, half to myself. Holmes gave a small laugh.

"Henry has been ever thus. Life hasn't always gone his way. One hopes that purchasing your practice will finally make something of him – or help him make something of himself. Either would be acceptable."

He shifted so that he was facing me. "And how are you, Watson? Selling your practice, although the right decision, is still quite a change."

I thought about it, but just for an instant. "It was the right decision," I replied. "With Mary gone . . . ." I considered elaborating, but all that I might have said had already crossed Sherlock Holmes's mind. "In any case," I concluded, "it isn't the first time I've sold this practice, so I should be used to it."

Holmes nodded. "And as I recall, after that transaction was completed, you dined at Simpson's. May I suggest that we do the same? I think that something nutritious and tasty would not be out of place."

*The idea was appealing, as the completion of that morning's transaction seemed worth celebrating. "As long," I added, "as the meal isn't followed by gunfire . . . ." **

And it was not. We chose to make the short pleasant walk from Gray's Inn to the Strand, cutting through Lincoln's Inn Fields and thence along the Kingsway. The restaurant wasn't very crowded, as it was somewhat before midday, and we easily obtained a table looking down upon the street, where Holmes, as was typical, made various amusing but no-doubt correct deductions regarding the passers-by. Upon the conclusion of our meal, we returned to the street, whereupon I realized that I had the entire afternoon free, stretching out before me and suddenly no longer tied to the routine of keeping office hours or visiting patients. I was about to suggest a walk when the Great Clock of Westminster chimed noon. It stood not-quite a mile to the south and the day was bright and blue, so the familiar musical tones were very clear. I don't know why I paused to listen, as I'd heard that small tune more often throughout my life than I could count, but something seemed to hold me, entranced. And as I listened, I became aware that Holmes was very softly singing along:

"All through this hour,
Lord, be my guide,
And by Thy power,
No foot shall slide . . . ."

As he finished, the booming tone of the hour count rang forth, and I involuntarily counted along with it, all the way to twelve. I recalled something that I'd heard once when studying medicine – it seemed a lifetime ago – that if the bells ever tolled thirteen, some sort of doom is predicted, although it was never made quite clear for whom.

I glanced at Holmes, who smiled and asked, "Were you unaware that there were words to that notable little melody?" When I shook my head, he added, "The tune is supposedly a variation of the Cambridge Chimes, itself taken from violin phrases within Handel's Messiah. *The words themselves are written on a plaque mounted to the wall of the clock room."*

I raised an eyebrow. "And I suppose that you noticed that during some dangerous adventure in the tower's belfry – perhaps a struggle with a madman and the ever-present danger of falling to your death, perched hundreds of feet above the Thames?"

Holmes gave a short laugh. "No, Watson! When I found myself in the Tower struggling for my life – an entirely different occasion, I assure you – I had no chance to notice the plaque. Rather, I had the opportunity, many years ago, to simply climb up the tower as a guest and inspect the Great Bell, Big Ben as it's known, in order to satisfy my own curiosity about something." He glanced up at the blue sky. "It's a fine day, and I'm unaware of any demands on either of us. I perceived that you were about to suggest we take a walk. While we do, would you care to hear the story?"

I started to ask which one – the death struggle, or when he read the bit of simple rhyme set to the bells' tune. Instead, I simply nodded, letting him decide. A walk suited me down to the ground, and so we set off, seemingly at random, meandering to the east, generally along the river toward The Tower . . . .

As you know, *[Holmes began]* when I was young, my father chose to take us on a great Continental Pilgrimage. I saw a great deal of Europe from the back of our wagon as we traveled the slow and obscure routes from city to city – Pau and Montpellier. Darmstadt and Stuttgart and Munich. Heidelberg and Berne and Lucerne. My father had notions of seeing much of Europe, but not just the cities, and with no set plan or route. He said it was to educate his sons – and no doubt it benefited Mycroft to a great degree, but I was quite a bit younger – too young, really – and I'm not sure what impressions were formed upon me.

It wasn't as if we were gone continuously from England during those years. We returned at various times to the family manor in Yorkshire, and we also visited other British and Scottish cities and towns – including occasionally leasing a house here in London.

Whenever we were in London, my father often took a house in Kennington – one of those solid, middle-class villas that sprang up south of the Thames. It was during one of those sojourns to the capital – in '64, as a matter of fact – that I first met old Sherman in Lambeth, adjacent to Kennington, and not too far for me to wander. You recall Sherman, don't you? I should think so! I was ten at the time, and had already formed the habit of rambling through London, with my father's encouragement and to my mother's dismay. You've been to Sherman's shop. I can assure you that it looked just as rough and distressed thirty years ago as it does today, were we to cross the river and pay him a visit. Ah, Watson – I saw that look of dismay flash across your face! Your ability to dissemble has not improved with the years, old friend! Fear not – this wandering tale of mine does not involve a visit to the noted bird-stuffer of No. 3 Pinchin Lane. No, I only mention old Sherman because this story has to do with his brother, a Whitechapel bell maker.

I perceive you've made the connection, though still tenuous – Big Ben, and now a bell maker.

To continue: By 1868, my health had collapsed, and father moved us back to Pau, but in 1870, we again returned to England, this time home to Yorkshire, because of several years of poor crops and mismanagement at the manor that needed his attention. And it was in the late summer of that year that I was sent to the Brompton Academy, in South Kensington – not all that far from the practice you just sold in Vicarage Gate.

Suffice it to say, I was miserable, and not a good student. Even at age sixteen, I already understood my own solitary nature, and also that my father's unusual method of education – tutored by my mother while driving the family from town to town for great stretches across Europe, only to be interrupted by returns to our remote Yorkshire home, or keeping to ourselves to ourselves in rented London houses – was not conducive to learning how to get along with fellows of my own age. Thus, my time at Brompton was not what I (or my parents) would call a success – but at least I was back in London, where I could resume my explorations, and renew my friendship with old Sherman.

He hadn't changed from when I'd met him six years earlier, and we quickly fell into our old friendship, wherein he, a lonely old widower who had grown ever-more eccentric with the passing years – was glad to have a curious young student with a hundred questions leading to a hundred more. I knew that his wife had died years earlier, and I had some understanding that there had also been a child, taken far too early by a fever, but I was surprised one day when Sherman mentioned that he had a brother – for I had thought him to be quite alone in the world – and even more surprised when I learned why I was told about him.

"He's gone missing, Mr. Sherlock," said Sherman one afternoon as the late October darkness blackened narrow Pinchin Lane outside the front window of the ground-floor shop. In all my time there, I'd never seen a customer make the trip there, nor had I seen any evidence that Sherman was doing any taxidermy work for a paying client. Rather, he seemed to make up the varied curious *tableaux* that decorated the shop for his own amusement. You've seen, of course, the stuffed weasel holding a young rabbit in the window. If you spend enough time there, you'll come across quite a few other oddities. An adder swallowing itself by the tail. A stoat wrapped by a slow worm. Between us, although Sherman bills himself as a "bird-stuffer", I've never known where his income is derived – and I've never wanted to! As you've seen, the place is more of a menagerie than a taxidermist's shop, and when I first visited there, I feared that he only kept the creatures to kill and stuff them. Later, I had to wonder where he obtains funds to feed everything that lives in that curious old building.

But I digress. On that autumn evening, Sherman told me some about his brother, John, although at first I was uncertain as to his reasons.

"You'll have heard me speak of my brother, Mr. Sherlock," he said, seemingly without reason. He had been showing me the differences in the paw-prints of various breeds of dogs. Glancing up from my lesson, I averred that I had not heard of any brother.

"No matter," he replied, and for a moment he went back to pointing out the difference between hare-footed, web-footed, and cat-footed canines. Not knowing what use such information might hold, I nevertheless found a place for it in my little brain-attic. It was with some annoyance, then, that a question on the tip of my tongue about that day's subject of study was prevented when he again mentioned his brother John.

"He vorks at the bell foundry," old Sherman explained. "In Vitechapel." You've met him – you know his strange method of speech – swapping his *V*'s and *W*'s as if one has met a latter-day Mr. Bumble. "He started vorking there before I was born – he's older than me, you see, by several years."

Sensing that this topic held some importance for my tutor, I sat up, set aside my question, and asked directly, "Is there some reason to mention your brother, Mr. Sherman?"

He looked up, his head bobbing on his stringy neck and the lantern light reflecting from his blue-tinted glasses. I suppose that he was rather shocked that I had jump ahead of him while he crept up on the subject.

"Vell, um, yes, Mr. Sherlock, I suppose there is. You've managed before to find some things that vent missing – or so you've told me."

I nodded, even as I frowned to myself. Apparently he'd been listening after all to my occasional conversational contributions about a few past incidents in which I'd been involved. It was a lesson to be more discreet in the future.

"That's right," I said, cautiously, sensing a trap opening up before me. But when Sherman explained what he wanted, it didn't seem so bad – although I had to wonder at his asking for help from a sixteen-year-old boy.

"My brother has disappeared, Mr. Sherlock," Sherman said, his eyes going back down to the bench where he shuffled around various dried dog paws. "He generally comes by here once a veek – to share a meal and talk about – vell, we talk about things, but he's now missed two veeks in a row. Last night being the second time. I'm . . . I'm vorried about him."

"Have you been to check on him – where he lives, or where he works?" I asked, getting a hint of where this was leading.

Sherman shook his head. "I cannot, Mr. Sherlock. I cannot go. You know I can't leave here. There are all the beasties to care for, and if I'm not vatchful, one of the dogs – I have over forty of them, you know – might get loose and go after one of the cats or badgers or rats, and you never know ven one of the raptors might swoop down and take a rabbit, or a wiper take one of the rats. And then there's the children."

Ah, Watson! Don't look shocked. It's not as terrible as it sounds. Sherman's building, as you'll recall, is bigger inside than it looks from the outside. It's rather like something a wizard would construct, and he has room for a veritable zoo, but never fear – Sherman doesn't keep caged children there. At least – not to my knowledge! Ha! A jest, Watson! A jest! You are far too gullible! Wipe that look of concern from your face. No, the neighborhood children used to spend far too much time taunting old Sherman, and he was in a regular daily terror of some of them getting inside and causing mayhem, or receiving injuries themselves. I had managed to mitigate that, by way of a few words with the Irregulars in the years before my travels abroad. I'll need to make sure that he's still being left alone . . . .

But I have again drifted off the path. In the end, (for our walk is progressing while my story has become mired in Pinchin Lane,) I was convinced to seek out John Sherman and find out why he had missed two dinner engagements with his brother. And so, with the addresses of Sherman's residence and workplace in hand, and rather than go back to school, I almost-gratefully returned to the north side of the river and walked east instead of west, toward Vite – umm, *White*chapel.

It was a beautiful October day, with the skies the most vivid blue you could imagine. There was a crisp and bracing aspect to the air, just enough to make me glad of my coat, and with the underlying warning of impending winter. A breeze from the river held some mysterious scent, always at the edge of my perception that made me want to keep walking. I was sixteen, and exploring London, it was wonderful.

My route was much like where we're walking now. I had crossed from Lambeth over the Waterloo Bridge and turned east along the Embankment – but it looked quite different then from how it looks now, as you will certainly recall. There were none of these benches back then. The Embankment had just opened to the public after several years of construction – but I don't need to tell you that. As I recall, you were already attending the University of London by then, so I'm sure you had a chance to amble along here as well.

There was a spring in my step, as I had no idea that this would be anything more than showing up at the offices of the bell foundry where John Sherman worked and asking to speak with him. I would relay my message and then take the long way back to South Kensington and Brompton. I had recently struck up a friendship with a retired teacher still living within the school, old Waxflatter, who was in some ways as eccentric as Sherman, and I hoped to pick his brain about a few esoteric science questions. He had degrees in Chemistry and Biology, was well versed in Philosophy, Mathematics, and Physics, the author of twenty-seven books – and most people thought he was a lunatic. Of course, I wanted to know what he could teach me more than anything I'd learn in the classroom lessons.

It was with these thoughts that I continued east – alongside the Temple and the different piers, all the way to and past the Cathedral and the Bank, and so into the East End.

If you'll recall, it actually wasn't quite as bad then as it became a few years later – during the times when all of the Rippers were carrying out their atrocities. While still terribly poverty-stricken, the number of immigrants hadn't yet arrived to the degree they would in the eighties, and neither had the country-folk who had been lured to town for better opportunities, only to find that none awaited them. The desperate overcrowding hadn't yet taken root, and even a rather bold sixteen-year-old such as myself could walk the main streets in daylight without too much anxiety. Before I knew it, I'd arrived at No. 34 Whitechapel Road, and the Whitechapel Bell Foundry, in business there since the 1500's. I didn't know much about it or bellfounding then, although I've had the opportunity to find out more in the years since. For instance, I was surprised, when traveling in the United States in '79 and '80, that the famed Liberty Bell in Philadelphia was cast at the Whitechapel Foundry. The fact that it later cracked has some small connection to my story, as you shall see.

I entered the office by way of a nondescript door, no different from any other on that street, and was met immediately by a rather harried gentleman who demanded to know my business. I later learned that he was George Mears who, at that time, was a co-owner of the business, along with Robert Stainbank. I stated that I was looking for John Sherman – "Mr. Sherman's brother hasn't seen him in a couple of weeks," I explained – and Mears immediately lost his temper, slamming a hand onto a nearby desk.

"He hasn't bothered to show up for nearly two weeks here either, and if you find him, tell him not to come back! First Albert Copper, and now Sherman – and with the Canterbury job to finish by the end of the month! One doesn't just reach out and pluck a skilled bell maker from off the street! What are we supposed to do?"

Seeing that I had no easy answer to his question, he cursed under his breath, turned, and went through a door at the back of the room, slamming it behind him. In the seconds that it was open, I could see that the building opened into a large working space with various curved molds stacked along one wall, drifts of sand and metal filings on the floor, and several men involved in pouring molten metal into a substantial bell-shaped construct sitting on a pallet.

Only then did I notice a young man sitting at a desk in a dark corner. He had wisely kept to himself during the previous tense moment.

"Don't mind Mr. Mears," he said. His tone was pleasant, and he spoke in an educated sort of way. "Just as we took on the big Canterbury job," he explained, "two of our senior men up and left."

"Mr. Sherman and Mr. Copper?" I asked, and the young man nodded. He stood and walked closer, and I could see that he was in his mid-twenties, unmarried, rather fastidious about his dress – a surprise in such a manufactory sort of location – and already a secret tippler of both the grain and the grape. If he wasn't careful, he'd be begging in the street outside before he was thirty.

"That's right," he confirmed. "You say that you were sent by Mr. Sherman's brother?"

"He has missed two of their weekly dinner engagements. So he's also disappeared from work?"

"That's right. We haven't heard from him in over week. The last time was just after Mr. Copper went home."

"'Went home'? And has he disappeared too?"

"No, no. Mr. Copper is a supervisor, you see. *Was* a supervisor, that is. He's been with us for years, just like Mr. Sherman, and he's been growing steadily more ill for a year. Some sort of wasting illness, you see. He tried to keep working, but it finally became too much for him." He lowered his voice. "The poor man went home to die." Then, his tone returning to normal, he added, "That was bad enough, but then the next day, Sherman never showed up, and that left us awfully short-handed. Mr. Mears and Mr. Stainbank – he's the other owner, and my uncle – are quite upset."

It was interesting, I supposed, that the two men had stopped coming to work at about the same time, but I couldn't see anything in one man being sick that would explain why the other had disappeared entirely. "Were they close?" I asked. "Would Mr. Copper's condition have upset Mr. Sherman to the point where he couldn't carry out his job?"

The young man shook his head. "Not likely. They clearly don't care for one another. Mr. Copper treats Mr. Sherman with great disdain. If the latter hadn't already worked here for so long, I'm sure he would have quit and gone elsewhere. A man with his experience could have easily found a job with one of our competitors. Truthfully, I'm not really sure why he's stayed."

Not knowing what other path to pursue, I asked for Mr. Copper's address, so that I could visit there if necessary after checking at Sherman's rooms, as there seemed to be some connection between the two men. The young fellow was suddenly wary. "Why would you want to pester a dying man?" he asked. "As I told you, they didn't get along. Mr. Copper can't tell you anything."

"Probably," I agreed. "But it sounds as if they have known each other a long time, and I need to tell Mr. Sherman – *my* Mr. Sherman – that I looked under every stone to see about finding his brother. I'm sure," I added, "that you understand."

Truthfully, I'm not sure that there was anything about that statement that had any legitimacy worth understanding, but the young man nodded as if convinced, if for no other reason than to get rid of me, and wrote an address on a slip of paper, and then told me how to find my way there. Then, with my thanks, he showed me out and the door shut.

There isn't much to report about Sherman's residence. The address was a small house near the London Hospital, in Raven Row. The landlady was rather enfeebled, both physically and mentally, and could tell me nothing. Knocking at Sherman's door brought no response, and it never occurred to me at that age to burgle his rooms. There were no obvious neighbors to question, and with some of the afternoon remaining, I set off for Mr. Copper's house, with a sigh, walking northeast toward Bethnal Green. My London exploration, now a duty rather than an adventure, was no longer quite as exciting.

I had only a fraction of the knowledge of London then that I would later acquire, but fortunately I was able to obtain directions as I went, and I eventually approached my goal, a modest house in the little thoroughfare of Parmiter Street. And once I was there, I realized that I was completely uncertain how to proceed – and somewhat unwilling to do so as well.

At that age, the idea of knocking on the front door of a dying stranger was quite intimidating. I stood for the longest time upon the front step, looking at the black door and deciding whether I had already done enough for my friend Sherman. After all, I had been to where he worked and lived, and what could I learn here? Just because this man had stopped coming to work at the same time that the bell maker went missing meant nothing. I had just about talked myself into making the long walk back to Brompton School when I heard someone in the distance clearing his throat. I turned to see a man across the street, standing behind a tall bush, leaning out and waving me over.

What choice did I have but to learn what he wanted?

As I approached, he stepped back behind the bush, clearly not wanting to be observed. I was a bit suspicious – wondering if I would be waylaid as soon as I stepped back there too. Instead, I found an older man facing me, his gnarled and scarred hands hanging in a most-unthreatening manner. And he looked so much like my friend Sherman that he must be the missing man.

"Mr. Sherman?" I asked. "John Sherman?"

He nodded and gave a smile. He had the same angular make-up and skinny limbs and neck as the bird-stuffer, and I could see how my Sherman would look in twenty years – much how he did look when you first met him, Watson, eighteen years later in '88.

I started to explain why I was there, but he interrupted. "Your brother sent me to find you – " I said, but he raised a hand to interrupt me.

"I'm not surprised that he vould send you, young Mister Sherlock."

The surprise at hearing my name from this stranger must have showed on my face, because he continued, stating, "My brother thinks a lot of you, lad. He says that you're the smartest pupil he's ever trained."

"Pupil?" I had to ask. I'd had no idea that my visits were anything more than a way for me to pick Sherman's brain while finding distraction away from school.

"That's right," said John Sherman. "He says that you immediately understand and remember vatever he teaches you."

He had the same curious speech habit as his brother. I don't propose to recreate it from here on out.

"Still," I asked, "how did you know it was me?"

"Two reasons – Because he has no other pupils, not anymore, and because of your hat, of course."

I nodded. Even then, I chose to wear this headgear, and it does make me recognizable when it serves my purpose. It had certainly helped make the connection with John Sherman. And now I could ask why he had disappeared, leaving his brother to worry in ignorance for over a week, and also placing his employment at risk.

"I've been to the bell foundry," I explained. "They told me that Mr. Copper – " Here I nodded toward the quite house across the street. " – has been away for about the same amount of time as you. And Mr. Mears – "

I didn't want to speak the next part, but John Sherman finished my thought. "He's no doubt fired me," he said. "Not surprising. But I had a task that's more important to me than working right now on the Canterbury bell job. I have to be here when Albert Copper dies. I have to get back what's mine."

He leaned out then, looking past the bush at Copper's doorway. Nothing had changed, and he seemed to feel that gave him a little time to keep talking.

"I agree with my brother – from what I can see, you're a likely lad," said John Sherman. "Would you be willing to help me? To get back what's mine?"

I didn't quite know how to respond. I had started the day with the plan of stopping by Sherman's shop to have a short visit before wandering on, perhaps to the British Museum, or possibly one of the stations to learn something new about trains. And yet, my feet were now on this path, leading unexpectedly across London. I had once read of a mountain in the American South, a great quartz dome in the State of Georgia, where one is tempted to walk out to the edge and look off. But there is a gradual slope as one progresses, the slightest of curves at the most infinitesimal of angles, that seems almost flat. One goes a little more, and a little more still, to get to the point where looking over the edge seemingly becomes possible – but then one finds that the slope has become more than expected, and getting back to the higher level has become nearly impossible. All that's left is to slide off the thousand-foot-high foot rock with the frantic fatal final knowledge that one has made a mistake. I was wondering if my day was running along that same sort of slippery slope, and if I kept taking small steps forward, at what point would I find that I couldn't return?

John Sherman pulled some coins from his pocket. "A few hundred feet back the way you came, you can buy some cheese and bread, and ale. Get some for both of us, and bring it back here, and I'll tell you a story."

I returned to John Sherman's covert in ten minutes and, as we ate and he looked regularly toward Copper's front door, he related a most curious tale.

"When were you born, lad?" he asked by way of a beginning.

"1854," I replied. "In January."

"Then you probably don't remember much from when Big Ben was cast."

I shook my head. I suppose I'd been aware that the Great Bell was made sometime during the years when I was small, but I'd really given it no thought. By the time that we were living in London and my mind was somewhat functional, the great clock tower and the bell within it were simply part of the City's landscape, and I gave its origin no more thought than I did to St. Paul's or Nelson's Column. John Sherman could see that I needed to be educated.

"The Great Bell, or Big Ben, was first cast by John Warner in 1856, in Stockton-on-Tees, and brought to London by sea. The clock tower wasn't finished yet, so they mounted it in the nearby yard of Westminster Palace – and when they tested her, she cracked. Four feet up one side. They should have hired the Whitechapel Foundry to cast her from the beginning instead of Warner, but at least we were given the job of repairing her.

As we ate and he looked regularly toward Copper's front door.
(Illustration by Thaddeus Tuffentsamer)

"We re-cast her in 1858 – in that same foundry where you visited before finding me here. The original bell was sixteen tons, but we had a better design and reduced her to thirteen-and-a-half. That's still a lot of bronze – twenty-two parts copper to seven parts tin. And there was a little something extra added in . . . ."

He fell silent then, as if seeing a far-away vision of long ago. Then he took a drink of ale and continued.

"I'd been working for the foundry for ten years by then, and so had Albert Copper. We grew up alongside one another, and found jobs there on the same day. We were the best of friends for so long – and then we met Alice Denney.

"She was the daughter of our supervisor, and I don't know how we went so long without knowing about her. But when we finally met her – on a day when she brought her father his forgotten lunch – it was as if all my life had been lived under a cloudy sky, and finally the sun was visible. Where all had been gray, now there vas color. I felt as if every breath woke me up a little more than the one before.

"And Albert Copper saw her too and felt the same way. Thank God it was me that she loved and not him.

"We were to be married in the spring of '58 – just when the remains of the first Big Ben were ready for recasting. After she had first cracked, she was broken up into scrap, brought to us, and melted down. I don't know if you've seen a bell made, but we make forms, inner and outer, out of sand, compressed and then covered to hold its shape. We add whatever is supposed to decorate the outer side of the bell to this mold – lettering, raised edges or grooves, and so on. With inner and outer molds constructed, we put them together and pour the molten metal into the space between them. In a week or so, the bell that has formed inside is cool enough to hold its shape, and we take the mold off to see if we were successful. It's never a certainty, you understand.

"The evening before the bell was to be cast, Alice and I were strolling towards the river near The Temple, down along King's Bench Walk, talking about our future and what we each dreamed for it. It was then that she looked down, having seen something shining in the light of the setting sun. She pointed me in that direction, and I bent to find two rings, a man's and a woman's, tied together with twine and dropped into the ditch beside the roadway.

"Our first thought was to see if anyone had noticed us. When I decided that we were unobserved, I looked at them more closely. They weren't of any great worth, although there was some gold inlaid into the lesser base metal. They could still fetch a pretty penny for us if sold, but my thought was that with a little adjustment, they might make fine wedding rings instead – for we weren't able to afford any on our own.

"I explained my thought with enthusiasm, but Alice was always of a different and much more-practical cast. She reminded me that wearing rings while doing my work was dangerous and discouraged – more than one man had seen the skin stripped from the bone when a ring was caught, or lost a finger entirely – and that she herself had never had any interest in wearing a ring.

"'We can sell them, then,' I said. 'We can start out with a tidy little nest-egg.' But she shook her head at that too. A different notion had popped into her head, and the more she thought about it, the more she liked it.

"'We can always make money," she said. I thought that was being a little optimistic, but she had been raised by her father, who had always enjoyed a comfortable living, and she didn't understand some of the hardships of life. But she continued, explaining, 'We don't need these rings – but we can do something with them that will be a much greater reminder to each other of our vows than simply looking down every day and seeing them around our fingers.'

"Now she had me intrigued. 'What do you have in mind, my love?'

"She gave a clever smile – one of the many reasons I loved her – and said, 'The Great Bell is being cast tomorrow. Push them into the molten metal. Thereafter, whenever we hear the bell ring, we'll be reminded that *our* rings are up there, in the bell tower, part of the sound that echoes across all of London. I can't think of a more romantic reminder of our love than to hear it toll every hour.'

"Now, while I was the more practical of the two of us, and liked the idea of having whatever money the rings would raise to be saved for a rainy day, I couldn't say no to her smile. So the short side of it was that the next day when the molten metal was poured into the new form, I opened one of the little side doors low down on the bow near the bell's mouth and quickly pushed in the two rings, side by side. No one saw me. Then I closed the hatch, screwed it shut, and waited the week or so for the cooled bell to be revealed.

"Alice was standing with me the day the molds were removed, and it was better than we could have hoped – or so we thought. There, on the side of the bell where the little door had given me access, was a patch of just the slightest different color, not much bigger than the size of two side-by-side coins. The rings had melted, and the gold and base metals in them gave a slightly different cast to that part of the bell. Now, not only would we *hear* the bell every time and think about our love, but we would know that the proof could be *seen* for anyone who knew where to look!

"We were so happy, and even the growing jealousy and ill will from my former friend, Albert Copper, couldn't take away from it. Life went on, and we prepared for our wedding, and I couldn't imagine how anything could go wrong – but it did.

"A few months after she was recast, Big Ben was hung in the tower. At that time, it was the biggest bell in the world. It, along with four other smaller bells, were tuned to play the song you've heard so often since then, probably without thinking about it. The clock was required to be accurate within one second of the time kept at Greenwich, and the works are adjusted to run fast or slow as needed by placing or removing pennies on the great weights.

"1858 passed by, and in the fall, Alice and I were married. That finished any remnant of my friendship with Albert. He'd never had a chance with Alice, but he didn't see it that way. Meanwhile, he gained more responsibility at the foundry, taking on supervisory roles and making my life difficult. I thought of leaving, but remained because Alice's father still worked there, and he served to keep Albert in check. It was something that Alice and I discussed often – Albert's various actions against me – but they didn't seem all that important as we enjoyed our new married life. Then, just a year from our marriage, came an omen that seemed to foretell all that came after. In September of 1859, Big Ben cracked.

"Officially, it seemed as if it was caused by using a hammer that was far larger than what had been specified. But I was part of the crew that was summoned to the belfry to examine the bell, and I was horrified to see that the horrendous crack, several feet long and running from the mouth and up the side, passed directly through the spot where the change in color indicated that our rings has been placed. Later that afternoon, back at the foundry, I pulled Alice aside to let her know. She was often a visitor there, bringing both me and her father lunch. As we whispered about it, wondering if somehow the metal from our rings had created a flaw in the great bell, we didn't realize that we were overheard by Albert – he understood completely what we'd done. He didn't mention it then. He held onto the knowledge and hoarded it until it could do him the most good.

"Not long after, we found that Alice was expecting – but within a few months, it was obvious that something was wrong. The baby hadn't rooted in the womb, but instead had settled elsewhere in her body. As it grew, it was killing them both, and there was nothing that could be done. By the end of the year, she was dead.

"I was broken, and went through the sad motions of my life in a haze of grief. Meanwhile, debate raged as to what to do about the bell, and whose fault it was that the crack had occurred. The foundry blamed the man who hung a too-heavy hammer, and he blamed the foundry. Of course, I never hinted that I had possibly damaged the bell by pushing in our rings, and Albert never said a word about what he knew. It was finally recommended by Sir George Airy, the Royal Astronomer, to use a smaller hammer – which should have been done from the beginning – and to give the bell a one-eighth rotation so that the hammer didn't hit on the crack. Then Albert suggested one other repair – although I didn't know about it until afterwards.

"A week or so later, Albert called me aside at work and, seeing that we were alone, pulled a metal piece from off his, a thick square measuring several inches on each side. I'd seen such things before, cut from old bells or left over from different metal tests. But he held it in such a way as if he didn't want me to grab it away from him.

"'Did you hear? They took my suggestion about fixing Big Ben.'

"Hearing that, I paid more attention, suddenly wary.

"'In order to keep the crack from expanding, I suggested that we cut out a piece – *this* piece.' He turned it in his fingers, catching the morning light. I had a horrible premonition where he was leading.

"'It was a good idea – and I didn't even mention that there seems to be a flaw of some type with this piece of metal. Almost as if something were added to the molten brass during casting, something spoiled and defective and rotten that cursed the bell and made it crack.'

"He smiled then, cruelly, and I understood that he somehow knew what we'd done, and that he'd found his revenge. 'I heard you talking,' he explained. 'About how you ruined the bell by pushing in your filthy cheap rings.' He leaned closer. 'They say that the crack, and this cut-out, have both changed the tone of the bell. That its overtones aren't quite right any longer, and that it will always have a distinctive sound. I agree – I can hear it every time she rings. Can you? Have you heard the difference? I expect that you have. If not, you will from now on. Every time you hear that bell ring, you'll know how it's off, and out of tune just a little bit, because something *cursed* it! And you know what cursed it – and you'll always know. *Every time!*'

"I felt like lunging toward him, to take back the metal piece containing our rings from his soiled and scheming grasp, but I was frozen. This somehow fit with everything bad that had already happened, and I was overwhelmed. I couldn't fight it – or Albert. Just then, he had won. He had taken something that we had meant to be so meaningful, and that had already been spoiled, and further desecrated it. But I vowed then that someday I would get back our rings, mine and Alice's, no matter what it took. And now – " He glanced across the road, where the front door of Copper's house was opening. His voice lowered, and took on a new urgency. " – He's kept our rings from me for years. I was never able to get them back. But now that he's about to die, I'll have my chance!"

It appeared that he truly would, and very soon, for a solid and plain middle-aged man was just then stepping out of the house, carrying a medical bag. He turned around and shook hands with someone who appeared to be the butler. They shared a few words and then each nodded gravely. Then the doctor stepped down to the street and walked in our direction while the door shut. John Sherman abruptly lurched past me, into the view of the physician, blocking the man's path.

"Albert Copper?" he asked, his voice almost a croak. "Has he died?"

The doctor, apparently thinking we were just arriving to visit before the end, but now tragically too late, nodded with a sad sympathetic expression. "Only a few minutes ago," he said gravely. "He was unconscious at the end. There was no pain."

John Sherman cursed softly, and I believe that the doctor gave him the benefit of the doubt, as if my companion were upset at missing some chance to see the dead man one last time, when in fact I understood that Sherman wished that Copper had indeed suffered. Then, Sherman nodded an acknowledgement and the doctor moved along. Before he'd reached the corner, Sherman was looking back at me, his gaze fierce and raptor-like while he gripped my arm with sudden urgency.

"Will you stay?" he asked, his voice raw. "Until nightfall? And will you help me retrieve our rings?"

What Sherman was asking could not be true – that he apparently intended to break into the dead man's house on the eve of his passing and take the metal piece that had been kept away from him for nearly a dozen years. But there could be no other explanation. Not knowing what else to say, and continuing along that gradually increasing slope from which there was no return, I nodded in agreement.

Sherman pulled me away from the neighborhood, as if now he feared that we might be seen, and around several corners to nearby Bonner Road, not far from the hospital. There we found a small pub that served hot food, apparently to a regular crowd of men who plied the nearby Regents Canal and managed the upkeep of the Bonner Hall Bridge. He was recognized, and it seemed that Sherman had become something of a regular in the days that he was watching Copper's house, waiting for the man to die. Over a tasty stew of meat, carrots, and onions, strongly flavored with paprika and garlic, he explained more about how his life had become strangely tied with that of the dead man.

"I should have just left the foundry," he explained. "Alice was dead, and I could have found similar work at other bell foundries. But knowing that Albert had cut out the piece of the bell that contained our rings – the symbols of our love – and that he was holding it like some evil charm drove me mad. A thousand times, I thought of killing him and taking it back – but that would have been even worse. Nothing that I did could be allowed to soil our rings in that way. So I had no choice but to wait him out, putting up with his abuse for the last twelve years. And then, suddenly, he was sick. He was dying. One day, he wasn't at work, and they said he wasn't coming back. Hearing that, I departed immediately, back to watch his home as I've done so many other times. Before, I was watching because I had nowhere else to go. This time, there was a reason. This time, I would finally get what's mine – mine and Alice's."

He looked from one side to the other, as if he were about to impart deeper secrets. I knew not who he was looking for. Surely no one here knew him very well, or cared about his business.

"It was a chancy thing," he said, his voice lower. "Whether I could wait out Albert or not. You see, young Master Sherlock – I'm dying too. Have been for quite a while, as a matter of fact. I haven't told anyone, not even my brother. Soon, I'll be with my Alice, and we'll both be young again, and together forever. And it's a very lucky thing that my brother sent you to find me just now."

He paused, as if waiting for me to take in what he was telling me. Apparently, there was more to come, besides helping him burgle the dead man's house. I chose not to rise to his bait, and instead took another bite of stew. He watched, waiting for me to respond, but when I did not, he shrugged and began to talk more about the great bell – Big Ben. But I knew that the topic of his next favor wasn't abandoned.

"She's a beauty," he said. "My brother says you're a musician. Do you understand music, or do you just play by how it sounds?"

"I play by ear," I replied, "but I also read music, and I understand compositional theory."

He nodded. "As a bell maker, I had to learn some music as well – although when I was very young, it never occurred to me that I'd acquire such knowledge. So you understand musical keys then?"

I nodded, and he continued. "Big Ben strikes an *E*. The original bell, before it cracked, was an '*E*' too, and it's lucky that that the re-cast bell turned out to be the same note, as the four smaller bells were also cast in the key of '*E*': *E*, *B*, *F-sharp*, and *G-sharp* – the first, second, third, and fifth notes of the *E* scale. There was some worry when the new bell was re-cast that its tone would be wrong, since it used over three-thousand pounds less brass. Normally you make a bell heavier than you need for a deeper note and then shave away until it gets lighter and its pitch rises to what you want – but in this case, we hit it spot on. Almost a miracle, some would say.

"Did you know about tuning a bell, Mr. Sherlock? Some think that it rings just a single note, but there are other notes present, underneath the dominant or prime note that the human ear hears. The harmonics of the different parts of the bell – the mouth, the waist, and the shoulder – all have different notes, and as the main note – the fundamental – fades, you hear hints of the other notes. A minor third and perfect fifth in the first octave, and the same in the second octave, all tapering off that the last lingering tone, the *hum*. If your bell is made right, that is."

He went on to share with me a number of other bits of working knowledge – both bell-making and metallurgy – and I was enjoying myself in the way that I did when spending time with his brother, knowing that I was learning from a true craftsman. Still, I knew that he was working around to asking for his favor before our meal came to an end.

"So, Mr. Sherlock," he said, when it was fully dark outside and our food was gone, "I crave a boon. Two, actually. First, will you help me search Albert's room tonight?"

I had already decided that I would, and told him so, but I was curious about the rest of his request, and I asked him about the second favor. "Soon enough," he said. "One thing at a time." He wiped his mouth and stood. "I know the routine at Albert's house well enough by now. No worries – we'll be in and out before you know it. Time to go."

As we walked through the darkness back to Parmiter Street, we didn't meet a soul. Sherman softly explained that Copper only had two servants, a husband and wife, who slept in the rear of the house's top floor, while Copper's bedroom was on the opposite side, with a ground-floor entrance. "They'll be in bed, and we can get in and out without anyone knowing."

He'd clearly thought this through during his time watching the house, and it did go as quickly and easily as he predicted. He led me to the rear of the building, where he used a long-bladed knife to jemmy open the door, and then we were inside a comfortably furnished bedroom, lit only by a low-turned lantern on a side table.

There was a bed, a few chairs and a table, some bookshelves, a bureau and dresser, and a great desk covered with papers. What hadn't been expected, and to Sherman's surprise as well as my own, was the sheet-covered body of the former master of the house, lying on the bed.

"I thought that the undertaker would have been and gone while we ate."

He stepped across and lifted the sheet, looking down at the face of his former friend, who had spent a dozen years tormenting him. I thought about walking across and seeing him for myself, but there was no need. Instead, while Sherman silently exchanged whatever private goodbyes he had for the dead man, I turned toward the desk.

I had started to open drawers and push through piles of papers, looking for the piece of metal cut from the Great Bell. In those days, not knowing that I should do so, I hadn't formed any sort of method for successful searching, but I still tried to approach the desk in a scientific manner, moving to one side as Sherman joined me.

"How," I whispered, "does a supervisor at a bell foundry afford such a house?" I asked.

Sherman snorted, shifting papers from side to side. "He inherited money, and he worked hard at the foundry, to the point where he participates in the company's financial successes. With his assets, I've often wondered why he stayed, and I can only conclude that it was to remain and torment me."

That seemed a bit unlikely, I thought at first, but then I remembered John Sherman's obsession, and decided that it was quite possible for Albert Copper to have had something similar from his different perspective.

At that moment, I moved a long flat box that turned out to be quite heavy, and which gave a metallic ring when I set it down. I handed it to Sherman, who opened it, sliding out a flat rectangular piece of brass. Tied around it was a note.

Sherman simply looked at it for the longest time, his breathing ragged, as if he'd just finished a long race. Then, he slipped off the note and unfolded it. After a moment, he crumpled it with a curse.

"He saw me watching," he said. "For the last week, he knew I was watching – and that I'd come for our rings. Rather than destroy it or hide it where I'd never find it, he left it for me – and in doing so, he laid his final curse on the metal!"

Not knowing how to respond, I said, "There is no curse. Don't give that idea any credence. Instead, consider yourself blessed that he knew you were planning to retrieve the rings, and yet he didn't destroy them."

I have to confess that I wasn't convinced that Copper hadn't switched one metal piece for another, with his final revenge being that he let Sherman steal back the wrong object, but I didn't want to take the idea that he'd at least finally achieved his goal away from my new acquaintance.

Somehow my words gave Sherman the comfort he needed. He nodded and, without a look back or another word, he put the metal piece back in the box, walked to the fireplace where he tossed in Copper's final letter, and then led me back outside. I pulled the door shut behind me, knowing that the evidence of burglary would be obvious, but realizing that when nothing was apparently found missing, it would just be considered a minor mystery.

Outside and across the street, near the bush where we'd previously tarried, I was prepared to take my leave and return to Brompton, and I was starting to remind Sherman to go visit his brother when he finally spoke. "About that other boon, Mr. Sherlock . . . ."

I had hoped he'd forgotten, or that it was no longer necessary. I started to ask him what it was, but then, considering just how far along the slope I'd slipped so far, I realized that I wanted to know how the story ended. I simply nodded, and in the darkness I could see him smile in appreciation. Then he led me back toward Whitechapel.

I became more aware as we progressed that this was a much different district at night than during the day. I was not altogether ignorant, even at that age, of the various wicked misdeeds and vices pursued by our fellow man, but that walk, short as it was, remains in my mind as something of an education. Still, I could only observe with one part of my brain as Sherman spoke softly.

"My position at the foundry is – *was*, that is – also quite responsible, after so many years of service. I also have a comfortable living – but I chose to devote my resources elsewhere. Specifically, to making sure that Alice has had a comfortable resting place – and me beside her, when my time comes. To do so, I've spent quite a bit of money to obtain a proper tomb, and to make sure that we'll keep it after we're both gone."

I'll admit that I was puzzled, uncertain as to where he was leading me, both physically and conversationally. He sensed it.

"I have to deliver our rings now – tonight. It cannot wait until I'm gone. Someone might steal them from my rooms, and once . . . once I'm dead . . . ."

It was becoming more clear, and it was no surprise when my guide led me through the gates of the Brady Street Cemetery. He walked with purpose and certainty, and in just a silent moment, we stood before a modest tomb, marked simply with the word *Sherman.*

He fished out a key, unlocked the narrow iron door, and stepped inside. I held back, uncertain. In a moment, he had lit a lantern hanging inside the door, and I took a deep breath and joined him.

He was already standing alongside a coffin, on a bier at the left side of the small stone chamber. A matching spot, *sans* coffin, was at the right, awaiting my companion's occupancy. In Sherman's hand was the metal piece, which he was holding up, not where he could see it, but rather as if he were showing it to someone, proof that his mission had been accomplished.

"Do you . . ." I asked. "Do you want me to wait outside?"

He looked at me, shook his head, and smiled. "No, Mr. Sherlock. This way you can see where I put them, and their importance to us both. My other favor is for you to find a way, after I'm gone, to come here from time to time to make sure that she still has them – that no one else takes them from us. When we're done here, you can have this key – it's my own copy. You can check here every once in a while – if you're agreeable. It will be our secret."

What else could I say, Watson? I wanted to ask why he couldn't make this request of his brother – but before the words crossed my lips, I knew that he had his own reasons. Perhaps he had planned to request this same boon from his brother, but when I unexpectedly wrote myself into his story, the plan changed. Possibly he had some reason to doubt his brother's sense of responsibility, or his longevity. Or possibly the bird-stuffer had already refused him, convinced that he was unable to leave his menagerie for the same reasons that he'd sent me on the quest to locate his missing sibling. In any case, I simply looked at him and nodded. A look of peace crossed his face.

Despite what he'd said, I left him alone while he opened the coffin and slipped the piece of metal inside. Soon the lantern went dark and he was back outside, relocking the door. Then he solemnly handed me the key.

I left him with a handshake at Whitechapel Station, just south of the cemetery, and returned by late trains as far as I could to South Kensington, managing with no great difficulty to reenter the school and find my way undetected to the dormitory and my bunk.

The next day, I went to Pinchin Lane and told Mr. Sherman that I'd located his brother, safe and sound. I didn't share anything about the rings, or our visit to the dead man's house. It wasn't my story to tell. A few weeks later, I joined Sherman at his brother's funeral, and I thought I sensed the old man's peace when his coffin was placed in the tomb. Until now, I'm the only one who has known the story of what else is there . . . .

Our anfractuous walk had wound through Whitechapel, with Holmes pacing his narrative to match our progress, and by the time we reached the entrance to Brady Street Cemetery, I wasn't surprised to learn that it was our destination. We stood for a while in silence, looking at the Sherman tomb, while I considered what I'd heard, and what was hidden inside.

"Why tell me this?" I finally asked Holmes. "If it was a secret?"

"I saw no harm in it," replied Holmes, "and I don't think it was ever necessarily meant to be a secret in that sense. John Sherman simply wanted to make sure that the rings remained safe."

"And are they?" I asked. "Safe? Have you made sure over the years?"

Holmes nodded, but it was a moment before he spoke. "Three times," he finally said, "and no time is ever any easier. I enter, and remain just long enough to barely raise the lid to Alice Sherman's coffin – it isn't sealed. There, tucked in the linens, is a piece of metal – the same one that John Sherman left there in October 1870."

"Have you ever examined it?" I asked. "Taken it out to see if it really does show indications of being discolored from the presence of the two rings?"

He spent another moment's silence spent staring at the tomb. I wondered if Holmes somehow had the key with him that day, manipulating our walk with the intention of making another inspection of the coffin after being away for three years. But then he took a deep breath and straightened his back. "You know, Watson, I have not. I prefer to believe, along with John Sherman, that he found the correct and unsubstituted piece of Big Ben on Albert Copper's desk that night, and that's what he brought back for his wife."

He turned then and led me back to the street, and then west, generally in the direction of Baker Street.

"But you said that you made a trip to see the bell." I noted. "To see where the metal was removed."

"I did. Just a month or so after John Sherman's funeral. Mycroft arranged it – although I didn't feel like telling him why, and he was perceptive enough not to ask."

At that moment, as if on cue, I could hear – at the very periphery of my senses – the great bell striking the hour of two o'clock.

"You can hear it if you listen," explained Holmes as we paused. "The slight 'offness' of the tone, after the crack and the piece of the bell that was cut out. It's actually a rather beloved feature of the bell, or so I've heard. They say," he continued, "that under the right conditions, one can hear the bell from five miles away."

I nodded, and we resumed walked along in silence. After a few minutes, Holmes laughed softly. At my inquiry, he explained.

"I had thought I was telling you the story of John Sherman and the rings because we heard Big Ben chiming earlier, but perhaps there's a deeper reason than that."

"How so?"

"I encountered John Sherman in October 1870. Just a couple of months later, not long before Christmas, was when I first met Henry, when he came to the Brompton School after his previous school in Carlisle finally succumbed to a mountain of debt and unpaid fees. Perhaps seeing him today at the lawyer's office awakened memories of that entire period of time somewhere in my mind."

"Perhaps," I agreed, my tone recalling that my opinion of Dr. Henry Verner was not of the highest.

Holmes, of course, recognized this and said with a smile, "There's more to Henry than you might think, Watson. Perhaps, on the walk back to Baker Street, I might tell you of what happened that Christmas, not long after he arrived at Brompton – the murders of a series of old men with a secret connection. And on our way, we might detour past the remains of a certain warehouse, which you'll be surprised to learn once held a fully reproduced pyramid, maintained by an Egyptian death cult of most-deadly Osiris worshipers."

Then the smile faded. "It wasn't all fun, however. It also ended up being the first great tragedy of my life . . . ."

By the time we were finally back at Baker Street, and having heard about these curious adventures of a Young Sherlock Holmes, I had no doubts that selling my practice was the best possible decision I could have made.

NOTES

* More about Watson's first sale of his Kensington practice and the incident involving gunfire in front of Simpsons can be found in *Sherlock Holmes and The Eye of Heka* (David Marcum, MX Publishing, 2021)

Dr. Verner

Very little is told to us about Dr. Verner in the Canon. In "The Norwood Builder", it states:

> *At the time of which I speak, Holmes had been back for some months, and I at his request had sold my practice and returned to share the old quarters in Baker Street. A young doctor, named Verner, had purchased my small Kensington practice, and given with astonishingly little demur the highest price that I ventured to ask– an incident which only explained itself some years later, when I found that Verner was a distant relation of Holmes, and that it was my friend who had really found the money.*

In a series of tales brought to the public by Sam Siciliano, it's been established that Dr. Verner is actually *Dr. Henry Vernier*. In these various adventures, narrated by Vernier, Holmes's cousin, we see the Great Detective from a different perspective. Sadly, Vernier is a rather petty and unlikeable fellow, constantly and irrationally jealous of Watson, and inaccurately portraying himself as Holmes's best friend. But aside from Vernier himself, the adventures are quite good.

I've determined that Dr. Henry Vernier is actually the young Watson-like fellow that accompanies Holmes in the filmed and novelized adventures *Young Sherlock Holmes* (1985). Since Holmes and Watson first met on January 1st, 1881, the events of *Young Sherlock Holmes*, set in December 1870, cannot also be their first meeting, and if Holmes didn't meet Watson in 1870, who did he meet? *Dr. Henry Vernier*, of course.

It wouldn't have been unusual in those days, especially considering Holmes's many boyhood travels, if the two cousins hadn't previously encountered one another. When the script and associated novel for *Young Sherlock Holmes* were written from Vernier's old notes and diaries, the filmmakers correctly perceived that there would be less commercial interest in a *Holmes and Vernier* film as compared to a *Holmes and Watson* film, so Vernier's name was changed. If Vernier was still alive when the film was made, this would no doubt be yet another one of his unfounded grievances against Watson – even if this, like the others, wasn't Watson's fault.

Much more about *Dr. Verner* being identified as *Dr. Henry Vernier*, and also his participation in *Young Sherlock Holmes*, can be found in my essay, "Actually, That Wasn't Watson: Some Notes Eventually Circling In Upon the Major Obfuscation in '*Young Sherlock Holmes*'", which originally appeared in a *The*

Watsonian, Fall 2016, Vol.4, No. II, and then in a slightly different form as an entry in my online blog, *A Seventeen Step Program*:

> *https://17stepprogram.blogspot.com/2017/03/actually-that-wasnt-watson-some-notes.html*

The Crack in Big Ben

As described, a crack did occur in Big Ben in September 1859, and it has had a slightly unusual but famed tone ever since. Rather than remake the bell (after it had already been recast following its first crack in October 1857), a smaller hammer was used and the bell was given a one-eighth turn. Also, a piece of metal was cut out of the crack, which can still be seen today.

Until finding this narrative in the vast amount of Watson's papers which were entrusted to me several years ago during one of my Holmes Pilgrimages to England, I hadn't give much thought to Big Ben. Now, knowing the truth of the crack, the metal cut-out, and the bell's unique sound, I'll never be able to hear it without thinking of Alice and John Sherman's rings and the love it represents – which I like to think would have pleased them both quite a bit.

The Swapped Names of the Saviour

Yesterday, I read in The Times *that Reverend Rayford Chinnor Longwick had died at Gallipoli. When the war began, he volunteered immediately as an Army Chaplain, and from what I've heard, he never hesitated to place himself where he could do the most good, even at the greatest personal risk to himself. I was greatly saddened by the news that he is lost, and now, four years after we first met, I'm still shamed at my first reaction to this brave man, when I initially thought him to be nothing more than a pompous, ineffectual, and silly* poseur. *This, in truth, was the same hero who raced into a contested plaza, the bullets flying like maddened hornets, to lead out a mother and child who were trapped in the deadly crossfire. Only when he knew that they were safe did he allow the thread of his life, nearly severed by the four bullets he'd taken from the Turks' Mausers, to fray and drift part, and he went to his reward, so I'm told, with a smile upon his face.*

– JHW
6 June, 1915

An adage that never loses its efficacious wisdom is that one shouldn't count upon the weather. The seasoned traveler understands this, and heaven knows that I – nearing the middle of my seventh decade as I recall these events – am certainly one of those. However, on that day in early autumn 1911, my planned holiday to Beachy Head, on the Sussex coast where I would spend a few days visiting in the cottage of my friend Sherlock Holmes, had established itself in my head with visions of bright blue skies and bracing walks across the countryside. Despite the accumulating daily evidence to the contrary, I continued to picture it with high anticipation, even as London, seventy-five miles nearly straight to the north from that piece of coastline, settled further into an interminable repetition of dank and foggy days.

I knew better, of course, with each day's weather predictions, but still my imagination would drift toward that idyllic image, even as the facts negating it mounted. The newspapers reported that the same conditions were in place in Sussex – deteriorating, and likely to remain so for a week or longer. Still, each morning, and each day closer to my short holiday, some primitive part of my brain fooled me into thinking that circumstances could possibly still improve even as the glass was falling.

My practice in Queen Anne Street had, by that point, become rather reduced, as I only saw a handful of old patients – by then it might hardly have been called a practice at all. My wife was away for a visit to a long-time friend, and it had seemed to be a perfect solution to my daily malaise when Holmes had invited me to journey south. (I found out later that my wife had wired him and suggested it, should it be convenient to Holmes's schedule.) I needed the change, and amongst my traveling bags I had packed some of my notes, hoping to question my friend regarding a few points concerning his past investigations with the possibility that the narratives might someday appear in *The Strand* – which, it cannot be denied, was always a useful supplement to my income.

I'd convinced myself early on that I would hazard the journey in my automobile, and had made sure beforehand that it was adequately prepared for the trip – fuel tank filled, rubber tires pressurized, and lamps in good condition – but as the day approached, I understood that these plans were also doomed to failure.

The night before my departure, it began to rain in earnest.

Notifying the garage that I wouldn't be taking the car after all, I instead entrained at Victoria Station and settled into a private first-class compartment, thankful at least that I was on an express. It was no use looking to either side as we progressed – the weather made sure that none of the usual pleasant scenery was visible. Instead of daydreaming the journey away by watching raindrops streaking along the windows, or sleeping – The temptation for that bled away too much of my time already! – I settled in with the last-minute editing of the manuscript that I was preparing for publication within the next couple of months – that of the rescue of Lady Frances Carfax from the clutches of the thoroughly despicable "Holy" Peters. The story hadn't ended quite as well as the version I'd recorded – as Doyle insisted on a "happy ending" – and the lady had suffered from terrible and crippling recurring nightmares after being nearly buried alive in a coffin, sidled up alongside another dead body, but there was no need to subject the poor woman to worse scrutiny than she'd received from the press at the time.

The train arrived on time, and I was soon ensconced in a rackety old cab and rattling west along the narrow road to East Dean. The weather was breaking up for just a little while, and at times I could see glimpses of the angry churning sea in the distance. I knew the driver, Beauchamp, from previous journeys, and he told me of some of the recent local flooding, including a wash-out on one of the roads upon which I would have driven. I had made the correct decision to leave my automobile in London.

We turned south at Crapham Hill and soon passed the old inn and then the coaching establishment before veering back west, with the ground sloping dramatically upward on our left to the edges of the high chalk cliffs. Meanwhile, the road itself was steadily dropping toward Birling Gap, with its limited access to the sea at the Coast Guard station. However, before we reached it, Holmes's small farm – a "villa" as he liked to call it – came into focus on the right, a rectangular plot of five acres, surrounded by a low wall made from the local quartz, with open fields stretching behind it to the north, used only by those locals walking from here-to-there and the many sheep that dotted the nearby landscape.

Beauchamp delivered me right to Holmes's door, which was thrown open before I reached it by Mrs. Hudson. At the time of Holmes's retirement, she had initially thought to stay in London, but as time passed, she agreed that her days would be better spent in the countryside instead of the smoky and unhealthy capital. (It was a lesson that I hadn't seemed to learn.) At the time of her relocation, Holmes had arranged to purchase her lease of 221 Baker Street, to use as a base of operations whenever he needed to return to the capital – for his "retirement" was more often than not a convenient fiction used to cover his activities as he went all over on errands for his brother Mycroft, preparing for the ever-certain impending war with Germany. (In fact, within a year from the events that I describe, Holmes would take on his identity as the mysterious "Altamont", a bitter and disaffected Irish-American willing to spy for the Germans. But that is a tale I'll reserve for another time, when the end of this war is in sight.)

At that moment in time, a war with Germany seemed much more likely after the previous April's Agadir Crisis, and finally the common-folk were beginning to understand a bit more about what was coming, although none could realize to what extent. I had the benefit – or curse – of both being a veteran of and a witness to a particularly terrible battle, and also the keen insight of both Sherlock and Mycroft Holmes to explain just what a modern conflict with so many entangled nations – and such modernized weaponry – would be like. We had worked long to avoid it entirely, but now it was clear that such a more-pleasant outcome wasn't possible. We could only hope to delay the war's inevitability, and to place ourselves on the best possible footing when it arrived.

But none of that was on my mind when I entered Holmes's warm cottage that day and hung my coat and hat to dry. I chatted with Mrs. Hudson for a moment before she bustled toward the back of the house to finish up lunch, which she promised would be something special. Leaving my bag at the door until later, when I would carry it to my room, I wound through the house to Holmes's study, where I found him, standing near one of his shelves, a book opened in his hand.

"Have you read the new *Britannica* article on recidivism?" he asked, looking up, his tone critical, as if we were continuing a conversation already begun that morning. "It refers to '*some ardent reformers*'" – and he glanced back at the book, reading, "'*recommend a system of indefinite imprisonment or the indeterminate sentence, by which the enemy once caught is kept perpetually or for a lengthy period, and thus rendered innocuous. Habitual offenders, it is argued, should be detained as hostages –* ' Note that phrasing, Watson. ' *– until they are willing to lay down their arms and consent to make no further attempt to attack or injure society. The theory is sound and has been adopted in part in several countries, especially in the United States.*'" He looked up while closing the book. "A bit harsh, don't you agree?"

"Indeed. Besides the idea that such a system would basically encourage a prison industry, how would one determine who is an '*habitual offender*', worthy of an open-ended sentence – perhaps for life?"

Holmes shook his head and returned the volume to the shelf. "The United States adopted such a system two or three years ago. Here in England, we've been much more tentative about it, but the procedure is in place to add '*habitual offender*' to a criminal's charge. Of concern is the fact that this decision is likely left up to the local police."

I nodded. "You're thinking of that constable in Bostock, back in the eighties, who framed several of his rival suitors."

"Which goes to show that even our noble law enforcement officers are still just men, with all the faults that are possible as such."

"We were quite lucky," I replied, "that so many officers with whom we worked – Lestrade, Gregson, Bradstreet, and such – were men of honor *and* little imagination."

"Yes. Thankfully, it never would have occurred to Lestrade to frame one of his enemies. Lack of imagination is sometimes a blessing."

We continued with our discussion, with one topic passing easily to another, uninterrupted through Mrs. Hudson's excellent lunch, featuring one of her fine pork roasts. Although it had only been a month or so since I'd last visited, I felt very much the guest of honor – and also quite sleepy afterwards. Rather than let me slide into an afternoon of wasted dozing, Holmes suggested a walk along the Downs. I had some wariness when considering the recent weather, but I agreed, retreating to my room long enough to change into more appropriate boots and then grab my coat and hat.

Within fifteen minutes, we'd made our way across the narrow road and then up the meandering paths that wound back and forth through the gorse, rising to the cliff-top. Both of us were canny enough to stay well back from the edges, which were always dropping way in great chalky chunks, and especially likely with the ground so saturated, the rain reaching deeply into the countless cracks we crossed. Many was the time that one would take a walk and find the perch from the night before, where the view of the sunset had been most beautiful, simply gone – dropped away into the water hundreds of feet below. Even well back from the cliff, the ground was striated with fissures extending to unknown depths, certainly filled with groundwater which would freeze and expand in winter, and indicating where some future fracture would inevitably occur.

We walked west, and the stiff sea breeze finished chasing away any of the sleepiness that I might have retained. In the distance, we could see the dip the cliff line where the Cuckmere reached the sea, and beyond it the Seven Sisters. Much closer and more accessible was the small settlement at Birling Gap. As we passed the old abandoned lighthouse and started down the slope, I could make out, at the far end of the Gap, the distinctive corner tower and slate roof of The Gables, where the Bellamy family had once lived. I'd had occasion to meet them on several occasions, including a few times after Holmes had related to me the events of their tangential involvement in a schoolmaster's death by way of an encounter with a misplaced creature of the sea. The young lady of the house, Maud, was quite the beauty, and I was unsurprised to hear that she had since married and moved to London.

At the Coast Guard barracks, we repeated our familiar discussion – wondering why they were located at that spot, a location where the sea could only be reached by a makeshift and occasionally shifting staircase (as the natural gap where the land sloped down to the ocean had long since vanished as the cliffs receded) and no boats could be moored. It was always a puzzle that such a station wasn't re-located to Eastbourne, or perhaps at the nearby mouth of the Cuckmere River. As always, we had no solution, and Holmes, his interests elsewhere, had never bothered to pursue an answer.

The barracks were where the road turned north, and in another mile we were in East Dean and passing through the low door of the Tiger Inn, a favorite visiting spot. We were both greeted with warmth and spent the next couple of hours in conversation, sometimes just the two of us, and at other times joined by various patrons. A portion of our visit was spent with a fellow named Patrick, manager of farm not far north of Holmes's villa, discussing a number of Satanic symbols that had been maliciously chalked on various buildings. He'd apparently consulted Holmes about it the previous week, and Holmes was able to confirm that his investigations had revealed the culprit to be the owner's eleven-year-old daughter, half-British and half-American, who seemed to have an unhealthy preoccupation with religion. The introduction of symbols had recently stopped as the family, who traveled more often than they were in England, had departed on another journey. Holmes recommended that the child see an alienist before she progressed to killing animals, but Patrick shook his head, agreeing that she "wasn't quite right," yet feeling unable to relate such a recommendation to his employer. As he shuffled heavily away, Holmes shook his head. All too often after his advice was ignored, the result of which was nearly always tragedy for someone. This matter would come back to pester Holmes greatly in a few years, but neither of us could know that then.

By late afternoon, with the threat of rain returning, we hired a local named Steed to drive us back to Holmes's farm. We were soon returned to his door and, as we approached, Holmes touched my arm and nodded towards the building. The lamp in the front parlor was lit – which wasn't always the case – and we could see the shadowed silhouette of a visitor perched on the front of a chair near the large front window.

I glanced toward Holmes, thinking that he might evince some of his enthusiasm of the old days in Baker Street, when we would return to our rooms to spot a similar image outlined against the pulled shades in the sitting room windows above us. His reaction then would run the gamut from barely suppressed excitement to impatience that he might have missed the opportunity for a new case by being away unnecessarily. But now I could perceive that he was the least bit irritated. Clearly he didn't need the stimulus of new problems as he had in the old days – or more likely, he didn't need *this kind* of problem, whatever it turned out to be.

As we placed our hats and coats to dry on the hooks by the door, Mrs. Hudson joined us from the back of the house, handing Holmes a card and explaining softly that his visitor had come all the way from London.

Holmes glanced at it and then passed it to me. *Rev. Rayford Chinnor Longwick, BD, DD*, it said, with a Mitre Court address.

"Poor man," she murmured. "He seems most distressed, and he berated himself terribly when he found that you weren't here and that he'd neglected to send a wire asking for an appointment." She lowered her voice even more. "He must be quite absent-minded. He suddenly became concerned that he'd misplaced his umbrella, looking from side to side as if it might have dropped at his feet, never noticing 'til I told him that he still held it gripped in his left hand." She shook her head. "He's only been here for ten minutes or so, and I've served him some tea – he wanted nothing stronger. Now I'll go finish fixing something warm for all of you."

We entered Holmes's study to find a tall stork-like man in minister's garb, standing in the center of the room, facing away from us and apparently listening to something that wasn't perceptible to my ears, nor to Holmes's from his expression. Normally when one spends time waiting in a strange room, activities range from sitting quietly, perhaps smoking or sipping something, or if in a location as interesting as that one, examining the various objects sitting haphazardly on shelves and table-tops, or possibly perusing one of the many eclectic volumes on the densely packed shelves. But not this fellow.

He appeared to be about my age – nearly sixty – and his hair, though silvered, was thick and combed from his left to right. His matching eyebrows were tangled and tufted, perched out on a rather prominently ridged brow. He had a pair of *pince-nez* sitting upon his notably long nose, deeply grooved lines running on either side of his small dark-lipped mouth, and a prominent chin that left his similarly jutting Adam's apple in shadow, although quite visible over his clerical collar. His voice was high, and unfortunately unpleasant and quarrelsome when he spoke.

"Do you hear her?" he asked softly, turning toward us, his tone rather stressed.

"No," I replied, sounding sharp against the silence. "She is in the back of the house, preparing some refreshments."

"No, no!" the curious fellow snapped. "Not the housekeeper. It's the lady's *shadow* – the woman from *before*!"

I glanced at Holmes and saw the expression I'd expected: One corner of his mouth pulled slightly to one side, and the opposite eyebrow lifted in skeptical irritation at Mrs. Hudson for admitting some spiritualist crank who thought that he could communicate with ghosts. He'd had enough of that foolishness the previous spring, when Doyle and his wife wanted to pick a fight with anyone who dared doubt that she wasn't receiving messages from the crew of the *Wiln* after it sank in the Bristol Channel, and had dragged Holmes in by thoughtlessly mentioning his name in a newspaper interview.

Holmes opened his mouth to speak, but the man quickly raised a hand, forefinger extended, and cut him off. "She is a *Gray Lady* – I see a gray bonnet and dress. She lost her child – crib death, I expect. She wanders here in despair – and has done so for nearly half-a-century I would guess. What do you know of her? Have you seen her?"

"I've seen no one," Holmes snapped. "If this is why you've traveled all the way from London – "

"*I've* seen her," said Mrs. Hudson, entering with a tray. "The Gray Lady. Sometimes she passes at the end of the hallway, or occasionally I come upon her in the small room upstairs. I've also sensed that she's looking for a child that died, and she cannot rest. I just let her be – for I believe that she does not see me. She only sees the shadows of the cottage the way it was when she lived here."

Observing Holmes's scowl, she set her mouth and scowled back. My friend and I had learned over thirty years earlier that Mrs. Hudson was not a woman to back down from what she believed. I suspected that this topic, curiously avoided until now, would be a source of much discussion between the two of them, some of it possibly even polite, and I hoped that they would refrain until I'd departed.

"Nevertheless," said Holmes, turning back to his visitor, "if this is why you've traveled to Sussex, Reverend – " He glanced at the card, still in his hand to refresh his memory. " – Longwick – "

"So sorry," said the fellow quickly, seemingly jumping back into his skin from a great distance, and now with an amiable smile in his eyes and the harshness completely vanished from his tone. He pulled another card from his pocket and handed it to me, stating, "Reverend Longwick. I have a small ministry in No. 7, Mitre Court, off Fleet Street, leading through to the Temple. No, no – it isn't a church. Rather, my efforts are spent preparing and distributing religious materials and providing them to the various immigrants that continually wash ashore in London." He glanced my way. "You must be Dr. Watson. I'm so fortunate that you're here as well." Then, accepting more tea from Mrs. Hudson, and indicating that he simply couldn't say no to a piece of her lemon seed cake, he sat where indicated and continued speaking.

"No, I'm not here about anything related to restless spirits. It was only when Mrs. Hudson placed me in this quiet room that I couldn't help but become aware of your ghost – although I do so hate to call them that. I've always had a gift, you see. I choose to call it a gift, although there are times . . . I can sense them, particularly when they are unable to move on due to some unresolved grief. That's what afflicts the poor woman here at your farm, Mr. Holmes – unresolved grief."

"I've neither heard nor seen anything," Holmes rather growled, glancing at Mrs. Hudson, who met his gaze firmly while departing. "If you aren't here about ghosts, then – "

"Yes, yes. It's something much more prosaic than that. You see, I publish various foreign-language versions of the Bible for immigrants, and after many years of creating a system that works quite well, I've become aware that the works have recently been altered – not necessarily in a bad way. Nothing like changing the meaning of the text entirely to something that welcomes the Antichrist or the insertion of naughty words. No, it's more subtle than that, and I'd like to know why."

"You didn't say you'd like to know *who* did it – perhaps because you already know?"

"I think so. I'll get to that in due course."

As we settled more comfortably, partaking further of the tea and cake, the wind and rain increased, and I could only imagine conditions out upon the Channel, just a few hundred feet away from where we sat – sloping up to the top of Beachy Head, and then dropping abruptly over five-hundred-feet straight down to the water. Although I knew better (because it really was too far), I liked to think that on a clear day I could see France when standing at the cliff-top, but now, visibility would be negligible – up there one might be hard-pressed to see the very edge of the precipice – and I was thankful, for the benefit of others who needed it, that the great lighthouse at the base of the cliff was there. It had been commissioned in 1902, just a year before Holmes had retired to this area, replacing the old Belle Tout lighthouse on the rise just to our west. I knew that the old light had never worked as planned, often being obscured by sea mists, which required its replacement. I could only imagine when it was still functional, and its beams would have doubtless cruelly illuminated the windows of Holmes's villa whenever it was lit.

Holmes, his mood now more relaxed after learning that the reason for the minister's visit was earth-bound, settled back and asked for more details.

"As you probably know," Longwick began, "there are different versions of the Bible – various translations besides our own King James version, and different arrangements of the ancient texts. The Protestant Bible has sixty-six books, the Catholic has seventy-three, and the Orthodox eighty-one. Some of those included in the Catholic version are part of the Protestant *Apocrypha*.

"Years ago, I had the idea of publishing the Biblical books separately as individual pamphlets, in different languages, to be handed out among the London immigrants like periodicals. Now, I know what you're thinking, and many have pointed out to me before that wouldn't it be better just to print Bibles in the different languages in their entirety, instead of in the manner of monthly installments, but this format actually has its uses. A number of Bible study groups have been established across London through the years, and having the books presented in this more-digestible manner tends to be less overwhelming for some, and breaking the narrative into small pieces, so I'm told, ensures that the participants return regularly to the meetings, becoming used to studying one isolated and less-formidable portion of the scripture at each session.

"We use translations of the Protestant version, sixty-six books, and some of the shorter works like *Second* and *Third John*, or *Philemon* or *Jude*, being just one chapter each, are combined in pamphlets with longer books so that we publish fifty-two issues per year, one per week, and start all over again in January. Initially, I thought about dividing the Bible evenly by the number of chapters – there are nearly twelve-hundred, not counting the Apocrypha – but dividing by fifty-two caused some awkward arrangements, breaking one book at a crucial point and joining it to something completely unrelated." He looked at both of us over his *pince-*

nez, as if giving good advice. "If you're going to set yourself a schedule to read the Bible once per year, as many do, three or four chapters a day is a good plan."

Longwick gazed upon each of us for another few silent seconds to make sure that we were following. We both nodded, and Holmes added, "I recall seeing a number of your publications over the years, when passing through various East End sanctuaries for immigrants – coffee-shops and churches, and the back rooms of pubs. You'll be happy to know that your influence has penetrated into the worst of the East End Hell-holes, populated with some of the most angry and revolutionary types to walk upon our shores."

The minister seemed intrigued. Leaning forward like a long-bodied water bird with a black body and gray top-knot, he said, "Knowing some about your past work, Mr. Holmes – I've read a number of your stories, Doctor – gives me some sense of just where you've been when you say 'Hell-holes'. The Bar of Gold, for instance, in Upper Swandam Lane just off Upper Thames Street. I won't ask you to elaborate upon why you were in such places, beyond what was shared in *The Strand*, but I thank you for letting me know about my little volumes. I, too, have been in those places as part of my ministry, but going in as a minister does not provide the same perspective as one who is disguised to fit in with those needing guidance. I've learned that even the darkest of hearts may be reached – but the effort must be ventured or nothing will be gained. I feel that the work of the publications has done some good, and that's why I'm angered that someone has been altering the texts."

"In what way?" I asked. I had been inclined to first think the man something of a fool, but as he spoke, I was reassessing my initial impression.

Longwick finished his tea and set the cup aside. Recrossing his long legs, he explained. "Just as there are many books of the Bible, and alternate versions with more or less books, each language also has different ways of spelling our Lord's name. In English, and German and Portuguese, it is *Jesus* – as we have known all our lives. But this isn't the universal spelling. In Albanian it's *Jezu*, Turkish is *Isa*, Romanian and Russian is *Iisus*, and in Croatian and Serbian it's *Isus.*" He spelled each, and pronounced them so we would understand the difference. Some were quite similar, but there were small variations. "Italian is *Gesù*, Ukranian is *Icyc*, and Slovak is *Ježiš*, spelled with accent marks upon the *Z* and *S.*" He illustrated these accents with a flick of a finger.

"The list goes on and on. Years ago, when the idea for this ministry was first conceived, we – and by 'we' and 'our', I mean myself and whichever staff member I'd hired at the time – went through the process of having the Bible translated into a number of different languages, and then setting up each of the individual pamphlets. It was a great deal of initial effort, but once the system was in place, we've been able to print as the need demands ever since. For instance, I simply have to place an order with the printer, with whom I've worked for years, telling him that I need so many copies of a certain month's booklet in Turkish, and he prints what's required for distribution. That way, we don't have to store a massive amount of already-printed materials. Basing the printing on the demand is really a revolutionary and valuable idea, and the greater publishing industry would benefit from taking a look at it.

"However, having done this work so long ago, I became rather complacent, thinking that aspect of the operation need not ever be reviewed again. Therefore, it was with some surprise that I was stopped on the street two days ago by a man named Josef, a long-time associate who is employed in distributing the pamphlets. He informed me that the latest set of booklets – we're late enough in the year to now be publishing *The New Testament* – had an error. In the *Italian* edition, where Jesus' name is supposed to read *Gesù* on page 92, it now said *Isa* – the *Turkish* spelling."

He reached inside his coat and pulled out several pamphlets, all about eight inches high. Each was folded once, long-ways, and when opened, they were about five inches wide. He opened one of them to a page marked with a folded corner and handed it to Holmes. I rose and looked over his shoulder, observing the word in question, circled in red ink. It was as the minister described, but I would have to take his word for it that the word had been swapped.

I sat back down, but Holmes continued turning the pamphlet this way and that before noting, "The printing plate has been altered," he said. "Adequately, but not without certain peripheral and careless flaws. The letters spelling *Isa* look a bit ragged and don't quite line up, and the spacing to each side is incorrect. " He laid the pamphlet on the table beside his own empty teacup. "I assume that you investigated further."

Longwick nodded. "I did. Not having any pamphlets stored at the office, I began visiting the different distribution sites located throughout the city. Not only did this month's version have the substitution of Jesus' name to the Turkish spelling in the Italian edition – and from what I can tell, only once, on page 92 – but it was the same way in the German and Russian editions, and also only on that particular page. And I found that last month, the spelling in those three editions – Italian, German, and Russian – Jesus was spelled with the Albanian *Jezu*, but this time on page 84. You can imagine that researching this took some time – flipping through each version to see when an incorrect usage appeared."

"But there were no changes in other printings?" asked Holmes. "Romanian or Croatian, for instance?"

"None that I could determine – and I made a careful examination of all of them! But you didn't let me finish. I also found that two months ago, in July, the spelling of Jesus in those three language editions was the Serbian version – *Isus.*

"And before that? How far back does this go?"

"Only those three editions – the current, and the previous two months – July and August. Nothing beyond July that I could find – and I checked all the way to the beginning of the year."

"And what page did the error occur two months ago?"

"On page 77."

"Do you have any idea as to how this happened?"

"I do," said Longwick, now sitting forward upon the edge of his chair, his long legs and bony knees supporting his folded arms as he leaned forward. "I went 'round to the printer – a friend named Millhouse that I've used for years – and we looked at the plates for this month together. We found that each one of them has been repaired, and now all of them once again have the correct word in the correct language for *Jesus* on page 92, Millhouse could see where the plates had been altered. We looked back at the August and July issues as well, and they have also been repaired."

"You said that you knew who had done it," I said, puzzled at the apparent senselessness of such an obscure action.

"That's correct, Doctor," said Longwick, now leaning back and crossing his arms. "About four months ago, I hired a new assistant. It's always just me and a single assistant – it's been that way since the beginning. I take care of the ministerial side of things – visiting the locations where the pamphlets are placed, and seeing the people where they live, and particularly raising the funds to support this endeavor – and the assistant deals with Millhouse, as well as seeing that the orders and deliveries are made, and paying our office rent and the printing and delivery costs." He looked from one to the other of us. "I tried to keep my investigations discreet about the alterations, but my assistant seems to have discovered that I was asking questions. He didn't come to work this morning, and when I went to his lodgings, the landlady said he'd abruptly packed up and left."

"And who was this assistant," asked Holmes.

"A fellow named Fred Curll – with two *L*'s. There was once a famous British publisher named Curll, but my assistant isn't British. He speaks English very well, but he has some sort of accent – German or Dutch, if I'm correct. I'm usually good with languages, but I had a difficult time working out just where he was from. I never did, as a matter of fact. I didn't want to ask him about it, as he kept to himself and wasn't easy to get to know – very much different than my last assistant, Ian Murchison, who left last summer when his gout became too much to manage."

As Longwick explained about his vanished assistant, I saw Holmes's attentiveness increase from the usual curiosity he displayed during the description of a puzzle to sudden keen interest. I had no idea why, but the answer to his next question seemed to fix an idea in his mind.

"Tell me, Reverend Longwick: Was your former assistant – Curll – well-dressed, and with somewhat long hair combed down beside his thin face, oversized bad teeth, a large red nose covered with tiny broken capillaries, and similarly lined red cheeks? Does he have an arrogant expression with odd light-brown eyes, and with the whites around the pupils discolored and bloodshot, as if each entire eyeball is a solid muddy marble?

Longwick's jaw dropped in surprise. "How do you know that, Mr. Holmes?" He leaned forward again. "That is so specific! That's Curll to a *T*!"

When Holmes waved away an answer, Longwick continued. "When I discovered this matter, it concerned me more and more, although I'm not sure why. Perhaps I've been more nervous than normal – I'm always a nervous fellow – because lately there has been growing unrest among the immigrants. I talked it over with Millhouse, and he suggested consulting a detective. I've been hearing good things about a young fellow near Paddington – since he set up shop three or four years ago, they've been calling him 'The Sherlock Holmes of Praed Street' – but I became convinced that I should actually seek out the *actual* Sherlock Holmes. I'm most grateful that you took time to see me and hear my story without an appointment, and from your reaction, I believe that there is more to this than I previously suspected . . . ."

He paused, his last words almost a question, waiting for Holmes to provide some explanation, but instead my friend simply answered, "I believe that I'll need to return to London with you." He cocked his head at the sound of the still-rising storm. "This is a terrible night to travel, although I understand that the worst of it will pass before morning. Will you stay for dinner? Then I can put you up overnight so that we can travel back together early tomorrow."

Longwick immediately accepted, and when Mrs. Hudson had shown him to his room in order that he might prepare himself for dinner, Holmes turned to me, asking, "I hope you don't mind running back up to London for the day."

I shook my head. "Not at all. Apparently you see something serious in this business."

"Quite possibly – although . . . Of course, I could just be imagining things, but . . . ." He shook his head. "No, I don't think so. Do you recall the aborted riot last week in the East End? By Turkish immigrants? It took place on the second."

I nodded.

"There were similar Turkish riots on that same day in Berlin and Rome and St. Petersburg – and they were brought under control much more violently than our local version was. I believe that our home-grown riot was suppressed before it ever really started. The previous month, on the fourth of August, Albanian immigrants rioted here – again, a small affair hardly worth reporting, but also much worse in St. Petersburg and Berlin and Rome – particularly the latter. And on 7 July, it was the Serbians that were rioting in London and the other three capitals – again just a skirmish here, but quite ugly upon the Continent.

"I don't understand."

"I don't either – not yet – but it can't be coincidence that on the 7th of July – which might be written as '*7-7*' – there were Serbian riots in the capitals, and the alteration in the July edition of Longwick's monthly Bibles – on page *77* – was a *Serbian* spelling in those printings. The next month, on 4 August, the error was the *Albanian* spelling – on page *84*. As in August 4th."

"But we write August 4th as '*4-8*'."

"But in Germany they write that date with the month first, as '*8-4*' – as they do September 2nd: '*9-2*' – the same as page *92* of the most recent edition, which had Jesus spelled in the *Turkish* way . . . and this time it was the Turks who rioted."

"Hold on," I said, raising a hand. "I'm trying to understand this. Loosely pieced together, it seems as if a man with a vague foreign accent, Fred Curll, took a job as the latest assistant at Reverend Longwick's ministry, wherein he was in charge of the printing and business side of things. Soon after, small changes were made to the long-standing printing plates, altering the language of the word *Jesus* to fit with certain groups that have been rioting in London, Rome, Berlin, and St. Petersburg, and that the dates of these riots correspond with the page numbers on which the errors appear."

Holmes smiled. "Essentially, yes."

"That's quite a stretch."

"True, but you'll recall that it's no more so than the messages that Maybrick was placing in the newspapers during late August '88."

I nodded. "You were also able to describe Fred Curll – 'to a *T*' as Reverend Longwick put it. How did you know who he is?"

"I didn't *know*, necessarily, but his name is something of a clue. The Reverend was very perceptive when he said that Curll's accent sounded German or Dutch. The latter is correct."

"You've heard of him. Is he mentioned in your scrapbooks?" I asked, nodding toward the shelf which held the many and varied volumes, brought down from London when Holmes retired."

"Yes, but not under that name. This fellow took the name *Curll* – or rather, it was assigned to him – as something of a little inside joke – and I happen to be in the group that would understand it. As the Reverend mentioned, there was a famous eighteenth-century publisher named Curll – Edmund Curll – who became synonymous with many unscrupulous practices like publishing accounts of scandals and pornographic materials, and generally anything that would make money. Calling this fellow *Curll* has always held an element of irony.

"You seem to already know what's going on."

"To a great degree, although there are still edges of the painting to fill in. But by tomorrow, you and I will know what's happening – although I doubt that we can share the true story with Longwick."

The next morning, Holmes telephoned for the local cab, and Beauchamp had us in Eastbourne with time to spare for the first train back to London. The night before, dinner had been an interesting exchange of ideas, as Longwick explained more about his mission, comparing notes with what Holmes had seen in disguise throughout the poorest parts of London as compared to Longwick's experience visiting there as a recognized man of the cloth. The minister was fascinated and somewhat saddened, and rather surprised as well, to learn that in many cases, the people he'd met over his many years of service didn't behave the same with him as they did when he wasn't around. The knowledge actually left him rather shaken, as if a rug had been pulled from underneath him. At the end of the meal, he thanked Holmes for the information, stating that aside from the help he was receiving in determining who had altered and then repaired the printing plates for his pamphlets, what Holmes had conveyed to him about his "flock" was worth more than he could repay.

He appeared to have been affected by learning that he hadn't truly connected in quite the way he'd always thought, and he excused himself after the meal to rest and get his thoughts in order. He promised to be up on time and, as he'd left us, I noted that Holmes had successfully distracted him so that he hadn't been asked to elaborate on what might have taken place in the minister's operation. Likewise, the minister had shown the good sense to avoid mentioning the spirit he'd sensed haunting Holmes's villa. I myself had never seen her, and I didn't see her that night, but my many varied experiences over six continents had given me an open-mindedness to such things that Holmes refused to acknowledge within himself.

I thought that Longwick had retired, but later that night, I passed down the hallway and saw that he and Mrs. Hudson were having a discussion over cups of tea. I wondered if the topic was the cottage's supposed spirit, or if they had more in common, and whether Longwick might became a somewhat-regular visitor at the villa – although not to confer with Holmes.

When we arrived at Victoria Station in the middle of the next morning, Holmes led us outside and waved down one of the newer automobile cabs. There were still hansoms and growlers about, but less of them, it seemed, with each passing week. Although I could see the sense of the automobile on that rainy morning, I think I would have preferred a four-wheeler, as it was roomier than the three of us trying to fit into the tightly constructed metal contraption. It was one thing to have your own automobile, as I did, and to be in control of where it went and how many souls were crammed into it, but I found that the sudden unexpected accelerations and stops associated with such *taxis*, when in the hands of a stranger, were a much more unnerving and unpleasant experience.

Holmes had explained to me that, while he knew much about what was going on, he had to make a show for the minister of carrying out a full investigation, not wanting to reveal anything too soon. I was beginning to have the sense that before the day ended, we would probably end up in Whitehall or Pall Mall.

Holmes asked that we first be taken to Millhouse's printing establishment, located in an unmarked passage off Chancery Lane, not far from Longwick's Mitre Court office. We found the printer to be a solid and bluff man in his mid-fifties, his sleeves rolled up on his great forearms, and ink stains of long standing up and down his fingers and wrists, underneath his short nails, and across his high brow and unto his thinning hairline. He could tell us very little beyond confirming what we'd already heard.

"This Curll was in and out of here quite a bit over the last three or four months, several times a week, since the time he was hired, but that ain't unusual, is it? All of the Reverend's assistants have checked in the same way over the years, keeping track of each month's printings. No, it would have been easy for Curll to get in after hours if he'd wanted. The Reverend and I have an arrangement, seeing as he's my oldest and steadiest customer. His Ministry has a key so that the Reverend's man can drop in anytime and pick up the printed pamphlets directly here, instead of me sending them over to the Mitre Court office. It saves him some money by not paying for delivery, and me from not needing to hire delivery people. That's right – it's no secret where the plates are kept, and anyone who had tolerable skill to make the changes could alter them and then just as easily fix them back again."

Holmes turned Longwick and asked about the key's whereabouts.

"I don't know," he admitted. "It's normally in the assistant's desk at the office. I didn't think to check that. We can go look, if you'd like."

Holmes nodded, but first he and Millhouse examined the plates, each making a series of comments that elicited nods of agreement from the other. Then, thanking the printer, we walked down to Fleet Street and across, and so through the passage leading into Mitre Court. I glanced just south, toward where our old friend Thorndyke lived, where the Court opened into King's Bench Walk, and was considering suggesting that we ask if he'd noticed anything unusual about the minister's curious assistant, but Holmes, seemingly reading my thoughts, shook he head, stating, "5A is too far away through the passage to expect that anyone there might have seen Mr. Curll, and in any case, I happen to know that Thorndyke is away right now – some dire business at the Chelmsford Police barracks."

How Holmes kept up with these things while in Sussex was a mystery, but that he did so didn't surprise me. Though supposedly retired, he still had any number of strings in hand leading to who-knew how many unlikely spots.

A quick search of Longwick's office showed that everything was in its place, including the key to access Millhouse's printing operation. In fact, the assistant's work area was so tidy that Longwick commented on just how unusual that was.

"Curll wasn't the neatest of men, although he could always lay a hand on any invoice when I asked. The fact that he left everything cleaner than he found it means to me for sure that he's gone. But what could making these alterations have accomplished?

What indeed? I wondered. While I had a dim grasp of what Holmes had explained to me, I could find no purpose to it. And yet, we continued our investigation, with Longwick walking us eastward to the missing man's lodgings in Fore Street, almost evenly situated between the Guildhall and Moorgate Street Station. His landlady, a very fat and wheezing woman named Mrs. Evans, was limited in what she could tell us.

"He showed up yesterday afternoon," she said, catching her breath, "early home from work and all het up about something. He went upstairs and came down with two bags – I guess it was all that he had – handed me the key, said he had business that was calling him away urgently, and left.

He still has two weeks left on his rent, but it sounded as if he won't be back, so I've already advertised for a new lodger."

She agreed to let us see the room, which she informed us hadn't yet been cleaned, and she fetched the key from somewhere in her own chambers and sent us upstairs on our own. We ascended the two narrow flights, and I could only imagine the poor landlady trying to do the same. I doubted that the room would be ever be cleaned if she was the one required to do it.

Holmes made his usual systematic search, but the room had apparently been swept clean, for there was neither scrap nor crumb to give any indication about the previous occupant – except for one object left precisely centered upon the desk: *The Strand* magazine from the previous April, which had featured my most recently published story, "The Red Circle".

The magazine was open to the first page of the story, and the first line had been altered. Originally reading: "*Well, Mrs. Warren, I cannot see that you have any particular cause for uneasiness*," the words *Mrs. Warren* had been crossed out and *Mr. Holmes* written above it in red ink.

"What does it mean?" asked Longwick, his eyes widened. "What is going on?"

"It means that your Mr. Curll is sending me a message – that he knew you intended to seek my opinion, and that since his scheme was discovered and he was forced to move on, possibly sooner than he expected, he wanted to gain my attention when we searched this room."

"But for what purpose? None of this makes any sense!"

"It does, Reverend Longwick – but I'm afraid that we cannot share with you the reasons why. I'll need to confer with someone about this, to see what needs to be done." He looked around the room once more, seemingly deciding that there was nothing more to discover. Then he refocused his gaze upon the minister.

"You said that you tried to keep your investigations discreet, but somehow Curll found out. What did you do to make him suspect?"

Longwick looked as if he'd been caught doing something shameful and was loathe to admit it. "When examining the back issues for alterations, I didn't seek his help, for he wouldn't know what to look for – or so I supposed. But as I found altered pamphlets, I set them aside, and he would have certainly seen which issues I'd pulled – and if he was the one who changed them, their significance would have been obvious. Then, when I decided to seek your help, Mr. Holmes, I made a telephone call to a fellow that I knew in divinity school – Dr. Thorneycroft Huxtable. I recalled from seeing his name in *The Strand* some years ago and, knowing you were retired, I wondered if he could tell me where. He has kept up with you, and was able to point me toward your Beachy Head cottage."

"And no doubt," I said, "Curll put all these pieces together and knew that his scheme was discovered, and he absconded."

"Perhaps that word is a bit strong," said Holmes, "but we shall see." With that, he led us back outside. Thanking the rather confused minister, we abruptly left him standing there with a promise to let him know what we could. Then we hailed a cab heading west.

I made a point of pulling out my watch. "Too early for your brother to be at the Diogenes. Are we going to one of his offices?"

Holmes's eyes widened with surprise, and then he gave a bark of a laugh and slapped his knee.

"Oh, Watson, you are well-and-truly caught up, aren't you? Well done!"

"Not all the way," I assured him. "Your knowledge of this Curll fellow, and the message to you in 'The Red Circle', and this scheme's relation to riots in foreign countries, gives me some sense that Mycroft must have a finger in the pie somewhere – or if he doesn't already, he probably should have. We're either going to ask him some questions, or to relay information to him."

"The former – for Curll is one of Mycroft's agents. I have some vague sense of what might be happening, and if I'm right, it's a very fragile construct, and I hope that our involvement, by way of Longwick's tumbling to what's going on, hasn't spoiled anything. But be prepared, for I suspect there's an ugly shade to this whole business."

But our visit to the man who sometimes *was* the British Government was unexpectedly delayed as – to our great surprise – we found that not only was Mycroft Holmes not in his most-likely office, but he wasn't in the others as well. Nor would we find him in his Pall Mall lodgings, or in the Diogenes Club across the street. "Urgent business," we were told by his secretary, and not even Holmes's brotherly connection, and the knowledge that he often carried out the most confidential tasks for Mycroft and The Crown, could get the man to provide any additional information. He did, however, state that Mycroft should return that same day, and we received the promise that we would receive a message at my Queen Anne Street home when Mycroft was available.

Outside, Holmes stated that he would continue to fill in the edges of the painting while checking with me throughout the day about Mycroft's availability. "If you don't mind spending the day here in London," he added, "and interrupting your holiday."

I assured him that the change in plans was not a difficulty, and he replied that he would be in touch. Then he walked away while I found a cab.

I puttered the rest of the day, answering some old correspondence, and considering what new story that I might prepare for publication, having left my notes of the nearly-finished Lady Frances Carfax matter with my luggage in Sussex. I had a plethora of material from which to choose – an overabundance of a plethora – and despite his earlier attempts to disassociate himself with Holmes's adventures, my literary agent had come to recognize the continuing financial value related to their occasional publication, and he was constantly pressing for another one – although too often he wished for those that seemed to have some supernatural bend, and when the solutions were solidly down-to-earth (as they always were) he too-often tried to insist that they be edited – "punched up" as he called it – in order to add false spiritualistic aspects, satisfying some broken need within himself. I could only hope that he never heard the story of the Gray Lady at Holmes's cottage, or he and his wife would be on the first train south to set in motion one of their ridiculous séances – no doubt claiming that Phineas, Lady Doyle's spirit "guide" and their resident pet phantasm, was along with them.

Although well able to keep myself occupied, the house felt lonely when my wife was away, and at some point I gave up on my efforts and settled down for a nap – planned, and not an accidental dropping-off where I would wake confused, and vaguely irritated that the afternoon had slipped away. I had awakened not long before the doorbell rang. Beating the maid to the door, I opened it to surprisingly find Holmes – along with his brother, and an ugly man who could only be Fred Curll.

"I came across Mycroft as he was returning to Whitehall," Holmes explained, "and since he was already untethered from the temptations of his nest, I suggested that we come here, rather than asking you to get back out and journey to us. We stopped along the way to collect Mr. Curll."

"Pleased to meet you, Doctor," the curious man said. I understood what Longwick had meant about his puzzling accent. Dutch, as I'd been told, but there was something else that was odd about it. However, all was soon explained when the fellow spit forth an appliance from his mouth – a construction of bad and distracting false teeth that covered his own, while also affecting his manner of speech. "There, that's better," he said. Fortunately he'd caught the false plate in his left hand, as it was his right that he offered to me. We shook, and then Holmes suggested that we adjourn to my study.

After brandies and whiskies were shared, and chairs were claimed – including the settee for Mycroft – Holmes's brother looked my way. "Of course, Doctor, what we're about to discuss is not for sharing."

I agreed, as he knew that I would. He was still somewhat nettled that I had mentioned him in print without consent back in 1893, nearly two decades earlier, when publishing my earlier efforts to memorialize my supposedly dead friend. My wife, Mary, had died by then, and writing seemed to be the only way to fill my empty hours and avoid following the grim destructive paths of my late father and brother. With Doyle's encouragement – "The public will eat up the idea that Holmes had a brother!" – I had given no thought that such a revelation might shine an unnecessary light on just what it was that Mycroft Holmes did . . . and was still doing, apparently, since this entire business had turned out to be one of his many schemes.

Sherlock Holmes took the reins. "Correct me if I'm wrong, Mycroft," he said. Then he looked my way. "I've refrained from asking any questions." Back to Mycroft: "This is some convoluted intrigue that is designed to provide legitimacy to one of your agents infiltrating German Intelligence."

Mycroft nodded. "I'm rather proud of it. There were seven other ways to go, but Longwick's monthly Bible books presented the easiest path forward."

As usual, I had to raise a hand for attention, as if I were politely drowning off-shore while the two Holmes brothers stood on the beach having a discussion about politics without sparing a glance my way. "Can we begin at the beginning?"

Holmes smiled and nodded to his brother.

"We have an agent who has penetrated German Intelligence. He has found a path to a very integral position – a nexus of several of their interconnecting data-gathering agencies. But he needs to retain his value to keep that position, so occasionally he must bring some grist for their mill – something useful and unique to win their trust and admiration. Recently he was able to predict riots in London, Rome, St. Petersburg . . . and Berlin."

"Riots planned and instigated by you," interrupted Holmes.

Mycroft nodded. "With varying levels of intensity. Those in London were quite minor – essentially stopped before they began. Rome and St. Petersburg were somewhat more . . . escalated. And the Berlin riots – as foretold by our embedded agent – were lessened due to the knowledge that our agent provided from his 'secret' source."

"That source being you," I said.

"That is correct. After I identified Longwick's monthly Bible books, and their translation into various languages and how they were spread throughout the immigrant community, I saw a way to insert coded messages. We manipulated events so that only Curll applied to become Longwick's new assistant – by preventing Longwick's advertisement for help from actually being published – and then, when he was in place, Curll set about making the alterations.

"However, having a coded message without anyone being able to read it was useless, so word was spread throughout the immigrant community that the coded messages would reveal the location of the next riots – Serbian immigrants in July, Albanians in August, and most recently the Turks. Then, our other agents in the different capitals arranged for those riots to be planned and to actually occur, providing legitimacy to the coded messages, and for our agent who was seemingly able to predict them, based on information from his mysterious source. His reports allowed his German masters to diminish the riots, while they observed that the London, Rome, and St. Petersburg riots also occurred – exactly as prescribed by the coded messages."

"The codes had already served their purpose," continued Curll, "and I was due to leave Reverend Longwick's employment soon in any case, and in a more orderly manner, so as not to inconvenience him. But then he found out what was happening, and I could tell that he suspected me. When I overheard him trying to find you, Mr. Holmes, I vanished – but I left a copy of *The Strand* in my room for you to find, knowing that you'd certainly head in the right direction."

Holmes nodded, and Mycroft finished his brandy, setting the small glass upon the nearby table. He was clearly finished and ready to go, but I had one further thought – for both Holmes brothers.

"Longwick cannot know about this."

Mycroft looked as if I'd said something stupid. "Of course he cannot. It is a State secret, and the operation is still ongoing. Our agent in Berlin cannot be discredited."

I shook my head. "No. I mean that some legitimate-sounding tale must be contrived to satisfy him. He is owed that. And it must have no aspect related to the riots being planned from his periodicals – no half-truths about that included to make the lie more believable. I'm aware that the London riots were very small, and quelled before they really began. Am I also right that the Rome and St. Petersburg riots that you fomented were larger, and more violent?"

Sherlock Holmes turned his head toward his brother, cocking it to one side as if the question hadn't occurred to him, and now he wanted an answer too. Curll dropped his eyes to the whisky glass held in both of his hands.

Mycroft's lips tightened and he nodded. "That is correct. Both of those riots quickly spiraled into full-scale street battles – rather along the lines of Bloody Sunday. And before you ask your next question: Many were injured – both rioters and police – and three were killed in Rome, and four in St. Petersburg . . . including a mother and child trampled by the crowd."

My gaze darkened. "A crowd that you stampeded."

I had known Mycroft Holmes by then for nearly a quarter-century, and I had gone from being curious about Holmes's rather idiosyncratic brother, to awe at his power and position, to something approaching friendship as the years passed and Holmes and I worked with him in the nation's interests. But I never let myself forget that he was much more of a cold calculating machine than his younger brother, and that he had no compunction about making cold calculating decisions. I knew that he was a good man, and that the death of the mother and child weighed upon him, but at that point in his life, a thousand-such decisions were already upon his broad shoulders, and Atlas-like, he showed no signs that his stamina was failing now after the thousand-and-first.

"That is correct, Doctor." His voice softened. "And it will always be tallied against me, Watson. But hopefully, for the greater good, it will have been worth it."

I could only nod, but my agreement had varying levels of nuances, which was understood by the others sitting there in the waning daylight.

We found Longwick later that night, and Holmes gave him some story about how Curll was a known trickster who had an arrest record at Scotland Yard as long as the minister's skinny shanks. That explained how Holmes knew of the man, while completely avoiding the reasons that nothing more could be revealed.

Longwick shook his head. "I must be more careful." Then he proceeded to tell us of other times when other assistants had also violated his trust, and it took too long to extricate ourselves, leaving the man with another learned lesson – which I could tell wouldn't count for much.

Earlier that afternoon, at the conclusion our discussion when Mycroft and Curll were preparing to depart, we were standing up prior to moving toward the front door. "What happens if you run across Reverand Longwick once again?" I asked Curll. "He's bound to recognize you. After all – " I stopped myself without mentioning the man's unfortunate and notable ugliness.

He smiled and held up the false plate of crooked teeth. "These aren't the only part of my disguise, Doctor," he said, the curious Dutch accent now completely gone, and replaced with another that implied that he was a lifetime resident of Yorkshire. I'd occasionally heard hints of these same tones and pronunciations from both Sherlock and Mycroft Holmes, as Yorkshire was the land of their birth, but mostly they never gave any indication of it, as they had both traveled abroad for much of their formative youth, and each had later worked hard to homogenize their way of speaking to something that might be called "British Neutral".

"I think that it's about time Fred Curll retired. Don't you, sir?" he asked Mycroft, who nodded.

"He has earned that, I suppose – but more importantly, he is becoming too recognizable. I have an idea about his successor. Be in my office tomorrow morning to discuss it."

The man known as Fred Curll grinned, slipped the false teeth back into his mouth, nodded my way, and turned to depart. It suddenly crossed my mind to wonder if I'd met the man before, in some other guise, but before I could stop him and ask, Mycroft looked at us both. "Would you join me for dinner at the Diogenes? I have an idea that I wish to run by the both of you. Never fear, Doctor," he added for my benefit. "It will involve a small trip to Staffordshire in the morning, and then you'll back to your Sussex holiday by the weekend."

Later, when Mycroft explained what he wanted, I thought that he might be right – a short but essential errand, and then back to my interrupted plan. But on Saturday night, when Holmes and I were hidden in the hold of a ship crossing to Calais on stormy tossing seas, with the likelihood that our upcoming rendezvous at the Au Calice brasserie on the Boulevard Jacquard would shunt us even further eastward, I suspected that Mycroft had deliberately misled us – for surely a man with his undisputed omniscience had known when he recruited us the previous week that this mission had no easy solution.

Holmes seemed to read my mind, and when we heard the rough tone of the boat's engines change their pitch, indicating that we would soon be docking, he smiled. "Once more unto the breach?" he asked.

Reflecting that, were we not here at this moment and in this place, we would have likely spent the rest of the week wandering the Downs near Holmes's villa, or too much time imbibing in The Tiger Inn, I nodded.

I had to admit: This holiday had turned out to be much better than I'd imagined, and there was no end in sight.

The Debt to Jabez Wilson

"If you could stop by and see the poor man, Doctor, it would be a comfort – to him, and to me as well."

Mrs. Hudson looked expectantly at me, and how could I say no?

She had arrived at my Paddington doorstep just five minutes earlier with her request, explaining that she had business in the neighborhood, and that a chance to stop by and say hello was more welcome than taking time to explain the whole business in a note. I agreed and asked if she would stay longer, and have some tea. I still had several patients to see, but I would make them wait a moment or two for a chance to visit with my former landlady. She declined, however, reminding me to be in Baker Street at nine o'clock the next morning. Then, stating that she would pop in and say hello to Mary on her way out, she left my consulting room, and I fell into a brown study, staring at the card that Mrs. Hudson had pressed into my hand.

I had first met the man two years earlier, nearly to the day, when I'd stopped in Baker Street to visit my friend, Sherlock Holmes, and found him engaged with a new client. A series of quick deductions about the fellow had led to the sharing of his apparently comical story, and Holmes and I had burst out laughing. The humor had faded, however, when Holmes heard enough to suspect that there was villainy afoot, hidden behind the man's curious tale. Before we were finished, a notable criminal had been captured, and a bold plot to steal a fortune from the cellar vaults of a bank had been prevented. It had been an interesting case, and I had recorded it in my notes and then used it the following year when publishing a series of sketches about Holmes in a rather new periodical. But as to the original fellow who had first brought the unique problem to Holmes's attention – ? Why, I confess that I hadn't given him a moment's thought since, assuming that he'd settled back into his old life.

What new problem, I wondered, *has Jabez Wilson gotten himself into?*

The next morning was overcast, and several times on my walk to Baker Street, a cold October wind whipped a hint of rain into my face. Depending upon the direction of the streets I traversed, the wind seemed to be intensified, as if it found a path that it preferred, allowing it to speed ahead unimpeded. It was a stark contrast to the pleasant weather I'd enjoyed just the day before, with a sky so pure and blue that it looked like that of Scotland in my boyhood – the same blue as on the Scottish Saltire, but with an additional glow from the autumn sun.

Sherlock Holmes was dead. It hit me yet again, as it always did throughout every day since early May of the previous year when he'd fallen in combat at the Reichenbach Falls. This time, I was reminded as I crossed the intersection of York Street and Upper Montague. I felt that if I looked just right, I could see the time back in '88 when Holmes and I had been cornered there by four toughs, sent by Lord ----- when he felt that we were getting a bit too close to identifying one of the Rippers. A proud Mason when required, and a wastrel always, Lord ----- had been tasked with shutting our mouths, but he sent the wrong men to do the job. I wondered if I could still find any of the biggest one's teeth if I looked in the nearby gutter. He'd certainly left that night without any of them still in his mouth. The second had lingered for a week before peritonitis took him. I'd seen the third a year later, when I'd had reason to visit Newgate Prison, sitting on a little cart in the yard because his legs no longer functioned. The fourth was a craven coward, and his testimony helped to definitively send Lord ----- to the gallows. Holmes and I were there that day, and the man refused a hood, staring at my friend as he dropped into his eternal punishment. I wish that he'd spared a glance for me as well. There were dark thoughts that I wished to convey to him before he departed.

It seemed that over the last few years, some of these dark thoughts found their way into my head far too easily. The events of the investigation and destruction of the Rippers cabal were some of the darkest that I've ever witnessed, and I found myself rather changed afterwards, as my belief in the innate goodness of mankind was cracked. That was in the dark autumn of 1888, and not long after, Holmes's investigation into the terrible web of Professor Moriarty had accelerated. I believe that Holmes's defeat of The Rippers – evil men at all levels of society, from the cess-pool bottoms to the highest seats of power – was his finest hour, even greater than when he ended Moriarty's reign. The latter might have been even more worthy and far-reaching, but I couldn't completely say it was a victory, for it ended with my friend's death.

Now, in October 1892, I was faced with further opportunities for despair as my dear wife, Mary, seemed to be sliding deeper into ill health, and I didn't know what to do to prevent it.

I threw myself into my work during the day, and otherwise made sure to save time for my beloved wife. I'd been through too many previous losses, and I'd learned my painful lessons about wasted opportunities. I still maintained my interest in the detection of crime – How could I not? – and Mary often encouraged me to wade a little deeper, making myself available to my friends at Scotland Yard when they came calling. (And it was fortunate that I did, because it cemented my friendship with them, and they lifted me up when I could not otherwise be lifted the following spring, when Mary passed.)

During this time, I occasionally visited Baker Street, usually to see Mrs. Hudson, but sometimes when it was necessary that I retrieve some item from the abandoned sitting room. Curiously, it was maintained nearly as it was before Holmes died, looking much as it had when he and I had departed London on 25 April, 1891 – with only one of us to return a couple of weeks later. The only differences in the room from the way it had been before, likely noticeable only to Mrs. Hudson and myself, was where Mycroft Holmes had paid to have it restored following the fire of 24 April, the night before we left, when Moriarty had a fire set and tried to burn Holmes out. Some of the items and papers lost that night were now gone forever, but otherwise, the room looked as if Holmes could return at any minute. (If he did, he'd be dismayed to find that Mrs. Hudson was dusting it regularly in his absence. He always set a great store of value upon the levels of unremoved dust.)

I had seen Mycroft Holmes on a number of occasions since Holmes's death, some sombre, and others quite dry and businesslike, but I'd never had the courage to ask him why he paid to maintain his brother's rooms, as if it were some museum that only the landlady and I could see. Mrs. Hudson once told me that Mycroft never visited the place, so he wasn't keeping it as his own effort to find connection with his late brother. Perhaps I didn't ask because I didn't want to force Mycroft into admitting he had a soft and sentimental side. I liked to think of him, in those days when my thoughts were often too dark, as the cold blunt edge of the British Government, using his agents to deal with any problems that arose.

Soon, I would find myself in that same position, to a lesser degree, directing my own agents to right a wrong.

I arrived just at nine, even as a hansom cab discharged its fare. I paused on the doorstep, the key I still possessed out to open the door, and waited for Mr. Jabez Wilson to join me.

He had aged terribly in the two years since we'd last met. Then, he'd been elderly and florid-faced, but now he was pale, as if his heart was giving him trouble. His once bright-red hair seemed dull and rusty, and there was a great deal of white around his ears and in his weepers and streaked up and across through the rest of the mass – now also a bit thinner than before. He had been stout. Now he looked to be down at least two stone. His previously shabby clothing looked to be even more so. He still had the curious square Chinese coin upon his watch chain, but his Masonic tie-pin was gone.

"Dr. Watson?" he said, peering up at me as he approached. I confirmed it, and he shook my hand. Then, noticing my up-and-down examination, he frankly stated, "I've come down a bit in the world since we last met." He shook his head and passed a hand up and down to display it, as if to say, "Look upon me and despair!"

At that moment, the cold wind pressed us, and I urged him to come inside, ringing the bell as I unlocked and opened the door. As we entered, Mrs. Hudson came from within her ground-floor demesne and helped take and hang our coats. Then, I indicated that Wilson should proceed me up the stairs. He did so, wearily, two and three steps at a time, and pausing at the turn of the landing to catch his breath.

At the top, he stepped aside so that I could lead him into the sitting room. Before I could do so, however, he spoke with a small laugh.

"It really is seventeen steps," he said, causing me to turn my head curiously.

"Eh?"

"Seventeen steps," he explained. "You and Mr. Holmes remarked on it in one of your stories – the one about the German king."

"Bohemian," I corrected. "A nobleman from one of the moribund houses."

He nodded, but he wasn't really listening. "Do you report everything that happens? Are you completely accurate?"

Leery of which way this seemed to be drifting, I answered with a cautious, "Yes."

He nodded again. "Umm-hmm. Umm-hmm. And the story about snake? Was the wicked doctor's name really 'Royal'?"

"Well, it was 'Roylott'," I corrected.

"So you changed it for the magazine!" He said it with vigor, and not as a question.

"No, you misunderstand. His name was 'Roylott', and that's how it was reported in *The Strand.*"

He seemed a big deflated then. "Oh. I'd hoped to find that you – at least sometimes – made changes when you prepared Mr. Holmes's cases for publication. After all, you stated that my pawnshop was in Saxe-Coburg Square, when it's actually Charterhouse Square, near Barbicon, and when describing where the interviews for the League took place, you called it 'Pope's Court' instead of Mitre Court."

In fact, I did sometimes make minimal changes, and I had altered these place names as he indicated – not willingly, but upon the advice of my literary agent, who felt that identifying the real locations might serve to irritate the other residents of those spots. I sometimes altered a name as well, but in this case, hadn't felt that it was necessary. But for the purposes of this conversation, to keep things simple, I merely replied, "Mr. Holmes wouldn't have appreciated if I fictionalized important details. He always argued for a scientific presentation of his work."

Wilson frowned, and a pair of vertical lines formed below the corners of his mouth. I didn't recall them from when he'd been heavier – even when vexed by the machinations of the Red Headed League.

"I am disappointed to hear it," he said. "I'd hoped to bring action against you – No offense, sir! – for being willing to change details when relating some people's misfortunes, but choosing to reveal every accurate aspect of my little problem for the world to see and ridicule. I saw you glance to my missing Masonic tie pin." I nodded. "It was taken from me – the Masons kicked he out for being a fool – which they discovered by reading your story!

"I spoke to an attorney – Although one can't buy much advice for what I can afford these days! – and he said that I have no case, but I thought that I would try anyway. Not knowing how to reach you – The offices of *The Strand* magazine are singularly tight-lipped! – I attempted to see Mr. Holmes here in Baker Street, but the housekeeper – "

"The landlady," I interrupted. "Mrs. Hudson owns the lease on the building. Mr. Holmes – and I before my marriage – were tenants."

He nodded and went on, politely waiting until I was done, but not listening. "The housekeeper told me that Mr. Holmes was unavailable. I returned several times to the same story, and finally she suggested that she could get a message to you – which was what I wanted all along, but never quite thought to convey. My mind is all over these last few months, you see, and I'd hoped that, by bringing a lawsuit for defamation against you – No office intended, sir, I assure you! Nothing personal – Just a matter of business! – that I might gain enough coin to get out of my unfortunate situation and move along. I've considered it anyway – simply walking away from the shop and never looking back – but I'm too old to start over somewhere else, and they would know what I was planning should I start to sell things in order to raise capital."

I raised a placating hand. "Hold up, Mr. Wilson. I'm interested in your story, but you must tell it in order." We had been standing near the doorway, and I gestured toward the fireplace and the familiar chairs grouped there. "Would you care to have a seat and share the details?"

He suddenly looked wary, as if suspecting a trap. "And see it told in next month's *Strand*? No thank you, sir!" Then, as if hearing himself, he sagged a bit, stating, "I apologize, Doctor. Two years ago, you and Mr. Holmes came to my aid – even though I didn't suspect how much I required it – and you couldn't have known what it would lead to. And your story: I know that you were simply relating one of Mr. Holmes's more interesting cases. It probably never occurred to you how it made me appear to my neighbors and customers – just a gullible old fool, easy to bring to a disadvantage. Not the most optimal position for a pawnbroker!"

By then I'd led him to the basket chair. There was a cheery fire going, and the room was already warm and cozy, courtesy of Mrs. Hudson. I stepped to the open landing door, called down for tea, and then seated myself in my old chair to Wilson's immediate left.

Under no circumstances would I have instead chosen Holmes's armchair. I still half-expected to look over and see him sitting there again someday.

"You allude to unpleasant circumstances," I prompted. "May I ask you to elaborate?"

He sat up straighter – he had been abjectly slumped – and looked around. "Where is Mr. Holmes? No offense, sir, but I'd prefer to wait and just tell it just once."

I let a silence fall as I considered my response. Over the past year-and-a-half, I'd had to explain more times than I could count that Holmes was dead. It had been reported in the press at the time, but one must remember that while he was widely known in certain circles – those he'd helped and those he'd defeated, the good and the bad, the police and the criminals – many others hadn't yet heard of him, and whatever appeared in the press was likely ignored. So many people still came looking for him, having heard his name and reputation, and they had to be convinced that he was no longer available to look into their varied problems.

Clearly, Jabez Wilson was one of those people.

"Mr. Holmes is no longer with us," I said, my mouth stumbling as usual to find a more gentle euphemism for *dead.* "Early May of last year. It happened while he was investigating a complex case on the Continent."

Wilson chewed on that for a moment, and was still silent until after Mrs. Hudson had come and gone. He held his quite-sugared tea for a number of long moments before raising it, giving the cup a couple of gusty cooling puffs, and then drank it all down. Licking his lips, he set the cup aside and made to rise.

"Well, then," he said, clearing his throat, "if there's no help to be had here, I'd best be returning to my shop."

I rose as well. "Hold, Mr. Wilson! At least tell me your story. Perhaps I can suggest something."

He gave me a suspicious look, as if still believing that I was seeking more fodder for my magazine narratives. Then, with a shrug, as if to say that he had nothing better to do, he sat back down, put his hands on knees, rocked forward and back a couple of times, and told me of his life since October 1890.

"In some ways, the morning that I visited here, and told my curious story to you and Mr. Holmes, [1] was my last easy moment. Before then, I was able to fool myself that all was well. Oh, I don't blame you. If my young assistant, Vincent Spaulding – I mean *John Clay* – had been able to successfully rob the nearby bank, then the tunnel back to my shop would have been found, and there would have been so many questions, and suspicions that I was also involved, even though I hadn't fled. It would have been assumed that I knew about the tunnel, and gave permission for it. And no one would have believed that farrago concerning the League. In hind-sight, I can barely believe it myself.

"Afterwards, I had no assistant, and seemed to have no luck finding another. The girl that had worked for me left as well. I suspect she – let us say that she had a . . . a *fascination* with John Clay. My wife having died years ago, I was alone, and thus could only open the shop in a limited capacity. On top of that, the City and Suburban Bank slapped a bill on me for repairs caused by the tunnel intruding into their cellar! That ate up the last of my savings, and I was forced to take a small loan besides, which I could barely repay.

"And then last Christmas, I had a visit from Fraser Guy."

He said it and then paused, as if waiting to see my reaction, but I had none, for I'd never before heard the name. *Perhaps Holmes knows of him,* I thought, glancing without thought to my friend's chair. But he wasn't there.

When I didn't react, Wilson continued. "He is a dangerous fellow in those parts, there on the edge of the East End and only a mile from where the Ripper roamed, and he'd smelled my weakness and came to take advantage of it. 'Ho, Mr. Wilson!' he said that first visit as if were friends. 'I hear that your days have been dark of late. I'm here to change that – to throw you a life-line, you see.' He took a look around, stepping here and there and prodding my meager wares as if he were poking a finger into a refuse pile. 'What you need is a *partner*, and I'm that fellow! Congratulations, Mr. Wilson!'

"Then he rubbed his big hands together briskly and proceeded to explain what this 'partnership' actually meant. You look as if you don't know him, Dr. Watson. I envy you that safety. He is a notorious fence, and he rightly perceived that setting up in such a shop as mine – nearly destitute and empty, and ridiculed to boot – would make it the perfectly anonymous place he needed to carry out his activities. 'And I even hear that you can provide me with a tunnel into the bank on the next street," he said, and laughed and laughed. I was too despondent to offer any correction, or truly any resistance at all. This seemed to be the natural progression of my sad life since that day I'd dropped by here, sitting in this very chair, to ask about the sudden cessation of the Red Headed League. Oh, for those carefree days!" And he threw up his hands dramatically. If he'd been a minister, the sincerity of the action might have been enough to win over a soul, but instead I was simply left with an uneasiness, feeling somehow responsible for this mess.

"This 'Fraser Guy'," I said. "He's still there?"

"Oh yes," was Wilson's emphatic reply. "He's infested my cellars like the filth in King Augeas' stables. It would take a Hercules to force him out, but – " And he now glanced toward my old friend's empty chair. " – as you say, the only Hercules that I've ever met is gone." He then shook his head and stared at his feet. "No offense, sir."

I chewed my lip, wondering if I was about to bite off something too big to swallow. Then, "Mr. Wilson, are you still residing in the building?"

"I am. Guy lets me keep a room upstairs. 'Wouldn't do,' he says, 'if someone comes knocking, not to be able to show them the owner.' But no one has ever asked. Either they don't know or care, or they're afraid of Fraser Guy and will never come knocking."

I stood and he looked up, my sudden motion leaving him rather confused. "I will help you," I said. "I don't quite know how, yet, but I will." I gave him my card. "This is my home and practice. A message there will reach me. In the meantime, just return to the normality of your days, such as they are, and I'll set some plans in motion. I'll . . . I'll come up with a plan."

He stood then as well, peering up at me. He seemed to see something that he could accept, for he stuck out his hand and shook mine firmly. Then he turned and, without a backward glance, opened the door, stepped onto the landing, went down the stairs – seventeen of them, as I re-confirmed from counting his solid descending footsteps – and so out the front door and back into the passing masses.

"Well," I said aloud while sighing heavily and glancing again at Holmes's chair. Once again I was amazed at how nothing is ever truly finished. Wilson's brush with the Red Headed League had been two years earlier, and now it was back. Holmes had died on the fourth of May, 1891, and still his affairs reached out to involve me.

And perhaps Mr. Fraser Guy had also had previous involvement with Sherlock Holmes – and now he'd learn that the connection wasn't severed for him either.

I found an entry for Guy in Holmes's scrapbooks. It had taken me a while to decipher his system, but by the time of his passing, I'd become fairly comfortable with locating what I needed. I lamented that the volumes hadn't been updated since he left England, but they were still a valuable resource, and I wondered that Mycroft, in preserving the rooms, hadn't at least seen about donating them to the Yard. Some there wouldn't have known what to do with them – but others would appreciate their value.

Guy was forty-four years old, a transplant to London from Manchester. As of early 1891, he was unmarried, but had four sons ranging from twenty-eight to thirteen by three different mothers. This was attributed to his unexplained animal magnetism over some types of women, and his aggressive abuse of others. All four sons served as his lieutenants. He was a big man, and his sons nearly as large, even the youngest, and they, along with four or five other men of the lowest character, made up his gang, which was fancifully called "The Stepney Saints". (Holmes had once wasted some time in tracking down the origins of the names of different London criminal gangs, thinking that as he perceived a pattern, it might reveal some truth that he could record in a monograph, but he lost interest when it appeared that names were randomly generated for irrelevent reasons.) As Wilson had mentioned, Guy's specialty was fencing stolen goods. A spot in Wilson's stagnated pawn shop would make a perfect location for such work.

"Doctor," said Inspector Lestrade, apparently on his way out, but willing to stop and talk when I unexpectedly arrived at his office door. "You were right – when Wilkins went back to where Harbolt's body was found, the grass was dead, indicating that he'd been there for several days longer than we thought. It must have been Trigiani that stabbed him, since his alibi – now proven false – was the only thing keeping us from arresting him."

"That's good news," I said, "but I'm actually here about something else."

"Oh?" He shifted his focus away from the Harbolt murder and invited me to a chair, which he uncovered by moving a foot-tall mound of leaning files. "How can I help you?" he asked, shutting the door.

Since Holmes's passing, I'd formed closer friendships with a number of the Yard's inspectors. For quite some time I'd worked with them, and I'd always had a great deal more patience toward them than the late detective. Also, I felt something of a kinship with them, possibly due to my military days, as they themselves had the same respectful camaraderie, despite their rivalries, that one found in the service. "*We few, we happy few, we band of brothers . . . .*" Sadly, it took Holmes's passing and removal from the equation for my connection with the inspectors to truly grow and solidify, for he was always like the gravitational pull of great celestial body whose transit affected all the other smaller objects around it.

"What can you tell me," I asked, "of the Stepney Saints?"

Lestrade leaned back and eyed me speculatively, saying "They aren't a bunch that you should be messing with." He declared it without need for consideration. "In the last year, Fraser Guy has proven himself to be a master at the art of fencing, and since he's also demonstrated that he's a master at the art of murder, he's eliminated his competition. He's smart enough to do it without leaving any evidence that ties him to what we can prove, and he's become the leader in his field, one might say."

"And how has this been allowed to happen?" I asked. "If he's so well known, then why not arrest and prosecute him?"

Lestrade shook his head, apparently at my *naïveté*. "Knowing and stopping – or arresting and prosecuting, as you say – are two different things. One reason – and this is not something we're proud of – is that the villain you know about is easier to deal with than the one you don't. We've rather let Guy run the table – for a while – so that he's a monopoly unto himself. That way, when we are ready, we only have to take him down and not worry about the concurrent small fry – because just then, there aren't any small fry left. He's eliminated them for us. Of course, taking him out of the game means that there's a new vacuum to fill, and a new set of criminals inevitably arise to fill it. That's how Guy found his place: When Professor Moriarty's organization was destroyed, all of the little fish that were left, as well as the organizations from elsewhere that were slavering to get into London, having previously been kept away, now had an opportunity. We let them thin the herd, in a Darwin-like way, to see just who we'd be facing at the end of the day. That was Fraser Guy. He's had his year. Now it sounds like he's ripe enough to pluck – that is, if you have something for me that we can use."

"I don't know," I said. "I met with someone today – one of Holmes's old clients – whose business has been unwillingly subsumed into Guy's enterprise, and he seemed rather hopeless – enough so that I said I'd help. Afterwards, however, I realized that my skills in this type of fight are limited." I then told him of Jabez Wilson, reminding him of the events of October 1890, and relating what had occurred to the poor fellow since then. "I cannot disguise myself and go loitering about the East End as Holmes would have done, putting in my hand at just the right spot and plucking out the one person with the one fact that can unlock the puzzle. However, I have some ideas of who to approach – and you and the Yard were at the top of the list."

Lestrade nodded. "Rightly so." He stood. "Let me go find Peter Jones. That red-headed business was his case, and Fraser Guy falls squarely in his bailiwick."

With a promise that he'd return in a moment, he stepped out, leaving the door open. I sat quietly in my chair, my mind wandering from meeting Jabez Wilson that morning, and back two years to the first time I'd seen him. It was easy from there to drift into other memories, good and bad. The laughter Holmes and I had shared when first hearing Jabez Wilson's curious story, and his understandable embarrassment and anger. The subsequent visit to Wilson's shop in the southeast corner of Charterhouse Square. The discussion the previous year with my literary agent about renaming that location for the published story, as someone nearby tenant might have objections (without either of us ever considering renaming Jabez Wilson).

I thought of the branch bank on Aldersgate Street, just behind Wilson's shop, which had been the location of a second robbery attempt just three months later – partly because, Holmes thought, its weaknesses had been identified during John Clay's defeated attempt. Holmes had been consulted on that affair as well, quickly resolving it to the manager's complete satisfaction. Then there was the matter of the street drain a quarter-mile far west, in the intersection of Charterhouse Street and Farringdon Road, opening downward into the lost River Fleet. I would never forget when Holmes and I had tracked the Smithfield Market Skinner, that terrible murderer who mutilated his victims to steal as much as he could of their largest bodily organ. When cornered, he had fled under the street to the lost Fleet, and we had followed down and through the darkness, finding his lair in a dank chamber far back and below Fetter Lane, where the horrors we'd seen before that day were only a precursor. Holmes had pushed me aside when the Skinner came for him, and if I hadn't found my service revolver in the darkness and pulled the trigger when I did . . . .

A constable leaned in abruptly, interrupting my reminiscences. "Seen the inspector?" he asked. I didn't know him, but he seemed to recognize me. I said that Lestrade should be back shortly, and he nodded. "Big break in the Molesey case," he said before vanishing back the way he'd come.

Lestrade rejoined me just a moment later, bringing with him Inspector Peter Jones, a fellow that I didn't know as well as some of the Yarders, but whom I very much respected nonetheless.

"A constable was looking for you," I said. "He said there's been a break in the Molesey case."

"Ah!" A smile lit his face. "Big doings. A pity you're tied up with this Fraser Guy business. Fancy a side-trip down to Molesley? You've never seen a victim done up quite like what we found in nearby Hampton Court Palace."

"Perhaps I'd better not," I said. "I'll forego it his time. My regular duties are where my efforts must lie."

"Don't be too sure," Lestrade responded. "Your surgeon work is much more trusted that of Fernard. I'm still not going to be satisfied until you're working for us full-time." He turned to Peter Jones. "Fill me in when you have a plan. I want to go with you." Then back to me: "Feel free to use my office. Now I must hurry to Waterloo. Good luck to both of you. Fraser Guy is a villain whose time has come."

Then he was gone, and Peter Jones was saying, "Fraser Guy, eh? What can I do to help?"

I hadn't seen Jones for some time, as his duties had gradually altered since the arrest of John Clay. Saving the French gold – albeit with Holmes's guidance – had been quite the feather in his cap, but Clay's capture had also been something of a burden, as the fellow was one of Professor Moriarty's mid-level creatures, and therefore, Jones was indirectly drawn into the escalating multi-front investigations into the Professor's affairs. As such, Jones, who had previously shown an aptitude for the tedious work required when chasing down obscure and twisted financial records, was shunted onto an administrative path that meant more responsibility and prestige within the Yard, but a disconnection with his previous police duties – something that I felt did not entirely please him.

When I began, mentioning Jabez Wilson, Jones shook his head.

"Poor fellow," he said. "His pawn shop was barely squeaking by. If Clay hadn't worked there practically for free, it would have already closed before the robbery ever occurred. How does Fraser Guy enter the picture?"

I finished relating Wilson's story, and then Jones excused himself for a moment. When he returned, he explained. "I telephoned the station that's responsible for the area around Barbican, Smithfield Market, Charterhouse Square, and so on, and spoke to one of the constables. He stated that Wilson's shop is doing a steady business, but he sees nothing suspicious – just the usual pawn-broking trade going in and out, and the store is filled with more items than it's had in years."

"So does this mean that Wilson simply spun a story for me, for some reason of his own? Perhaps related to the publication of his indirect involvement in the gold robbery?"

Jones shook his head. "Not at all. This is exactly the type of thing that Fraser Guy would set up, and if he's using the pawn shop as a cover for his fencing operation, then he'd want the shop to appear somewhat successful, to cover when people on his business go in and out. If the shop was nearly dead, the neighbors might pay more attention when Guy's people show up." He tapped his lip and said, "I take it that the point of this is to get poor Mr. Wilson out from under."

"It is, but that's only half of it. I also want to make sure that he still has a good business left when Fraser Guy has been excised from his life. I have an idea about that, separate from what the Yard can accomplish."

Jones nodded. "Give me a day or two, and I think we can come up with something that you'll like."

I took a moment to explain what I was thinking and, as it would serve to pull in tandem with what Jones had planned, we shook hands, and I left the building and turned east along the Embankment, seeking a Wiggins.

After meeting with Jabez Wilson that morning in Baker Street, I had arranged to have my practice covered for the rest of the day by my obliging neighbor. It was something that he'd done quite regularly just a few years before, when it was typical for Holmes to request my presence, either at the Baker Street rooms for some appointment, or when stopping by my Paddington home and practice unannounced to pick me up as we set out for what might be a couple of hours or a couple of days.

Although I was nearly certain that Holmes wouldn't – without prior warning – commit me to weeks away from London after I was married, as he had during my bachelor days in Baker Street, there was always the shred of worry that he *might.* He'd had no compunction about volunteering my extended services in the fall of 1888 during the Dartmoor expedition, or the time in '84 when I learned on the morning of my departure that I was to spend nearly two weeks in Bath, watching for the passage of a one-eyed man along the north side of the Abbey. My time was wasted – the fellow never even went to Bath – but Holmes did acknowledge that my efforts weren't mispsent and that his case was bolstered ten-fold when I was able to report that a beautiful woman was there every day, waiting with ever-increasing disappointment for the same man who never arrived.

My journey was nearly two miles, and a cab would have been quicker, but I wanted time to think. Since Holmes's death, I hadn't remained entirely unconnected to the world of investigation. Knowing my long association with my late friend, his acquaintances were occasionally desperate enough to seek my help when they found themselves in situations beyond their control. In most cases, relying on my own intelligence guided by experience, I was able to assist them. Sometimes these same people recommended me to strangers, and I did what I could. More often, the inspectors at Scotland Yard sought to include me. We had become friends, and also they were often frustrated with the police surgeons that they were forced to use, like Doctor Fernard, so they asked for my outside opinion. I was flattered, and did my best, but there was never an instance where at some point, I didn't ask myself, "*What would Sherlock Holmes do?*"

Because of this, I used my time walking from Scotland Yard to Gray's Inn to consider Wilson's story, and what I recalled of the area of London where his shop was located. But my observations were of limited value. I needed something better.

I followed the Embankment to Waterloo Bridge, and then turned north and east alongside Somerset House, working my way toward High Holborn, and thence into Gray's Inn, and the chambers of my attorney, Marchmont. He was glad to see me and asked what I needed, and I pointed to one of his clerks. "Can I borrow him for half-an-hour? I need to talk something over with him."

Marchmont, always a fine fellow, readily agreed, and the clerk followed me out and down to the passage leading to Gate Street, just northwest of Lincoln's Inn Fields, and thence into The Ship, where we found a quiet corner for a talk.

Michael Wiggins was looking prosperous and happy, and I was glad. I'd always worried that he was too thin, but he now looked fit and healthy. I congratulated him upon noticing the wedding ring on his left hand, recalling that he'd been married just the year before, and he proudly told me that he was to be a father in the spring.

I had first met him sometime in the early eighties, when he was one of the ever-changing group of lads (and occasional lasses) that made up Holmes's unofficial Irregulars, a band of street children ranging across various ages whom he had recruited to serve as his eyes and ears, seeing and hearing what others could not. He'd already had this organization in place when I met him in 1881, having formed them up several years earlier during the time he was establishing his practice while living in Montague Street.

One of his first Irregulars was a lad named Wiggins, who had quickly demonstrated his quality and settled in as the leader of the bunch. Holmes had performed a service for the Wiggins family – namely, saving their mother from a charge of murder [2] – and afterwards, a firm bond had formed between them and the detective. As the Irregulars grew, older members departed while younger took their place – many of them members of the extended Wiggins family, and usually with a Wiggins in charge. Michael Wiggins, while never a leader, had been an important and effective member of the troop nearly ten years before. Then, when he reached adulthood, Holmes found him a position as one of Marchmont's clerks.

One aspect of Holmes's use of the Irregulars that is often forgotten was that he didn't simply pay them the random shilling for following someone or confirming some obscure fact. He made sure that they were clothed and fed and schooled, and then he found places for them – jobs, or even careers for the ones who were willing to work hard and study and pay their dues. London was full of former Irregulars who owed their success to Sherlock Holmes, and his death the previous year hadn't negated that. When I explained why I was there and what I wanted – namely, for a report on Wilson's situation from an Irregular perspective – Wiggins understood immediately, and knew exactly who to involve and what to do.

Finishing our drinks, I walked Wiggins back to Marchmont's office and then continued east, three-quarters of a mile or so to Barts, to confer with The Sphinx.

Passing through the Henry VIII Gate on Giltspur Street, I wound through the dark passage and then right across the hospital's inner court to the modest side-door, opening into a wing of the great hospital. From there I went up the bleak stone staircase and the down a corridor, and so into the chemical laboratory.

The Sphinx was Henry Barth, a chap who worked as a laboratory assistant, alongside the student physicians, to clean up their messes and help set up experiments as needed. Due to a congenital handicap – the poor fellow had been born with a hunched back – he'd had difficulties all his life, but his steady work ethic and bright intelligence had led him to a position in which he seemed most satisfied. He'd already been at Barts for quite some time when I was a student, and he was still there now.

The origin of his nickname, "The Sphinx", was much debated when I was a student, and that likely hadn't changed amongst the current crop. Some said it was due to his physical shape, somewhat similar to the Great Sphinx of Giza. (Having been there and having seen The Sphinx, I didn't see the resemblance.) Others claimed it was because of his round-about way of answering questions that could grow tedious, as they resembled riddles more than definitive responses. Whatever the case, there was one thing about him that I required that day: His knowledge of local criminals in that area.

I believe that I'm the only person that Henry ever told about his secret. He was a model hospital employee in every way – except that sometimes he stole inconsequential medical supplies. Nothing more than small amounts of bandages, for instance, or needles and suture for sewing up wounds. The only way I knew is that once he'd needed help for a procedure that was more than his informally acquired skills could conclude. It was then that I learned about Henry's informal clinic, where he provided care for those in society who would not receive it otherwise, either because of their lowest stations, or their fear of approaching anyone in authority, even a doctor.

Henry had a brother, Albert, and both had been born within a mile of Barts. That was their world. While Henry had displayed the gumption to work hard and find a position, using his intelligence to overcome his difficulty, Albert had become a petty criminal, and not a very good one. He got by through his loose attachment to local gangs. He never made many ripples, except for once, when he was shot by being in the wrong place at the wrong time. Henry tried to treat him, could not, and recruited me. That was when I learned his secret. I recognized the stolen materials, and Henry confessed. I kept the knowledge to myself, knowing that Henry Barth was too good a man to lose over such small potatoes, and that Albert Barth was harmless and helpless, and didn't need to be thrown into the indifferent arms of the Law. For this Henry was ever grateful.

Now I wanted to ask him a question – unrelated to the information that Wiggins was assembling, and something that could be best obtained by a long-time resident, since this was Henry's part of London, and he could locate the answers I sought.

I explained why I was there and what I needed, and why I needed it, not worrying that Henry would betray me, or the fact that Jabez Wilson was seeking to escape from someone as dangerous as Fraser Guy. Henry frowned and nodded, understanding the implications.

"What would happen to the man who bites the hand that feeds him?" he vaguely asked, from which I assumed he referred to Wilson and Guy, should the latter find out that the former had looked for help from a friend of the late Sherlock Holmes. "Will all who seek answers be satisfied, or will the only response be the monotonous sigh of the unchecked and indifferent winds?" A moment's consideration led me to think that possibly he meant that I might or might not be content with whatever he learned.

I nodded as if that was it, told him I'd be back to see what he'd found in a couple of days, and left – glancing, as I always did whenever visiting here, over to the old chemical table where I'd first met Holmes on that New Year's Day over a decade before. How often does one realize that he or she is in a moment that will change life's direction forever? On battlefields, of course, and when attending births or deaths, or at terrible accidents where lives are lost or ruined. But what about the quiet moments, such as when I was first introduced to Sherlock Holmes at that table? I had no intimation then of that moment's importance. I'd awakened that morning, worried about my finances and ill-tempered. I'd met an old friend and we'd gone to lunch. He'd mentioned someone who was seeking to share lodgings – which was exactly what I *needed*, even if it wasn't what I *wanted*. I'd been doing fine by myself in a hotel off the Strand – except for the small qualification that my expenditures were running ahead of my limited income. I'd gone along to Barts to meet a possible future co-lodger, not realizing the precipice that I approached, or that I was stepping beyond the edge and jumping headlong into a different life.

That old table had been used hundreds – nay, thousands – of times since I was introduced there to Sherlock Holmes. It was just a table, and it was in just a room, but it was where I'd taken a momentous step, and I could never see it without remembering all that happened after.

I had one more stop that day. I wanted to see Jabez Wilson's old pawn shop.

Upon exiting the hospital, with St. Paul's in view just to the south, I worked my way through a couple of passages to the east, whereupon I set my steps on Aldersgate Street toward the Underground Station. Just a short walk past it, I turned left toward Charterhouse Street, and almost immediately reached Charterhouse Square.

It was much as I remembered it from two years earlier. When I'd published the narrative related to Wilson's curious experience, I'd described it as "*a poky, little, shabby-genteel place, where four lines of dingy two-storied brick houses looked out into a small railed-in enclosure, where a lawn of weedy grass and a few clumps of faded laurel-bushes made a hard fight against a smoke-laden and uncongenial atmosphere.*" There was nothing royal-looking about it, and I had to wonder at the obscure reasoning behind my literary agent's insistence that I change the location name from *Charterhouse Square* to the royally associated *Saxe-Coburg Square.* But he had lots of strange and curious "fancies", as he called them when our disagreements over his editorial notions became heated, and he often sullenly retreated by insisting that his "fancies must be consulted, Watson. They must be consulted."

Wilson's pawnshop, No. 42, was at the southeast corner. The woodwork was painted black, and three gilt balls beside a brown board lettered *Jabez Wilson* marked the place from its neighbors. Two years earlier, I had wondered how such a business might thrive in this dull little pocket, with no cross-traffic from the nearby busy road besides the residents, and no reason to come here – it wasn't even a square, but rather a pentagon – unless some historian wished to gaze upon the enclosed grassy garden, which had once been a fourteenth-century plague pit.

Wilson's shop seemed more prosperous than before, and now I understood why. I considered going inside – I could ask for a quote to pawn my brother's old pocket-watch before deciding to keep it after all – but I realized that seeing the inside of the building would add nothing to my limited knowledge. Fraser Guy was almost certainly not there, and I might encounter someone that I had met before, which would jeopardize whatever scheme we were trying to assemble. Perhaps even coming to the Square had been a mistake – but I had inexplicably felt the need to see the place once more. Perhaps it was because I knew that Sherlock Holmes would have wanted to survey the field before the battle, as he had that day in October 1890 when we'd stood there and faced John Clay, while Holmes sought indications of a tunnel.

Having taken my look, I retraced my steps to the station and had a noisy unpleasant ride back to Paddington.

For two days, I went about my usual affairs – seeing patients at my practice and in their homes, helping at the nearby St. Mary's Hospital, and most of all, spending time with Mary, worrying to myself at her worsening health while staying cheerful and positive to hide my fears.

And I also made and kept one appointment with a banker of my acquaintance that might do some good, or might be a waste of time, depending on how the campaign against Fraser Guy progressed.

It had been a Tuesday when I met with Jabez Wilson in Baker Street, and on Friday, I attended a conference at Scotland Yard. Lestrade was there, and Inspectors Gregson and Bradstreet as well. Athelney Jones had invited himself, and I appreciated it, for what he lacked in intelligence was more than balanced by his exceptional character and thirst for justice. He was speaking with Michael Wiggins, who seemed completely at ease, even laughing at one of the inspector's asides – something about how young Michael had once vexed him, but now "All water under the bridge, lad!" Peter Jones opened the meeting, speaking for just a moment before turning over the reins to his colleague, Inspector Patterson.

"After your visit the other day, Doctor," Peter Jones explained, "the first thing I did was seek out Patterson. He has an encyclopedic knowledge on the criminal classes, and I knew we'd want him involved, now that it's Fraser Guy's turn to walk the plank." He nodded to Patterson and sat down.

There were many who dismissed Inspector Patterson as an "odd duck" – though less since the destruction of Professor Moriarty's gang than before. Upon joining the Yard, he'd been an introverted and often absent officer, and when one did encounter him, it was an awkward event. The man wasn't eloquent or loquacious by any means, and he preferred being out in the shadows to spending time in the office.

Holmes had spotted Patterson's talents immediately – his ability to disguise himself, and then insinuate whatever identity he'd assumed into the criminal element. As this was also one of Holmes's gifts, he had found a kindred spirit. It was during this time that the confrontation with Professor Moriarty was escalating, and Patterson was an early and eager recruit to Holmes's specialized little army, filled with only those that he could truly trust. After Moriarty's defeat, one might have thought that Patterson's major work was done, but he'd stayed busy, using the same methods he'd perfected over the previous years.

Unlike Jones, Patterson remained seated when he spoke. His tone was low but clear, and everyone in the room held to his words.

"Like most of them when they get so successful, Fraser Guy has gotten arrogant and careless," Patterson explained succinctly. "He doesn't try to hide anything anymore, and we have more than enough witnesses – solid witnesses – to charge him with everything from receiving stolen goods, smuggling, intimidation, beatings, theft, and murder. For a time, he's useful to us, as watching the comings-and-goings of his foot soldiers, and those doing business with him, has let us keep accumulating evidence while seeing which further trails to follow. It was a method that Mr. Holmes and I worked out a few years ago. It was successful when boxing in the Professor. It was foolproof against Guy.

"Now is the time to remove him, because his successor is already positioning to make a play, and we'll be happy to see him fill the empty spot when Guy is gone: Sidney Fulworth – 'The Blade' he likes to call himself, playing up a knife fight he had when he was young, winning only because his opponent slipped in Sidney's blood. But he's a fool, and even as he seizes control, he'll mismanage everything as if it's a music hall comedy.

"I believe that the warrants are prepared?" Patterson glanced at Peter Jones, who nodded. Then Patterson leaned forward to see Michael Wiggins. "And you can tell us where to find everyone?"

Wiggins nodded, sitting up straighter on the edge of his chair. "After Dr. Watson visited the other day, I found some of the other lads – grown now, like me, but still interested in helping. We spread out and asked questions. We can tell you where everyone you're seeking can be found – lead you right to them."

"Good, good," said Patterson, leaning back satisfied. "Best to take them completely unawares, with nary a shot fired."

I had again arranged for my accommodating neighbor to watch my practice – "Just like the old days!" he'd chortled. "Will you tell me about it when you're done?" – and I went with the inspectors to arrest Fraser Guy – for all of them wanted to be there when the evil man was taken.

While a small army of constables, sergeants, and other inspectors spread out over London, each led by one of the former Irregulars to where Guy's various lieutenants would be found, I rode in a growler with Lestrade, Gregson, and Wiggins, while the other inspectors followed in another. There had been some cursory concern about including Wiggins in our group – "You never know who might start shooting," Lestrade had declared. – but in the end, I felt that the young man had earned his spot. Additionally, I knew that Marchmont dabbled enough in criminal matters that it wouldn't hurt for his rising clerk to have some additional experience associating with the police, and seeing an arrest of this importance first-hand was invaluable.

Fraser Guy's abode was in the first-floor rooms above a Cecil Court bookshop. Following Moriarty's organizational arrangement, he was only accessible to a few trusted lieutenants. In turn, the next level down in this unlawful hierarchy reported to the lieutenants, and so on. In this way, there was never a constant and suspicious trooping of numerous shady characters along the narrow street. Instead, the five men who reported immediately to Guy were the only ones who visited his lair, and they were always taken for bookstore employees or customers.

Police officers stoppered both ends of the narrow passage, and surrounded the back as well. There were even constables on the roofs of adjoining buildings, should Guy try to escape by going up, and Patterson had researched the cellars as well, making sure that there were no forgotten entryways into the city sewers. ("I learned that lesson when Mr. Holmes and I nearly missed taking Constance Riddick," he explained to me in a soft tone as we took our positions at one end of the court. "She was a snake, that one, and would have escaped clean had not Mr. Holmes been willing to go down after her. Nearly took a stab wound for his trouble, but it all worked out. They say that slipping on the soap was what broke her neck, and no loss it was, but I know that it was the other prisoners that done it. They never could abide a child killer among them.")

Then the signal was given and the officers charged forward, in overwhelming numbers that could not be answered or denied. I'd wanted to join the scrum, but Lestrade forbid it, and he was correct. I had other responsibilities.

I hadn't known what to expect when Fraser Guy was dragged into the light, and at first I had difficulty believing this soft fat man was any sort of danger. He seemed comical and rather foppish. But when the constables holding his arms stood him up in the street, and I was able to walk closer and take a look into his eyes, I could see that he was something else indeed, a wolf that had been left free for too long to grow fat among the sheep. His eyes even had a wolfish cast to them, with a wild feral aspect to their shape, and an inhuman yellowish turn to both the irises and the surrounding *sclera*. He had a small pursed mouth, now pulled back to expose similarly yellowish teeth, each just a bit too pointed, and a very red tongue that darted around like a skinned rodent trying to break free from its toothy cage. The corners of his mouth were flecked with foam, because he was ranting like a madman, threatening death to whoever fell within his gaze. I don't know how, but he knew my name along with everyone else's, and he promised to flay me alive, and my wife as well. I was more relieved than I would admit that Patterson had done so well to build an airtight capital case against this monster. I was in attendance when he was hanged later that year, and I freely confess my relief that he was gone.

Jabez Wilson had stood no chance against one such as him, and he probably had no idea how close to the edge he had skated, should have made any kind of open resistance. Fraser Guy was not the sort to tolerate opposition.

Following Guy's arrest, I had one other bit of business to conduct on Jabez Wilson's behalf. Michael Wiggins joined me, this time as a representative of Marchmont's legal firm.

We obtained a hansom and headed east. We took a moment to find a post office, where I could send three telegrams, and then we rode to Threadneedle Street, specifically to the offices of Holder and Stevenson, the second largest private banking concern in the City of London. Upon identifying myself, we were led deeply into the building where we were received by Alexander Holder, Senior Partner.

I had arranged to meet with him two days before, on Wednesday, and was shocked to see how he had aged so considerably since early 1888, when he'd first shown up in Baker Street, acting as a madman. [3] His expression then had been of overwhelming grief and despair, and he had swayed and mumbled and pulled at his hair before unexpectedly rising and beating his head upon our wall. We had calmed him enough to get his story – a valuable Royal heirloom that was deposited with his bank as collateral for a loan had been stolen from his home, and he feared that his reputation, and all that he'd worked for, was gone in an instant. Holmes had recovered the stolen coronet fairly easily – although it had been damaged during the theft – but Holder's grief was deeper than before when he learned that it had been stolen by a trusted family member – his niece – who had fled with the true villain before being confronted.

Holder welcomed Wiggins and me into his spacious office quite graciously, asking if we wished for refreshments, which we declined. I thanked him for his time, as I had two days earlier when he'd agreed to see me. I'd traded on his debt to Holmes, seeking the appointment and then a favor, and he'd been most willing to oblige.

I was pleased to see that my telegrams had all served their purpose. Besides alerting Holder to our impending arrival following the successful arrest of Fraser Guy, they had also successfully summoned Jabez Wilson, puzzled and confused but present as I'd previously asked him to be. With him was The Sphinx, Henry Barth.

"The villain?" asked Holder when we were seated. "He is in custody?"

"He is," I confirmed, before providing a few bare details. Wilson's eyes widened, and he shook his head as if disagreeing that it was so easy, but he didn't offer any comment.

I turned to Barth. "What did you discover?"

He settled into the chair as best he could, his short legs dangling above the floor, and said, as if the pawn-broker wasn't sitting there beside him, listening, "Mr. Jabez Wilson has the highest reputation in that part of London. Time was when his shop was the by-word for honest dealing." His countenance turned a shade sad. "His business suffered some – Well, in truth, quite a bit – when his wife passed ten years ago. It's like the heart just went out of him. But even as his prosperity declined, and the shop dried up, and even after that criminal took advantage of him to dig the tunnel into the adjacent bank, his own personal reputation never declined. No one blamed him or thought him criminally involved. People simply understood that, for him, times weren't what they had once been."

Throughout these comments, Jabez Wilson had been becoming more and more focused, taking in what was being said and working to understand its relevance. I felt that it was time to explain.

"Mr. Wilson, you have been the victim of a series of unfortunate events: The death of your wife. Taken advantage of by the criminal, John Clay – and then worse, by Fraser Guy. But your reputation is still excellent, and I have no doubt that you can rebuild your business. That's where Mr. Alexander Holder here comes in.

"Several years ago, Mr. Holder needed help from Sherlock Holmes to retrieve a stolen object."

Wilson nodded. "I read of it in *The Strand*."

"Holmes found that the thief had already sold it to a receiver – a most dishonest pawn-broker – from whom he was obliged to buy it back at a most inflated price. When I recalled this aspect of the affair to Mr. Holder last Wednesday, he agreed that there is a place – a *necessity* – for someone honest and discreet in your line of work for his type of client – not like the broker who bought and sold the jewels from the Coronet – and he's interested in becoming your partner. That is, if you are willing to work hard to rebuild your business. I think that you are. After all, your name is on the sign, painted in large white letters, and it's your reputation that needs to be restored. What do you say?"

When Wilson appeared to be overwhelmed by the sudden unexpected opportunity, and found that he could not speak, Holder prompted him.

"What say you, Wilson? Don't turn it down. I've made my own investigation and heard nothing but good things. You've just had some deuced bad luck, that's all – and I certainly understand that. Say yes, and then let's get to work."

He stood, walked from behind his great desk, and offered his hand. Wilson looked from it to Holder's beaming face, then stood himself, and shook, sealing the deal.

It was a profitable undertaking. Within a year, Wilson's business had been restored, and more. Soon, with Holder's support, he pivoted to specializing in antiques – specifically furniture – and it wasn't so many years after that when the small pawnshop metamorphosed into *Wilson and Holder*, whose sterling reputation needs no explanation.

But perhaps most of all, the two old widowers became the best of friends – a most unexpected result to the long chain of events that began several years earlier, when the criminal John Clay spotted the interesting juxtaposition between red-headed Wilson's dying pawn shop and a nearby bank that had been chosen to temporarily hold a fortune in French gold, and plotted how to connect the two by way of a tunnel and the creation of a clever but bogus Red Headed League.

"Life is infinitely stranger than anything which the mind of man could invent," Holmes had once told me. "We would not dare to conceive the things which are really mere commonplaces of existence. If we could fly out of that window hand in hand, hover over this great city, gently remove the roofs, and peep in at the queer things which are going on, the strange coincidences, the plannings, the cross-purposes, the wonderful chains of events, working through generations, and leading to the most *outrè* results, it would make all fiction with its conventionalities and foreseen conclusions most stale and unprofitable."

He was correct, of course, and I wished very much that I could have shared with him just how well this particular chain of events had turned out.

NOTES

1. See "The Adventure of the Red-Headed League", occurring on 25 October, 1890, and originally published in *The Strand* in August 1891.
2. See "The Adventure of the Gower Street Murder" in *Sherlock Holmes: Tangled Skeins* and *The Collected Papers of Sherlock Holmes – Volume II: Records.*
3. This was described in "The Beryl Coronet", 3-4 February, 1888, and published in *The Strand* in May 1892.

The *X*-Marked Boxes

I had joined my friend, Mr. Sherlock Holmes, late one cold night in a Great Russell Street wool shop. The owner, Mr. MacGregor, was an old acquaintance of his from those long-ago days when Holmes had lived most meagerly in nearby Montague Street. MacGregor's problem might have been considered a small case and (at that point in his successful career) not really worthy of Holmes's time – an intruder was finding his way into the shop during the wee hours when it was closed – but Holmes was fond of the old Scotsman, telling me that the shop owner had once gifted him with a tweed scarf which had subsequently held great sentimental value.

Holmes explained that MacGregor had visited him in Baker Street earlier that day to relate that for the past several mornings, his carefully arranged stock had been shifted, ever so slightly, but still obvious to the canny owner. As owner and sole employee, he knew every inch of the store and its contents. Worse – when MacGregor had straightened the items, his hands had blistered. Holmes had visited the store later that day, and an examination of a few pieces of the displaced stock – in this case some woolen scarves that were midway down in a stack – showed something unusual: Fine organic dust that, when he touched it, also caused his own fingers to blister and itch.

Separating and removing the sabotaged scarves, Holmes took them 'round to the laboratory at Barts where, with the help of a couple of old acquaintances who had worked hard to cultivate certain specialized knowledge, and also making use of assistance from the old medical librarian, he was able to ascertain that they had been dusted with crushed pieces of mucuna pruriens, *a legume native to Africa and tropical Asia. The plant's seed pods and young leaves were notorious for causing itching – as evidenced on Holmes's still-affected fingers on his right hand, the backs of which displayed small red bumps for several days.*

Fortunately, MacGregor confirmed that no scarves from that stack, including those doctored with the itching plant, had been sold. As other nearby stock also showed evidence of tampering, and because the shop had been violated three nights in a row, it was hoped and assumed that the next night would evince a fourth intrusion – for if the intruder had successfully entered that many times, wouldn't he be tempted to try for another? On that assumption, Holmes invited me along to lay in wait. Eating an early meal and kissing my wife goodbye for the night, I made the short trip from Queen Anne Street to Bloomsbury and entered the shop from the front as if I were a customer, hoping that no one was watching closely enough to observe that I didn't similarly exit by closing time. Holmes was already there, hidden comfortably in a back room. MacGregor had laid in sandwiches, jugs of tea, and a bottle of whisky brought down from his last trip to Inverness – "Made with the pure waters of my homeland!" he had declared with a challenging eye. I informed him of my own northern heritage, and he gave me an approving nod. Then the old Scotsman said goodnight and closed the shop as usual, locking the front door and walking away down the now-mostly empty street. We heard his echoing footsteps recede into silence, leaving the only sounds around us coming from the daily settling of the building as it cooled.

The front of the shop, just a few doors east of the Alpha Inn and directly across from the British Museum, was moderately well-lit, and we agreed that entry by way of the main door was unlikely, as foot traffic there was thin but steady and constables made regular passes along the perimeter of the Museum. Rather, the intruder was certainly going to come in by way of the single rear door that opened from a dark mews. Holmes had already confirmed fresh scratches around the keyhole, and in order to give the illicit visitor as much freedom to act as possible, we were waiting in a side room, in a nook behind shelves holding MacGregor's stacked items. The wool smell was both comforting and overwhelming, and more than once I had to stifle a sneeze. On other occasions, I would have expected Holmes to rebuke me, at least with a judgmental glance, but he had softly sneezed several times as well, and I knew that he understood that in this case, such a reaction was unavoidable.

We talked very softly of this and that, with long comfortable silences in between in the way of old friends who have known each other for two decades. He asked after my wife and my practice, and also about a mutual friend, my neighbor in Queen Anne Street, who had recently suffered an injury and sought Holmes's help in redressing the grievance. Holmes then caught me up on a few recent cases of his own, including a recent attempt to steal a sizable trove of securities from the City and Suburban Bank near the Barbican Underground Station. "A dozen years since the thieves last tried," he said, "and they almost got away with it this time. Can you believe that the bank never filled in John Clay's tunnel running from Wilson's pawn shop? [1] At the time, the bank had discussed buying out Wilson's lease, using his shop for storage, and enlarging the tunnel between the two cellars and making it permanent, but they could never come to an agreement amongst themselves, let along get to the point of approaching poor Wilson with an offer, so the plan drifted into an eddy, spun around quietly for a while, and sank – forgotten, except by thieves who read your story and had the idea to find and re-use the tunnel."

That led to our discussion of the recently departed Mr. Wilson, and I recalled a time when Wilson came to me for help during that period in the early nineties when Holmes was believed to be dead. Holmes had never heard the story, and of how Jabez Wilson came to be associated with a certain noted City banker, and that helped to pass a half-hour or so. [2]

Gradually our talk drifted to MacGregor and how Holmes had first met him. I already knew that there had been a presentation of the scarf from the store's owner to the needful young man – but as was often the case, there was more – much more – to the story. Refilling our small glasses of whisky, and confirming that there was no noise to alert us that anyone was trying to enter the shop (for Holmes had set a few small indicators in the alleyway that would let us know when someone arrived), we settled back, and Holmes shared the events of that cold January of 1875, during the first winter after he'd moved to London to attempt to establish himself as a consulting detective . . . .

I'd first come up to London in the summer of '74 [*Holmes related*] to spend the remaining weeks of my long vacation from school, as my original plan – rusticating for that entire time at Donnithorpe, in Norfolk – had collapsed following that ugly and uncomfortable incident at the Trevor home. Mycroft was already living in Montague Street then – Number 24, before he moved, for just a little while, to No. 42 Chad's Street, [3] and then eventually to Pall Mall – and he made room for me, mistakenly assuming that I planned to return to school in the fall, while I actually intended to remain in the capital and pursue my new profession – as soon as I built up the courage to inform my father of my decision. It must be recalled that I was but twenty years of age, and to go against the plans and wishes of one's father . . . .

Our space at No. 24 was already cramped for one – even though Mycroft wasn't quite so large in those days – and fitting in the two of us was quite the strain – although I was willing to sleep uncomfortably upon the floor, up against one of the walls and out of the way. In any case, Mycroft was already weaving his webs within the Government and making himself indispensable from morning to dusk, and I was out for most of every day, either wandering the city or spending time across the street at the British Museum, or working on chemical experiments in the laboratory at Barts – access to which being courtesy of a friend of my father's.

As I've told you before, our landlady at No. 24 was the widow of one of my father's first cousins – and this Mrs. Holmes was certainly no Mrs. Hudson. She'd obtained the lease on the building years before, when her husband passed – almost certainly a desperate move to escape her – and she made do by renting the top three floors to a variety of tenants. On the first floor, in the most easily accessed rooms, was a tiny old woman named Mrs. Coombes, who had a small independent income, and also a proclivity for taking in small dogs and cats, in equal balance. Should she obtain a new pup, she would balance the scale by soon finding a new kitten. She worked hard at her mania, and was altogether a good neighbor. I can't recall there ever being a noise complaint, or the slightest hint of an odor problem. On the middle floor was a young chap about my age who worked across the street in the Museum – Isaiah Beddings – and Mycroft and I were on the top floor, which was useful in those days before he moved out in keeping Mycroft's weight down, as getting up there was rather like climbing a ladder into a church belfry.

It was Isaiah Beddings' situation that drew me into the business where I met Mr. MacGregor.

Holmes paused in his tale. "But you lived in this neighborhood at one time as well, as I recall," he said, "between when you graduated medical school and joining the Army. It was always a cozy little district – we all seemed to know one another to varying degrees. Yet you and I never ran across one another – that we remember. How is it that you didn't meet MacGregor in those days?"

I shifted in my seat and took a sip of whisky. "When I graduated in '78, I had enough saved, along with a small inheritance, to rent the small practice in Southampton Street. From my lodgings and practice at No. 6, I did venture up this way on occasion to drink at the Alpha – and we've discussed before how odd it was that we didn't meet either there or at Barts, where I also spent time between patients, instead of several years later when we did *meet after I returned from Maiwand. But in truth, patients were few and far between, and instead of roaming north and west into Bloomsbury during my free time, or doing as you did between clients, working on increasing the breadth of my professional knowledge, I generally headed down toward the Strand or the theatre district to pursue less-improving paths. After a year or so of waiting hopelessly day after day – rather like Hatherley when he set himself up as a hydraulic engineer, sitting along in his office for someone to seek him out, or when Doyle filled his time between rare patients scratching out his tedious historical novels – I decided to try something else and joined the Army."*

Holmes nodded. "And it all worked out for the best."

Recalling the pains from my military experiences that still assailed me from time to time, and that never entirely went away, even after more than two decades, I could still only agree.

I had stopped into the Alpha [4] one evening, [*Holmes continued*] having just earned a few shillings for a small piece of work much like what we're doing tonight – hiding and waiting for a bad fellow to show up where he wasn't supposed to be. I had spent most of the past three days down in the crypts of St. Paul's working out a little problem for the Bishop of London. It isn't worth retelling – I know that look, Watson, but the truly interesting part of the tale is that the Bishop decided to hire me in the first place. Just twenty years old and with no professional reputation to speak of, I should have been the last person he approached for assistance, but he'd heard of me from a friend of a friend . . . In any case, having located a long-buried lock-box alongside one of the eight support piers, and also having trapped the man who had learned of it and then led us to it, I was ready to return to the surface world. What shocked me was the bone-chilling cold that had settled upon London while I was down for so long in the relatively warm cavern of the cathedral's vast cellars.

I realized when I surfaced that my birthday [5] had passed during one of the days I was hidden in the crypt, but that was of no account. I had a tidy little fee in my pocket, but with the next month's rent due, I didn't want to waste part of it upon a cab, so I chose to walk back to my lodgings. It isn't much over a mile from St. Paul's to Montague Street, even with the twists and turnings of the streets, but I painfully felt every step as I faced into the icy wind, seemingly blowing from whichever direction that I turned, holding my hat to my head, lest it be blown eastward into the darkness. I recall that the skies were clear that night, with a bright moon that in contrast made the streets and alleys and areaways seem especially dark with menace. I also had the sense that there was a hint of dampness in the wind that promised rain by morning, or – if these bitter temperatures continued – snow.

Realizing that opportunities for a warm meal upon reaching my lodgings were very limited – due to both the late hour and my landlady's sour disposition – I made the decision when I reached Great Russell Street that I would part with a few coins after all and turned toward the Alpha. Walking the short distance down the dark street, I was soon inside and settled into a table near one of the windows looking into Museum Street.

Even at that time of night, the place was still halfway full, and there was a low steady murmur of conversation all around me. I was faced with the choice of what to order, and I was jealously hoarding my funds, for the rent was nearly due. By then I was responsible for all of it, Mycroft having moved out several months before. This was less than a year after my decision to become a consulting detective, you'll recall, and in those few months, circumstances had greatly changed. After my decision to become a detective, I threw myself into studies that would benefit my new profession.

I knew all of this, of course, for I'd heard it before, but Holmes was in a narrative mood, and revealing the details of an old case – which always interested me, and wasn't too common of an occurrence – so I was more than happy to pass the quiet moments letting him tell it his own way, in an uncharacteristic and comfortably rambling fashion.

I spent my time studying at the Museum and at Barts and other hospitals. I intruded on as many police investigations as I could, even if I simply stood in the crowd and watched over shoulders as the officers shuffled about where the crime had occurred, carelessly destroying evidence like a wandering herd of moor ponies, blithely going where they would. And I realized that to truly learn what I needed, I'd also have to seek out the criminals and get them to teach me their skills – all while hoping for the occasional case that would give me both practical experience and funds for food and lodging – and the occasional excellent beer at the Alpha.

When I'd told my father that I was changing professions, he was predictably unsupportive – and literally so as well, stopping my funds entirely. The plans he had for his sons required that I become an engineer, and no variation was allowed. Mycroft was more accepting – or indifferent – and he arranged for me to retain the Montague Street rooms when he moved to Chad Street in late '74, as his position required that he reside in better lodgings reflecting his increased responsibilities. His support then was crucial, and there were many times when his charity supplemented my income – and what he provided to me during some months, along with an occasional brotherly lecture, was all that kept me from starving or being evicted.

But January 1875 was neither the best nor the worst of my times in Montague Street, and I had some spare change, and my trip to the Alpha that night led to an interesting case.

As I waited for my sausages and potatoes and a pint of beer, I let the warmth of the room thaw me out – except for the back of my head, which was near one of the large plate windows looking out over the street. I could feel the cold radiating off the glass, and I pressed forward over the small table to get away from it. I was considering a move to a better, warmer spot when I heard a low argument in the back of the pub, gradually rising over the other conversations.

I glanced that way to see Old MacGregor and Isaiah Beddings, both seated at that table in the back – you know the one, where everyone prefers to sit because it's away from both doors. They were both leaning in to speak intensely, their attempts to remain quiet negated as they tried to talk over one another, getting louder and louder. MacGregor was then in his early fifties, and much more invigorated than the man we know now. Isaiah Beddings, about my age – about twenty or so – was doing most of the talking, but when McGregor would sometimes get in the occasional word, it would make the young man respond all the more vigorously.

There was always something very naïve about Isaiah. It wasn't just his wide-eyed view of the world, an expression that looked perpetually surprised. He truly was often surprised, expressing it in a multitude of ways, even during short conversations. He was tall, several inches above my own height, with broad bony shoulders that were hunched forward, taking away several inches, and more were lost by the way he held his head forward instead of upright on his long thin neck. I knew from his uniform that he was something of an apprentice guard at the Museum, although I'd never actually seen him in the public areas during my time there. What I didn't yet know was that, at that stage of his burgeoning career with the Museum, his time was spent in the bowels of the building, crating and uncrating exhibits, and the only guarding that he did was of those unseen items which were not being displayed on the public floors of the building.

Their discussion went on for some three or four minutes and, while it didn't have the effect of shutting down the rest of the conversations in the room, it did cause many to glance that way a number of times as people paused, trying to catch a sense of what was being said – and whether they should be concerned if it escalated to violence. Finally, having apparently heard enough, Isaiah abruptly pushed his chair back and stood. It seemed as if he had another thing to say, but he instead bit his tongue – he actually tucked it between his front teeth and held it there – and turned and departed, passing just by my table as the waiter brought my food. There was nearly a disastrous accident as they almost collided, but fortunately the waiter pulled back just before he was overrun by the angry young man.

My food was placed before me, and I was in the process of sawing off the end of a perfectly browned sausage when MacGregor also went rushing past my table, seemingly following after the young man who had just banged out the front door. But then, just past me, the older man slowed and stopped, looking ahead uncertainly as if locked in indecision. The rest of the patrons had returned to their own interests and conversations, but I continued to look up at MacGregor, observing him as I chewed thoughtfully.

I knew of him in a most casual way, as I was aware of so many in that neighborhood, but I didn't *know* him. I had walked by his shop countless times over the last few months since my first arrival in London, but I'd never had any thought of stopping in, and never foresaw a reason that I ever would.

I took another bite of the sausage, and then the potatoes, swirling both in the brown onion gravy that even then the pub made so well, aware that it was already cooling too soon and that I needed to eat faster. It was then that MacGregor turned back to his table. But as he passed by me, he stopped and turned his stern gaze my way.

"Ye would be that fella that fancies himself a detective," he growled in his strong brogue.

My mouth full, I could only nod.

"Wait here," he said – As if I would abandon my sausage! – before walking to the rear, retrieving his half-empty glass from his table, and then returning to my own. "If you don't mind," he said, sitting down without a response, his back to the bar.

"Ye saw what happened," he said in a low growl.

I nodded. "An argument, apparently. But I couldn't hear what it was about."

His eyes narrowed. Clearly he'd sat down to share some of his business – but he didn't like the idea.

"Isaiah is my grandson," he said. He saw my raised eyebrow. "Oh, I know he doesn't sound Scottish, but he was raised in the South – near Oakamoor, in Staffordshire. My daughter – my only child – married a sassenach who worked there in the nearby Alton train station – the Churnet Valley line, serving Morton's copper works. He and my daughter . . . they were killed a few months ago in a railway accident in nearby Crewe." He cleared his throat. "The sassenach – that is to say, my son-in-law, Stephen – he tried to save a poor woman trapped in the wreckage who had come back to England from India not long before. My daughter was initially uninjured, and raced to help him . . . and then . . . Well, there was an explosion . . . ."

He fell silent for a moment, and I felt that it would be impolite to saw off another bite of sausage just then while he gathered his thoughts back to the Alpha on that cold January night. But then he refocused on me, and I continued with my meal.

"I don't blame my son-in-law. He was doing his duty – even if it did get them both killed. After the accident, Isaiah came down here, to London, and I found him a job in the Museum, and rooms in your building. It wasn't my first choice – dealing with that shrewish woman – " Then he stopped himself. "But you're both named Holmes. The landlady isn't your mother, I hope?"

I shook my head and swallowed. Then, after taking a drink of beer, I said, "A distant relative. And shrewish is a polite way to describe her. You were speaking of Isaiah. He and I – we know each other just well enough to speak in passing, but that's all."

"He's a good boy. I'd work him in the wool shop if it would support the two of us, but it won't. The same for a place to stay – my rooms are only big enough for me, and not another full-grown man. But I found him a place in the neighborhood – right across the street from the Museum and just around the corner from me – and it doesn't get much better than that. Or so I thought – but now he's in trouble, and that's what I want to ask you about. In your capacity as a *detective*."

He said the last word with a bit of emphatic distaste, as if he were forcing himself to speak with some sort of low criminal. And in those days, I suppose that might not have been entirely wrong. I had set myself up as a "consulting detective" – what I perceived as the first of that profession – but there were already lots of government detectives and lots of private ones, and some weren't fit for the job due to lack of knowledge or experience or ability, and others were corrupt. Too many displayed all of these aspects. I had the sense that MacGregor had dealt with some of these before, but now a situation had arisen with his grandson where he needed help – and I had been sitting right in front of him at just that moment.

"Isaiah is worried about his job, and he wants to do the right thing – but he's also worried about getting his new Museum friends into trouble, and being seen by them as untrustworthy. I told him that he has to report whatever it is that he's seen, but he became angry. He said that he wished he'd never told me about it, and that it was a mistake, and that – but you saw. He stood up and walked out and refuses to talk any more."

I had nearly finished eating by then, having hurried the latter half a bit more than I would have liked. I held up a hand. "Wait – Please tell me exactly what he said."

MacGregor nodded and raised his glass. Finishing it, he said, "Wait a moment," and rose, nodding toward my glass. I shook my head. He obtained another beer at the bar, returned to his seat, and spoke again.

"Isaiah has worked at the Museum since November, not more than a couple of months, starting just after he came to London when his parents died. I had the job lined up when he arrived, thinking that it was best for him to jump right in, and not waste time grieving. He's a smart lad, and had a year or two of university before deciding that it didn't suit him. To be honest, Mr. Holmes, he doesn't yet know what does suit him, but he had to do something. I know McGinty, who is a guard of supervisory standing, and he obtained an entry job for the lad, with an eye toward being a full guard, once he's learned all the ways of the place and paid his dues.

"One doesn't simply start in the Museum proper, you understand, dealing with the public on the first day. Instead, a new guard is trained for several years behind the scenes, becoming familiar with the workings and the hidden parts. Isaiah has already seen a lot, and all that he tells me is fascinating. I've been in my shop for over twenty-five years – down here in London, while my brother keeps track of the other end of the business in Edinburgh – and I never knew a fraction of what Isaiah shared with me. Cellars upon cellars of things that may never be exhibited. What they show to the public, young Mr. Holmes, is just a fraction of a fraction of what they actually have in storage, brought back from all over the world. Egyptian things, and Oriental, and African. Old idols and books and artworks and sculptures – the best from every land that we've touched, all right here in London, preserved and safeguarded from those natives who wouldn't appreciate or take care of it if left where it was found."

I nodded, but chose not to interrupt him by either replying that the idea of appropriating art from other nations was ethically questionable, or by stating that I was already aware of what he related about the Museum, having made my own friend among the young guards who had managed to sneak me inside and below-stairs on a few occasions.

"And Isaiah stumbled across something dishonest?" I prompted.

"He has – but I don't know what. He started to tell me about it – said there's someone there that's a wrong 'un – but then stopped. I spoke too quickly. I said that whatever it is, he has to report it. That's when the argument started, and – Well, you saw. He left."

We were silent for a few moments, and I finished my beer. One would be enough for me, but MacGregor finished his and rose for yet another – the third that I knew about, and who knew how many he'd had before I arrived? Still, he showed no signs of inebriation. Then he sat back down, took a long pull, wiped his mouth, and said, "Will you help me? Help us? Help Isaiah?"

I considered all of the unanswered questions. I really knew nothing about the situation – but that was a challenge, not a hindrance. I had the payment from my last investigation in my pocket, and the rent was covered for the month, and part of the next as well, and most of all, this seemed like an opportunity to gain further experience. Not only did I have to find the solution to Isaiah's problem, but I also had to determine what exactly the problem was. It seemed like a good chance for me to add to my so-far limited experience, as another case, no matter how large or small, would help me improve my skills

I nodded. "I'll look into it tomorrow."

MacGregor nodded. "Thank you, young Mr. Holmes. I'll be forever grateful."

Although I was tired, and it was time to return to my room, I had one stop to make – at the nearby lodgings of Foster Belkirk, the young guard who had managed to get me inside the Museum on a few different occasions for an unseen tour of its non-public treasures.

Foster was always a pleasant fellow, heavy-set with wide naïve eyes, startlingly blue, and reddish hair and cheeks. By the time I met him the previous summer, he'd already worked at the Museum for a couple of years, and had navigated his way through the apprenticeship that Isaiah Beddings had just begun. Foster was smart, having won the Fortiscue Prize several years before at the College of St. Luke's before deciding that, rather than pursuing an academic path as was laid out for him, he instead wanted to retain his amateur status and seek enlightenment elsewhere. We had that in common, as I had also turned aside from my proscribed professional training – but his father was much more supportive than mine, being simply proud that his son was happy and making his way.

Foster had married several months before I met him, and now his wife, Violet, was expecting their first child. Based on how the child was being carried, they were certain that it was a boy. When I expressed skepticism one night when invited to dinner at their humble flat, they had explained the old wives' tale that carrying low and in front means to expect a boy. "My granny is sure of it!" Violet said with sincere urgency, and I didn't want to argue with her, although I was tempted to respond that Granny certainly had a fifty-per-cent chance of being right. Still, it crossed my mind that there might be some scientific reasoning behind these claims, and that there might be some study to be undertaken someday comparing predictions as based on presentation during pregnancy versus the actual birth results. It might be of some value – but with all I already had on my plate in terms of things to learn for my new profession, I had no time to waste on that.

"Good thing, too," I interrupted. "That idea is poppy-cock."

Holmes smiled. "Watson, if you keep saying things like 'poppy-cock', you'll end up being one of those calcified relics who can't climb out of his club chair, covered with Trichinopoly ash from where you fell asleep while smoking it. Turned fifty recently, didn't you, Old Man?"

Before I could respond, he held up a hand. "Peace, Watson. Now, to continue . . . ."

I'd once had occasion to help Foster and Violet find her wedding ring – a simple bit of deduction after questioning her and realizing that she had taken it off while baking and left it behind the flour tin. Ever after, they felt that they owed me greatly, and when I explained what I needed the next morning, Foster readily agreed and, even though it was getting late, he immediately set about obtaining what I'd requested.

My vigilant landlady, Mrs. Holmes, heard me when I entered, indicating that I needed to improve silent entry as one of my burgeoning detective skills. She stood in the doorway of her parlour, castigating me as I crossed by her to reach the narrow stairway. By the time I'd fully ignored her, she was snarling and pacing like a frenzied dog while I climbed upwards to the next floor and, had she truly been a canine, I have no doubt that her ill-temper would have caused her to freeze onto my ankle and cause a ten-day injury.

I had thought of MacGregor's problem during the very short walk back to No. 24, and by the time I turned out the lights and went to sleep, I knew that my plan would be, first thing in the morning.

I was up early – as is my way when there is work to be done – and before seven o'clock, I was back at Foster Belkirk's modest rooms, where he had obtained a Museum guard's uniform for me to wear. I was to accompany him to work that day, ostensibly as a new trainee, to see what I could see. "It won't be a problem," he explained. "There are always new faces about, and some don't last very long. Besides guards for the main facility, there are other sites where objects are stored – space at the Museum is limited, you understand – and you can pretend to be one of those other guards, transferred over for a day or so. No one will give you a second glance. Pay attention, jump in and help once in a while if needed, and otherwise keep an eye on Isaiah."

Although Foster tended to gossip a bit more than he should have, I felt that I had to confide my reasons for seeking his help, and he understood that whatever was going on needed to be kept quiet. "I haven't seen anything odd myself," he said, "but then I haven't been looking. It's a fault of mine, I suppose – I assume the best. It makes the days much more pleasant, you understand."

He kept looking at me with a grin on his face until I warned him to stop. I was in disguise, having altered my features with a false nose, makeup to provide different planes to my face, and pads to change the shape of my head. I felt that it was necessary so that Isaiah wouldn't notice me. While not up to the level of disguise that I managed to achieve in later years – especially after my time touring America with the Sasanoff troupe – it would be sufficient for a day or two in the dark bowels of the Museum.

We walked from Foster's residence in Guilford Street, near the foundling hospital, and around to the big rear entrance in Montague Place, with my uniform serving as a badge of entry. No one looked twice at me and, when Foster led me to where Isaiah generally worked, he left me to it.

I won't describe the full nature of my day, but in learning to be an apprentice guard, I felt that I was instead practicing to be a uniformed stevedore. My time was mostly spent moving boxes, opening boxes, emptying boxes, refilling boxes, nailing boxes shut, moving and opening and emptying and filling and closing more boxes, and so on. It was January, but quite warm in that hidden part of the Museum, and the ill-fitting borrowed wool uniform was most unpleasant. A great deal of the day was focused on worrying about whether my disguise would give up and slide down my face at an inopportune moment, but fortunately no one seemed interested in paying me any attention at all, once I had answered a summons to present myself at this or that box and do something useful.

Over the course of the day, I constantly shifted myself around to keep Isaiah in site, and I was pleased to see that he was one of the hardest-working young men in the group. But even has he did all the things that I was doing, with much-more practiced ease, he also kept his eye repeatedly on another fellow – and thinking that this must be the "wrong 'un" that he described to his grandfather, I gradually pivoted my attention to keep him in sight as well.

The supervisors called him "Todd Allen" – always by first and last name: "Todd Allen, grab that pry bar," or "Todd Allen, load that dolly with the small black boxes." I almost began to wonder if it was a hyphenated first name – it was not – since many other of the apprentices were addressed by just one name. My false name was "Victor Trevor", the first that had come to mind, and the few times it was called, it was simply, "Trevor!"

Todd Allen was also in his early twenties, but already bald. He had a very round head and weak chin on a thin neck, and a film of short-shorn whiskers upon his face. His eyes were squinty and rat-like, and this matched his thick lips, always in a half-grin that displayed his yellowing buck teeth that looked as if they needed to be worn down some. He looked like an earless rat. He stayed on the move, but I also noticed that he worked much less than the others, finding sly ways to stand back when his peers turned toward some more-difficult task. And I was fortunate enough to be watching when he took great pains to take possession of one of the smaller flat wooden boxes sent up from the basement, mark it surreptitiously with a faint chalk "*X*", and set it to one side.

As part of our work, we moved loaded boxes from delivery carts that had come from off-site storage areas, containing objects being brought in for new exhibits, and likewise we shifted boxes outward, to be carried away and back into storage. I was lucky enough to be watching when Todd

Allen picked up the *X*-marked box and carried it to a furtive little driver who waited to one side, nothing else on his cart. He couldn't help looking around to see if he was being noticed, actually drawing more attention to himself than if he'd simply accepted the box without any indication that something was going on. He didn't see me watching – nor did he notice Isaiah, who was also looking with great interest. The furtive man laid the box in his cart, covered it with a dark tarpaulin, mounted the driver's seat, and departed.

This, I was certain, must be the activity that had worried Isaiah Beddings and, seeing it for myself, I also concluded that something illegal, or at least questionable, was afoot.

I also knew that I would have to return the next day and attempt to find out what Todd Allen was up to.

That night, I stopped by Foster's apartment to tell him that I needed another day in the Museum. I described what I'd seen, and he was in agreement that something wasn't right. "I spent my apprenticeship in that room," he agreed, "and there's no reason for a single box like that to go with a single driver. If there weren't so many new employees down there, they'd likely recognize which ones are the regular Museum-hired drivers who shuttle the big loads to and from storage."

After speaking with Foster, and turning down Violet's offer for a hot meal, I found a few of the neighborhood lads and hired them for the next day. This was a couple of years before I met Wiggins, and there was no thought then of organizing them into what would become the Irregulars – but as I occasionally used them, I did get more and more used to the idea, and then began to count on them for certain types of jobs. Following a cart through the streets of London was an ideal use of their special skills. Then I directed my steps to the wool shop, to report to Mr. MacGregor – but even though I was able to tell him about Todd Allen and the odd box, he seemed unimpressed with my progress, so I finished our conversation quickly and returned to No. 24.

I had neglected to recall that I was still wearing the guard uniform, though Mrs. Holmes was quick to notice it.

"So you've found a real job, then?" she sneered. "Your father will be pleased, I suppose."

"Are you spying on me for him, then?" I asked, forgetting my primary rule of avoiding any engagements with her at all cost. It was worth it, however, to see that she reacted with unexpected guilt, as if in mentioning communications with my father, she had revealed something secret. I pressed my advantage.

"How quickly will you tell him?" I asked with apparent enthusiasm. "About my new job? It looks to be the start of a promising career." It was my hope that she would make a quick report, and that when the truth was discovered, she would lose all credibility. The plan was doomed, however, when she quickly progressed in a different direction.

"I'll tell him, all right," she said. "And I'll also mention that you're likely to lose the job in less than a week!"

She had outplayed me. By framing her news in that way, the subsequent report that I wasn't actually working at the Museum would be taken that she was correct, and that I'd been sacked before I could truly begin.

She was still baying and growling at me when I turned away and mounted the steep steps.

I was up early the next day, as I wanted to consult with Mycroft before my day at the Museum began. He didn't appreciate me arriving while still carrying out his morning ablutions, but I was able to snare some of his breakfast before he could eat it – not for the first time. Fortunately he had more than enough to spare, despite his bluster.

Unlike Mrs. Holmes the night before, he instantly perceived that the uniform I was wearing did not indicate that I'd found new employment, and I told him something of the case. He listened, but didn't turn his great mind toward offering any useful suggestions, as he also knew that I was there to see him for a different reason.

"If you continue living there," he said, cutting to the chase, "then you'll either have to learn to put up with her, or find more creative ways to get in and out without encountering her."

"You know that's impossible," I said. "She has a most meaningless existence, with nothing to do but rise up at any noise and start barking. She'd make a wonderful watchdog, but she's a terrible landlady."

"Nevertheless."

"Did you . . ." I had reached the central nugget of my concern. "Did you know she is reporting on me – to Father?"

"Of course I knew," he said. "Are you truly surprised? Just because he's cut you off doesn't mean that he stopped taking an interest in you, or caring about you – or hoping you'll come to your senses, according to his lights."

"But all he'll ever hear from her is the worst – twisted to present me in the worst possible manner!"

"And I," he said with a look of mostly concealed fondness, "will continute to counter whatever she tells him with my own more-positve reports."

I found that my jaw was agape. "Close your mouth," Mycroft commanded. "Surely you aren't surprised that I would also be enlisted to send news about you back toYorkshire. Father knows, as well as you do, that whatever I report will be factual and untarnished, compared to whatever the unfortunate Mrs. Holmes misinterprets or concocts. And never fear, Sherlock – on balance, what I've told father has been positive. And he's not as angry with you as you've feared. He only wishes to nudge you – most vigorously, I'll admit – back onto the path he laid out before you were even born. You have to decide whether you'll give in to him, or keep setting your own course.

"Now, aren't you due at the Museum soon?"

Foster didn't need to take me into the Museum that morning, as I was now already accepted as one of the new recruits. Knowing what to expect, I'd done a much better job on my makeup so that it wasn't a constant worry.

The day progressed much as had the one before, and I had time to recall Mycroft's words. There was much to ponder in them, but that would be something to examine at some other point, over a pipe. On this day, I had to pay attention.

Isaiah Beddings continued to watch Todd Allen, who continued to subtly shirk his tasks. As the day progressed, I began to fear that nothing would happen to advance my investigation. Then, in mid-afternoon, I saw that another *X*-marked box had appeared, apparently carried up from wherever all these other boxes came from. Clearly there was someone else involved in a different department, preparing the boxes and seeing that they were delivered for the next phase of the operation.

Over the course of a half-hour, Todd Allen worked around to pick up and carry out the *X*-box – and he took it over to the same furtive driver, who accepted delivery and laid it in the cart. My plans were in place, and I had the lads on either end of Montague Place ready to follow, whichever way the driver departed. But then I noted with horror that there were *two* carts of that type just then, both nearly empty and about to leave, and they wouldn't know which one it was. I raced back inside, grabbed my overcoat, hat, and scarf from the hooks along one wall, and ran back outside, thinking that whatever happened, it was unlikely that I needed to return to that temporary and uncompensated employment.

Luckily, Todd Allen had already returned inside and, in the milling confusion just outside the great door, I was able to get to the cart as the driver worked to turn it around and tie my scarf to the cart's back gate. No one seemed to notice, most importantly the driver, and in a moment he was ready to leave. Seeing that he and the other similar cart were both turning east toward Russell Square, I hurried out ahead of them and looked for young Garland, the boy watching on that side. He spotted me and came running over.

Out of breath, I hurriedly explained, "It's that one – with my scarf tied to it."

He nodded and, with nothing further to be said, set off in pursuit. I knew that the other boys would shift and follow, racing ahead and regrouping and adjusting their arrangement as the cart continued on its way.

Still in my borrowed uniform, I settled into a small teashop in Russell Square, knowing that I couldn't go back to No. 24 to wait for word, as the hateful Mrs. Holmes would never bother to let me know that a street urchin was waiting at the door with a message for me, and most certainly she wouldn't let him inside to deliver it upstairs in person.

In less than an hour, Garland was back, out of breath but with good news. "In the mews," he wheezed, "between Harrison and Sidmouth Street. Just near Regent Square. Martin and Lloyd are still watching."

I nodded, fished out some funds for Garland out of my earnings from the Bishop, and set off to take a look at where the *X*-box had ended up.

It was a narrow passage with empty stables on both sides. Many were padlocked, now used for storage of goods instead of shelter for horses. Knowing that many were likely now tenanted by costermongers, I wondered if the cart driver had that connection but, walking through the muse and casually glancing into the open stable, I saw that there was nothing like a costermonger's wares stored there – just a row of small empty boxes of the size that I'd seen marked with an *X* – and on a low rough-hewn wooden table, a stack of framed paintings!

I knew that I had to get a look at those paintings, but I was uncertain as to how. I was wearing my overcoat, so my borrowed guard togs were covered. Thus, if I stepped inside and initiated a conversation, there would be no indication that I had followed from the Museum. With no better plan, that's what I did.

The day was bright and bitterly cold, the temperature having dropped considerably overnight. Inside the chamber, the air felt twenty degrees warmer, though still bitter, but it was also quite dark, with only one lamp on the low table beside the frames. As I approached, I could see that they were all rather plain – like nothing that would have been hung in the Museum. Had I made some sort of mistake?

The driver had been talking to another fellow, over a foot taller, and dressed in an expensive-looking wool coat that looked almost warm enough for the January freeze. While much was hidden in the dim light, I could see that his hair was freshly trimmed, as was his short beard. He looked to be about fifty, and his voice sounded smooth and refined while he spoke to the driver, although I couldn't hear what was being said. He stopped speaking when he noticed my approach, turning smoothly to face me.

"What do you want?" he asked, and I could hear a trace of a German accent. "Be gone. This is private property."

"I'm just looking for my sister," I said, a whine in my voice, and continuing to approach. "She's been missing these three days. Disappeared just around here, she did. Thought maybe you might have seen her."

"We have not. Now get out."

But I kept walking closer to the table, sidling to one side to get a look at the stacked frames. I still couldn't see what they were, but in my inexperience, I suppose that I telegraphed my interest in the paintings too obviously. With a growl, and no other warning, the taller man took a step for me, suddenly swinging his stick, which I had not noticed him holding by his side.

It was lucky that I was able to lean back, as the weighted knob of the thing *swished* by my face with just a whisker's width of space. But in so doing, it connected with my false nose, knocking it askew and alerting the two men that I truly was not what I seemed, and worthy of their concern after all.

Then I was scrabbling backwards, trying to get away from the taller man as he pressed his advantage, swinging this way and that with his stick, and never a word being uttered by either of us. The little driver, however, started bouncing up and down as if he were at a prize fight: "Hit him!" he cried. "Hit him! Hit him!" – over and over again, as if the taller man needed this advice. In fact, hitting me was already his sole strategy.

I don't know how it would have ended if Garland and some of his friends hadn't been watching, having decided to see how this jolly affair progressed. In spite of their natural suspicion of authority, one of them sought a constable who soon arrived and waded in, swinging his own stick at the foreigner's head and blowing his whistle as he did so, summoning more of his brethren.

I didn't know any of them, and more importantly they didn't know me, so any explanation of who I was and what I was doing there was essentially useless. However, one of them did at least listen, telling the tall man to be quiet when he attempted to have me arrested and removed without any further discussion.

In truth, I wasn't sure that I had any good leg to stand on. When I was allowed a chance to speak, and explain how I'd arrived there, and to direct attention to the stacked frames, I had a sinking feeling. One of the constables started standing them up, one by one, to show that they were all amateur and poorly executed paintings of circus clowns.

I recalled Foster telling me that some of the items that regularly left the Museum were donations of poor quality that, while of great value to the donor, held no actual value from the perspective of the institution. Were these, then, that type of object – amateur paintings that were donated and then rejected, culled by a wise curator and summarily sent away to whomever would take them? Had the *X*-marked boxes been so designated because they held clown paintings that were of interest to some private collector, to be packed separately and put into the care of the little driver? Was the tall Germanic man with the lethal cane actually a collector of clown paintings?

That seemed to be the case, as he was confirming that the paintings had been sent to him from the Museum, and that he had a special interest in that unique topic. Meanwhile, my thoughts raced as I tried to weigh whether or not such a tale could be true, and whether I had committed a major and embarrassing mistake.

And as I considered what was happening, the constable still holding one of the paintings happened to turn it over, so that I could see the back – and I saw the solution.

The clown painting that had been visible had been poorly mounted, as if it wasn't quite squared before being nailed to the wooden frame, and thus it had a small loose ripple in the canvas running diagonally across the front. But when the back of the painting was revealed, that canvas was stretched tight – nary a ripple in sight.

I knew that further examination was necessary – and that if I asked permission, it would not be given.

Moving suddenly, I stepped to the table and picked up one of the framed paintings.

"Here now!" growled one of the constables, moving to prevent me, while the tall man cried, "What are you doing?" Ignoring both of them, and feeling on both the front and back of that painting, I realized that I was correct. The tall man continued yelling, trying to stop me, and the constables were all barking warnings, but I ignored them and pushed the canvas out of the back of the frame with my thumbs, dislodging the painting and causing it to pop onto the table. The small nails used to tack the clown to the stretching frame were exposed – and also the fact that underneath the clown canvas, the edges of a second canvas were just visible.

Just as I turned to show what I'd found to the constable in charge, explaining what it meant, the small driver bolted, which only served to confirm that something shady was going on. But Garland stepped forward and tripped him, and he sprawled for only seconds before he was dragged upright in the grip of two officers. Meanwhile, another placed himself beside the tall man while I worked the nails loose, peeling off the dreadful clown portrait to reveal an artwork of much finer quality – a landscape by one of the minor Dutch masters.

All of the clown pictures held the same secrets – lesser-known works from various Continental artists. The tall man, a German named Kreitzer, was a dealer who had set up the scheme whereby an agent of his named Daniels, working within the Museum, would identify lesser-known works that were in storage, as there was no room to hang them all in the Museum proper. He would reframe them underneath the terrible clown portraits and, now in cheap and unassuming frames, Daniels would log them as rejected donations, crate them and mark with an *X*, and then send them out by way of Todd Allen to the German dealer. Their operation had been going on for weeks, undetected, and they had become confident. There were so many stored minor paintings to steal that they had increased the deliveries to nearly daily. Dozens more works of the same value were found in Daniels' small basement room at the Museum, and there was really no defense when they were all tried and convicted later that winter.

With the thanks of the constables, and having given the one in charge one of my few cards so that I could be notified if needed, I once again expressed my appreciation to Garland, paid him more from my dwindling funds, and went around to MacGregor's shop to report. Though obviously disappointed after my previous visit the night before, he now seemed to be impressed – though it wasn't expressed in any effusive way.

"If you don't mind," he said in his northern manner, "I'll tell Isaiah that he doesn't have to worry about it any longer. It might embarrass him if we both let him know."

I nodded. The case was finished now, and how Isaiah found out what happened was of no consequence to me.

MacGregor then raised a thick eyebrow. "Your scarf," he said. "The one you tied to the cart – it seems that you left it behind."

I raised a hand to my throat. He was right – it had never occurred to me. As I considered whether it might still be in the mews if I hurried back, MacGregor raised a hand.

"Did it mean anything special to you?" he asked.

I shook my head. "Just something that I bought last fall, when the weather started to turn cold."

He nodded. "I saw it the other night. One tends to observe things like that, if you're in my profession. It was rather cheap, wasn't it?"

Without waiting for an answer, he turned to one side and reached across to a stack of wool scarves Taking one – a very fine one indeed – he shuffled back and handed it to me.

"We'll settle up what I owe you in a moment, but for now, take this – with my compliments, young Mr. Holmes . . . ."

"The scarf that you mentioned earlier," I said.

"This scarf," Holmes replied, waving a hand to the table where his Inverness, hat, and scarf were lying. "The one I lost had no sentimental value, but I wouldn't trade this one for the world."

I recognized it, of course, having seen it off-and-on for over twenty years. It was about nine inches wide and six feet long, fringed on the ends, and displayed a complex brown-and-black houndstooth pattern. I had long-ago noted that it was of the very finest wool. "This one is sentimental," I said, "but yet, you were willing to alter it – for that's the same scarf you've used in the past – that night on the docks, for instance, in '88, when we cornered a couple of the Rippers and you used the weights that had been sewn into the end as something resembling a Thuggee *noose."*

Holmes nodded. "When I asked, a few years later, MacGregor was more than willing to make the alterations necessary to add the weights. It's saved my life on more than one occasion. Yours too, as a matter of fact."

And then he abruptly stopped whispering, as there was a scratching sound coming from the rear door.

It was one of the easier captures we'd ever made: A bloodless runt of a fellow named Cyril Funt, who had conceived a hatred of MacGregor for not being willing to discount a hat to the price that Funt was willing to pay. There had apparently been a disagreement – though to hear MacGregor's later explanation, to him it had been so next-to-nothing that he barely remembered it. But Funt had brooded and festered after the encounter and, in his position at the nearby University of London dealing with various plants from beyond the coasts of England, he'd conceived the notion that he would taint MacGregor's stock, thereby ruining the store's reputation. It was a tedious little plan, poorly conceived, and he after he was caught, and when he'd lost his job and spent a few months in prison, he had an even greater grudge against the wool merchant.

"He will bear watching," advised Holmes that night, and MacGregor gave a dark nod.

Outside, with the little man in custody and MacGregor's shop once again buttoned up against the night, Holmes and I stood under a gaslight, facing the dark Museum across the way.

"Time for a pint?" Holmes asked, nodding down toward the Alpha.

My initial inclination was to shake my head. I was ready to head back to Queen Anne Street, as my consulting hours came early. Such a reply was on my lips when I suddenly changed it.

"Why not? Time for one, before they close."

I let him lead me inside, recalling the many times that I had been there, both as a medical student and during the short time after that when I'd had a practice nearby, and later in Holmes's company. Time was passing, but the old tavern never seemed to change, and it was a comfort, knowing that some places like that were always a fixed point and unchanging – or at least changing so slowly that they would seem to remain safe havens during the years of my own lifetime.

And as always, the beer at the Alpha was excellent . . . .

NOTES

1. See "The Red Headed League", 25 October, 1890, and published in *The Strand* in August 1891.

   Mr. Jabez Wilson's former pawn shop, 42 Charterhouse Square, London (as photographed by David Marcum, London, 17 September, 2013):

2. See "The Debt to Jabez Wilson" in this volume, and originally in *The MX Book of New Sherlock Holmes Stories - Part XLVII: Occupants of the Canonical Realm (1890-1898).*
3. For more details of the Chad Street residence, see *Enter the Lion*, 23-30 November, 1875. (Narrated by by Mycroft Holmes, and edited by Michael P. Hodel and Sean M. Wright)
4. The "Alpha Inn" is actually The Museum Tavern, located at 49 Great Russell Street, London, just across from the British Museum, and around the corner from both Holmes's former residence at No. 24 Montague Street and also Watson's first practice (before joining the Army) at No. 6 Southampton Place (now Southampton Place). The Tavern is sometimes called The Alpha Inn because of the various *A*'s worked into the outer woodwork – an example of which is shown in the photo on the next page, within the oval inset. (Photo by David Marcum, London, 1 June, 2024)

5. Holmes was born on 6 January, 1854. For those who consistently see him as fixed in middle age, he would have just turned twenty-one at the time of this narrative.

The Clue of the Undamaged Stones

"Many has been the occasion," said Sherlock Holmes when we spoke on the telephone that morning, "when you have recommended rest and a change of scene when I displayed signs of overwork. A short sojourn by the sea, to be alliterative, can only do you some good."

He wasn't incorrect, and I acknowledged that a few days rusticating in Sussex would not be unwelcome. For the last couple of years, there had been rising-and-falling surges of smallpox cases in the capital, and recently I had been heavily involved in getting ahead of the latest wave. Although my help was still needed, I knew that I would be more effective and useful if I returned refreshed.

By that afternoon, the twentieth of June, I arrived in Eastbourne and left the station to find a cab. The resort town was rather crowded at that time of year, and there was a mugginess in the air that forced people to slog along, dragging their feet and considering the possibly they should have picked somewhere else to holiday, or that they should have made arrangements to travel at a different time of year. Having served in much hotter climes a quarter-century earlier and still retaining my acclimation for it, I was indifferent to the temperature, which was no higher than the low eighties. However, but I knew that to the average Britisher, it seemed as if he or she had been unhappily transported to the tropics.

The cab took me to Holmes's small farm, approximately five miles from Eastbourne and not-quite five acres on the Downs, just north of the base of Beachy Head. He had acquired it during the course of an investigation, with the idea of retiring there. I'd always assumed that said retirement would occur at a much older age, but he had surprised me in early October of 1903, not quite two years before, when, at the age of forty-nine-and-three-quarters, he had unexpectedly announced his imminent departure from London.

Of course, "retirement" to Sherlock Holmes wasn't quite what it would mean to other people, as leaving his consulting practice meant taking on more clandestine investigations for the British Government, away from the prying eyes who would have observed his comings and goings from his old London lodgings. Still, since moving 56.69 miles as the crow flies from 221b Baker Street to his farm – he had measured the distance to the hundredth-deimal from a series of sequentially placed Ordinance Maps, providing explanatory commentary regarding making adjustments in his calculations to take into account the curvature of the earth – he'd settled in easily to country life, as if he'd been down there for years, dividing his time between learning the intricacies of being an apiarist and taking on various investigations – some rather publicly displayed and along the lines of those handed in his former Baker Street practice, while others were of a more discreet nature at the behest of his brother, Mycroft. These latter required that he sometimes slip away unseen, while giving the impression that he was still ensconced as a recluse behind the shoulder-high walls of his enclave, constructed from locally gathered quartz many generations before our time.

I spent the ten or fifteen minute drive between station and farm conversing with a fellow named Hibbert whom I'd met numerous times before since making this part of the world a regular stop. The fellow was in his fifties, and moved down from London nearly a decade earlier, finding a job as a cabbie – first with a horse, and lately with an automobile. As usual, the drive was mostly his lamentations along the theme that he'd never be accepted as a local. The rest was spent expressing interest in Holmes. Hibbert had first become aware of Holmes during the 1880's, when my friend was initially building his reputation, and it always pleased him to be able to drive Holmes or me when given the opportunity.

Hibbert seemed pleased as we approached Holmes's farm, as the retired detective was standing outside, in front of the house at the termination of the short drive that connected to the road.

"Well met, Watson!" he said. "Stow your bag inside, and then Hibbert can drive us up to the village. Tom Keller has something he'd like to discuss."

Keller was the owner and keeper of The Tiger Inn, located a mile-and-a-half to the north if we walked across the Downs, traversing the pastures and their *Ovis aries* denizens, and climbing stiles and passing through gates, or another mile longer than that by way of the winding road that went from Holmes's gate to Birling Gap, and then north toward the village of East Dean. Whenever I visited, we always ended up at The Tiger – but not usually so early.

I had also met Keller when Holmes relocated to Sussex. Holmes had performed several services for him, sometimes with my assistance, and just the previous June, we had been involved in the curious incident of the inn's ghostly "White Lady" – a matter that still generated some friendly disagreement over the interpretation of what I saw that stormy night. [1] But on that particular warm and muggy last day of spring, not long after my arrival from London, Keller wished to consult Holmes about a different manner, and someday I'll record the events concerning the German medal. It was a short and tidy affair, but it had implications for both an immigrant from the Continent, and Holmes's secret activities in the years leading up to The Great War.

We were back at Holmes's "villa", as he liked to call it, by suppertime, and I was feeling weary as the sun was setting at nearly half-past-eight. With a yawn, I said goodnight and went up to my usual room when visiting there. It seemed as if I'd barely gone to sleep when I was awakened by a knock. Fumbling for my tableside traveling clock, I saw that it was just after midnight. I sighed and bid Holmes to enter.

"Sorry, Watson. We've received an urgent summons. Dress quickly – Hibbert is already waiting for us downstairs."

When I descended five minutes later, Holmes was waiting by the door, holding my coat and hat and wearing his own. "Many apologies," he said with sincerity – which hadn't always been the case in our younger days when a nighttime caller would awaken Mrs. Hudson, who would then retort upon Holmes, and he would then share the experience with me. "We have a bit of quick traveling in front of us." He led me outside and walked to the waiting automobile. "I've received a summons – to Salisbury."

As we settled ourselves for the fast drive back to Eastbourne, I grumbled, "There are no trains running this time of night."

Meanwhile, I tried not to consider how little I could see of the surrounding night from the rear seat of the coach as Hibbert wrestled his rather battered four-seater Wolseley across the dark and narrow road.

"Arrangements have been made," said Holmes. "The client is a man of influence. He indicates that we'll have use of a special train. I have no doubt that he set about arranging it as soon as he sent the wire requesting my presence."

And such was the case. I can only imagine the effort needed to have a locomotive and tender, as well as a couple of coach cars, ready and waiting at the station, but we were able to depart within a minute of exiting Hibbert's cab and being ushered aboard. Only after we were seated on the train did Holmes hand me the telegram, that he'd received just before waking me up.

> *Come at once to Salisbury* [the wire read]. *Murder – Cannot draw attention from imminent important celebration at site. Will have special train immediately ready and waiting for your departure from Eastbourne.*
>
> *Antrobus*

I raised my eyes to meet Holmes's. He wore a slight smile, and his eyes shone with anticipation. Retired he might be to the public, and there was no doubt that he did enjoy his new rustic life, but his reaction to the promise of an intriguing case was no different than the old dog rising and stretching in anticipation upon hearing the call of the hunting horns.

"Antrobus?" I asked. "Sir Edmund Antrobus, the baronet?" Holmes nodded, and I continued. "Hence the connection to Salisbury. His involvement with the restoration of Stonehenge – somewhat controversial – has been in the newspapers." I recalled the date – it was now the next day. "The twenty-first – this is the first day of the Summer Solstice. Sunrise will be in just a few hours – "

"Three-forty-four," interrupted Holmes. "Less than three hours."

" – and the Druids will be gathering at Stonehenge."

"Surely the 'important celebration' referenced in Sir Edmund's wire."

I tried to remember what I'd read a few days before in a small newspaper article. At the time, it had seemed nothing more than a curiosity, scanned quickly, and I wished that I'd paid more attention.

"I recall that Sir Edmund started some work at Stonehenge a few years ago. A restoration to the site – for safety concerns, I believe – and he's received a lot of criticism for closing it to the public. This year, he's allowing the Druids to hold a sunrise ceremony there." A thought occurred to me. "How is it that – even with a murder – Sir Edmund can command your presence so easily? And of greater interest, how can he arrange a special train with such ease?"

Holmes leaned back, his mouth a thin line. After a moment, he said, "As you know, my relocation to Sussex had less to do with a need to actually retire, and more with the necessity of carrying out various tasks for Mycroft as we drift ever closer to war with Germany. You have been of vital assistance in helping me maintain the fiction that I'm now nothing more than a reclusive beekeeper. There are others who are living the same sort of double life, secretly carrying out governmental tasks – and one of those is Sir Edmund.

"He was involved in the Suakin Expedition in Sudan twenty years ago, and his quality was recognized. Since then, he's maintained a rather shadowy connection with the Government – and with my brother, who, as you know, sometimes *is* the Government. And more so with every passing week. Sir Edmund became the fourth baronet upon the death of his father six years ago, and since then his involvement with these surreptitious affairs – and his association with Mycroft – has deepened considerably. I can't say that he has any sort of authority over me – I report only to Mycroft – but he does have influence, and more important, I respect him. If he felt the need to summon me, then I am willing to respond. And clearly he has the influence to arrange a special train."

We were now speeding along, and with the lines being cleared ahead of us, and I had no doubts that we were making fifty miles an hour or better. At that rate, we'd likely cover the hundred-miles or so of our journey in just a couple of hours. From Eastbourne, the cities, towns, and villages flashed by in the night, and it was only by luck that I was able to read a few of the quickly passing signs that identified small stations, or to judge from context which bigger southern cities we were traversing. Eastbourne to Brighton to Southampton, and then we turned, more sharply curving to the northwest, arriving in Salisbury at five-minutes-to-two – surely not quite a record, but still quite fast nonetheless.

A man in chauffeur's livery met us as we stepped to the platform, briskly chivying us with no nonsense outside to a waiting automobile. I had a chance to look back at the modest red-brick station building, then just two or three years old, pondering with amazement how quickly one could now travel – turned out from a warm bed one moment, and then suddenly walking just a few miles from a mysterious historical site in the time one might take to watch a long play. Just a few hours before, I had been asleep in an entirely different part of England, and now I was relocated by way of modern technology – a fast train and telegraph communication to clear the way – to a different point in space and time in nearly the blink of an eye (in the great scheme of things), where I was climbing into a vehicle that would transport me – I assumed – to one of the notable ancient sites of the British Isles.

As we settled into the rear of the automobile, the man waiting inside, perched on the rear-facing seat, commanded to the chauffeur, who had also just settled himself behind the steering wheel, "Quickly, Clayton. As fast as you can." Then he turned back to face us, leaning forward to shake Holmes's hand, and then offering his grip to me as well, while peering with a look of stern curiosity.

"Watson, I presume?' He looked back at Holmes. "He happened to be in Sussex when my wire arrived?"

Holmes nodded. "Down for a short holiday."

"Pleased so meet you, Sir Edmund," I said.

"Antrobus," he said, settling back in his seat. "Edmund Antrobus. None of that 'Sir' business, please. I still don't like it. And I'm glad that you're here, Watson." He leaned back. He was in his mid-fifties, and appeared to be fit and in good health. He wore a wedding ring, and even in the first moment I met him, I could see that he still carried some of the authority that marks the military man for the rest of his life. Knowing that Antrobus was involved with Mycroft Holmes and the secret business of protecting the Kingdom didn't surprise me in the least.

"Rum business," said Antrobus, looking back at Holmes with a tight smile. "I suppose you've already deduced everything, and there's nothing for you to do but point the coppers at the guilty party."

He was serious, but there was still a look of warmth in his eyes, and I knew that he was teasing Holmes in his own way. Clearly the two of them knew each other rather well. Holmes shook his head with his own small smile.

"We aren't quite so fortunate to have reached that stage just yet. Perhaps you should provide a few more facts before we arrange the arrest. It often helps to have all the pins lined up *before* the accusation." Holmes's tone turned darker. "Murder, is it?"

Antrobus nodded. "We have ten miles to go – I'll just have time to tell you about it. You'll have heard of Sir Edvard Bilbrey?"

I turned my head in surprise. "He is the victim?"

"That's right. And it couldn't have come at a worse time."

I dimly perceived why, and wished again that I had paid more attention to the press reports. It has now been a number of years since Sir Edvard was regularly mentioned in the newspapers, and if he is recalled now at all now, it is only as a figure of fun. He was quite influential in those years just before and after the turn of the century, if for no other reason than his ability to stir up controversy. As a young man in the seventies, he'd had a rather undistinguished military career, noted only for losing several toes upon one foot when a locker was dropped upon them on his way out to India. Upon his return to England, he'd dabbled around the edges of his father's mining interests.

Upon the elder Bilbrey's death, a victim of his own unsafe mines when he was on a poorly timed site inspection, the younger came into his sizeable fortune, as well as taking over his father's hereditary position in Parliament. It was there that he gave the famous speech that defined him thereafter. When a number of hecklers interrupted him, he was moved to testily reply – quickly rising to anger as was his general response to most situations. He apparently meant to say that he greatly disliked individuals who displayed such rude behavior, or something along those lines, but he shook his fist and cried haltingly, overcome by emotion and in a breaking voice, "I . . . hate . . . *people* . . . !" He later claimed that he meant to add more qualifying information as to what sort of people he hated, but he apparently hated so many different sorts that he couldn't decide which group to specifically identify. By then the crowd was roaring, surprisingly with approval, and the quote became a rallying cry. He even attracted a group of unwanted followers who also espoused the "*I hate people!*" philosophy.

After that, his participation in Parliament waned – he'd never had much interest in it from the start – and he turned in other directions.

"I recall," I said, making a connection, "that a year or so ago, Sir Edvard aligned himself with the Druids."

"That's right," Antrobus agreed. "The Ancient Order of Druids, they call themselves. Not so ancient – they just formed in the 1780's. Rather more like imitation Freemasons than Druids, from what I can determine. I've had dealings with them lately, too – because of Stonehenge. Rather silly, if you ask me – chaps wearing masks, apparently because they're ashamed of themselves, demanding to wander the site in different routes and patterns, chanting and carrying cardboard sickles. Overgrown children," he spat. "And yet, some of these same men are respected members of society – politicians and doctors and lawyers and such – so I have to allow them some leeway.

"The property has been in my family since 1824 or 1825, and every generation, it seems as if the Druids come crawling out of the woodwork with some new kind of request or demand. Until recently, we've never kept much watch on the place, and I expect that they've come and gone in secret over the years much more than we've ever realized. But this 'Ancient Order' has become my particular cross to bear, as they've decided that they want to hold their Solstice ritual this year – today, in a few hours. I think that it's become more of an issue because this year they're vexed since I put up a wire fence around the place – twenty acres or so. And I hired a policeman to stand guard during the day. Blast! If only I'd thought to have someone professional here at night, too. But the daytime seemed sufficient."

"And you felt the need to have a guard because someone could get hurt" said Holmes. "Due to the restoration work,"

Antrobus nodded. "That's right. Back in 1901, I instituted some repairs – nothing major, and all of them working with The Society of Antiquaries, to make sure it's done right. I felt like I had to do something after one of the uprights and the lintel resting on it fell down. How much longer before they're all tipped over? So I paid to have the tallest trilithon stood back up – and that's when the Druids started howling. You'd think they'd be thankful, if the place really means that much to them, but no. And the worst of them has turned out to be Sir Edvard – although I think he was just looking for the latest cause with which to associate himself and garner attention."

"And now he's dead," replied Holmes, drawing our attention back to the present events. I glanced out of the window at the passing countryside. It was less than two hours until dawn, and there was nothing yet to be seen, as all was still in darkness. I thought that we had about five miles remaining before reaching the site. I didn't have a sense of where we were on the road between Salisbury and the famed stone circle, but I was fairly certain we had already passed Old Sarum, the ancient settlement and later Iron Age fort that – so I'm told – was the first known settlement in Salisbury. Holmes and I had many occasions when we visited Stonehenge, Old Sarum, and Salisbury on various cases, and sometimes I wondered if that spot was a focal point of crime, both new and ancient, in the same way that Holmes had once said some jewels are the "the devil's pet baits", seemingly created specifically to attract evil.

"Ever since I fenced off the stones and started the repairs," Antrobus continued, "the Druids have poked up their heads and pestered me about it. They wanted to be here for the Solstice, but I said no. It isn't safe, and I don't want the liability if one of them gets hurt. But Sir Edvard wouldn't be quiet, so I finally compromised and said that he and a few of his 'deputies', as he calls them, could come down and be there for the sunrise. And then he goes and gets killed!"

I thought that Holmes would ask for specifics related to the crime, as we seemed to be skirting the edge of the event, but first he had another question. "Not to negate any man's death," he said, "but why this urgency? The bother and expense of a special train in the middle of the night? It's overcast, but there's no sign of rain that might destroy vital clues. Is there some question that the killer might flee?"

"No, no. Although you may find something to the contrary, I think that we can narrow the killer down to one of three men – Sir Edvard's 'lieutenants'. Those deputies of whom I spoke. They're all prospective sons-in-law as well – interested in the dead man's daughter. No, the urgency is to get the matter settled before sunrise, because despite my wishes, a larger clot of Druids is planning to be there anyway – Who knows how many? – and we need to have answers before things have a chance of getting out of hand." He glanced my way. "No offense, Doctor, but I'm sure you're aware that there are matters of statecraft that cannot be shared with you – just as there are also currently investigations that Holmes here is carrying out at the behest of his brother in strict confidence. I, too, take on such duties, and there is one such event that's coming to fruition in the near future that would be spoiled by an incident this morning. I'm afraid that I cannot explain the details to either one of you.

"But know that this murder couldn't have come at a worse time. I'm being watched, and I don't need the kind of attention just now that an unsolved mystery will generate – or a riot by a bunch of Druids if they get stirred up. By the time the Druids learn of Sir Edvard's death, we need to tell them who is responsible – present them with a *fait accompli*, so to speak."

"Tell us more of these three lieutenants," Holmes said. I knew that in just a few moments, we would be arriving at the prehistoric structure.

"All three are in their early twenties, just a few years older than Sir Edvard's daughter, Rachel. Between us, she's a rather unpleasant girl, spoiled and sour as you might expect, but she has the advantage of being his only child and heir. And now she's an orphan, as her mother died years ago.

"The first suitor is Clifford Estes, the second son of Lord Estes. He's being groomed for some sort of Foreign Office position, but expectations are he'll end up being the primary heir sooner rather than later, as his older brother Gerald is a sot who will likely be dead from drink in just a couple of years."

I was beginning to see that Antrobus didn't believe in sugar-coating hard facts. As I came to know him better, I learned that this was his regular nature, as in his secret work, he was often forced to cut to the quick of the matter in little time, seeing and describing things with honest bluntness.

"The second of Bilbrey's followers is Andrew Garvey, of the Lancaster mill family. Also a second son, but it's no secret that there's so much money in the family that Andrew and his two brothers will all receive substantial fortunes. Still, he'd do well to align himself with Sir Edvard's resources.

"The third is Tyler Gilman. His father is Lord Randolph Gilman – you'll have read of his moral dissolution – and his mother is the American heiress, Wanda Gilman *née* Copeland, of the Boston Copelands. Like Andrew Garvey, Tyler Gilman is set to have a considerable amount of money bestowed on him, by way of his maternal grandfather, in less than a year – but he also wants that connection with Sir Edvard's daughter.

"From what I understand, all three likely joined The Ancient Order and curried Sir Edvard's favor solely as a way to win his endorsement of their interest in his daughter, and not because they have any true interest in Druidism. Wherever Sir Edvard has gone, they've gone, and when he showed up here yesterday, they were here too. And then, when he came up with the ridiculous notion that the stones needed to be guarded through the night, they were designated for the task."

"Guarded?" I asked. "From what?"

"That you'll have to ask them. Right now the local constable has all three in custody, under suspicion, in my local lodgings. But I see that we've arrived, and I've had the body left *in situ* for you to examine, Holmes."

The vehicle had slowed to a stop, and the chauffeur hurriedly exited to pull open the door. Antrobus climbed out, followed by Holmes and me. My eyes were now adjusted to the darkness, but the night was still too black to really see anything clearly. I had the sense that we'd stopped a dozen yards or so from the famed stones, but they were more of a looming presence felt than anything truly discerned.

Antrobus sought his bearings and then turned away from the great monoliths, leading us a hundred yards or so in the opposite direction until there was something of a long arcing ditch in the rough turf. There were two men standing beside it. In the darkness, I could barely make out that one was a constable, while the other fellow seemed to be dressed like a workman. As we approached, both took a few steps to one side, while the constable said to Antrobus, "No one has been here, sir."

As they moved, I could see an irregular shape in the ditch just beyond them, a darker blackness than the surrounding ground. Before anyone could ask, the constable turned on his electric torch, pointing it toward the form. "Pleasure to see you again, Mr. Holmes," he said, handing it to the detective.

Holmes glanced up. He must have recognized the voice, because there was no way to determine features in that gloom. I'd only been able to determine one of the men was a constable by the shape of his helmet. "Ah, Adams. I hope that the family is well. Still the one child?"

"Two more now, sir, thank you for asking. We're all doing very well. Hello to you, too, Doctor."

I recalled the officer from when I'd once set a broken finger after a scuffle with a raging cat's-meat lady, and I also asked a couple of questions about his current situation while Holmes knelt by the shape, which I could now see was a canvas tarpaulin. After giving it an intense examination, he pulled back the wrappings to reveal the body of a man.

I took a step forward, still staying out of the way, and yet able to make my own observations. Holmes moved the torchlight where he needed so that it never held in one spot for too long, but I was able to determine that it was a man in his fifties, about six feet, and in a suit of some dark wool. He'd still had his hair, even in mid-life, but it was going gray at the temples. He was clean-shaven, and in death, the frown lines which had made Sir Edvard Bilbrey so recognizable were only deepened, engraved there as his final epitaph. His lips were pulled back in a rictus of agony, frozen upon his face, revealing the significant gap between his front teeth – a feature that the newspaper artists had used for quick effect when illustrating him.

Holmes motioned for Adams to help him roll the corpse. As the dead man was turned up in my direction, I couldn't tell what they found underneath him, but I could see more clearly that there was a bullet hole centered on the body's chest. At that moment, Holmes motioned me forward for my own examination.

"Have a look," said softly. "And can you verify my conclusion that the bullet went straight through, likely avoiding hitting bone?"

Knowing what he was getting at, I quickly ascertained for myself that he was correct. "He was shot from the front, and the route taken by the bullet does appear to have gone straight through, as you thought. The exit wound is straightly aligned with the entry wound, and is slightly larger, as one would expect – although I doubt that this was an expanding lead slug, due to the small amount of exit damage. Likely a jacketed slug. And while an autopsy will confirm it, I believe that the heart and pericardial sack were both torn, leading to a great deal of immediate blood loss. You can see that it soaked into the man's coat and vest during the moment after he was shot, before the heart stopped – but neither this tarpaulin nor the ground below him any true staining." I looked over to where Holmes knelt beside me. "He was shot elsewhere and moved here."

Holmes nodded and got to his feet. As he did so, Antrobus spoke.

"This is Grieg, my caretaker. He discovered the body. Tell him, Grieg."

Holmes had left the pocket torch on, but directed it toward the ground so as not to blind us. However, it threw enough light to see better than before, even though our range of perception was limited to small lit circle in the middle of the vast inky night. The workman took a step forward and touched a finger to the bill of his wool cap.

"I walked up to give the site a once-over – normal thing every night, but more tonight, you see. I was told to do so about once an hour, all night long – because of the visitors, and the sunrise ceremony today. Those three lads were taking turns playing at guard duty, but we didn't know but what they weren't up to some mischief. It's just luck that I took the direction that I did – I was staying well back from the Stones, because we were told they were all armed – and came across this poor fellow lying in the ditch – about half-eleven or so. I might just as easily have missed him. Rolled in this tarp, as you see.

"Sunset was about half-after-eight, and the sky was full dark by then. Clouds out, like now – no stars or moon. A black night. Hard to see your hand in front of your face. I don't know which one o' them lads was on guard just then, but I didn't see anyone. Likely whichever lad was out here at that time was over by the stones, or sitting down on one of them. In any event, I decided not to alert him, but instead went back to the house double-quick – " He gestured vaguely in one direction which I was to later know was east, nearly to Amesbury. "It's about a mile. I woke up the master, and he got on the telephone and summoned the constable here, and we all drove back over quickly and found him thus."

"Is there a local inspector?" Holmes asked.

"He's away, sir," replied the constable. "Visiting family, up north in Alton. Won't be back for another week, unless we send word."

"No time for that," added Antrobus. He looked at Holmes. "I immediately saw the gravity of the situation and started making telephone calls – to London, and to you. London took care of the special train, and thank Heavens you got here as quickly as you could."

"Where has Sir Edvard been lodging?" asked Holmes.

"With me," Antrobus explained. "I own the house nearby – just to the east. It's where I stay when I have business down this way. When I decided to allow Sir Edvard access to the site this morning, I let him and his daughter stay there, and the three deputies as well. There's plenty of room, and it was all the better to stay on his good side and attempt to keep this as low-key as possible." He growled. "And then he goes and gets himself killed."

Holmes nodded, frowning and concentrating intently. Then he seemed to have reached a decision. "If I may, Adams, I'll borrow your torch once more and make an examination on my own. I believe that I've seen enough here. The body can be moved – back to the house, I suppose – so that it won't be here when people start to arrive for the sunrise event. Watson – can you join me?"

And with that, he turned and went into the darkness, toward the famed menhirs, the torch directed toward the ground. While Antrobus, Grieg, and the constable discussed the best way to retrieve and relocate the body, I trod after Holmes as his light illuminated the stones, and his investigation carried him into the center of Stonehenge.

I caught up with him. "As you noted," he stated without pause or turn, "based on the lack of blood at both the site and on the tarpaulin, Sir Edvard was killed elsewhere and then placed in the ditch." He gestured forward. "It isn't unreasonable to believe that such a notable site as this, on a night of extra impending importance, might be the location where the death would occur."

"Are you hinting at some sort of ritualistic execution?" I asked.

"Not necessarily. But if one of the three suspects, who were supposed to be on guard duty here, wanted to arrange a secret meeting of some sort, then such a site would certainly intrude itself in the making of the decision."

By then we had entered the stones – not our first time there, and not the first time we had investigated a murder there either, but certainly the first to occur in the middle of the night in those impending hours leading to the Summer Solstice. I thought of all the thousands of other solstices that had come and gone over the millennia since these monuments were raised, and the certainty that Death had been summoned to this spot countless times over the ages – but often it was part of some religious rite carried out with the primitive belief that shed blood was required to ensure fertility for the coming season. But how many other deaths had been accomplished here in secret – not by a priest with life-blood spilled in front of many witnesses, but instead carried out in darkness, the murderer creeping and slinking away with the hopes of eternal anonymity and avoidance of responsibility for the craven deed?

Having worked with Holmes for over two decades, I had good knowledge of his methods, and as he systematically examined the grounds, bent forward to see the ground illuminated by the torch as well as he could, I stayed out of his way. He was quite methodical: No haphazard dashes here and there. Instead, he traveled sequential and overlapping lanes, working one completely from my left to right, and then turning and going back in the other direction so that nothing would be missed.

I saw that he paused several times when passing the Altar Stone, seemingly locating something of interest, but he didn't cease his search until the whole site had been examined. Only then did he call me over to the Altar Stone. "Here, Watson," he said. "He was shot here. Look, there are footprints – this one matches Sir Edvard's size elevens. There was a unique cut on the sole of his right boot. Unfortunately, his killer's prints are much more indistinct. All one can see is that they are of average size. Still, perhaps we'll see something useful when we meet the three lieutenants. Possibly two of them will be eliminated by having unnaturally large or small feet.

"In any case, the killer stood here, his back to the Altar Stone, turned northeast – the direction where the sun will rise in an hour or so. Sir Edvard faced him – and it was there that he was shot. You can see the place on the ground where he fell, straight backward. Those are his heel marks, dug in when he landed on his back. There's a spray of blood beyond in the direction where his head would have fallen – what spurted from his body as the bullet passed through. More has soaked into the grass where his body dropped. Then, there are indistinct footprints as the killer moved around, taking one of the tarpaulins from the repair work over there and bringing it back to wrap the dead man. Then, you can see where it was dragged off in the direction of the ditch in which it was found."

He then led me to the northeast, over to the tall Sarsen stones that form the main ring of the structure. Beyond, and in spite of the overcast conditions, the sky was beginning to lighten with the first hints of false dawn. The great Heel Stone, farther in the direction in which we walked, was now visible to us as a great dark shadow against the brighter background. If we were to finish our investigations before the expected arrival of the Druids, it would need to be soon.

"We may have had a piece of luck," Holmes explained when we reached the Sarsen stones located in line with where the dead man had fallen. "The bullet went straight through Sir Edvard, and then traveled in this direction with impacting any of these stones – neither these here, nor on the Heel Stone beyond them. There is no marking on the stones where a bullet strike would have occurred."

"But how does that help us?" I asked.

"You are aware of some of the advances in ballistic science – specifically, that some identifying rifling marks can be found on fired bullets that can be linked to specific weapons. I myself have contributed some knowledge to the subject, and one or two of my own cases have turned on such a point. In this instance, the deadly bullet apparently wasn't damaged – that we know of – by the body or the stones, and if it can be recovered, then we may have additional evidence toward identifying our killer."

I shook my head. "'If it can be recovered'," I said. I gestured out past the Sarsen stones to the expansive plain beyond. "Quite the long shot. Finding it would truly be like locating a needle in a haystack."

Holmes smiled, a gleam in his eye. "Ah, I have an idea about that."

"And even though we were told that the three guards were armed," I continued, "they might have been sharing the same gun, passing it from one to another as their guard shifts ended and began. So even if you prove that gun was the murder weapon, how do you tie it specifically to one of the three men?"

Holmes raised a hand, as if to fend off my objections. "We'll see what other cards are doing to be dealt. Now, let's find our way to Antrobus's lodgings and meet our suspects."

Holmes set a quick pace, and I did my best to follow and breathe steadily. I would be turning fifty-three in a couple of months, and I found when moving at speed that daily city walking was not as efficacious at as I'd like in terms of retaining youthful vigor. I had let my life become more sedentary than it should have been after Holmes's retirement nearly two years before.

As we approached the well-lit house, we found Antrobus, Grieg, and the constable standing by an outbuilding. The knight thumbed toward it, stating, "The body is in there." He then led us inside, adding, "He'll be safe enough here, until he's removed to the morgue."

After a moment of thought, Holmes indicated that he now wished to interview the dead man's three myrmidons. We left Sir Edvard Bilbrey wrapped in the tarp upon the earthen floor – a humble place to tarry at the start of the last journey that would lead to his rather overblown funeral a few days later.

Holmes succinctly explained the indications we'd found of where Sir Edvard had been shot and died. With Constable Adams' agreement, Antrobus ordered Grieg to get some buckets of water and wash away the blood at the Altar Stone to avoid stirring unnecessary speculation. "And find a lock for the shed door, and stay available." We left the caretaker there and walked toward the main house.

We entered by the front door, where two other constables stood unobtrusively on either side, backs against the walls. From where we stood in the entry hall, we could hear voices coming from an electrically lit parlour just to the left. We went in to find a another constable watching over a seated young lady, dabbing her eyes with a linen handkerchief, and the three grim young men seated along a different wall to her left.

Antrobus stepped forward. "With the absence of the local inspector, Constables Adams and Cable here have authority over the investigation, but with their approval, I've called in Sherlock Holmes." He nodded toward the famed detective. "He has been given authority by the constables to conduct the investigation. Please answer his questions accordingly." Then he stepped back, indicating that Holmes should take his place.

Instead, Holmes remained where he'd stopped upon entering, causing the three men to sit turned slightly in his direction. I knew that this was intentional, causing them to be somewhat uncomfortable while he asked his questions.

Before he could speak, the young woman sat up, a harsh look upon her face. "Where is the inspector? Get him here – or another one. Father was *killed*! That requires more than a pair of *constables*, or some private detective! Father is – *was* – a man of importance, and his murder should be treated accordingly, and not left to some *amateur*!" The last was snapped with particular viciousness. But she didn't save all of her frustration for Holmes. Looking at the three men, she continued. "It was one of *them* – Find out which one! I'll see him hanged, and cursed for the killer he is!"

I had no notion of the relationship between this woman the her three suitors prior to that moment, but it seemed that whatever esteem that might have been held between any of them up to then had vanished, and if the bitterness displayed was indicative, it would not be restored. Rachel Bilbrey's tone was vicious, and it seemed that even if one of the young men were singled out as the killer, the rest were damned by association.

When the lady had settled, Antrobus introduced the three young men. Clifford Estes was a rather squat type with a permanent smirk upon his face. My friend Mortimer would have classified his skull as *brachycephalic*, and it did nothing to make him pleasing to the eye. He had thin sandy hair combed down over a high balding brow, and he seemed amused by Miss Bilbrey's outburst.

Tyler Gilman was a complete contrast – lanky with a permanent frown, and a long thin head that nearly looked like he'd been sat upon as a baby. Whatever he was thinking kept him firmly distracted, as he hadn't glanced up at either us or the lady.

Andrew Garvey looked like his mill-working ancestors. He would have passed for solid peasant stock but for his clothing, which betrayed the fact that, as Antrobus had said, there was much money in the family.

I noted that each of the three men had average-sized feet – no help there.

Holmes seemed to be aware of Antrobus's concerns about solving the crime quickly, because he didn't waste time fencing with the different players, instead jumping immediately to the heart of the matter.

"Sir Edvard was murdered within the last six hours or so by a bullet through the heart, fired at him in the center of Stonehenge, near the Altar Stone. As I understand it, you three were sent out to stand guard, so presumably one or all of you were there when the murder occurred. Were you all together, or working in shifts?"

Garvey and Estes looked at one another, while Gilman didn't react. Then Estes replied, his voice a sneering drawl. "We were separated – in shifts. Sir Edvard thought it better that way."

"Why? What were you guarding against?"

Clifford Estes shrugged. "Who knows? The old fool was paranoid – absolutely certain that someone would try to disrupt the sunrise ceremony, although for the life of me, I can't tell you why. He – "

At the use of the word "fool", the lady once again erupted into shrieks of anger, defending her father most vigorously. She abruptly rose, and likely would have approached and clawed at Estes if Antrobus hadn't signaled for Constable Cable to step forward and have her replaced in her seat.

"You always resented Father!" she snarled. "You weren't fit to wipe his boots! You – "

Andrew Garvey talked over the girl, and she fell silent. "We were sent out alone, in shifts. We were supposed spread out the watch over the course of the night – sunset to sunrise. Gilman was the first, to cover nine o'clock or so to eleven. Then Estes until one o'clock, and then me through to the finish. But we thought it was silly, so we talked it over amongst ourselves and shortened our watches to just an hour apiece."

"And you kept to the one-hour shifts?"

"That's right. Well – I was in bed by eleven-thirty. I'd taken the last shift because we had to be up by sunrise, and since I can usually get by on less sleep than the others, I could be in bed by midnight, and still get back up and be out there by three-thirty or so, when Sir Edvard planned to arrive. That way, he'd think that we'd all done our parts, all night long. But I saw no sense in staying to the last minute, so I walked back early."

"And were you all there as you'd planned? Mr. Gilman? Did Mr. Estes relieve you at the end of your abbreviated shift?"

At this mention of his name, Gilman finally shifted his eyes toward Holmes. Following a pause and a deeper frown, as if seeing his questioner for the first time, he muttered, "Yes. Yes, he did."

"And what time was that?"

"Oh, probably about ten, as we had decided. I got out there sometime after sunset, and didn't stay more than I was supposed to – just until Estes walked over." His voice was low and deep, and had a rough edge, as if he'd damaged it at some earlier time in his life. "It wasn't too unpleasant," he added.

"And Mr. Estes – Did Mr. Garvey arrive at his agreed revised time?"

Estes nodded, his mouth pinched as if enjoying a private and unpleasant joke upon his two comrades. "He did. Before eleven. I wasn't out there much longer than an hour, and I was more than ready to leave when he got there."

"And you," Holmes said to Garvey. "Did you actually stay until eleven-thirty, or did you leave as soon as you were left alone?"

Garvey frowned, shook his head, and said shortly, "As I said, I saw no need to stay the entire time, but I did serve some of my sentence. We'd already agreed that being on guard was ridiculous, so what did it matter if I stayed until eleven-thirty, or if I went back even sooner? But I chose the latter. I enjoyed the idea of being alone at night at Stonehenge. I smoked. I listened to distant sounds. I wished that there were no clouds to block the stars. And then I returned to the house, let myself in – quietly, so that my arrival wouldn't be noticed. As I said, I planned to get some sleep, and then dress and slip back out for the sunset, since I was supposed to still be there for the morning watch. But then, just an hour or so after I went to sleep, one of these officers rousted me, and I've been awake ever since."

I considered that I understood how he felt.

"You were armed for your period of guard duty," Holmes continued. "Did you each have a gun, or did you share one between you?"

"We each had one," replied Estes. "When we became Sir Edvard's 'enforcers', as he liked to call us, he bought three identical Lugers from Westley Richards in New Bond Street."

Holmes looked toward Constable Adams. "Where are the guns?"

"In the next room – tagged when we collected them so we know who had each one."

"Excellent. Have any of them been fired?"

Adams started to answer, but Estes cut him off. "No help for you there, Sherlock. All of them have been fired. When we arrived yesterday, the three of us had a bit of fun shooting at bottles out by the stables."

Holmes frowned and looked toward the constable. Adams nodded. "I'm afraid so. All three fired, none cleaned."

"No matter," Holmes said. "There is still hope." He turned back to the three men. "You realize that all of you, by way of your scheduled presence at the Stones around the time when the murder occurred, are the most-likely suspects." There was no reaction. "Which of you had the most reason to kill Sir Edvard?"

There was still no response, and Holmes pressed further. "Come, gentlemen, this is your chance to undercut your rivals and provide us with damning information. I understand that you were each in competition for the lady's hand – and the fortune that comes with it. Who among you had made the best case? Who was the least effective? Who felt like murdering her father? Which one of you would think that killing Sir Edvard would make the path forward easier rather than more difficult?"

Estes smiled. "I thought you were more clever than that, Sherlock. Of course, none of us will rat out the others. Why should we? Certain of my own innocence, I'll wait and see what happens. I can't speak for the others. Perhaps, when you do find the killer – one of my *friends* here, it sounds like – the lady will finally realize that she and I have been the best-suited for one another the entire time – No offense, fellows. Anyway, you're just trying to pick the low-hanging fruit, holding all of us as suspects. I've heard nothing to indicate that the killer couldn't have been someone from the village, or a stranger here to see the sunrise, or some tramp or gypsy who was wandering across the plains. I suspect that's it – Sir Edvard came out after we'd all abandoned our posts to check on us, and that's when he stumbled into his killer. He likely picked a fight with the fellow and got shot for his trouble."

Rachel Bilbrey growled, but stayed still and otherwise quiet.

"Did any of you see or hear anything suspicious during your watches?" asked Holmes, ignoring Estes' points.

"No," said Garvey, glancing distastefully at Estes, as if in confirmation. "But why would we? I've heard nothing to indicate that Sir Edvard was killed during the time when we were there."

"Don't believe them!" erupted the young lady, now moved to lean forward as if she were about to roll upright and charge at her former beaus. "They all hated him! And they never cared anything for me, except for what they thought they might get by marrying me! I told Father, but they were always trying to win him over, and he wouldn't listen. They – "

"That's enough of that, Ma'am," advised Constable Cable, laying a hand upon her shoulder. She subsided, glaring at the three men. I was uncertain as to what peace had been arranged between this peculiar group during the odd courtship, but it appeared to have irretrievably ended with the death of the girl's father.

Estes shifted in his seat, as if preparing to rise. "Now, if there's nothing else – "

"You aren't going anywhere," advised Antrobus.

"Oh, really!" the young man sneered. "By *your* authority?"

"No," countered Constable Adams. "By mine."

Holmes had been thinking to himself, and seemed to ignore the brief quarrel that had bubbled forth. Instead, he caught Antrobus's eye and said, "Can we speak in the other room?"

Our host nodded and turned to walk out. "You as well, please, Adams," added Holmes, and the constable joined us, leaving Officer Cable in charge of the four detainees. In the hall, Adams paused to have the two constables by the door relocate closer to the parlour.

In Antrobus's study, we four stood and faced one another, not bothering with finding seats or getting comfortable. "That was inconclusive," said Holmes without preamble. He looked at our host. "I'm afraid that I cannot name the killer before sunrise."

Antrobus started to speak – to disagree, or to urge him to try harder in the name of national security – but he held his tongue, and then said, "What do you advise?"

"Without taking time to conduct a much deeper investigation into the backgrounds and relationships of those people, to learn the truth about their convoluted relationships, we're at a standstill in that direction. Likewise, the fact that all three guns were fired means that we can't use that fact to narrow down the killer. But there is one possibility, as we've had a bit of unexpected luck: The bullet that went entirely through Sir Edvard and then between the Stones is likely undamaged, and resting somewhere on the plains beyond the Heel Stone."

Antrobus looked at him with a cocked head and said, "And you consider that to be *lucky*?"

"It is. It's a chance, and if we can find that bullet, I can name the murderer. In the meantime, you'll have to go ahead with the sunrise ceremony, and if anyone asks about Sir Edvard's absence, put them off. That should avoid the immediate scandal that you fear might disrupt your greater plan." He looked at the desk, and back to Antrobus. "Might I use a sheet of paper?"

"Of course."

Holmes quickly moved around the desk, pulled over a sheet of stationery and a pen, and made a couple of short notations. Then he blotted the paper and folded it in half. He returned to the three of us and handed the sheet to Constable Adams.

"Please obtain these items as soon as possible. In the meantime, we'll be watching the sunrise and awaiting your return."

For those who have never had the chance to attend the Summer Solstice at Stonehenge, I heartily recommend the experience. There are other megaliths throughout the Isles that are also laid out along similar lines as lunisolar calendars, such as the one at Swinside in Cumbria, where Holmes and I once rescued the kidnapped newborn that had been designated the *Electus Puer* by the sinister *Cultus Tenebris*, but Stonehenge is certainly the most famous. (I expect the Winter Solstice, when viewed there, is just as striking, and perhaps more dramatic with its somber connotations of death and darkness, but I have no desire to stand out upon that unbroken plain in late December, with nothing to stop or deflect the wind except possibly the ineffective Normanton Down Barrows half-a-mile to the south, should the wind be blowing from that direction and no other. The dead who haunt that place no longer feel the cold, but it's all too real for those of us still among the quick.)

Antrobus's fears of being inundated by a crowd of Druids, all somehow scenting the death of Sir Edvard Bilbrey and causing a notable riot, turned out to be the merest moonshine. The Ancient Order of Druids, of which Sir Edward was a part, failed to show. Antrobus muttered to himself, irritated that he'd worried for nothing, but he was also clearly relieved that the incident he'd feared, whatever it was, had been avoided.

"And in any case, I'm glad," he added to me in an undertone, "that Holmes is here. Not disparaging the local Constabulary, but I don't see that they would have been able to make much headway with that unpleasant Cerberus known collectively as Sir Edvard's 'lieutenants'."

As the sunrise approached, there were only a few quiet locals in attendance, and I was sure that some of them were likely true Druids, there to quietly contemplate the event. They stood off to themselves, unobtrusively, but positioned in such as away as they could see the sun through the specific stones placed to line up with its first appearance on the Solstice. The day was cloudy, with a uniform gray dimness all around, making the cool morning breeze seem that much more brisk and more unpleasant. But fortunately, as the specific hour and minute approached, there was a break in the clouds to the east, and the sun triumphantly showed through. At the exact moment of sunrise, I was standing in the right spot to see the light lined up through the stones. After looking and glancing away, I noticed that many of the locals in attendance had closed their eyes and seemed to whisper silently to themselves – prayers, perhaps, related to their ancient and personal beliefs. Then, after the moment passed all too soon, they silently drifted away.

I could only imagine the spectacle if The Ancient Order of Druids – that clownish and costumed amateurish group of fakirs down from London, playing at ancient beliefs that held no meaning for them – had actually decided to make the journey.

When we'd first gone back to the menhirs from Antrobus's house, Holmes had taken up a spot to the east, past the Heel Stone, to keep watch over the area where he felt the bullet had landed. He kept his back to the rising sun to protect his vision while he made sure that no one else wandered in that direction, possibly looking for the missing bullet, or simply exploring, but taking the chance that they would somehow make it more inaccessible, perhaps by treading upon it and driving it into the turf.

I had offered to keep watch with him, but he generously waved me back to the central circle where I could see the sun come up – something that, once the moment had passed, I was profoundly glad to have witnessed for once in my life.

As the day grew brighter and the observers departed for their homes, Holmes came back and we walked over to join Antrobus. Holmes explained that we were now waiting for Constable Adams to return with the items he'd requested. To pass the time, Holmes showed where Sir Edvard had been standing when he was killed, and demonstrated how there was no sign that the bullet had hit any of the stones in that direction.

I knew that, like me, Antrobus wanted to ask what difference the undamaged stones made, but he knew enough to possess himself in patience and wait. And it didn't take long, as the constable quickly arrived and pulled to a stop nearby.

"I have everything you wanted, Mr. Holmes," he said. "In fact, I picked up some extra to make a few more, to help it go faster."

"Excellent initiative, Adams! While we get started with our preparations, would you run over and bring back our suspects? It might be instructive for them to watch our investigation – and for us to watch them."

We began to unload various items from Adams' battered Humber, before the officer drove over to Antrobus' residence. Holmes didn't bother to watch him depart. Instead, he began to sort several rolls of copper wire, half-a-dozen iron pipes, one inch in diameter and two feet in length, and a matching number of bulky lead-acid batteries. I dimly began to perceive Holmes's plan, impressed that his mind would have instantly leapt to such an obscure solution to the problem.

By the time Constables Adams, Cable, and the two others returned with the four "guests", Holmes, Antrobus, and I had had constructed three rather unwieldy electromagnets, one apiece, and we had the pieces ready to assemble three more. Holmes had explained that we might as well make the extras while we had the time and materials, in case one of the others failed. Adams had also brought some straps, which we used to fashion handles for carrying our homemade devices.

Construction was an easy-enough affair. We each cut long lengths of copper wire, and then began to wrap it tightly into a coil around the iron pipes. When finished, we connected each end of the wire to the terminals of the battery, thus magnetizing the pipe.

The policemen shepherded the three men and Sir Edvard's daughter to one side, and Holmes began to explain as he finished up his second magnet. Just as he'd done a few minutes before with Antrobus, he indicated where Sir Edvard had been standing when he was shot. At this, the man's daughter began to softly weep, and as Holmes talked she continued to stare at that lonely spot, dramatically facing the Altar Stone. Estes, Garvey, and Gilman seemed fascinated, with Estes seemingly poised to interrupt with some snide remark, but Holmes continued to steadily explain, and he never got the chance.

"We had two bits of good luck," said Holmes. "It might almost seem to be mystical, if one credits the atmosphere of this place. First, the bullet went straight through the body, and east, out of the circle, without hitting any stones. And second, Sir Edvard chose Lugers to arm his three agents, and he used steel-jacketed bullets – a recent innovation by Luger – which mean that the slug didn't deform – and that the bullets are magnetic. This is further confirmed by the straight clean path of the bullet through the body. When we find the bullet, we can examine it to determine which gun fired the shot."

There were a number of curious faces, and Holmes continued.

"In the last few years, there have been significant advances in the science of ballistics, and especially identifying which gun fired which bullet by way of microscopic examination, but the initial work on the subject is seventy years old. In 1835, Henry Goddard, a Bow Street Runner, linked the marks on a deadly bullet to the mold in which it was formed. In the American Civil War, it was seen that the type of bullet that killed the Confederate traitor, General Stonewall Jackson, came from one of his own men, and not a Union soldier. In the last five years, there have been several other cases in the United States where rifling marks made on the bullet by the gun's barrel have provided important evidence. And I myself was able to clear a man early in my career by comparison of two different bullets." [2]

The three men were watching Holmes carefully as he finished up the construction of the magnet and then picked up the strap to lift it. He walked to the automobile, holding the iron bar pointed in front of him. When he reached the vehicle, the bar pulled his arm forward, attaching its end to the iron fender-work with a metallic *thud.* The magnets were activated.

Leaving the four young people with the other two constables, Antrobus, Adams, Cable, and I also picked up our electromagnets and walked east, past the Heel Stone, and began slowly trying to detect the metal in the ragged plains grass. We made a curious spectacle in the early morning light, bent over like scavenging birds, waving our magnetic wands this way and that inches over the turf in wide sweeps while throwing long shadows back toward the stones from the slowly climbing sun.

We all looked back frequently to make sure we stayed relatively lined up with where the body had fallen and the space between the two relevant Sarsen stones. All the while, there was some discussion, as the sun rose behind the clouds and somewhat brightened the early morning, about how far a jacketed Luger bullet might be expected to travel, particularly after passing through the soft tissues of a body. There was no clear consensus, and the search continued.

I was more than amazed when, after no more than ten minutes, I heard a small metallic *clic*k at the end of my metal wand. I had wandered a bit farther than the others, knowing from my past experience in Afghanistan that bullets had an uncanny way of going past where one thought they could. I had treated too many men, and seen too many others who were dead, who had all believed themselves safe due to their supposedly adequate distance from the shooter.

I had begun to worry that the bullet wasn't in the line we expected, perhaps having been skipped up or to the sides by a bit of turbulent air along its passage. I almost didn't credit that I'd found it, but there was no mistake: I had the steel-jacketed killer resting in the palm of my hand.

I signaled to the others and hurriedly walked back to them. They crowded around, looking in the dim morning light at my discovery. Antrobus crowed and patted Holmes on the back. "Brilliant!" he repeated, over and over, while Adams looked at my friend with even more awe than he had when Holmes had showed him and Inspector Youghal the recovered Irish Crown Jewels from the lonely middle-aged deviant, Christopher Heydon.

Holmes immediately led us back toward the Stones. In addition to the supplies needed to make the magnets, Adams had obtained a microscope from a local physician, and we now planned to relocate to Antrobus's house where a comparison would be made between the bullet and the guns – but it proved to be unnecessary.

When we walked through the Sarsen stones and rejoined the group, all attention was turned to the foot of the Altar Stone, where Tyler Gilman was lying, curled into a ball on his side. He was muttering to himself. The rest watched him in shocked silence.

"We saw you find something," explained one of the constables who had been guarding the group. "We assumed it was the bullet. It was then that Gilman there collapsed. With a moan, he started to sway, and then made it a few steps to the stone, where he laid down . . . like that."

I stepped closer to examine him and found that he felt feverish. He ignored me when I commanded that he unfold himself so that I could see what else was the matter. Instead, over and over, he simply repeated, "He deserved it. I had to. He left me no choice. He deserved it. You all know it. He deserved it . . . ."

A later examination revealed that Tyler Gilman's gun had indeed fired the bullet. He never recovered enough to provide an explanation, or to answer any questions at all, and he was found "Guilty but Insane" and remanded to Broadmoor, where he would likely remain for the rest of his life.

Holmes's subsequent investigations revealed that the young man's father had brought the family to near ruin, and that the house of cards he'd constructed was just about to collapse. Gilman had been under immense pressure to rescue his family by securing a marriage to the heiress, Rachel Bilbrey. It seemed that the apple didn't fall far from the tree in terms of personal character, as it was easily determined that Gilman himself had a number of detestable habits, not much different than those that brought about the ruination of his father. Although not proven, it was speculated Sir Edvard had either discovered this aspect, or suspected it, and was about the bar Tyler Gilman from pursuing any engagement with his daughter.

A note was found wadded in the pocket of Tyler Gilman's coat – simply written, unsigned, in block script, advising *Meet me at the Stones at midnight.* It was felt that Gilman had arranged an appointment this way with Sir Edvard, luring him there to his death when the last of the guards had departed. Then he'd rolled the body into one of the tarpaulins that littered the site related to Antrobus's restoration work and moved it to a seemingly out-of-the-way place. He'd retrieved the note and returned to the house, and then to bed. But the matter had preyed on his mind, as reflected in his introverted behavior while being interviewed. Seeing that his guilt was about to be revealed had caused the weak-minded killer to crack before the accusation could be leveled and proof produced.

I later heard that Andrew Garvey left London and returned to the bosom of his Lancashire family. Three months after her father's death, Rachel Bilbrey married the disagreeable Clifford Estes, and their life since, while undeservingly wealthy, has apparently been as unhappy as one might expect.

Antrobus, who hinted that he'd seen Holmes in action before, could not have been more impressed. Curiously, for one so centered and grounded, he soon threw himself in an entirely different direction, allowing The Ancient Order of Druids to hold their first ritualistic meeting at Stonehenge the following August, and for himself to be enthusiastically initiated among their number on that sane memorable day. From the impression I'd formed of Sir Edmund Antrobus upon our initial meeting, I could only think that this new role was simply a performance, a part of some mission that he was undertaking for the Government. Of course, I would never ask him to confirm or deny it, and I watched with curious amusement in the following years as he continued along that path – until he passed away ten years later. As there was no heir – his son having been killed the year before in Belgium – the estate passed to his brother, who sold Stonehenge soon after.

Holmes and I were back on the train by lunchtime – this time in a first-class carriage, but by the usual means and methods: No special trains to return us from where we'd started. It certainly took longer than our outbound journey, but I used the opportunity to catch up on my sleep. It's a good thing, as we were met on the platform at Eastbourne Station by Inspector Bardle of the Sussex Constabulary.

"I'm fairly up against it, and make no mistake," he explained, and then he continued to lay out the events related to a corpse, a wool scarf, a rare book, and three sisters – one blind, one deaf, and one mute.

It was two further days before I made it back to Holmes's villa for his "recommended rest and a change of scene".

NOTES

1. See "The Two Different Women" in *The Collected Papers of Sherlock Holmes – Volume IV: Narratives* and *The MX Book of New Sherlock Holmes Stories: Part VIII – Eliminate the Impossible: 1892-1905*
2. See "The Two Bullets" in *The Collected Papers of Sherlock Holmes – Volume V: Chronicles* and *Sherlock Holmes and Doctor Watson: The Early Adventures – Volume I*

25 August, 1905: Sir Edmund Antrobus (and others) at Stonehenge, being led blindfolded to be initiated into The Ancient Order of Druids

Some of Sir Edmund Antrobus's restoration work at Stonehenge. (Photo: 1914)

Personal Notes

My father, John Marcum, spent most of his adult life in law enforcement. He served as an MP in the United States Army during the Korean War, and then returned home to attend college under the G.I. Bill. In the late 1950's, he became a Tennessee State Trooper, and in the late 1960's, he became a Special Agent for the Tennessee Bureau of Investigation, covering several counties, with his office located in our home.

When I was growing up, he let me read his files, and he taught me about criminal investigation, including how to take a person's fingerprints, and how to lift them at a crime scene. I learned about plaster casts of footprints, and I was able to accompany him on a number of investigations, watching him conduct interviews and work with both witnesses and other law enforcement officers. Once, he even let me accompany him on a murder investigation. He finished his TBI career by becoming the State's first polygraph operator – and he taught me how to do that too.

After he retired, he held a number of other law enforcement related positions. At the time he left the State, he was commended for many of his investigations. In one, his diligence was exemplary when he found a bullet casing in a front yard that proved to be the key piece of evidence – somewhat like what Holmes accomplished on that day in June 1905 as the sun rose over Stonehenge.

David Marcum and his Deerstalker at Stonehenge
Holmes Pilgrimage No. 4
June 9th, 2024
(Photo by Dan Marcum)

Soiled Doves

She knows that I love her, but it makes no difference.

"Wiggins," Kitty often says, rubbing the fingers of her left hand with her right, squeezing and twisting them. But there is never really any relief. "I'm a soiled dove, ain't I? You don't know the life I've led."

"I do know," I tell her, and she knows that I know, but she goes on in the same way, every time we talk about it.

Kitty is stubborn – it's part of what makes her who she is – and she doesn't back down.

"Well then," she'll say, "you've seen what I'm capable of. You don't want to associate with the likes of me. Go find yourself a nice girl." Then she'd squeezes her fingers some more and closes her eyes, waiting for the pain to ease – or for me to get tired and leave. But I never will.

When Kitty Winter tossed the acid into Adelbert Gruner's face last autumn, some splashed on her hand, and in the rush to escape, there wasn't time to clean it off or treat the wounds. Mr. Holmes, for all of his observant ways, didn't see that she was in pain before he sent the two of us fleeing back to London, or how her hand was being damaged while the acid kept eating into her skin – but it wasn't his fault, because Kitty hid it from him. She's strong like that. She just sat quietly while the acid did its damage.

She's always maintained that it was worth it – punishing Gruner like that – and that she'd do it again a thousand times if necessary – or if she ever gets another chance – but she's paid her price for it, and that's certain. She won't ever admit how much pain it's caused, but the damage to the nerves in her hand ended up being more severe than anyone thought, because sometimes, when she thinks no one is listening and the pain comes on suddenly, she gives a little gasp or cry or even a moan, and the only thing she can do – or will do – is twist her fingers.

When I suggest wrapping her hand in hot cloths, or dipping it into warm water, she replies that heat doesn't help, and it's obvious that cold makes it worse. I saw how bad the pain was last winter, in the months following the vitriol throwing, and I'm worried, as next winter is getting closer. Early on she sought the help of doctors, but when they just offered laudanum or morphine – or worse – she rejected them. We've both seen how that's the start of a slippery path that likely ends in a bad way.

Dr. Watson is the only one who is willing to tell her the truth – even though it isn't what she wants to hear. Me either, for that matter. Her hand might get better, he says, or it might not, but if so it will take time – maybe a long time.

So Kitty lives with the pain, and the slim hope that it will subside as time passes. I once told her about the scar across the back of one of my fingers, where I'd once sliced myself open to the bone with a knife so sharp I never felt the pain. She looked at my hand and shook her head. I'd foolishly looked away while sawing at a piece of leather – just something that I was doing so I'd look busy and not be noticed – and then I looked down and saw the yellow-white finger bone, with one slim blade groove running across it. I only saw it for a second before the blood pooled over between the cleanly split-apart skin, but I knew what I'd done. I should have sought help and had it stitched up right then, but that was when the person I was busy following for Mr. Holmes bolted, so I could only wrap it in a clean-enough rag, holding the skin flaps in place until the slice scabbed over.

Later, I showed it to Dr. Watson, but it was closed by then. "You'll certainly have a memorable scar," he said with a sympathetic wince. "It must hurt like the devil. You're lucky, Wiggins, that you avoided infection." I just grinned as if nothing could bother me, for I had a newly earned shilling in my pocket. The doctor was right, though – the scar was impressive, and it did hurt something awful. I only had to brush the back of my finger against something – a door jamb or wall, or reaching into my pocket – and it sent a jolt through me like I was being branded with a red-hot iron. It ran up my arm in a way that, for just a second, pushed out any other thought. I learned to be careful with that finger, and being careful was still something that I did without thinking, long after the nerve had either healed or died. All I knew was that after a few years, the pain went away, even when I'd run another finger along the scar to see if anything was left of it.

I knew that Kitty felt pain like that, and I saw how she was careful to protect herself. Her whole life had been one of pain, and she was protective of that too, flinching at getting too close to anyone else. But she seemed to take some comfort from my story – and she has little enough to comfort her.

And I love her, and I wish that would help, but so far it makes no difference.

People see how I feel for Kitty, and they have differing opinions. Mr. Holmes shows it in his dubious expression, but he doesn't say a word. Dr. Watson encourages me, because he still believes in happy endings. Porky Johnson just smiles knowingly, as if he's heard some good news but he can't share it. Hilda Bane is practical – she thinks that the longer I stay around, the more I'll become something of a habit to Kitty, like a favorite cat or tea mug. I supposed that's the best I can expect for now.

I stay because I love her, and also because Kitty has made powerful enemies – and though it's far from the first time she's had one of those, they seem to get worse – especially recently in the form of one man.

I tried to convince her that he was dangerous, to explain and reason that he was more powerful than she's seen, but she was indifferent. I hate to think that her recent successes have somehow made her believe she's invincible, but there are hints that such is the case. After her trial and subsequent release for throwing acid in Gruner's face, destroying his features forever and leaving him blinded and broken and shunned by everyone who knew about him, it was almost as if she received the thanks of the Court. Since then she certainly feels powerful. And after she started helping the other mistreated women who've had no one to champion them, she has become confident.

But Justin Marley was a different kind of enemy.

We first encountered Marley last August. It was hot and dry, although there was finally a little rain after the middle of the month. Kitty was lounging in her rooms, wearing her favorite red dressing gown, reading the morning paper and commenting about the new Poor Prisoner's Defense Act. "'*Desirable in the interest of justice*'," she read sarcastically. Dropping the paper onto the floor, she added, "That's a fine idea, ain't it, Wiggins? Now someone just needs to tell them what 'justice' means."

I nodded. I'd seen injustice all my life, and since Kitty formed her little "agency" some months ago, my eyes had been opened even more.

The noises of the street were louder for some reason that morning, but I didn't want to shut Kitty's window, on the chance that a breeze might spring up. I was about to hope so out loud just making conversation since she seemed to be in a mood to talk, when there was a knock at the door. I opened it to reveal a middle-aged woman, well-dressed, and looking like she was in trouble. Most women who find their way to Kitty's door have that expression, but this one was the best-dressed of them so far.

Her name isn't important. I'll call her Mrs. Smith. She sat down and then waited, likely afraid to go any further than she'd already journeyed, and hoping for Kitty to take the reins.

Kitty sat up straighter and asked the lady what was on her mind.

"They say that you help people – women – like me, who have nowhere else to go. No one to whom they can turn in times of trouble. That after your trial . . . after what happened with that Baron, you made it your mission to assist those who have no one else."

Kitty nodded. The mention of the trial seemed to bring on the pain in her hand, for she began to squeeze her fingers once again. "What's the problem?" she asked. "I ain't a mind reader, am I?" Kitty doesn't have much patience for shooting all around the target. "Get it done in one," she says.

"It's my brother," the woman replied. "He was in the newspaper – about his murder. He was – Gerald Jones was his name." Jones wasn't his name either, but it'll do. Mrs. Smith glanced at the newspapers on the floor beside Kitty's chair. "You'll have read about it?"

"Something or other," Kitty replied. "The police think it was suicide. You've told them that it was his partner who killed him."

Mrs. Smith nodded. "Gerald would never kill himself! He had too much to live for! He was engaged to a girl he loved with all of his heart."

Kitty leaned over and shuffled through the newspapers until she found the one she wanted. "The police say that he took poison."

Mrs. Smith shook her head. "He was poisoned, that's true, but they also didn't find any evidence with him, or in his rooms, to explain how he did it. No bottle, no flask – nothing. It was strychnine poisoning, and after he drank it, death would have been almost immediate. He was alone in his rooms in Rathbone Place, and the door was locked, and the key was in his pocket. If he killed himself in his room, how did he get the poison there? There was no bottle," she repeated.

After a moment when she was seeing something in her mind, maybe Dead Gerald, she went on. "I hadn't heard from Gerald in several days. Ordinarily, not a day went by without one of us reaching out to the other. We grew up orphans, you see, and even after my marriage, we remained close. My husband understood and tolerated it. After the first day of not hearing anything I was worried, and it was much worse after the second. I went to where Gerald lived, and the landlady said she hadn't seen him. That's when I summoned a policeman, and the landlady gave us her key. I was with the police when they went in and we found him . . . He was there, in his chair by the window. He . . . he . . . ." Then she began to cry.

Kitty let her be. She has little patience for women's weaknesses, having shut off that part of herself so long ago, but she also knew that letting Mrs. Smith weep then would likely free her to answer more questions later.

When the lady had control of herself, Kitty asked, "What do you want from me? I ain't no detective, am I, crawling around looking for clues, and then calling everybody together to tell them that it was Colonel Limp who done it with a knife in the parlor maid's *boudoir*? If you're here to see me, then you know what I do."

Mrs. Smith nodded, her eyes still wet with tears. "I do know. It was Cynthia Rutledge-Nelson who told me – who sent me to you after you helped her last spring."

I remembered that one very well. April 1903. The lady, a tall thin woman, made fragile and brittle by life, had become involved with a man she barely knew, and found out that he jollied from beating women. All too common – but after Kitty Winter became interested in the fellow, the only beatings occurring in his life were those he was now receiving in Pentonville Prison. A word discreetly placed meant that he received his lessons daily.

"It's Justin Marley," continued Mrs. Smith. "Gerald's business partner – although Gerald did all the work and Mr. Marley just sent him clients. He's the younger brother of Lord Marley. I don't know the details, but Gerald found out that he's been involved in something illegal. Gerald was going to report it, even if it hurt the business."

"And that's what you told the police," I said, speaking for the first time. "And the newspapers, too, and they printed it, and Marley didn't like it. I'm told that there's such a thing as libel laws."

Mrs. Smith's mouth tightened. "It will be worth it, naming Justin Marley in public, if he's caught and punished for Gerald's murder."

"Has he threatened you?" asked Kitty.

"He has."

It was then that I saw the light flicker up in her eyes. Another "case", as she'd taken to calling them. She sat up straighter. "I'm going to need to know more about it, ain't I?" she asked, and I pulled out my notebook and pencil.

It's been a strange year. After Kitty's trial, she was at a loss. Having just met her a few weeks before, in September 1902, I didn't know much about her – where she was from, where she lived – but I knew even then that I loved her. So when I saw that she was still in pain, and somehow at a loss following her release, I stayed around – running errands, getting underfoot, but always there to protect her as well.

We didn't talk much then, but she knew how I felt. Sometimes it amused her, sometimes it made her sad. One afternoon, she was telling me yet again that I should let her be – she had sinned far too much in her past for someone like me – and I was again arguing that it didn't matter, when there was a knock on her door.

It was a girl named Cora, a maid from one of the nearby houses. Since the trial, Kitty has lived in the first-floor rooms of a house in Marchmont Street, near the corner of Great Coram Street. It was a place that Porky Johnson found for her, saying that she couldn't go back to where he'd found her just a month before. I never tried to learn where that had been. To me, her life started over when she revenged herself on the Baron.

Cora entered timidly, asking if the lady seated by the window was Miss Kitty Winter. When Kitty nodded, barely interested and tired of it all, Cora introduced herself with a look in her eyes as if she were seeing someone famous.

"My name, ma'am, is Cora Wishum, and I heard what you did. We all heard about it – how you stood up to that evil man, that Baron, and made him pay. I just want to say how much we all – how much *I* admire you for it."

Kitty waved her hand in a dismissive gesture, but I could see that the girl's words surprised her. I knew from whenever I went out that there was still a great deal of public interest in Kitty, and curiosity, and that she was generally perceived in a positive light. I would hear women whispering about her admiringly in the markets or in passing on the streets. But Kitty didn't know any of that, as she wasn't leaving her rooms just then, a shut-in, having seemingly given up on life.

What I only learned later was that Porky and Mr. Holmes had made an effort to turn the ship of public opinion about poor Kitty by dropping a word here or there, showing her story in a positive way and making her a hero and not a villain. It took a while, because that ship has a small rudder, but it was clearly working, and when Cora showed up that day in late 1902 to heap her admiration on Kitty, I could see that it made a difference in healing her.

"It was so brave what you did!" Cora was saying, her words coming faster and faster. "We read all about your trial, and how that bad man had a diary, and how you punished him for what he did."

Kitty was becoming uncomfortable with the praise – I could read her moods well enough by then – and she was about to have me usher Cora out when the girl added, "We – the other maids and I – we need your help. There's a . . . the Master's son has been mistreating us. And the Master too . . . We need someone . . . we need someone to stand up for us. Someone strong like you, Miss Kitty."

And little did I know then that Cora's visit was just the tiniest first spark toward giving Kitty a new purpose in life – as an advocate for oppressed women – something like a consulting detective, but with a vengeance.

When I first met Kitty, and though I loved her at first sight, I had no idea of the steel in her spine, or what she would go on to accomplish.

Porky first told me about her, and I only knew that she'd found herself in a dangerous spot. I was recruited to help keep an eye on her, in case she was attacked in retribution for what she had just told Mr. Sherlock Holmes about a dangerous man named Gruner.

I've known Mr. Holmes since I was a small boy. As a Wiggins, that was rather inevitable. I'm not *that* Wiggins – the one that people know about from a couple of Dr. Watson's stories. That one is my cousin, and he grew up a long time ago. He was the *first* Wiggins to assist Mr. Holmes, back in the days when the detective was a young man himself, in his mid-twenties and living in small rooms near the British Museum. As he eased himself into his chosen profession of "Consulting Detective", he began to see the value of using various street lads – some of them *urchins*, just as Dr. Watson stated, and some of them of a little higher class, living in houses with their families, fed well-enough and in decent clothes, but still able to roam free and look and watch and report while having some sort of fun and earning a few coins. Years later, when I read *Oliver Twist*, I wondered if Mr. Holmes hadn't unconsciously taken Fagin's idea of using lads to do his work for him – but instead of stealing people's wallets, he had them gathering information. Fagin's crew, while all criminals to greater or lesser degrees, had ended up as something of a family, crossing generations and looking out for one another, and so did Mr. Holmes's *Irregulars*, as he called us.

The first Wiggins to work for Mr. Holmes had ended up being the leader of the group and, after Mr. Holmes saved his mother from a charge of murder, [1] the family was so grateful that a number of the children – brothers and sisters and cousins – ended up as Irregulars. (That title wasn't official for the longest time. Apparently Mr. Holmes initially used it when describing the group to Dr. Watson, maybe because of its military connotation and that the doctor was just back from a war, and the first Wiggins, hearing it and liking it, appropriated it.) The arrangement was not one way, with Mr. Holmes simply buying the Irregulars' time and information. He gave back to us.

For all that was done for Mr. Holmes, and the sometime-danger that accompanied it, there was more provided to the various lads and lasses than just a daily wage and the occasional bonus shilling. Mr. Holmes took it upon himself to see that all of us were educated – he required it – and that those of us who didn't already have homes had warm places to sleep, good food to eat, and clothes to wear – including shoes for those who would tolerate them. I used to wonder how he could afford it – he started using the Irregulars when he was just in his twenties, and surely before he had two farthings to rub together – but then I realized that, after the first few years when he was working to create his profession, his income became more steady, and then more profitable. I've heard tales of some very substantial rewards that he and Dr. Watson received for their efforts, in cases where no solution would have otherwise been found – and in others where the crime itself might not have been spotted but for Mr. Holmes's intervention.

When the Irregulars reached an age where their usefulness dwindled, or when their interest in such games faded in favor of more adult needs and thoughts, Mr. Holmes always made sure, if he could, to find a good profession for those who had served him so well. Some of them, despite all his efforts, simply drifted away without taking advantage of the opportunities that Mr. Holmes was offering them.

I took advantage of my opportunities.

Mr. Holmes noticed that I had an understanding of numbers, so he arranged to have me tutored. Fortunately, my teacher, a little lady who lived in Lambeth, worked to see that I had a rounded education – not just mathematics, but literature as well, and a knowledge of current affairs. She made me read and write, which gave me an understanding of words that has helped me as much as anything else I've ever learned. In 1902, I was seventeen years old, and if all went well, I would begin my studies in a year or so toward becoming an engineer. But I still helped out as an Irregular when I was able, and that's how Shinwell "Porky" Johnson recruited me to help watch and protect a lady who, as he described it, "has crossed a wrong 'un that may want to pay her back."

Sometimes – well, really most times – the Irregulars took on jobs without knowing much of anything other than the specific task. Watch a building and follow who comes out. Canvass a neighborhood to find a specific man or woman. Scour through the trash of a neighborhood to find a discarded object or sheet of a newspaper. Listen everywhere to hear talk or rumors about some event – past or upcoming. But by 1902, I was an older Irregular, and big for my age. And I had seen some things. So Porky told me more about the job. "The girl – you may have heard of her. Kitty Winter? Well, no matter. She gave information to Mr. Holmes about a very bad man who wronged her. And when this man, a baron, finds out what she did, he may try to get revenge on her. In fact, knowing his type, it's almost certain that he will." Porky rubbed a large hand across his whiskers, his big and meaty red face looking troubled. "I was the one who convinced her to talk with Mr. Holmes, so I can't let her be hurt. You and a few of the others will help watch. The others will be hidden to see if she's approached, but you'll stay right with her – to keep her safe." And he handed me an old revolver. It wasn't the first time I'd gone armed on one of these expeditions.

God knows what paths that gun had taken before reaching my hand, or what mischief – and worse – it created along the way. I didn't like having it, and hoped that nothing serious enough to make me use it would occur. It turned out that when I might have needed it, I forgot that I had it. Good thing, too.

I was introduced to Kitty in mid-September, in The White Hart in Whitechapel High Street, across from Commercial Road. It was dark both inside and out that day, and I didn't expect that it would be such a momentous meeting in my young life. The pub is long and narrow from front to back, the bar on the left side, and Kitty was seated in the back by the left wall with one of Porky's friends, a big quiet man who slid out and walked away when Porky and I arrived. Porky sat down on one side of the table, leaving me to slip in beside the small girl, facing outward so I could see in either direction.

She was in a plain dark coat, and wearing an ugly mashed-down hat. At first I dismissed her, glancing to my right toward the bar when Porky held up three fingers. Then he started to talk, saying that I would be taking over for Beakins, who had just departed. At that moment, the owner set down three mugs of beer, and I slid one over to the girl, beside another empty mug already there. As her head turned my way, I saw her face, and I was lost to her.

Kitty isn't pretty, exactly. Her face is lean, which matches her thin body. In certain light, there's a starved look to her, almost feral. She has big eyes and high sharp cheek-bones, more noticeable from the sides – then they almost come to a point. Her face tapers to a rather sharp chin, and she sits or stands with her head pushed forward and her shoulders rolled in as if she's cold. Overall, her features when taken separately aren't that pretty, but together, along with some spark that she carries, there's something that makes her stand out. And it isn't just me (who loves her) that thinks so. Every man I've met seems more aware of her.

She's very pale, and even though she's probably only five or six years older than me, the years have left a coarseness to her skin – small lines around her eyes and mouth, and dark circles under her eyes. Her skin looks thin, and in the right light, small blue veins are visible – especially if she's tired. When she smiles – usually not because she's happy, but instead because some bad man has been punished – her teeth aren't as straight as some would like, and they aren't dazzling white, but rather that shade that one often sees in true red-heads. (Dr. Watson told me that red-heads actually do have thinner skin and less tooth enamel, which explains it.)

And it's her red hair that serves as the focus of those other features, and makes all of them – even those reflecting her weariness and care-worn years – suddenly beautiful. Then one can see that she's like a delicate flame that must be fed and protected, and that any sin and sorrow she carries is irrelevant – it just doesn't matter – when instead seeing her intensity and intelligence.

Porky saw me staring at her and gave a gruff laugh. "Quit gawping, Wiggins, and listen to what I'm trying to tell you!"

Kitty smiled at me then, though just with her eyes, and not altogether happy, but I knew that *she* knew – that from then on, I was hers. God knows it wasn't the first time someone had looked at her that way. I wasn't the only one to show her that look, but unlike the others, I've stuck with her, and will continue to do so, and God willing, she'll change her mind about us some day.

Porky explained that later that night, Kitty would be going with Mr. Holmes down to Kingston, and the house of the baron who was a danger to her. "Is that a good idea?" I asked. "To take her into the lion's mouth like that?"

Porky shrugged. Like me and so many others, we had learned not to question Mr. Holmes.

After Porky was gone, Kitty and I remained seated. I nervously drank my beer, taking too many short sips to avoid speaking. Finally she looked around at me. "Ain't you going to move to the other side of the table? We ain't friends, you and me. I don't even know your name."

It was the first time I'd heard her voice, and it made me shiver. With a muttered apology, I quickly scuttered around the table, wondering why I hadn't done so before, as now I could look upon her without turning my head. She was as fair to me as spring sunshine after a long dark winter. I introduced myself, and she muttered something about, "Another d----d Wiggins!" She had a scoffing tone, almost teasing, so I explained how I was related to the family, and the ways in which I'd first helped Mr. Holmes so long ago. I probably talked too fast, and had to keep making my voice softer as my enthusiasm grew. I shut up after I could see her attention was wandering, and now that she had the chance to say something, she replied that she'd only just met Mr. Holmes, but of course she'd heard about him for years. And so we talked some more, one thing leading to another, in a way that became easier and easier. But I've never lost the feeling when looking at her that there's a tingle in my middle, in the way that the air is filled with electricity on a charged summer night, and lighting is about to strike somewhere.

It seemed too soon when I looked up to see Mr. Holmes standing beside our table. "Wiggins?" he asked. "What are you doing here?"

I was ashamed that I was supposed to be taking care of her, and that I'd had no notion that he – or anyone else – was close around us. He was wearing a bandage upon his head, low and tight enough that it didn't interfere with the placement of his fore-and-aft hunting cap. I recalled that he'd recently been beaten by several toughs outside the Café Royal in Regent Street. The newspapers had acted as if he were near to death, but the Irregulars had received word that it wasn't that bad. Still, Mr. Holmes didn't look up to his usual fighting stance that night in the pub.

I explained that Porky had arranged for someone to guard Miss Winter, and he smiled. "An excellent precaution," he explained. He turned to Kitty. "I apologize for recruiting you again at the last moment – especially after our unpleasant visit with Miss de Merville. Tonight, I'm slipping into the Baron's house while Dr. Watson distracts him, and I may only have a moment to try and retrieve the Baron's diary. I want you there in case I need any last-minute information about the layout of the house and so-on. Are you ready?"

Kitty's lips tightened and she nodded.

What happened next is related quick-enough. We took a four-wheeler to Waterloo, and Mr. Holmes asked Kitty practical questions about Vernon Lodge, the Baron's home. He told me later that he observed the little packet that she carefully caried under her coat, but I never saw it. He also mentioned that he regretted not asking about it, as he might have known what Kitty planned beforehand. He said he regretted it, but I don't think that he really did, as he's never seemed too dissatisfied with what happened.

At the station, we boarded one of the trains that travel all the time back-and-forth to-and-from Kingston, and they continued their conversation while I enjoyed myself by staring at the red-headed girl across from me. Sometimes I'd have to remind myself to swallow – such was my fascination with her. As is so often the way, especially as a trusted Irregular, much was said in front of me of a confidential nature, and I soon became aware of a terrible portion of Kitty's history – just how she knew this Baron Gruner, and what he had done to her.

I was angry – but not at her. Everyone's life takes unexpected turns, and she had been the target of an evil man. Nothing could diminish the new feelings that I'd carried since meeting her. But I hated the Baron.

We arrived at the Kingston station and then took out-of-the-way seats in the small buffet. A half-hour or so later, Dr. Watson's later train stopped and he stepped from a carriage, confidently leaving the station and obtaining a cab. As soon as he was out of sight, Mr. Holmes rose and urged us to follow in one of our own, and in ten minutes or so, we were standing on the road outside a six-foot wall surrounding a long, low, and ugly building marked by several sprawling wings and unsightly turrets. "I've already been here once," Mr. Holmes explained softly. "The Baron, in his arrogance, has no guards. Follow me."

We slipped through the shrubbery along the inside of the wall until we reached a garden on the east side of the building. Through a window to our left, we could see Dr. Watson just getting seated, a small box held in his hands. He opened it and then handed what looked like a little blue saucer to someone just out of sight. I glanced to my right, looking to see if Mr. Holmes had observed this, but he'd vanished. Then I saw that a darkened window was open just to the right, and the drapes were moving as if someone has just passed through them.

Kitty saw it too, her lower lip bitten between her teeth, and she drew closer to the building. I wondered how she felt, being this close to the man who had done so much to ruin her life. When she and Mr. Holmes had discussed it on the train, her voice had been flat, as if she was talking about someone else, but I already felt that I knew her, and I could feel the pain that she was holding in so tightly.

It was only a moment or so after Mr. Holmes vanished that I heard voices raised in the other room – Dr. Watson's, and some slimy-sounding man, presumably the Baron, with a low-pitched oily and sneering tone that was increasing in volume as he spoke. He was angry now, accusing Dr. Watson of something. Then there was the sound of a slamming door, and the Baron yelled something, immediately followed by the reappearance of Mr. Holmes jumping back through the side window beside us, now carrying a brownish-looking book.

The moon that night was full, or nearly so, and there wasn't a cloud in the sky. In fact, it hadn't rained in weeks. Everything happened as if we were in harsh daylight, with only the colors washed from the scene, leaving all of us playing our parts in pure white and black, and every shade of gray in between.

I felt that I could see every check in the pattern on Mr. Holmes's deerstalker hat. The bandage around his head, visible underneath the hat, seemed to glow with its own pure light. On the front of the book in his hand was some sort of Coat of Arms – a knight's helmet that looked more like a rooster head atop a shield with a left-facing crescent moon. I could even see the grip of Mr. Holmes's fingers upon the book, his knuckles almost as white as his bandage, and shadows around his fingers where he was indenting the book's leather cover. He was moving and turning back as if to defend himself from the dark-suited man who had pursued him through the window.

It was then that I might have thought to draw out my revolver.

And that was when Kitty stepped past me.

She, too, was illumined in the cold pure light. Her lips were pulled back and her teeth were clenched, and the moonlight was hotly reflected in her big eyes. She was focused purely on the man who was going after

Mr. Holmes. I have little impression of him – a thin mustache, and his dark hair slicked back. His eyes widened when he saw Kitty moving toward him, and I think he recognized her. Kitty's expression was so compelling that I never noticed what she was doing with her hands. I couldn't remember then, and still can't, to this day. But there's no mystery as to what she did.

With her left hand, she pulled the stopper from a glass bottle that she'd apparently been holding out of my sight, the little package that Mr. Holmes had noticed, and with her right, she forcefully and accurately threw the clear contents directly into the Baron's snarling face.

His momentum carried him forward toward Mr. Holmes a few more feet, but then he planted his feet, his hands abruptly rising and clawing at his face while he bent backward and howled under the moon like a man going through the torturous process of changing into a wolf. It seemed as if his features were erupting into smoking foam, while his mouth opened and closed into a rictus of agony. As the Baron screamed and screamed, Mr. Holmes took a step toward him, instantly perceiving what had occurred. Then he turned back toward us, grabbing Kitty by the arm and pushing her my way while hissing, "Wiggins! Get her away from here! *Now!*"

As I hurried her away, I parsed what I'd just seen. This girl, this small beautiful girl that I'd only known for a few hours, had a hard and sharp unexpected edge. I'd had no idea of what she was capable of if pushed, and for the right reasons. But it didn't shock or offend me, because I'd known men and women with that same edge all my life. I already loved her, and maybe this made me love her even more.

I have little memory of the rest of that night. As we ran away, I saw Dr. Watson joining Holmes, and then leaning toward the injured man. Kitty and I reached the station in time for an up-train to the city, and she never spoke a word, just folding her arms tightly across her chest with her hands tucked in. I had no idea then that her silence was covering the suffering she endured as the acid that splashed on her left hand continued to eat into her flesh unchecked. Mr. Holmes didn't join us, staying behind as he apparently had other business elsewhere that night, but he must have had time to send a wire, because one of Porky's men met us at Waterloo and took Kitty in charge, whisking her into a waiting carriage. She looked back at me once, her face expressionless, as she was led away. I wouldn't see her for days.

Not long after, there was a trial, but the normally strict punishment for throwing acid was tossed out. Porky told me that it was because of what had been found in the diary, which Mr. Holmes had retrieved from the Baron's bedroom while Dr. Watson distracted him in the adjacent study. Kitty's canny lawyer had threatened to introduce the diary into evidence, and no one wanted those contents revealed, for there were too many women of noble backgrounds whose awful histories with the Baron were recorded there.

No one had expected that Kitty would take the opportunity to exact her vengeance upon the man, but after what I'd heard in the train ride that night when we went down to Kingston, I couldn't blame her. If I'd known beforehand just what the poor girl had been through, I would have likely brought my own bottle of acid to also punish the wicked man who had caused so much pain.

In the weeks that followed, while I'd worked so hard to insinuate myself into Kitty's life, I pondered just how toughened she had become. Her past experiences had tempered her into something much stronger than she might have ever been otherwise. Some would say she was *damaged*, but I saw her as *improved.*

Cora Wishum seemed to sense that too, for it was to Kitty that she'd come for help.

It was a typical seamy story, and I watched as it roused Kitty's interest. I would learn that she had a great sympathy for those women who have been mistreated, and a great anger against those who took advantage of women who were too weak to defend themselves.

As Cora tentatively told her story, Kitty sat up with a growing light in her eyes – for the first time in weeks – asking questions and drawing out more and more details from the girl. In hindsight, it was as if I was seeing the initial flames that would grow into a great fire.

Cora's visit ended with Kitty's surprising promise to look into the matter, and then she settled back as she had been before, twisting her acid-burned fingers – but this time with a far-away look in her eyes as she considered what to do.

Within a day, she'd sent messages for a few other women that she knew, asking them to visit her Marchmont Street rooms. They all looked at me with amused interest as they arrived and I let them in. At first they were only names to me, but I've since come to know them better. Hilda Bane, tall, angular, and sarcastic, acquitted from poisoning her husband after a number of his mutilated mistresses were allowed to testify in court. Tilly Fanshaw – silly, bubbly, and blonde – someone who would never be taken seriously, which is vital to her self-appointed task of coldly serving as an East End Robin Hood, taking money from rich – at their insistence – and then giving it to the poor. Mary Sarah Vaughn – as small as Kitty, but dark and turned inward. She had been a nun once, I'm told, but she abandoned her vows when her disgust overwhelmed her at how the organized church cared for itself before the poor. She's made a specialty of moving in the shadows in order to effect the changes she desires – obtaining a job at a business with unjust practices to get a look at their records, for instance, before altering them to the company's detriment, or perhaps revealing them publicly (and anonymously) to the same end.

I was allowed to stay and observe, noting with interest how all of these other "Soiled Doves", as Kitty called them, listened with interest when she explained what Cora Wishum and the other girls in her house were facing.

It was the start of something unique.

Kitty related the basic facts – how Cora and several other girls worked in the Campbell household. Mr. Campbell was a banker, and his wife was a tyrant – demanding and abusive. This in itself was not unusual, but Mrs. Campbell kept order by way of constant threats to ruin the servants' reputations should they try to leave her employment – as she apparently believed that now they were bought and trained, and that they were hers to abuse forever. That was not atypical in some London households – but their only son, the very-spoiled Alec Campbell, had begun to abuse the girls in a far different and amoral manner, as if it was his right as the only child of the Lord of the Manor to do so. And then the father had started hinting that he had the same inclinations.

Cora Wishum, under Kitty's pointed questioning, had revealed more than she'd ever planned – explicit things. It was nothing new to me, growing up as I had, and Kitty displayed no discomfort upon hearing it, but Cora had glanced at me as all was revealed, initially hesitant and shameful, but eventually telling all.

And it was clear that Alec Campbell – indeed, all the Campbells – needed to be punished.

And so Kitty assembled her team.

Over the next week or so, Kitty obtained more information, finding a way to talk with the other girls who worked in the Campbell house, gaining their confidence and learning all that she could – not only about how the house operated, but also the secrets that the Campbells didn't want known. Servants see everything, but sometimes they need a champion like Kitty to know how to best use that information. It was no surprise that several of the girls who had been in the house much longer than Cora had also been intimidated and abused in inappropriate ways.

Kitty decided that it was time to proceed.

Tilly found where Alec Campbell spent his time and created ways to intersect with his path, attracting his attention. Hilda spoke with a number of people who had dealings with the Campbell parents, asking questions in such a leading way that they began to whisper to one another, asking their own questions about the Campbells so that a distrust of the family grew from a small seed into a tree within days. And Mary Sarah used her contacts to reveal the Campbells' unearthed secrets in places where even total strangers would also know all about them – thus providing answers to those questions first prompted by Hilda.

After a couple of weeks, when the whisperings about the Campbells had reached a fever pitch – in their neighborhood, at Mr. Campbell's place of employment, and in the locations where they socialized – Kitty wanted to explain to them exactly *why* their downfall had occurred. I was against it – "Just let them continue their collapse," I'd said – but she needed for them to *know* what had happened. And so she arranged an appointment at the Campbell's Cavendish Square home – with just the two of us.

It was ugly – there is no other way to describe it. Mr. Campbell denied his part, and his wife glared at him, but it was obvious that she really knew the truth already. Alec Campbell rose and threatened violence upon Kitty, but I put him upon the floor in a way that rattled the windows and jarred the lamps and he didn't try it again. At one point, the shrewish wife tried to buy us, as if the genie could be put back in the bottle with Kitty's say-so, but that didn't interest Kitty. She led us out of the house – me, and the girls who no longer worked there, as new jobs had been found for them without need of any reference from the now-soiled Campbell family.

And then Kitty settled back into her malaise in the Marchmont Street rooms, her work complete, and I feared that once again she was sliding into a dark hole. But Mary Sarah heard about a woman who had been beaten by her husband, and we had a new task – and Kitty reawakened once again with grim enthusiasm.

It went on that way for several months, moving from success to success. Word spread of Kitty and her *Soiled Doves*, ready to step in and seek justice, sometimes brutal, for those women who were otherwise unprotected in the world, trapped in circumstances where there was seemingly no escape. One after another, the women beat a path to Kitty's door, where I willingly did my part.

I didn't do anything more for Mr. Holmes after that. Everything that he'd taught me was now useful for what Kitty needed. She and I became closer, but still there was a distance – for I loved her, while she still urged that I go find a "nice girl". But when I stayed, she seemed fine with that, and I believe that she didn't really wish for me to go.

1902 rolled into the next year, and things only became more and more interesting. There was the affair of the mistreated mop-woman at the British Museum. And the sad matter of the Farringdon clerk – that one was in the newspaper when the lady's employer was killed by his business partner to cover up their sins, and she was framed. She was rescued from a nasty set of circumstances. Not all of Kitty's cases were successes, of course. In one instance, a middle-aged wife named Mrs. Fain, though rescued from her abusive spouse, was so tragically unsettled afterwards that she abandoned her lonely home for the streets, taking up a spot as a beggar on the steps of St. Paul's, selling little two-pence bags of seed and crumbs to passers-by with her sing-song chant to "Feed the Birds . . . ." Kitty could never pass by and see her there without a feeling of sadness – one of her cases gone wrong.

But there were more than enough other successes to make up for it, and she quickly gained a reputation, whispered from one to another by those who needed her, for being London's first *Consulting Avenger.*

And all went well until she and the other Soiled Doves took on Justin Marley.

With the information she'd learned from Mrs. Smith, Kitty assembled the women that she trusted, and they began to dig deeper into Marley's affairs. In most ways, he wasn't very much different than a lot of other men of his station. The younger brother of a lord, he had too much money and too much time, and not too much in the way of decency. He gambled and traveled and misbehaved. His brother insisted that he show a certain amount of responsibility, so he'd found his way into a few business opportunities – one of which was partnering with Gerald Jones. According to Mrs. Smith, Gerald – who worked as a bookkeeper for several small businesses who couldn't afford one of their own full-time – had appreciated Marley's unexpected interest and financial support, and willingness to send new clients his way. But then something had quickly changed, and Gerald would only refer to his partner with scorn and anger. And yet, his sister stated, something prevented him from severing ties with the man.

Once everyone was ready to report, there wasn't much mystery left.

Hilda told us what Gerald's older clients had reported. "He seemed to have less and less time for what work they sent him, but he was spending more money. He kept apologizing when he'd put them off, or when he was slow getting back with them, as if he didn't want to be doing whatever it was that was keeping him busy."

"No question what that was," added Mary Sarah. "The police didn't tell his sister, but they were getting ready to arrest Gerald. He'd been stealing from one of his smaller clients – altering the books. They noticed and had a separate accounting of the records, and they could see what Gerald was doing. If he hadn't died on Tuesday, he would have been arrested on Wednesday."

Tilly had the boldest task of all – ingratiating herself with Justin Marley. And when he was drunk, he liked to talk. "Justin Marley killed Gerald," she said matter-of-factly. "He admitted it to me when his guard was down and his belly was full of whisky. He'd bought into Gerald's business so that Gerald could alter the books for several large warehouse owners – all of them almost certainly smugglers. When Marley and his friends found out that Gerald was about to be arrested for small-time embezzlement, they were afraid that he would reveal their crimes to the police, trading his cooperation for a lighter sentence. Marley visited Gerald that afternoon, poisoned his drink, and locked the door on his way out with a skeleton key. He was too stupid to leave the strychnine bottle to make it seem like a suicide."

Knowing that, it was time to ruin Justin Marley and, using her tried-and-true methods that had worked for the past year, Kitty began spreading the word about the real circumstances of Gerald Jones's death, trusting that Marley would soon be arrested once all was commonly known.

But she hadn't counted on the reach and strength of Marley's influence. He, the brother of a lord, had his own resources, and the arrest didn't occur. And it didn't take him very long to learn who was working against him.

He determined that he would remove the threat.

I like to think that, despite my young age, not much will surprise me. But when I opened Kitty's door to find Justin Marley glowering at me, filling the hallway, I may have taken a small step back.

"Where is she?" he growled, and then he pushed past me to where Kitty was reclining near the window.

He was a huge man, half-a-foot over six feet and twenty stone at least, and all of it muscle. He was one of those who are born that way, some throwback to his laboring ancestors. He had never worked on his own to achieve his natural strength. He was born to it, and he threw it around as if he were a gorilla. His hair was dark and thick and grew very low upon his forehead. Dark hair matted the back of his hands as well. He had no beard or mustache, but his rusty-looking facial features were stained with beard shadow, and I suspected that he had to shave more than once a day to try and look less like an ape. One wondered why someone of his sort didn't just give in and grow a wild black beard to save the time. But we're all funny animals, and it never pays to ponder how a person sees themselves, and how it can motivate their behaviour.

Kitty's only movement was to turn her eyes in the man's direction shift her arm. "You won't need that gun," Marley snapped, somehow spotting the small pistol that she always kept with her, resting in one of her pockets. "Or do you have a bottle of acid in the other pocket? That's your way, you poisonous shrew."

"Mr. Marley," Kitty drawled, looking him up and down. "You have less intelligence than I was led to expect," she said, seemingly unperturbed at his intrusion. "Ain't that right?" Meanwhile, I had slipped to one side and opened a side-table drawer, retrieving the old gun that Porky gave me last year.

Marley noticed. "You won't need that," he growled. "She won't die right now." He took a step closer to Kitty. "You crossed my path, again and again, over the last couple of weeks. Did you think I wouldn't find out that it was you? Or that your foolish efforts would amount to anything? Do you know who I am? And who I keep in my pocket?"

"What do you suggest?" asked Kitty.

"Drop it. You hope to see me ruined. It will never happen. There are tides rising against you that you don't even sense. It's probably already too late for you to save yourself, but I thought to warn you."

"If you were that confident," countered Kitty, "then you wouldn't have come here. Now get out. I know where to find you when it's time to crush you."

With a growl, I thought then Marley would charge her. His fingers were already curled, as if ready to bury themselves in her throat. But he froze, released his breath, and visibly relaxed when I clapped the old revolver to his head.

Then he raised his hands in surrender. "I'm leaving. But you're finished, Kitty Winter."

"The same old song, ain't it?" she murmured wearily, closing her eyes. But Marley didn't hear her, for he had already departed.

Afterwards, I tried to talk about what had happened. I wanted Kitty to be concerned, to match my urgency, but she seemed indifferent. Finally, I sent word to Porky to send someone to watch my love while I went on an errand.

To Baker Street.

I was doing something that hadn't crossed my mind before, in all the months that I'd been with Kitty. I was seeking help from someone outside our little group. Before, it seemed unnecessary, for we had all been quite sufficient, successful in whatever we set out to accomplish. And as I crossed London with hurrying footsteps, I realized that I was just a bit ashamed to visit Mr. Holmes, knowing that Kitty's methods hadn't always quite been "fair play". (I knew that Mr. Holmes didn't always play fair either, but mostly he worked within the law.)

I considered my position as I crossed from Bloomsbury into Marylebone. Something about Justin Marley just felt more dangerous than those men we'd broken before. They had all seemed thin and vague against Kitty's strength and certainty. When she turned her attention on them, they'd wriggled and scrambled like half-stepped-on bugs, stuck to the ground in their own juices, their legs pushing and pushing without effect, unable to escape the next footstep that would finish them. But despite Kitty's efforts, Marley had enough influence to avoid arrest. This time, there were forces at Marley's control that seemed to reach beyond what Kitty could accomplish.

I'm not sure what I hoped for, going to see my old mentor, but I was dismayed to enter Mr. Holmes's sitting room and discover absolute chaos.

Boxes were piled everywhere. Bookshelves were emptied, and the table in the chemical corner stood bare. The familiar furniture was still in its place, but clearly Mr. Holmes was preparing to depart.

"He's retiring," said Dr. Watson from his old chair, at the left side of the fireplace. Meanwhile, I could hear Mr. Holmes moving around in his bedroom, speaking to himself.

"Retiring?" I asked when I found my voice. It didn't seem possible. I knew that he wasn't yet fifty years old. I also knew how much he loved his work, and that doing nothing had always seemed to sicken him."

"He's relocating to Sussex," continued the doctor. "It's a combination of things . . . ." [2]

"Sussex?" I asked, dumbfounded. "But he always says that he hates to be away from London – "

At that moment, Mr. Holmes leaned out. "Ah, Wiggins. It's been too long. Has Justin Marley been by to threaten Miss Winter?"

My jaw was slack and agape. It seemed I'd never learn not to be impressed by what Mr. Holmes knew, and what he could figure out.

"As you see," he went on, waving his arm, "I'm rather distracted right now, but I'll take time to put a few words in a few ears before I depart."

Then he turned and went back into the bedroom, leaving me to nod at Dr. Watson.

Feeling as if I'd accomplished something, though I didn't know what, I left and made my way back to Marchmont Street – opening the door to find Hilda and Tilly and Mary Sarah, along with Porky and Beakins. It was a Council of War, and I hoped that I hadn't missed the important parts.

"Been to Mr. Holmes, ain't you?" asked Kitty. She didn't wait for me to acknowledge it. "No matter. We'll handle this one on our own." She turned to Tilly. "I suppose he knows by now that you were working against him."

"No doubt," she agreed, tossing her blonde hair. "He'll be kicking himself for talking too much."

"Not likely," said Hilda. "He's too sure that he can't be touched."

"That can be fixed," said Mary Sarah, and Kitty nodded.

"Exactly. He's protected two ways – by the brother, and by the criminals he works with."

"Then how do we cut him loose?" asked Porky.

"This way," said Kitty. And then she explained.

It was only a few days before Lord Marley distanced himself from his younger brother, Justin. At least, that was the story which came from the Lord's servants – the Lord had kicked the younger brother out, and there was nothing shielding him any longer. The servants all gossiped about loud arguments between the two siblings, wherein the older raged at the younger concerning the damage being done to the family reputation, and how any protection that the family name had previously given to Justin Marley was being removed, leading to certain prosecution by the authorities. "Better to lance this boil now before it gets worse," Lord Marley was reported to have told Justin Marley before the latter stormed out of the mansion.

Of course, none of that was true. There were no arguments, and Lord Marley, always distracted from life by hunting and riding, was completely unaware of and indifferent to what was going on in London while he was away in Scotland. Certain servants had only repeated the fabricated stories of the brothers' fights, per Kitty's instructions. In any case, the story spread like wildfire through the London servant classes, and up and down from it as well to the other social levels. Everyone loves an interesting story, especially when it involves a man's downfall. Within days, word came that Marley had lost whatever charm was warding him, and that if the police didn't take him first, his partners would certainly eliminate him. That started an avalanche on Marley that couldn't be stopped.

Through Kitty's network of informers, we knew when Marley surfaced, and we were in a closed carriage outside The Hawk and Tortoise in Holborn when Marley's luck ran out. It was the police who found him first, dragging him outside, and Kitty made sure to lean forward and show herself through the carriage window as Marley was being locked in the back of the Maria. He saw her and tried to break free and run toward us, and he was pulled down by six policeman as he screamed that he would kill her. But it was all for nothing. His partners were afraid he would talk. He was shivved in his cell before the next sunrise.

I was never sure whether it was Kitty's efforts that destroyed him, or something that Mr. Holmes did on his way out of town, or a combination of both. In either case, I was satisfied. A bad piece was removed from the board – one that had scared me like none that we'd encountered before. Justin Marley's position in society had given him protection of the likes we hadn't encountered. I had to wonder what others like him were out there in our path.

Kitty and I were arguing about it a few mornings later. The early October weather had turned cooler, and the windows were closed.

"How long do you think you can get away with this?" I was asking her, exasperated. "Going after these evil men? You're going to bite off something too big!"

"And if I stop?" she said, her tone cross. She squeezed the fingers of her left hand, which happens more when she's agitated. "What do I do then? Go back to the East End and wait tables in The White Hart or The Ten Bells? Something worse? I've had a taste of this now, Wiggins – helping women who can't help themselves. And if I ain't going to do it, then who will?"

I started to reply that maybe it wasn't just the helping she was holding onto. Maybe it was the fact that she liked playing God, and what happened if one of these times she got the wrong version of someone's story and was manipulated into directing her skills toward ruining someone who didn't deserve it. But before I could get it out, there was a knock at the door.

Reluctant to turn loose of the argument, I nevertheless opened the door to reveal a small and mousy woman, in her forties and poorly dressed. She introduced herself as Mrs. Willis, adding, "I need your help."

I showed her to a chair, and Kitty straightened up. "I went to see Mr. Holmes," said Mrs. Willis. "Just before he left town, and he sent me your way. He said the kind of help I need is just your specialty."

Kitty looked at me and smiled with her eyes. Even though she didn't say it aloud, I could hear her anyway. "You see, Wiggins? You see? Even Mr. Holmes knows it. I'm right, ain't I?"

And she was, of course. She almost always is. Except for not wanting me to love her. She still fights me on that. But she knows that I do, and someday that will make a difference.

NOTES

The Adventures of Kitty Winter

As related in the foreword to *Sherlock Holmes and The Eye of Heka*, I was fortunate to encounter one of Dr. Watson's distant descendants while my deerstalker and I were in Queen Anne Street during my second Holmes Pilgrimage to London in 2015. This person still held the lease for Watson's old house there and, seeing my obvious interest in the lives of Holmes and Watson, made available to me a massive amount of Watson's writings. Inexplicably tucked into these papers was this narrative, penned by Wiggins, along with a number of others relating the adventures of Kitty Winter and her Soiled Doves. (Wiggins didn't provide a title to this narrative, and I chose "Soiled Doves" for obvious reasons.)

These tales aren't exactly detective stories – there isn't a lot of crime-solving or brilliant interpretation of clues. Rather, Wiggins' somewhat meandering notes record how abusive men were taken down by Kitty and Company. Along the way, one sees glimpses of Wiggins and Kitty's evolving relationship.

They're fascinating to read, and hopefully one day, when I have more time, I can break away from releasing more of Watson's writings about Sherlock Holmes and instead prepare a few other reports for publication of what Kitty Winter and Wiggins and the rest of her Agency were able to accomplish during the early decades of the Twentieth Century.

1. For more about how the *first* Wiggins became associated with Holmes, and how his mother was rescued by Holmes from a charge of murder, see "The Gower Street Murder" in *Sherlock Holmes: Tangled Skeins*, and also in *The Collected Papers of Sherlock Holmes – Volume II: Records*
2. The "combination of things" that led to Holmes's unexpected "retirement" in early October 1903 included the death of Irene Adler in a railway accident on October 3rd, and also Holmes finally relenting to increasing pressure from his brother Mycroft to devote much more of his time toward preparing for the inevitable war with Germany. Both Sherlock and Mycroft Holmes had seen this coming for a long time, and they, along with Watson, worked tirelessly to prevent it, or if that wasn't possible, at least to delay it until England was on a much firmer footing. By giving the impression that he was retiring and leaving London for a reclusive life as an eccentric apiarist, Holmes was actually freed to move in the shadows – spending time in Sussex, but also coming back to London occasionally, ostensibly for a more typical investigation – or disappearing entirely for great periods of time while carrying out one of Mycroft's complex and urgent tasks.

The Uncle's Cryptic Clues

"I expected your . . . office . . . to be a bit more . . . impressive." The young man's tongue darted out to lick his lips, and he tried to explain further. "I mean – this. It' so . . . unassuming." He cleared his throat and started to stand. "I apologize. I must have received the wrong information. I meant to visit your office, and obviously this is your residence."

Our visitor, J. Danforth Hutton, looked to the left and right around our sitting room. It didn't take him very long, as the space was only about twenty feet wide, and fifteen or so deep. It was no different than any similar room that could be found in that type of house all over London. Known as a "two up, two down", the first floor consisted of a sitting room with two tall windows overlooking the street in front, and the back half was the stairwell and a bedroom – in this case, Sherlock Holmes's room. My own bedroom was one flight up.

I recalled when I first saw this sitting room, on the second day of January 1881. I was not long returned from the war in Afghanistan, and grateful for the opportunity to have found affordable and comfortable rooms. I'd had no thoughts then that it wasn't impressive enough for, despite its modest size, it was soon a veritable museum of curiosities, with a chemistry table in one corner, shelves groaning with books – both professionally published volumes and hand-assembled scrapbooks – and an overwhelming number of fascinating criminal relics, such as a small porcelain leprechaun which had been coated with a sticky poison, and a polished human femur seamlessly joined to a polished mahogany pole to form a most unique walking stick, and an unassuming little collection of teacups, gathering dust on the back of a table. Each – as I was told – had been used in different successful cases of murderous poisoning. The fact that Holmes now possessed them testified that none of the murderers had escaped justice. Some men collect butterflies – Holmes sought criminals. "A pin, a cork, and a card, and we add him to the Baker Street collection!" he would sometimes say with a laugh.

Now, thanking our landlady, Mrs. Hudson, for fresh coffee and motioning to our uncertain visitor that he should sit back down, Holmes said, "Our little agency has not yet seen the necessity to take separate offices." There was a twinkle in his eyes as he leaned back in his chair and observed young Hutton, seated between us in a basket chair across from a cold fireplace, the morning light from the window behind Holmes illuminating the lad's smooth and care-free features. "Since I first began offering my services here, this location has been more-than-sufficient.

Having an office staff, and maintaining a waiting room and consulting rooms and all the trappings of such a business like some sort of Harley Street specialist, would only be an unnecessary distraction. Much of what is discussed here is of a confidential nature."

The young man simply blinked, as if considering what he'd been told before committing to his next reaction or response. Meanwhile, it gave me a chance to more closely observe the prospective client.

Over the years, since first accepting the offer to share lodgings with Holmes in Baker Street, and then beginning to take note of his methods, I had attempted to improve my own observational skills. And there were several occasions where I had noticed this or that odd fact that saved my friend and me from some unwanted grief. The unmistakable odor of an unexploded bomb. A misshapen coat that concealed an undeclared weapon. A sudden flight of birds from an otherwise peaceful-looking copse that signified a likely ambush. But even after all those years, I understood that I still had far to go.

I knew that Holmes had seen all that I had, and certainly more. I was satisfied to note that Hutton looked to be in his early twenties, sturdy and possessing solid rude health, and right handed. He was somewhat careless with his moderately expensive attire, his necktie askew and a few picks and loose threads upon his coat, but that could be attributed to his wide-eyed callowness. His handshake had revealed that he had no acquaintance with manual labor, while he did have the long-term ink-stains of a man who wrote extensive pieces by hand.

"I did recognize this as a residential-type structure when I arrived," Hutton explained, "but I supposed that the building was just the modest front entrance for something larger – that it opened to a building on the adjacent street, and I would be led through to something a bit . . . umm, nicer to the rear." He smiled apologetically. "Oh dear. Have I put my foot in my mouth?"

"Just a little," smiled Holmes. "Your heart was in the right place, I think. How old are you?"

"Twenty-one." Hutton took a deep breath. "Just the other day. That's why I'm here."

"Because of your birthday?" asked Holmes with mock surprise.

"Because of my inheritance," Hutton replied. "Although that isn't related to my birthday, which just happened to be the other day. Oh, I'm confusing things. Perhaps I should explain."

Holmes gestured for him to continue. "Please do."

Hutton took a sip of the coffee, spent part of a moment to order his thoughts, and then began.

"I'm an orphan," he stated. "My parents died when I was ten – a railway accident near Basingstoke. They were returning from the West Country – just the two of them. Father was a civil engineer, and did work for the Royal Navy, and it was something of a working holiday for the two of them. It was the only time that I recall that they went away together without taking me along. I had remained in London. I've always wondered if Father had a premonition to leave me behind . . . ."

"You are an only child?" Holmes asked.

Hutton nodded and took another sip. "During my parents' trip, I stayed with my Uncle Jonah, my father's older brother. Actually, we – Father, Mother, and me – had all lived with him for several years before that, upon our return to London from the Continent.

"Uncle's house is at the top of Mayfair – No. 57 Green Street. It originally belonged to my grandparents, and when they died thirty years ago, they left it to Uncle Jonah – that is, Jonah Hutton – as he was the older son, along with the substantial part of their fortune – and it was substantial. It still is, I suppose, although I've never had much cause to consider it until recently. Having that to tide him over, Uncle never really had to work, and he settled into an idle life, pursuing his interests in writing and drawing. He was never very good, I suppose, but it helped him to while away his life – although I don't know if he was ever very happy. He never seemed so. He did manage to have a few of his novels published when he was younger, but they didn't create a ripple. Rather, he established a connection with some publisher-type who produced the physical books from my uncle's works in exchange for an infusion of Uncle's cash into the publisher's business. But there was nothing dishonest about it, and it gave my uncle some joy. He was always proud to point to the little bookshelf where his books were kept in a place of honor, and he felt that it gave him some footing to claim that he was an *Author* – with a capital *A* – whenever he would attend local literary society meetings."

On some occasions, Holmes displayed impatience when a client didn't drive straight for the point, but on that summer morning, with no urgent business on hand and memories of the previous evening's Wagner concert still echoing in his mind, he seemed inclined toward tolerance.

"My father," continued Hutton, "although just as loved by his parents, was left a substantially smaller inheritance, and he had to find a career – which suited him, because he was smart and hard-working, and would have never settled for sitting around and doing nearly nothing like my uncle. In fact, Father always said it was his parents' greatest gift to him not to have burdened him with the money that sustained my uncle's idleness.

"When I was very small, the three of us – Father, Mother, and me – traveled all over in relation to Father's job. Up and down the British Isles, and to America, and on the Continent. When in London we would stay with Uncle Jonah, and after our permanent return here, we moved in with him. All was well, never a cross word, and after my parents were killed, I remained with my uncle – it simply seemed to be understood – and he finished raising me to adulthood.

"I attended university, obtaining a place at Camford in my father's old school, but I'm sad to say that maybe there is too much of my uncle in me, because I couldn't settle down to my studies, having more interest in pursuing my own literary and artistic interests than the rigid coursework required to follow in my father's more-technical footsteps. After a couple of years, I left school and, a year ago, moved back here, to London. I had an allowance from Uncle, and found my own rooms in Bloomsbury where I could write. I've had a few things published to good reviews – just minor pieces, you understand – but I have the sense that I can make my name with a lot of hard work and patience.

"Over the last year, I tried to visit Uncle as much as I could, but you know how it is – the days fill up, and then the weeks, and there's always next week with the best of intentions. All the while, while I didn't know it, he was becoming more and more ill, and just a week ago, last Wednesday, a couple of days before my birthday, he died."

"Your birthday was on Friday?"

Hutton nodded. "I was able to see him, at the very last – the day before, on Tuesday. Word was sent to me by the old couple who served as his butler and housekeeper, and I went 'round to the house. Uncle was weak, but glad that I was there. He could barely talk, but he was very serious – he knew he was running out of time. He explained that I was his heir – this wasn't a surprise – but then he said that he wasn't going to make it easy for me. He didn't offer a better explanation than that, and I didn't press him. I don't know if he meant to tell me more or not, but he fell asleep then, and that was all I had from him before he passed. Then, two days ago, on Monday, I met with Uncle's attorney, a chap named Harrell who has an office in Lincoln's Inn Fields. He gave me a . . . well, a clue is the best way to describe it. I have a week to solve the riddle – starting from the time Harrell put it into my hand – returning to his office by noon next Monday, delivering something or other to him, some object, or the house in Mayfair will be sold and the entire estate will go to charity."

Hutton took another sip of coffee, now surely gone cold. "I'd never met this Harrell fellow before last Monday – never heard of him, actually – but he told me that he'd been Uncle's lawyer for years. He told me in confidence that, as Uncle's attorney, he'd had an obligation to draw up the conditions as requested by my uncle, to arrange the test, and to do so in the best and tightest legal manner possible, and for that he apologized. He would have to strictly follow the conditions, and he also said that he had no idea what the riddle meant – that hadn't been explained to him – but he would know the object when it was placed into his hand, fulfilling Uncle's requirement."

"I went away with my head spinning, returning not to my own rooms, but instead to the empty old house."

"Empty, you say?" interrupted Holmes. "What of the staff?"

"Oh, they had already gone. It was just the old couple, Mr. and Mrs. Linkous. They were there for years, and I'd known them all my life. But they each received a legacy from Uncle and had wanted to move on immediately – or so Lawyer Harrell told me."

Holmes nodded and waved for Hutton to continue.

"I wandered through the house for hours that first day, trying unsuccessfully to get a line on what my uncle was thinking. Eventually, I went back to my own apartment in Bloomsbury, but I couldn't sleep. That was on Monday, and I spent all of yesterday – Tuesday – in a similar fog, roaming around the empty house. Another day wasted. It was only early this morning, when noticing the newspaper and the story about how you were responsible for clearing up the murder of a salesman in a house down in Sotheby, that I realized you might be able to help me. Some say that you like odd puzzles like this."

"Some do, I expect," replied Holmes. "Might I see this odd clue to which you referred?"

"What? Oh, certainly." And he fished in his waistcoat pocket, pulling out a much-folded and abused sheet of paper.

Holmes took it, looked at both front and back, holding it to the light, and then under careful examination by way of his magnifying glass.

"That's a copy Harrell made for me – that's his handwriting and paper. It was taken directly from Uncle's will that he signed on his deathbed a few days before . . . before he was gone. No secret messages or invisible ink there – just that mysterious jumble of words."

Holmes, with a gleam of interest in his eyes, passed the sheet across to me. I confess that I was dumbfounded.

hftpvcnlqodxehdbfoqlokqoveyxnIrfeqwogocfnzgkvbt

"Do you have any idea what it means?" I asked, handing it back to Holmes.

Hutton shook his head. "No, but whatever it says is the key to my inheritance."

Holmes was intently staring at the string of letters, his heavy dark brows pulled into a concentrated frown. Finally he shook his head and looked up. "Was your uncle fond of puzzles and riddles – and had he ever made use of codes before?"

"Not to my knowledge. He did read a great deal, however, and many things fascinated him."

Holmes took a deep breath. "I've made a study of cryptology and, at first glance, this doesn't resemble any complex code that I recognize. It certainly isn't a simple substitution – *Z* for *A*, *Y* for *B*, and so on. It may be based upon a specific word or phrase. Was there some word that your uncle used regularly – something that he'd know that *you* would know?"

Hutton frowned, his gaze drifting into concentrated reminiscence. Then he shook his head. "Nothing special. Sometimes he said 'Eureka!' or 'Brilliant!', but not to the point that I'd specifically associate those words with him.

Holmes nodded and returned his gaze to the sheet. After a moment he gave up. "No, those two words don't generate any sort of easy solution. I didn't expect that they would. May I keep this sheet?" When Hutton nodded, Holmes straightened in his chair. "I believe that Dr. Watson and I will need to speak to the attorney – Harrell. If you would leave his address, as well as your own information – ? Thank you. We shall be in touch – hopefully with good news."

The young man seemed surprised that we were suddenly at the end of the interview. I suspect that he'd pictured spending a greater amount of time at 221b, answering more of Holmes's questions and trying to guess what word or phrase would unlock the secret message. But such was not Holmes's way and, within a few moments, J. Danforth Hutton had departed. I watched from the window as he turned southwest, likely back toward Bloomsbury, and then looked back to Holmes, who had arisen and was preparing to depart.

"Will you join me?" he asked. "This may be of interest for a few hours."

I nodded. "Certainly of more interest than that fish-monger's problem last week," I said with a smile. "He almost seemed angry that you solved it so quickly – as if he wasn't getting his money's worth, in spite of the positive resolution to the affair that you provided."

"Mr. Waddell is an old acquaintance," Holmes explained, taking his fore-and-aft cap from the rack, "and I would have expected nothing else from him. Perhaps if you knew how I first met him, and the desperate hide-and-seek game that I had to play between here and Stoke-on-Trent in order to find his thieving brother and unfaithful wife, you'd understand why he takes that attitude." And he then told me the story during the cab ride, finishing just as we pulled to a stop outside Harrell's legal chambers.

We stepped to the pavement in front of a shabby brick building on the north side of Lincoln's Inn Fields. On the tenant plaque, I noted that all but one of the metal plates were rather new, indicating that these lawyers had recently moved in. Only one name, T. Claiborne Harrell's, indicating residence on the top floor, showed signs of long occupancy. The other newer plates were polished with pride. Harrell's was not so, being badly weathered over a period that was certainly decades instead of merely years.

We climbed the narrowing flights to the top floor, and the building became warmer with each upward level. Although just mid-morning, the early summer sun was already warming the old red bricks.

A knock upon the door prompted a distant and gruff, "Come in!" We entered a windowless anteroom, dark and illuminated only by the light of an office beyond. Although my eyes hadn't adjusted, and were somewhat affected by the bright office doorway opposite where we stood, I could see that the front room had a desk, piled high with files, and a number of cabinets, some with the drawers pulled open and emptied.

There was a scrambling sound from the opposite doorway, and a lean tall figure appeared, silhouetted against the light. "Yes? It will be that desk and the cabinets, and then the furniture in the inner office as well."

We stepped forward and, seeing us more clearly, the figure retreated – not to lead us through, but more out of nervousness. I could understand his viewpoint. From where he stood, we were two shadows advancing slowly toward him. But we continued to move steadily into the office, where all of us could now look upon one another.

We faced an exceedingly thin man in his early sixties. Like so many of his physical type, he leaned forward like a construct of sticks and tensioned wires, his bony head perched on the end of a long sinewy neck, and dipped downward as if he were a carrion bird. His arms were folded and held up to his breastbone, where his long fingers were intertwined, not below his long pointed chin, as if he were about to pray over his next meal like some sinister minister. He was dressed well-enough in a nice wool suit of an older style, and it did something to moderate the overall effect he projected, though in spite of his clothing, I somehow seemed to see him in a musty Dickensian outfit, as if he were a younger Ebenezer Scrooge, still undergoing his full transition into a miser, and several decades before his Christmas encounter with a series of grim ghosts.

"Yes? Yes? What can I do for you? The office is closed – permanently. Are you here about the furniture?"

Holmes shook his head, introducing us. "I am Sherlock Holmes, a consulting detective, and this is my associate, Dr. John Watson. We have been retained to look into the matter of J. Danforth Hutton's curious inheritance."

The man blinked, markedly, and then once again, as he considered our presence. "Yes. Well. Indeed." Then he seemed to relax a bit, unloosening his fingers and waving a hand to one side and then the other.

"Many apologies, gentlemen," he said. "You catch me at an awkward moment. I'm in the middle of closing down my practice. I'm retiring, you see. Mr. Hutton's uncle, Jonah, was my very last client. He was a dear old friend, and I only remained in practice to finish up his final affairs. He left a generous bequest for me, you see, something of a recompense for helping him manage his accounts and such for so many years – since 1884, to be exact – all the way through to the bitter end, poor fellow. Now I'll be able to travel as I'd always hoped."

He peered at us. "I thought you were the furniture men, here to collect the desks, chairs, cabinets, and shelves."

"We won't take much of your time," said Holmes. He looked beyond Harrell toward the inner office. "May we have a seat? You can tell us about the odd clue left by Jonah Hutton for his nephew?"

Harrell didn't look too pleased, but he gestured us toward a pair of heavy wooden chairs, and then he went around his large desk and sat down, the only window in the office behind him leaving his face in shadow while we were well-lit. It was an old trick, and an effective one. In fact, Holmes had the same arrangement in our sitting room, with his back to one of the windows, while the client sat in a chair somewhat facing him, looking into the light. My chair in the sitting room was opposite Holmes, so I also faced the window. *Perhaps,* I thought, without much sincerity, *my own deductive abilities might be significantly heightened if I was able to fully see the clients too, instead of squinting.* Then I had to admit to myself, *Not very likely.*

"The clue," prompted Holmes. "When was it added to the will?"

"Not long before Jonah died. He called me late the week before, with new instructions – to revise the will, and leave a blank space in the middle where he could handwrite the clue. I told him that I wasn't sure it would be legal – adding a holographic segment to a typewritten document – but he insisted. I offered to type in the clue, but he insisted on writing it himself just before he signed the will."

"And you hurried to accommodate him, I take it? To complete the will, as his health was failing."

"I did. He telephoned me several times to make sure I was working on it – and he had his butler and housekeeper, Mr. and Mrs. Linkous, call me once or twice as well. They'd been with him for many years. He insisted that they be his witnesses. He also left them a sizeable bequest – a thousand pounds each."

"How large is the estate?"

Here the attorney became rather reticent for a moment, but I couldn't blame him. Finally he said, "Sizeable. Let us use that word to describe it."

"You knew Mr. Hutton a long time," said Holmes. "How would you describe him? Eccentric?"

Harrell rubbed his thin jaw. "That fits," he said. "He's always had his own ideas – and sometimes I would have to talk him away from the bad ones. I remember once during the Boer War, he heard something from Lord Carnarvon that convinced him of the need to invest in a bicycle factory, because he'd worked out to his own satisfaction that there would be a need for them in South Africa, and that quickly and cheaply produced and shipped bicycles would be a way to quickly make a financial killing."

"Possibly he recognized something that others did not," I said, and the lawyer frowned.

"It would have been a waste of his money," he responded gruffly. "And I had a professional responsibility to preserve his capital to the best of my ability."

"Can you give any further examples of his personality?" asked Holmes.

"Jonah Hutton was a pleasant-enough fellow when things went his way – but he often sulked and got down in the dumps when they didn't. He had a negativity about him that seeped through in whatever he did – in his amateur art and writing, and mostly in conversations and his dealings with other people. He could never simply be happy, or wish you 'Good morning'. It was always, 'Good morning – although it looks like rain is coming.' Or 'The veal was good last night – which was a surprise, since anything from that butcher is usually mostly inedible.' That sort of thing – always a dark lining to every cloud. Is that what you're looking for, Mr. Holmes?"

"Possibly. It's still early days."

"Not so early. I gave Danforth notice on Monday morning, and now it's already been – " He glanced at the wall clock. " – approximately forty-eight hours. He has just five days left."

Holmes crossed his legs. "Do you *want* Mr. Hutton to succeed?" he asked bluntly.

Harrell was silent for a long. Although his face was shadowed to us, I could see that Harrell's mouth was tightened in irritation – and the lines upon his face showed that to be his normal countenance. "I'm not sure that it was in the spirit of Jonah Hutton's last request that Danforth hire consultants."

"Indeed," replied Holmes. "And was there specific language in the will that prevented such an arrangement?"

"Well, no, but Jonah wanted the lad to think his own way through the problem – to use his intelligence and *earn* the inheritance." Harrell frowned at him. "I see what you're doing, you know – trying to find out how Jonah's mind worked, to break that code. Well, as I said, I'm not so sure that it's ethical for me to help you do so. As the deceased's legal representative, it was my duty to follow his wishes, and to make the legal instrument expressing them as tight and foolproof as possible."

"And yet," countered Holmes with a smile, "it sounds as if you neglected to include a specific requirement that Danforth Hutton solve the clue without any outside assistance."

Harrell didn't speak for a moment, and then he folded his fingers and placed his hand before him on his desk, as if willing himself to sit very still.

Holmes continued. "Do you not consider it an intelligent action when, finding that the task was beyond him, Mr. Hutton had sense enough to hire workmen who *could* complete the job successfully? It's no different than if he needed work on his pipes and hired a plumber instead of doing it himself."

"Well, yes, I suppose so. But still – "

"May we see the will?"

Harrell shrugged. "The document is already placed with the proper officials – filed on Monday just after I spoke with Danforth. I don't have it. Now – " He stood abruptly, as if he were some long-legged mantis suddenly unfolding in preparation for leaping away. " – as you can see, there is much to do here, and – "

At that moment, there was a knock on the outer door and, without comment, Harrell quickly left us, walking through to other office, a look of sudden relief upon his face. We heard the front door open, some muted conversation, and then a middle-aged fat man and two lanky workers followed Harrell back into the office.

"The furniture men are here," Harrell said to us. "Now, if you don't mind . . . ?" He was clearly glad that the interview was ending.

We stood and thanked him, and then walked out. I thought that I saw Holmes and the fat man exchange a subtle look, but then we were in the hall, the office door shut behind us, and I realized just how quickly our visit to the attorney had passed.

"Now, Watson," said Holmes when we'd descended the narrow stairs and stood in the sunny street, "I have several tedious visits to make. I can offer you the choice of joining me, or returning to Baker Street until I have something to report."

"If it's all the same to you," I replied, "I would just as soon accompany you. My schedule just now is singularly devoid of activity."

"A fine way of describing it," Holmes said. "Then, knowing that we might not have an opportunity later, I recommend that we find some nearby lunch. Do you still enjoy visiting The Ship? A solid old tavern, just around the corner, and I think it will suit us down to the ground."

And it did, having been a favorite of mine since my student days. Holmes led me west along the wide pavement, past a large furniture van inscribed with *Burger Furnishings*, and then north through the small passage that was Gate Street. There, just at the turning where an alley leads on north to High Holborn, was the little pub, still in operation since its long-ago opening. As we found a seat, Holmes and I discussed some of the history of the place: Built in the mid-1500's during the height of the Reformation, it had been a secret place of safety for beleaguered Catholics. More recently, it had been designated a Masonic lodge in the late 1700's. As we waited for our food, Holmes pointed out various signs and symbols indicating the Masonic connection. "They believe they are being subtle and mysterious," he said with a silent laugh, and then he recounted a little affair there during his Montague Street days when he'd accidentally exposed the affairs of a Government agent. "It took me the better part of a week to make things right."

Over our excellent beef-and-mushroom pies, and with tall glasses of cider, Holmes shared his thoughts. "It is – shall we say – *curious* that Harrell is retiring just now, but then again, it could be perfectly natural. After we eat, we'll stroll around to Somerset House and get a look at that will."

"And then – ? The house in Green Street."

"That too. But first I want to speak with Alexander Burger – the moving man that was in Harrell's office. He's an old acquaintance."

"I thought that you two seemed to recognize one another. What do you think he can tell you?"

"I'm not sure – probably nothing, but he seemed as if he were trying to convey something to me."

We settled up and then walked south half-a-mile or so, passing along the western edge of Lincoln's Inn Fields and then through a tangle of streets until we reached and crossed the Strand. Holmes walked with confidence into Somerset House, leading me promptly to the Probate Office. The old white-whiskered man behind the counter, introduced to me as Mr. Fairlop, greeted him fondly, and in a trice had the document in question placed before us.

I didn't pretend to know what I was looking for, but I did my best to be observant, nonetheless. Holmes *hmm*'d to himself several times, looking at the simple two-page will for quite a while, turning it and holding it up to the light. Then he pulled out the sheet with the clue that Hutton had given him that morning. After another moment, let me have a closer look at the will. "What do you see?" he asked.

I stated that all I saw for sure was that the curious clue, shakily handwritten in a wide spot left for it on the second sheet, accurately matched what had been copied letter-for-letter and given to young Hutton. "What else should I see?"

"Well, look at the part referencing our new acquaintance, Harrell."

I read it again. "He received a ten-thousand pound bequest. Possibly excessive, but he had been the man's lawyer for over twenty years – and one presumes that he was doing a good job to have held the position for so long."

"Look deeper."

"Well, there's the dead man's signature on the second page, and also two witnesses – Mr. and Mrs. Linkous. I suppose that's legal? A husband and wife, employees of the dead man, acting as witnesses?"

Holmes nodded. "Anything else?"

Then I saw what he meant – the conditions of solving the clue. "If Hutton doesn't solve the riddle within a week, all assets are turned over to charity – but no specific charities are defined, and the entire process of distribution is under Harrell's direction, with no oversight."

"Not necessarily illegal," elaborated Holmes, "but certainly there's opportunity for mischief. Harrell might establish an entity to make *himself* as the charity, and there would be no legal rejoinder. There's also no instrument defined to make Harrell account for where the money goes. Do you see anything else?"

I didn't, and said so. "Ah well," replied Holmes, "there are a couple of other items, but perhaps one needs to be a bit more seasoned to spot them – or jaded and suspicious." He raised his voice. "Did you see them, Mr. Fairlop?"

The old man, who had never wandered very far, replied promptly. "I did, lad. But the attorney of record certified the document, so it's on him, until someone complains. We just receive and preserve documents here. We don't initiate investigations. In the meantime, we'll guard that document for its legal purpose – or if it should someday become evidence."

Holmes nodded. "The latter, I think. And this attorney, Harrell – Have you ever seen anything shady from him before?"

"Never at all, ever. Never heard of him, actually. This is certainly the first time he's ever submitted a will." He lowered his voice conspiratorially. "I did verify that much, Doctor. I thought that there might someday be a question arise from this document – the irregularities, you know, and the sizable fortune attached to it."

I looked back at the two pages, but couldn't see what Holmes or Fairlop were referencing. It was true that the conditions were odd, and questionable that the dissemination of the assets was vague and left under the lawyer's control, but then again, the rooms around me, filled with countless similar legal documents going back centuries, probably had many with the same vague conditions, leaving much in the power of the originating lawyers with no oversight or threat of punishment if criminal mischief occurred. *What was I missing*?

Holmes refused to elaborate and, with thanks to the smiling old man, we went outside and found a cab to take us east, into Commercial Street in Whitechapel, where we soon entered the used furniture business of Mr. Alexander Burger.

Up close, I could see that the fat man hadn't achieved his stout frame from too much eating. Rather, he came by it naturally, for it was obvious he was the physical type that, if was lined up with any of his forebears, would match their solid and heavy low-slung frames. He greeted Holmes with cool respect, and shook my hand when we were introduced.

"You have something to tell me?" asked Holmes as we stood in the wide open shop area at the front of the building's ground floor. Around us, men, women, and couples moved silently like aimless fish in a bowl, swimming amongst the furniture, looking at price information posted on cards atop each piece before moving on. A couple of salesmen stood off to the side, patient but predatory expressions in their eyes, ready to assist or transact when the need arose.

"Sorry to imply so," said Burger, with a faint Germanic accent. I had noticed that the sign over the front of his store – *Burger Furnishings* – was aged though well cared for. Seeing that the place looked relatively successful made me think that Burger had done all right.

"When I saw you there," continued Burger, "I knew that there's no smoke without fire. I don't have any information for you, that I know of, but if you want to ask me questions, or perhaps search the furniture? It's just been unloaded in the back . . . ."

"No need for that," Holmes said, "But I will ask a few questions. When did you get the call about purchasing Harrell's furniture?"

"Let's see. Would've been last Wednesday – a week ago."

"The day Jonah Hutton died," I said. "That was fast."

"Wouldn't know about that," replied Burger. "But it's taken me this long to see about getting back there."

"Back there? To the lawyer's office? Today was your second visit?"

"That's right. I went around a week ago, the day he called, and told him what I'd pay for the furniture. It was awkward, as it seemed to me as if the office was shutting down most unexpected-like. There was a mousy little fellow in the outer office – a clerk – who could barely keep from shedding a tear. He mentioned several times about how long he'd worked there, and he'd just found out that morning that the office was closing. 'What am I to do?' he asked me, as if I could tell him, and telling me, 'I had no plans to retire just now. What shall I do?' I felt badly for him, but I had to work out the details with Harrell – what I would take, how much I'd pay, when I'd be by to pick it up.

"I took a couple of the boys with me this morning, and you saw – Harrell wasn't nearly ready. Papers stacked everywhere, files still in the cabinets, books on the shelves. He apologized after you left – said he'd let his clerk go late last week, when he should have kept him a few more days to help clean out the office." Burger turned over his big calloused hands. "That's all I know, Mr. Holmes. I gave him a fair price for the furniture – less what he already owed me for moving the old couple out of the house in Mayfair – and my lads emptied the desks and shelves and cabinets, right onto the floor, and made quick work of loading them up. We settled up and left. As I said, the furniture is back in the warehouse if you'd like to have a look."

"No need for that, Alexander," answered Holmes. "But what's this about moving an old couple from a house in Mayfair?"

Burger nodded. "That's right. I'd never heard of this lawyer, but he called up and said that he needed to take care of some business quickly, including helping an old couple move from a house in Mayfair, where they'd been servants for years, until their master recently died. One of his clients, he said. We went over there later that day. Both the old husband and wife were upset, but they seemed to understand that their master had died just that day – the undertaker was taking him out, even as we carried out the old couple's few belongings – and it was over and done with quick-like."

"Do you happen to have their address – where you took the old couple's belongings?"

Burger nodded. "I'll get it for you."

He went into a small windowed office along the back wall, and when I started to speak, Holmes held up a hand to hush me.

"Here it is," said Burger upon his return. "A little house in Lambeth – the old lady's sister lives there."

"Thank you. And one other thing: Do you recall the name of the lawyer's clerk?"

"Hmm . . . *Dunwoody*. That's it. Don't remember his first name, though."

"That should be enough. I appreciate the information. There are several nuggets there that I can use. Now, you are on the telephone, I believe? I saw the number painted on the side of your van . . . ."

Burger led him into the office, and Holmes was soon speaking with someone. Then he made two other quick telephone calls. In the meantime, I had a short conversation with Burger, who seemed to think the world of Holmes. In the years since I'd known him, I'd encountered many like that, all around London, all benefiting from some help or service from the Baker Street consulting detective.

Shortly thereafter, Holmes rejoined us, thanking Burger, and then we were back in Commercial Street, hailing a cab.

"I reached Danforth Hutton," Holmes explained. "We're meeting him at the house in Green Street to have a look, along with a few other people, if we're lucky. I feel as if the solution to this riddle can only be approached with an understanding of Jonah Hutton. He left the clue with the belief that his nephew would understand."

"I wonder if there's any actual fortune to find," I noted. "There seems to rising suspicion about Claiborne Harrell and his actions."

"Possibly, but we ought not convict the fellow quite yet. I'll admit that the situation contrived by the will has dubious aspects, and those two circumstances I mentioned related to the will document are certainly indicative, but it could still be a set of circumstances that, while questionable from one angle, becomes innocent when taking a different perspective by way of a single step to the left or right. No, let us set aside the lawyer for the present, and take a look at the riddle instead."

It was a good thing that we'd taken time to eat lunch, because the rest of our afternoon was given over to solving Jonah Hutton's curious puzzle. We reached No. 57 Green Street around the same time as Danforth Hutton. He led us to the front door and pulled out his key. As he did so, Holmes stated, "You mentioned this morning that the housekeeper and butler had already moved before you spent time searching the house."

"That's right. They each received a legacy from Uncle, and Mr. Harrell told me that they had chosen to leave immediately. It rather hurt my feelings, as I've known them since childhood, but I understood that they were upset, and I assumed that they would get in touch with me soon, when things had settled down."

"We've been told," Holmes explained, "that their move was rather sudden and upsetting – and instigated by Mr. Harrell on the day your uncle died."

"What? I don't understand. I thought – "

"You can ask them about it yourself, hopefully soon. I've made arrangements to have them brought here from their new lodgings in Lambeth – assuming that they can be easily found." Holmes paused, having one more question to ask.

"When you visited Mr. Harrell's office two days ago, did you find it rather topsy-turvy?"

Hutton nodded. "That's right. He explained that he was closing up shop – that Uncle had been his last client, and that he was now ready to travel."

Holmes nodded, having confirmed that fact.

No. 57 was a tidy place, five floors (counting the attic level), and a basement that could be reached through an areaway guarded by a spiked iron fence. The doorway was on the right of the narrow building, in an arched recess reached by a five shallow marble steps. The bottom three floors, along with the basement, had lovely bow windows, one atop the other, on the left side of the building and, altogether, the house presented a most appealing dwelling. But when we stepped inside, there was already the faintest hint of abandonment, even though the owner had only been dead a week, and his nephew had just been there the day before.

Holmes immediately moved into action, walking left and into the front room, something of a parlour, and pulling back the drapes from the bow window. Then he paused to look around, as if considering where to search first.

Hutton started to say something, but I held up a hand. "Best to let him approach it in his own way," I explained.

After watching Holmes examine that room, and then hearing him as he moved through the rest of the house, I was considering asking Hutton about a cup of tea when the doorbell rang. Opening it, I found a heavy-set man in his forties, standing there with an older couple, both of them clearly nervous.

As I shut the door, the older man touched a finger to his worn cloth cap. "Afternoon, sir. Wilfred Deaver, at your service, with a delivery for Mr. Holmes – this husband and wife here, direct from Lambeth."

I heard Holmes approach from behind. "Ah, Deaver. Very good. Mr. and Mrs. Linkous? Please come in. Mr. Danforth Hutton is here and – Ah, here he is. Mr. Hutton – please take care of your old friends, would you? Perhaps a cup of tea while we wait for Mr. Dunwoody? Excellent."

As Hutton shuffled the older couple inside, Holmes turned to the man on the stoop. "Thank you, Deaver. Please wait – there may be some more work for you."

"As you like, Mr. Holmes." And he turned, stepped down to the street, and walked toward a plumber's van with his name painted on the side.

Closing the door, Holmes said softly, "Deaver has done a few errands for me in the past, down Lambeth way. He seemed the best bet to quickly locate Mr. and Mrs. Linkous and bring them to us."

"Have you found anything useful?" I asked.

"Looking around the house, I begin to have a sense of the late Jonah Hutton," Holmes replied, "and I see some light. But before I set about solving the riddle, I want to hear from the other involved parties. Ah!" he added as the sound of an automobile was heard, drawing up in Green Street.

We reopened the door to see a worn Winton stopping just outside. A heavily built man wearing dark spectacles was stepping from the driver's seat. He was strong-looking and firmly in middle-age. He walked around and helped a man of similar age, but of starkly different and weaker appearance, out of the vehicle.

"Right this way, Mr. Dunwoody," rumbled the big man, helping the little clerk toward the door.

"Excellent, Barker!" said Holmes to the former. "Any problems?"

"Not a one. A few telephone calls to a couple of lawyers that I know, and I had Dunwoody's information in no time. I went around and picked him up right away."

"And that other little matter?"

"I have men on it now."

"Wonderful. It's a pleasure doing business with you. Would you care to stay for the *denouement*?"

"With pleasure. Wouldn't miss it."

"Hello, Barker," I said, offering my hand.

"Doctor," he replied with a nod, returning my grip. "I trust you're well."

"Very much so. And you?"

Barker nodded. "Very well, thank you." He was a private detective with whom Holmes occasionally worked. My friend regularly called him, "My hated rival upon the Surrey shore," but it was meant with good-natured affection, and the two men had a deep respect for one another.

"Mr. Dunwoody," said Holmes, reaching for the man's hand and shaking it firmly. "Thank you for taking time to join us. Watson – Would you take Mr. Dunwoody inside while I catch Barker up?"

I agreed and left them talking on the pavement, wishing that someone would catch *me* up – although I suspected that such would be the case very shortly.

In the front room, Hutton was already serving tea to the former butler and housekeeper, having apparently insisted that they take chairs as guests instead of functioning as former servants. He spoke to Dunwoody politely, giving the tense little man some tea as well. At first I wondered why they seemed to be strangers, and then I recalled that Dunwoody had been retired by Harrell the previous week, before Hutton had been called in to receive his uncle's clue. I was offered tea as well, and though I'd had the notion just a few minutes ago that I'd like a cup, I declined. Then Holmes and Barker joined us.

"Thank you all for coming. I felt that this would be best handled by getting everyone together in one place for some quick answers." He then introduced himself, along with Barker and me. "Mr. and Mrs. Linkous, you, of course, know Mr. Hutton."

"That we do," said Linkous fondly, while his wife looked on proudly, as if he were her own grandchild.

"I'm sorry," said Hutton to both of them. "I didn't know that you were leaving so soon, but I was certain that we would soon regain contact with one another. I – "

"Please, Mr. Hutton," interrupted Holmes. Then: "Mr. Dunwoody, this is Mr. Hutton, who is the heir to Mr. Jonah Hutton."

The former clerk looked more closely at Hutton, and then nodded with no apparent change of expression, which – at least to me – indicated that he knew enough about Jonah Hutton's affairs to recognize the name and to have no strong feelings one way or another about the young man.

"Let us be about our business." Holmes said, turning to Mr. and Mrs. Linkous. "You were both let go rather quickly."

They nodded, and Mrs. Linkous replied, with sudden tears in her eyes, "It was so sudden – the very day the master died! And then there was no service for him – " Her husband reached and patted her hand.

"That was my uncle's wish," explained Hutton. "For no service, I mean. He'd always insisted that he simply be immediately cremated. That occurred on the day after his death, and at some point, I plan to scatter his ashes – when I can figure out where he would like to rest – and then I'll have a memorial service. You will both be invited, of course."

"Were you aware of the strange clue that Mr. Hutton wished to be included in his will?" Holmes asked the older couple.

They nodded. "He made sure that we saw it," explained Mr. Linkous, "and that we saw him adding it to the second page of the will before we witnessed it."

Holmes pulled out the folded sheet that Danforth Hutton had given him that morning. Showing it to both Mr. and Mrs. Linkous, he asked, "And was this the clue?"

They studied it and then nodded. "To the best of our knowledge, yes," said Mr. Linkous. "It is a curious jumble isn't it? I can't swear that it's exactly the same."

Holmes pivoted to Dunwoody. "And do you agree?"

The old man leaned forward, reading the letters and moving his lips. "It is. Or I believe so."

"And you know of the conditions of the . . . shall we say *test*, where there is a specific time within which Mr. Hutton is required to solve the riddle?"

"I am," Dunwoody replied. "One year."

Hutton stood abruptly. "One *year*? A *year*? But . . . I was told that I only had one *week*! I saw the will – it says one *week*!"

Dunwoody shook his head. "No, no. I prepared the document myself, on my own typewriter, from Mr. Harrell's drafted notes, per Mr. Jonah Hutton's instructions. It clearly stated that you had one *year* to solve the riddle from the time you were informed of it."

"Which," explained Holmes, "was why Mr. Harrell promptly retired you – so that when he filed an altered will, with the allowed time changed from a *year* to a *week*, you wouldn't be there to contradict him. Not knowing Mr. Harrell, but seeing that he was willing to play this dangerous game to steal Jonah Hutton's fortune, I propose, Mr. Dunwoody, that you're very fortunate you haven't been run down by a stray vehicle sometime in the last week to further ensure your silence. But perhaps I credit Mr. Harrell with more malice than he deserves."

The little old man blanched, becoming even more ill-looking than before.

"That's what you saw on the will when we examined it at the Probate Office," I said. "That the time limit had been changed."

"Not exactly. There was no indication of erasures or alterations of the word '*days*'. Instead, what I observed was that the specified time limit was mentioned but once – on the *first* page of the will, while the riddle itself, as well as the signatures of both Jonah Hutton and the witnesses, Mr. and Mrs. Linkous, were on the *second* page – so only the first page had to be revised and swapped out to change the conditions. And that page had, in fact, been swapped. The typing on the first page was clearly different from that of the second – as done by a two-finger typist, and not someone, like Mr. Dunwoody here, who regularly types with all ten fingers. You'll have noted the callosities on Mr. Dunwoody's fingers which confirm this. The typing on the first sheet, while skillful, showed entirely different characteristics from the typing on the second sheet. Clearly, two different typists had prepared the two different sheets."

"The first page was also slightly different from the second in that it was less-yellowed, as if taken from a different and newer set of blank sheets. I also noticed," Holmes said, holding up the sheet with the handwritten clue, "that this page provided by Harrell to Mr. Hutton, where the clue was copied from the will, was the same type of paper as the swapped first sheet. When Harrell wrote this for you, Mr. Hutton, did he retrieve the blank sheet from his desk?"

"He did."

"And that would be where he also pulled a sheet when he retyped the first page of the will."

"And then," I noted, "Mr. and Mrs. Linkous had to be moved along so they couldn't comment on any irregularities that they might have also observed."

"I expect so. You've both already received your thousand-dollar inheritances?" Holmes asked them.

They nodded. "The day we were moved out," replied the lady.

"Interesting, as that was *before* the document was even officially filed, let alone approved. Harrell may have paid you out of his own pocket – but more likely from the dead man's accounts in his care – in order to move you away from what he was planning."

"But he still had to notify Mr. Hutton about the will and the conditions," I said, "because with such a fortune involved, he couldn't simply steal it. He had to find a way to legally take control."

"Exactly. He hoped that Mr. Hutton would try and fail to solve the clue, giving up in the week that had been falsely allotted."

"Surely this is enough to have the entire will thrown out," said Barker, after silently taking in the direction of the discussion. "The case is solved."

"One would think," agreed Holmes, "and it's enough to have Harrell arrested as well. You're having him watched?"

"As instructed," said Barker. "With all his affairs winding up, as you've indicated, and with him thinking he's going to get away with it, he might decide to bolt, but he won't get far."

Hutton, who had remained standing the whole time, seemed stunned when considering what had happened so quickly. "So that's it, then? There's no need to solve the riddle?"

"Not so fast," replied Holmes. "Although the time limit was changed from a year to a week, we know that your uncle did truly intend for you to solve the riddle. That was still a condition of his will, and it could still be enforced. No, I think it's better to go ahead and solve it right now, while we're all here, and get this over with, instead of letting it drag on until next summer."

"Then . . . then you know the solution?" Hutton looked at Holmes with wonder in his eyes.

"I believe so – or at least enough to begin on the right track." He turned to the former butler and housekeeper. "Do you know what the hidden object is? What Mr. Hutton is supposed to find to gain his inheritance?"

The looked at one another. Then the old man said, "I . . . we think it was a small key – with a paper tag upon it."

"Excellent!" He looked at all of us. "I can tell you that the clue to figuring out the coded message is in this room. Do any of you see it?"

We all looked around, everyone in a different direction, hoping that something obvious would present itself.

The room was eccentrically decorated, with a number of odd sculptures scattered about on low tables and shelves. Likewise, the walls were filled with many artworks of dubious quality, likely painted by the dead man, in small frames hanging from nails in the wall, and larger works hanging by wire from a rather deep picture rail running around the ceiling.

Mixed in through all of these works were a variety of homilies and sayings, tired clichés all of them, written in varying styles and presented in frames of different materials and sizes. *You can lead a horse to water, but you can't make him drink* was framed on one wall. Another motto, *Life is like pounding water in a mortar*, had been crocheted and framed and hung by the door to the front hallway. *The grass is always greener on the other side of the fence* was painted over the doorway leading into the hall, and *Two steps forward, three steps back* was inscribed in large and lovely calligraphic letters upon the mantelpiece bricks over the fireplace. *It's better to be safe than sorry* was framed near the big bow window, and *It's just the tip of the iceberg* was in a frame standing on a table near one of the chairs. *Curiosity killed the cat. You can't have it both ways. You have to walk before you can run.* I noticed that, when viewed in a certain mindset, there was a similar subtle negative shading to each statement, hints of discouragement, and I commented upon it.

Hutton nodded. "That was Uncle's way – there was always something *disappointed* about him – as if he expected the worst."

Both Mr. and Mrs. Linkous nodded. "He'd say things like, '*There's always rain with the rainbow*.' Poor man – he had so much, and could never truly be happy."

I pointed to one, stenciled on the wall near the fireplace. "'*No news is good news.*' How is that negative?"

Hutton laughed and shook his head. "Uncle's interpretation was that '*No news*' – that is, no news of any sort at all – is *ever* good news. He used to rant about 'How can people offer that statement as a comfort – telling them that none of the news they receive will be good?'"

I turned to Holmes. "Is that it?" I asked. "Is there something to these statements that serves as the clue – that has allowed you to understand the dead man's intent?"

Holmes nodded. "Being here and seeing these credos and mottos – and one specifically – that so displayed the nature of the dead man were the clues that led me to understand the solution the riddle."

Then to Hutton he said, "Tell me – was the back bedroom on the first floor that of your uncle?"

"It was."

"Then I suggest we adjourn there."

There was a sense of electric anticipation, along with complete and utter mystified confusion, as our entire company relocated, climbing the steps to the first floor and entering the large rear bedroom. It was rather dim, despite the south-facing window, as drapes were partially closed. Barker walked over and threw them wide, while Holmes was busy turning on couple of electric lamps upon a nearby table.

Holmes looked at Hutton. "The electric power is still on."

Hutton nodded. "Mr. Harrell agreed to it – for a while – while I conducted my search."

"Mr. Linkous," said Holmes, turning to the old butler, "is there a step-ladder available? Thank you."

While the old man left to find a ladder, several of us began to toss questions in Holmes's direction, but he simply shook his head with a smile. At times like this, he was like a magician, and the trick was the thing. When Linkous returned, Holmes said, "I apologize – I should have requested the ladder before we came upstairs."

"No worries, sir," said the man, a note of enthusiasm in his voice.

"Please lean it there," instructed Holmes. "Against the north wall. Yes, there in the center. Thank you."

Then he walked over, mounted the ladder, and climbed the four feet or so until he could reach his hand back into the recess of the picture rail. We shouldn't have been surprised when he brought forth a small cardboard box – but we were.

"Is that it?" asked Hutton, stepping forward. "Is that the object I'm supposed to bring to Harrell to get the inheritance? Is it the key?"

Instead of replying, Holmes returned to the floor and handed the box to Hutton, who scrabbled to open it. There was no difficulty – it was just a couple of inches square, a box of plain grayish color, and an inch deep, much like something that might contain cheap jewelry.

The lid came off and Hutton reached in – pulling forth not a key, but instead a small folded piece of paper. He opened it and, with a groan, handed it to Holmes.

"It's just another riddle!"

"Not to worry," said Barker. "Holmes has an understanding of how to read them now."

And apparently Holmes did, for after just a moment he simply said, "Come with me."

As he led us from the room, he handed me the note, which simply read:

dbjfpavegyczmigcvigdqcveghkqeegkuqqsg

Without even wasting time to lament our incomprehension, we followed Holmes back downstairs, this time to the kitchen, where he turned on the electric lights and then walked directly to the stove. It was a handsome thing, resting on top of four sculpted legs. On the left side were two stacked ovens, and on the right a flat panel with three pot-sized burners – the latest electric model, and without a doubt costing a pretty penny. Jonah Hutton had certainly been willing to spend a bit to have nice things.

Kneeling on the left side, Holmes felt around in the space by the back leg, reaching up and underneath the oven compartments, and taking a minute to work loose another small box, identical to the first. He rose and handed this to Hutton as well. It was almost no surprise when Hutton simply said with boyish dismay, "Another riddle!"

Holmes, far from being frustrated, simply smiled as he matched wits with the dead man. After taking a moment to sort out the coded message, he passed it to me:

ulwqjtgpvzqopbtlhzginxt

"Is that the cellar?" Holmes asked, nodding toward a closed and unassuming white-painted door. When this was confirmed, he immediately stepped across, pulled open the door, felt around until he located an electric light switch, and then disappeared down the stairs. Of course we followed, and I reached the bottom and oriented myself in time to see Holmes in a dark corner, setting aside an old coal scuttle to reveal yet another small box. He stood and handed it to Hutton who, upon opening it and finding yet another folded clue, handed it right back to

Holmes. After just a moment of consideration, he simply stated, "Back upstairs," and away we went, returning to the front room.

Holmes handed me the small slip of paper, which read:

hoqkvoqloyqlmpjbncybuqyxnixlnrobhlwofbeIkkgccinoqjcku

Then, in just seconds, Holmes had liberated the next clue – this time a folded sheet, no box, placed in one of the volumes of Gibbons' *The History of the Decline and Fall of the Roman Empire*, recognizable by the distinctive decorations upon the books' spines. In reading it – now with apparent ease – the smile faded from Holmes's features for just a moment. Then, he seemed to reach some sort of understanding of the dead man's challenge. With a nod of satisfaction, he looked to Mr. Linkous.

"Do you have a hammer and chisel? A small one? Or if no chisel, then perhaps a screwdriver?"

"We have that."

"Good. Please get them, and meet us back upstairs in the master bedroom." And then, with no explanation, he charged back the way we'd already traveled.

By the time Linkous arrived with a hammer and screwdriver, Holmes had returned to the ladder, at the spot where he'd found the first clue. But he had climbed higher this time, his feet on the top rung, right to the ceiling, turning his head sideways and trying to see into the crevice over the picture rail. When Linkous handed him the tools, he reached up and awkwardly started to use the screwdriver as a chisel, pushing it into the darkened space over the picture rail and tapping it gently with the hammer to break up the plaster.

He only gave four taps before handing the tools back to the former butler. Then he reached into the hole, turned his hand from side to side, working something loose, and pulled forth another small box – this time covered with plaster dust. He blew on it, climbed down from the ladder, turned to Danforth Hutton, and placed the box into his hand.

Without a word, the young man opened the box and turned it up, dropping a small key with a paper tag onto his other palm. He dropped the box and picked up the key, holding it close to his eyes to read aloud, "*Capital and Counties Bank, Oxford Street Branch.*" He then looked up at Holmes. "This must be it – this will open a box at the bank, where I'll find what my Uncle left me."

"Something that he left you, at any rate," added Holmes, "in addition to the inheritance that you'll receive by solving the riddle and notifying your uncle's attorney – fulfilling the requirements of the will, even if you have to do so by speaking to him through his prison bars."

"Prison?" squeaked Dunwoody. "I wasn't involved! I didn't do anything wrong!"

"Well done, Holmes," growled Barker. "Very workmanlike."

Holmes nodded in acknowledgement, while everyone else started to speak. Two voices rose more clearly than the others: Hutton saying that he couldn't take credit for solving the riddle, and Mrs. Linkous, demanding that some explanation be given as to how Holmes could read those "foolish notes".

Holmes raised a hand, and the voices diminished and then ceased. "If we return to the front room, I'll explain."

When we had done so, Holmes resumed speaking.

"I knew that the secret to unlocking the clue was in understanding the dead man – how his mind worked. It was no typical code, so it had to be something specifically associated with him. I'd asked Mr. Hutton if his uncle had any specific words or phrases he used, but apparently there weren't any. It was only when we reached this house, and saw the manifestation of the dead man's somewhat negative attitude, in the form of all the framed mottos, that I understood how to solve the code."

He pointed to the mantel, where the credo was painted over the fireplace.

"'*Two steps forward, three steps back,*'" Holmes recited. "What seems to be just another clichéd phrase was actually the key. One can spot its importance when seeing that he chose to place it there, in the most prominent spot. And it *sounds* like instructions to solving a cypher.

"I just thought that it reflected his overall attitude toward life," explained Hutton. "That all forward progress is always negated by inevitably going backward."

"No doubt – but it was also the clue to solving the messages. As soon as I saw this phrase, I realized that it could apply to *letters* – specifically in the coded messages. The first letter in the first message is *H*, which is shifted *two steps forward* from *F*. The next letter, *F*, is backed up three spaces from *I*. The third, *T*, is two steps forward from – "

"*R*!" cried Hutton, and Holmes nodded.

"And *P is* three back from – ?"

"Hmm . . . *S*!"

"Correct. Now, without working out the rest of the message letter-by-letter, which you can do on your own if you don't believe me, the first message from the will spelled '*first floor back bedroom north wall picture rail center*'. When I realized that, there was nothing to do but go upstairs and see what we'd find. Disappointingly, we found another message which, when decoded, said '*behind the back left leg of the kitchen stove*'.

"As you saw, we found another message there – just as expected – directing us to '*southwest corner of cellar*', and from there to a bookshelf in the front room, and even a certain book: '*front room bookshelf west wall volume four decline fall romans*'. But then I was dismayed to see that the treasure hunt was suddenly stalled." He pulled out the sheet which he'd found in the book. "Would anyone care to decode the message that I pulled from the book?"

Hutton eagerly reached out his hand, as if to claim it before anyone else might, but in truth, no one was reaching for it, happy to let the lad work it out for himself, in some small way earning the right to claim that he had also solved the riddle of his inheritance.

I looked over his shoulder to see the following –

voaxixkkkqkpplvqjxvbcpaagixbfbgmgovekkm

– just as he stated, "It says, '*try again it is not that easy delve deeper think*'."

"And," explained Holmes, "that's when I remembered the nature of the clues we were solving – *Two steps forward, three steps back.* We had followed the clues to specific places, but the last, in the book, said to '*try again*' and to '*delve deeper*'. I was at a loss – until I remembered Jonah Hutton's philosophy – *three steps back.* And three steps back took us to where we'd been before. One step back from the book clue was the cellar. Two steps back was the stove in the kitchen. And three steps back was the bedroom – and specifically the space above the picture rail, where we were to '*delve deeper*'. Clearly the first clue had rested in front of the final clue – or rather, in front of the key, which was the item to be found and given to Mr. Harrell to fulfill the requirements of the will."

Barker's agents, who had been watching Harrell, stayed on his trail as he took a cab to Victoria Station. He wasn't fleeing the country – not yet – as he had to stay in London long enough to confirm that Danforth Hutton hadn't solved the riddle by the following Monday so that he could lay claim to Jonah Hutton's estate. But Harrell did visit the station to purchase railway tickets on the boat train to France so that he could leave as soon as possible.

A thorough investigation showed that Harrell hadn't actually stolen anything from Jonah Hutton's estate – either before or after the man had died – but he had certainly taken advantage of his position. Although recommending that Hutton not invest in a bicycle factory – this fact was confirmed – he himself had done so, and had made a financial killing. He was charged with changing and registering the false will, although events didn't proceed to the point where he actually benefitted from his actions. And his legal career – should he have needed to resume it after his unexpected reduction in ill-gotten income – was finished.

An examination of the funds that Harrell had managed, and hoped to acquire through his chicanery, showed that Hutton was indeed very wealthy by way of his inheritance. But that turned out to be just a fraction of the estate, as the key to a lockbox at the Capital and Counties bank revealed an incredible second fortune in the form of bonds, stock certificates, and jewels that old Jonah Hutton had purchased on his own over the years with money earned on investments from what he'd inherited from his own father.

In a letter contained in the box, the late uncle explained that he had always felt that his younger brother, Danforth's father, had been unfairly excluded from their parents' inheritance, and so he'd kept a secret separate fortune hidden away for his brother, and – when his brother suddenly and unexpectedly perished – for his nephew. But he wanted to make Danforth earn it by displaying cleverness, and also by showing an understanding of his uncle. After the fact, Danforth Hutton recalled that his uncle had quoted that one specific phrase – "*Two steps forward, three steps back*" – much more often than others, giving it special significance.

Fortunately, while Danforth Hutton did not inherit his father's technical skills, he also did not inherit his uncle's generally dark-turned frame of mind. The young man had a pleasant disposition and a bright attitude, and it was no surprise to either Holmes or me that within a few years, he had achieved a great deal of success in his literary endeavors. During that same period, he relocated to his late uncle's Mayfair house, which became a center of literary culture throughout the next couple of decades.

"Jonah Hutton didn't strictly follow his own motto," I said. "There were more than two steps forward – the clue in the will to the bedroom. The bedroom to the kitchen, the kitchen to the cellar, the cellar to the bookshelf."

"That's true," said Holmes, "but I think that we must give a little leeway to Mr. Hutton's arrangement – for if there were only two clues for progressing forward – from the will clue to the bedroom, and then the bedroom to the kitchen – how would one go back *three* clues? The kitchen to the bedroom, and the bedroom to the will, and then – to *where*? No, he had to build in enough clues to have a place to return and find the key."

In later years, Sherlock Holmes would reference this little case on other occasions, always having a warm feeling for it. "Once I understood the nature of Jonah Hutton," he explained as we walked back to Baker Street from Mayfair that summer afternoon, "it really wasn't complicated at all – rather like something that was devised by a certain turncoat Anzac major in Malta, back in '77, when he was being treated for a gunshot. I had a much more difficult time with that one . . . ."

He then dived deeply into explanations of symmetry and asymmetry, rule-based calculations, keys and substitutions, double and triple authentications, and other phrases and terms that went over my head. My hopes for a simple recounting of one his past cases soon nudged my mind wandering toward what refreshments we might find upon our return to 221b. Fortunately, Mrs. Hudson did not disappoint . . . .

The Adventure of the Flagitious Sire

Chapter I

"Perhaps, Doctor, a walk would clear your mind."

"Hmm?" I asked, somewhat startled that the long comfortable silence had been broken. In truth, I had slipped into a waking doze, aware that quarter-hours were slipping past like boats on a steady current, but without the will to shake myself loose.

Sherlock Holmes shuffled some papers. "On several occasions over the last few months," he explained, sitting in his chair across from me alongside the fireplace, "when I have found myself in a fog over this or that case, you have reminded me that a constitutional through London would serve to provide a better outlook, a resetting of one's mental perspective, and I've found your advice to be sound." He turned and leaned over to place the stack of bank records he'd studied for most of the morning and early afternoon onto the floor near the foot of the curious octagonal table where his empty teacup rested. "I find that, after spending far too long following the thread of Colonel Waller's disastrous financial miscalculations, I could certainly stand from resetting my own perspective for an hour or so. And you . . . ." He smiled and stood. "You were moments from starting to snore."

I shook off my somnolence, glanced toward my desk and the labors I had abandoned before lunch, briefly considered the problem which had vexed me off-and-on for two days, and sighed. "Perhaps you're right," I said, making ready to rise as well. "A walk would be pleasant." Then, with a groan, I was upright.

In those days, not much more than a year-and-a-quarter after Maiwand, I had to move with more careful deliberation than that relatively carefree era before I'd received my wounds. Sitting before a warm fire for much of the day had only served to make me more settled. In truth, I should have pulled loose from my nest hours earlier. I'd long before discovered the value of getting up and moving around, both as a recuperative measure, and for the sheer joy and sense of well-being that comes from taking a long ramble.

Sherlock Holmes, of course, didn't have the burden of war wounds, and when he decided it was time to arise and go, he simply did so with complete ease. Of course that wasn't surprising due to his own energetic nature, and also because he was just twenty-seven years old at that time, and a young man of that age generally displays a natural vigor.

To Holmes's credit, he was rarely impatient when waiting for me to gather myself and then throw my often-sore form into motion. I say "rarely", for when he was impatient to rush out the door and follow up on some newly recognized thread of an investigation, he disregarded whether I was finding my footing or finishing my breakfast.

I could see through the windows looking upon Baker Street that the weather was still bright and clear, but the early afternoon was upon us and it would only be a couple of hours until the early October sun set. Though it had been a day of moderate and pleasant temperatures, the clear skies would rapidly allow the earth to cool as night approached. If our walk was typical of some others that Holmes and I had shared over the previous months, I knew to wrap up, as we might meander here and there, impulsively turning right when the quicker path home was to the left, ranging quite far before returning again to our warm hearth.

For a time we simply ambled, our route being where one or the other of us seemed drawn. There was unspoken agreement as we traveled, turning this way and that without thought in the way that a bird murmuration seems to know which way to go by consensus. Our murmuration of two drifted south, and then west through Soho, and back up into Bloomsbury. For the most part we progressed in silence. Despite his idea of looking for a better outlook, I knew that Holmes was likely thinking about Colonel Waller's unfortunate situation, in which the old soldier had been defrauded of what funds he still retained after his long and adventurous life. I know that I was still wrestling with my own problem – one of my own making, as I'd willingly taken on a task when I didn't need to, and now, in spite of the difficulty I'd encountered, I intended to see it through.

We turned south, along the side of Bloomsbury Square, and passing between where New Oxford Street became High Holborn, we entered Finsbury and that maze of lanes alongside Lincoln's Inn Fields. Holmes was in a more talkative mood by then, relating one of the cases from when he'd lived in Montague Street, which we'd not-long-before passed, when we traversed the narrow passage that opened at The Ship tavern. Finding that I had also spent time there before the war, Holmes suggested that we stop in for a few minutes, as he had developed a thirst. I agreed.

When we entered, Holmes stepped to the bar and ordered two pints. As he handed one to me, the door opened and a man walked in. He glanced at us and walked past, over to the bar. After a moment, he received a drink, paid, and turned our way, approaching in a heavy-booted scuff.

He was about fifty, somewhat less than six feet and heavyset, and settled in a way that made him seem shorter than he was. He was bald, and there were a few old dark scars across the top of his sun-browned dome, flat like small port-wine stains. Clearly he was one of those who chose not to wear a hat, even in the hottest sun or the coldest winter. He had a short grizzled beard that didn't do very much at all to hide his weak chin.

He was carrying a tall glass of whisky, held in short, stubby fingers that didn't look quite long or supple enough to adequately grip it, nor quite clean enough to ensure against some kind of inadvertent intestinal poisoning should one brush his dark lips. There was a squinty shiftiness to him, his eyes beady and close together, and his natural facial repose had a marked and unpleasant slyness. There was also the carried sense of suppressed violence, as when meeting a dog that has been beaten, and may go mad with rage with no prior warning or provocation. I didn't like him on sight – and that was entirely due to my own initial impression, without Holmes's influence or advice, although it was clear that he didn't like the man either, as reflected in his tone when he spoke.

"Watson, meet Foxy Huff." Holmes's tone was short, as he clearly resented the intrusion. He shifted to face the man, looking down at the intruder. "You've followed us for half-a-mile. Well, you've cornered us, Foxy. Is there something you want to say?"

The fellow's mouth pulled back in a vulpine grin, showing a number of stained teeth, but there was no humor or friendliness in his expression. He shuffled another step forward, offering his hand to me in greeting. I had no choice but to respond. His grip was dry and rough, and while there was implied strength, it wasn't too tight – as if his fingers couldn't close all the way to adequately wrap my hand. I suspected that, were he able, he would be the type who would try to win points in a contest that only he perceived by squeezing as hard as he could to assert his dominance. Little victories in a life without very many of them to list would be important to someone like Foxy Huff.

"I'm not ready for you just yet, Foxy," continued Holmes before Huff could reply to his question. "I still have one or two witnesses to line up before your arrest. My case will be complete in just a day or so. Stay or flee – it's no matter. I'll find you."

Then Holmes turned to me. "I first became aware of Foxy when he stole Marion Terry's diary from the Haymarket Theatre, four years ago. If he hadn't sold out his friends and traded information with the police on who lifted the plate from that jeweler who lived in Chitty Street – "

Huff threw up a hand, as if deflecting a blow. "Whoa, whoa, Mr. Holmes! Stop right there! That's water under the bridge! Old water! That diary was just a-laying there. I didn't know whose it was – just a book, it was. I just picked it up – thought it was lost. You understand – a fellow tries to do the right thing, and what does it bring him? Heartache! Heartache, I'll tell you! And that idea I squealed on my pals – you've got that wrong. I'm the most loyal fellow you'll meet . . . ."

His unpleasant voice had the victimized and mosquito-like whine one would expect, and he looked back and forth between us, his shifty expression trying to ascertain whether we believed him. "When I had a chance to read it later," he continued, "and to see who wrote it, I would've have returned it, but you just caught up to me too soon, before I was able. I explained it to you at the time. You remember?" His tone had started as a whining wheedle, but then he repeated, with darker shades, "You remember," as if there would be a hard lesson taught if the answer was negative.

Holmes was having none of it. "Remember what? That you promised to get even? And yet, here we are. Is that what you want now? To reiterate your threat?" When Huff didn't respond, Holmes started to turn away. "I thought not. Begone with you. I'll reach out my hand and find you in a few days for the plucking when the time is right."

Although none of this conversation was loud enough to be heard beyond the three of us, there was an apparent tension that had attracted stares from several nearby patrons, as if they sensed trouble rising. However, when Huff spoke next, he seemed to willfully reduce himself, working to diffuse the situation, and the nearby onlookers turned away.

"You have it wrong, Mr. Holmes. I heard you were asking around about me, trying to pin me to that stolen plate business in Green Street, but you're on the wrong trail. It isn't me that's involved . . . You see, it's actually my son."

In the months that I'd known Holmes, I'd rarely see him surprised, but it had happened. The time Cecily Davies lunged across the room and stabbed her father through his black heart with a pair of sewing scissors. The terrible discovery in Mrs. Wenceslas' oven. The tragic truth of young Nick Evans' bicycle ride in the village of Wenalt. Holmes had blamed himself after each event, feeling that he should have foreseen the possibilities of what might occur. Generally, he usually held most of the threads in his hand, or he was two steps in front of everyone, but sometimes events turned too quickly, or facts were revealed in ways that he didn't expect. Such situations could frustrate him, but mostly he enjoyed the added challenge. On several occasions over the previous months, he'd explained that if one such as himself had the details of a thousand cases in his head, then it wasn't so very difficult to figure out the thousand-and-first. But I could see that there was a disappointment at the sameness of the thousand-and-first, and he craved the unusual and the *outré*. The outlandish and the idiosyncratic. And Huff's statement that his son was mixed up in the Green Street affair, whatever that was, had intrigued and startled him.

"In what way?" Holmes asked, his eyes narrowing.

"He's gotten himself mixed up with Abel Farris. You'll have heard of him, I suppose, if you've made any progress on tracking the missing plate."

"I know of Farris, but not in relation to the stolen plate. What is your son's connection?

"He fell in with a bad crowd – Farris' gang. One thing led to another – the same old path to ruin you hear about – and before we knew it – that is, his mother and me – our Reuben was part of the crew. He was the lookout on the Green Street job. That's how they rope them in – things like being the lookout, and then a little more at a time, until the guilt won't wash off. Now he's been asked to go along when the delivery to the buyer is made tomorrow night."

"And how do you know all of this?"

"How does a father know anything? I listen, and I snoop. We've tried talking with him, and tried keeping him at home, but he's old enough now to ignore us."

"What do you get from this – from turning in your own son?"

"Why, I hope to put a stop to all of it. He needs a hard lesson, Reuben does – something to scare him away from that life, and nothing me or my wife say or do is going to reach him. Not anymore. He's had a taste of it – just a little taste – but he likes it. I'm hoping that you can do something – catch him and scare him. Nothing more than that," he added hurriedly. And then he fell silent, looking from one of us to the other with slow, metronomic blinks, as if he were a reptile staring into the sun.

Holmes gazed at the man a bit longer than one might expect – as if looking into a petri dish to watch the bacteria spread. It was enough to make Huff glance away nervously. Finally Holmes answered, "Where will this delivery be made?"

"Behind the St. Giles Workhouse – at midnight. Halfway along Betterton Street, between Drury Lane and Endell Street. I hear that Reuben will be there with some of the gang. If you're there too, Mr. Holmes – with your policemen friends, and this one here – " He glanced at me. " – and pick him up, it will do him the world of good . . . And if you'll put in a good word for him, and make sure that he isn't treated too roughly – Well, he just needs a good scare . . . ."

"I hadn't fancied you for a caring father, Foxy," said Holmes with a shake of his head. Then, "I'll look into it."

"That's all I ask. I'd heard you were asking questions about me, and I wanted to make sure that you understood you're on the wrong trail."

The man glanced at me, then back to Holmes, before abruptly turning without another word. He stepped to the bar, turned up his previously untouched whisky glass to quickly drink the contents – clearly that much whisky had no more affect than a tall glass of water. Then he set down the glass and departed without looking back.

When he'd gone, Holmes snorted in amusement or disgust – or both. At my querying expression, he shook his head.

"There's no doubt that Foxy Huff is deeply involved in the Green Street theft. All of the pieces of the Old Sheffield Plate were stolen last Thursday night while their owner, Sir Norman Devere, was out of town. He returned the next morning, discovered it, and notified the police. I was consulted by Gregson.

The staff saw nothing, and I'm inclined to think them innocent. Sir Norman is a widower, and his only son died in the Second China War, so it's a small household: Just an old butler, his wife the housekeeper, a feeble-minded lad of twelve or so to do the general labor, and two young maids. Whoever took the plate managed to enter without alerting the house – it wouldn't have taken much skill, as the servants sleep in another part of the building and the latches are old. They carried off a number of items, including the Threlkeld Platter, which the Crown would like to get back – and they would have decades ago, but for a long-standing and convoluted document related to some loan by the Deveres to a member of the Royal Family in Regency days.

Sir Norman refuses to believe that the Crown might be behind this theft, to get the object back, but I'm starting to see signs to the contrary, and that Jimmy Farraday's crowd did the deed. There's a connection between Farraday and one of Queen's coachmen, and from there I can make a direct connection to Foxy Huff, one of Farraday's lesser lieutenants. There's no way a theft of this careful complexity was carried out by Abel Farris' gang. Farris is nothing more than a clumsy imitation Fagin, not even a score of years, and not much older than the lads he recruits. Nicking meat pies and breaking things for amusement is at the limit of their skills."

"Then clearly Huff thinks he's being clever to try and direct your attention elsewhere. But why implicate his own son?"

"Exactly. I hate to follow a trail laid out by Huff, but I'll make arrangements, just in case – if only see what kind of game Huff is playing." He turned his head. "You'll join me, of course?"

I considered that midnight in October in a most-insalubrious neighborhood might not be the wisest spot to place oneself. I was not yet fully healed, and the seeping cold that crept out of the cold air and the insidious fog and frozen pavement, standing still while hidden, watching and waiting for hours to observe something happening, could be quite unpleasant.

"Yes, of course." I answered promptly..

Holmes nodded. We finished our pints and resumed our walk.

Chapter II

We worked our way west along Great Queen Street, and then turned north along Drury Lane. For a quarter-hour, we prowled several of the streets behind the workhouse, including Betterton Street where the rendezvous was supposed to occur. Holmes refreshed his knowledge of the area while I was – yet again – introduced to a region that, while looking like so many other parts of London, still had its own peculiarities.

Betterton Street was a row of shabby four-story brick buildings, none with any outstanding feature. Looking at it, I was reminded of a narrow canyon in Afghanistan where several of us had been pinched from both ends by the natives. We had escaped unscathed and had laughed about it later, thinking ourselves indestructible, fooled by the idiocy of youth.

"Nasty place for a trap if they bottle us up," I noted.

Holmes nodded but didn't comment. He remained silent as he looked in both directions, doing his best to anticipate where the meeting would occur, and the spot from which to best observe it. Then, apparently satisfied, he led me on toward the Endell Street side, and a route that was relatively more wholesome in comparison. He shook his head.

"This area is a self-perpetuating engine of crime," he said, gesturing vaguely southwest down a narrow lane we were passing. "Five-hundred feet along that passage is Seven Dials. It, together with St. Giles, form one of the worst of the Rookeries. I'd be hard pressed to put Petticoat Lane or the Ratcliffe Highway ahead of this one, although parts of Whitechapel and Spitalfields are festering sores, just waiting for a match to ignite – to mix my metaphors. Just over a hundred years ago, the Paving Commissioners pulled down the Sundial Pillar, just over that way, but it did no good – the riff-raff still gather there, even if there is no monument to draw them. They say the Shaftsbury Avenue improvements to clear some of the slums will help, but I doubt it. Thirty years ago, Dickens spent a dangerous night touring the area with a Scotland Yard inspector, and wrote about it, but what has changed?"

Endell Street had become Bow Street. Holmes had fallen silent, as he was sometimes wont to do when considering the scope of misery in the world, and how attempting to stand against it was like plowing the sea. As we passed the police station, Holmes suddenly stated, "Still, Dickens had the right idea. Writing about things is important." Then he glanced at me and asked, "Will you finish your manuscript?"

By that point in our gestating friendship – I'd known Holmes just a little over nine months – I'd mostly ceased to be amazed when he seemed to read my mind. Still, I wanted to confirm how he'd done so.

"I suppose you've seen me staring at my desk off and on for two days."

I didn't look his way, but I sensed that he nodded. "And you glanced that way again, first thing when you woke up this afternoon." After a pause of a few steps, he added, "You don't have to do it, you know," he said. "Finish it, I mean. If you feel as if you've promised it to me – an enthusiastic declaration made in the moment – please divest yourself of that notion. There is no obligation. I do not see it that way, but if you do, I release you from the burden."

I thought of the manuscript to which he referred, three-quarters complete, but now lying unfinished on my desk, laid open like a poor autopsy study. For some reason, something was missing, and I was having difficulty bringing it to life – an unusual occurrence for me. Writing had always come easy, even as a youth, and I had long kept detailed journals, as well as making the occasional attempts toward adventurous fictions that at best were poor imitations of Sir Walter Scott and, later, Robert Louis Stevenson. I'd learned that my efforts to fabricate such fantastical and adventurous literature left much to be desired, while detailing the true events encountered along my path were quite easily described. Since my injuries and discharge from the Army, I found that I wrote even more – during the days when I was too tired or sore to venture out into the streets, or at night, when I could not sleep. Time spent on these efforts had allowed me to accumulate a number of narratives relating my military adventures and, more recently as I'd accompanied Holmes on his investigations, I was beginning to amass a sizable stack of those sketches as well.

"Your merits should be publicly recognized, and if you won't do it, I will."

"You have other things to write about," Holmes countered. I started to bluster, but he interrupted me.

"You are a *writer*, Watson," he said. "You must write – or you will burst. I'll admit that, if the signs of your recent overseas adventures hadn't been so obvious when we first met, leading me to conclude you'd been wounded in Afghanistan, I would have been tempted to deduce that you were primarily an author – and not just because of the signs of drink that were upon you at our initial meeting. Thankfully that was not your typical character, or our association would have likely been brief.

"Knowing you all these months has only confirmed my initial conclusions that whatever other titles and skills you carry – Physician. Soldier. – you are a *writer*. You display all the signs, you know – the shape of your fingers altered to reflect how you hold the pen for such long periods. The ink stains upon your fingers that are more permanent and prominent than the nitrate of silver on your right forefinger that marks you as a physician. The smooth cuffs that might lead some with less experience to frame you as a clerk entering figures in a ledger during most of your waking hours are just as easily achieved by writing prose. You write whenever you get the chance – when the weather is too foul to go walking, or when I haven't called upon your time to consult upon an investigation. When you cannot sleep at night, due to insomnia . . . or due to your nightmares."

Some might have flared at this last intrusive statement – a cold-hearted comment on such personal aspects of one's life – but by then, I knew that Sherlock Holmes meant no offense, and he perceived no boundary that he had breached.

"I could only presume," he went on, "without having looked, that you've resumed work on that narrative concerning the Jefferson Hope affair last spring."

"I have."

Before I could elaborate, Holmes reiterated, "There's really no need, you know. Lestrade and Gregson already have the credit. Let them keep it. What difference does it to me?"

"It makes a great deal of difference!" I replied with a sudden bit of heat, stopping on the pavement to face him. We were across from the pillars of the Lyceum. It was a discussion which we'd had before. "I know that you were bothered at the end of the Hope case when Lestrade and Gregson were credited with the solution, and when *The Echo* implied that you were simply some juvenile amateur who might someday learn a thing or two from the official Force – that in time, should you be so lucky, you might possibly achieve a fraction of their success."

"And you might also recall what you said to console me," countered Holmes. "Something like: 'The public hiss at me, but I cheer myself when in my own house I contemplate the coins in my strong-box.' What do I care if the newspapers give the police the credit, as long as the police keep seeking my advice and letting me pocket my fee?"

"But you also said – How did you put it? – 'I know well that I have it in me to make my name famous. No man lives or has ever lived who has brought the same amount of study and of natural talent to the detection of crime which I have done.'" Holmes glanced away, recalling the moment as well as I did. "I know you better now than then," I continued, "and I recognize that this was a true statement. You might allow the official force to take the credit, but you also seek acknowledgement for what you've accomplished. You *do* appreciate the praise. And making your name more well-known can only increase your reputation – and also increase the number of clients who seek your unique assistance.

"Clients? You know that I have many of those already."

"This is true, but I also see how you appreciate the interesting cases over those of little interest who seek your time during your routine daily consulting hours – to ask for guidance upon a lost pet or misplaced wedding ring. Those also give you a fee to pocket, but it's the interesting cases that stir your blood, the way a hound perks up when the horn sounds. Those cases when, as you put it, you have to 'bustle about and see things' with your own eyes are what pleases you most – and making the public more aware of your services can only open up more of those opportunities. And my promise to write about what happened during the Hope investigation, which I take quite seriously, can only help."

"But you've run into a difficulty," noted Holmes. "You were writing away, steadily and with purpose, and suddenly, yesterday morning, you stopped. You sat for the longest time making no forward progress whatsoever. Then you sighed, closed your journal, neatly replaced and set aside the pen, and took to your armchair, from whence you've regularly glared toward your desk ever since. What is the unexpected problem?"

"Jefferson Hope's narrative," I replied. "Relating his history, and his reasons for following those two men around the world, using up all the remaining decades of his life to achieve revenge . . . I have stumbled when it comes time to relate his aspect of the story – his background, and his motivations."

Holmes shrugged, his eyes looking ahead of us. "I don't understand the complication. Simply relate what he told us during our final interview, after his capture. It couldn't take more than a couple-of-hundred words. The Mormon leaders stole his intended bride, killed her father, and left Hope for dead. He dogged the two men most responsible, and eventually executed them. Or you can shorten it even more, if you're clever about it. I believe he stated something to the effect of, 'It don't much matter to you why I hated these men.' Surely that will suffice. Sometimes motivation is the key to understanding how to catch the criminal, but not always. In the end, it didn't matter why he was after those two men. He left enough clues that we were able to lure him into our trap."

I thought that it was generous of Holmes to refer to it as "our trap", as I hadn't understood what was happening whatsoever, even as it was occurring. "In this case," Holmes continued, "we were able to outthink Hope and he walked straight into our Baker Street web."

"It's considerate of you to state that '*we* were able to outthink him'," I said. "But I feel that the little we learned from him regarding his past – the story of the poor girl and her father, and Hope's great love for the young lady, and how Stangerson and Drebber and the others so ruined that part of Hope's life that he devoted the rest of it to destroying them – deserves more than a few hundred words."

Holmes turned a wary expression upon me. "Why," he said with a tilt to his head and a raised eyebrow, "do I have the sense that I should be uneasy about this narrative you're composing? It sounds as if you intend to fabricate some sprawling romantic fiction and graft it onto what should be a straightforward list of points outlining the bare investigatory facts."

I shook my head, suddenly chary as I carefully replied. "No, no. You misunderstand me. And in any event, I couldn't write anything of a fictional nature. I am no Scott or Dickens, able to generate such pretend events and conversations from my own mind. No, my journals – and now this slim volume – are simply my records of what I see and hear and understand. True narratives of true events."

He nodded, ready to take that as my final word . . . but there remained a whiff of suspicion and doubt. I didn't expand on my conclusion that the story *did* need more about Jefferson Hope – quite a bit more. The account required a substantial segment detailing the killer's past and his motivations, and what would drive a man to expend the rest of his days seeking vengeance. I'd reluctantly come to understand that to finish the story properly in the way that I felt it needed to be told, I'd have to find someone else – a literary partner – to write that segment. To flesh out the skeletal background that Hope had shared with us just before his death, and the tragic entwined destinies of those unusual people.

I'd written as much as I could from my own experience – a narrative explaining how I'd ended up in Baker Street and the beginnings of my friendship with Sherlock Holmes, and the events of the case, stretching from the day I was invited to get my hat and join Holmes when he examined the first dead body to the denouement when he and I had realized the Scotland Yarders were awarded the public credit for the solution. But I wasn't satisfied. There was the other aspect to be explored and expanded – Hope's narrative, which would almost feel like a separate book – grafted, as Holmes said, into my narrative. I would have to set the manuscript aside until such a time that I could find someone to help address my concern.

But now I had a new thought to worry me: When Sherlock Holmes finally read it, I greatly feared that he would object when discovering that it wasn't the dry and neatly scientific account that he envisioned.

Chapter III

Our walk continued for several more hours, working inevitably toward home. Upon reaching the Strand, we continued for a short time to the Embankment before Holmes plunged back into the quieter streets, leading gradually away from the river and toward home and hearth through a myriad of lanes, alleys, mews, passages, and paths, many without names, but all known to my friend. At one point we traversed Dean Street near Soho Square. Upon another, the long stretch of Titchfield Street to the east of Cavendish Square and the Langham. Our route led over to Devonshire Street, and thence to the workhouse near Baker Street Station, and so on, with the streets often – to me – appearing identical as the late afternoon grew more dark and cool.

Along the way, various spots suggested memories of Holmes's past cases. Once he pointed at a narrow building where Mansfield Street joins Queen Anne Street. "That was Sketch Rutledge's little temple. He wore a costume sewn from snake skins, and preached a unique interpretation of the Sixteenth Chapter of Mark, Verse Eighteen." And he then had a fit of that peculiar silent laughter of his which always boded ill for someone. He refused to elaborate, advising that neither the world nor his flatmate, despite my experiences on a number of continents, was ready for that story.

"And here," he provided a bit later, alongside the Castle Street marketplace, "was where Betsy Flynn tripped over a loose paving stone, unexpectedly revealing the Tavis-Gresham Hoard. You haven't heard of it, of course. The nasty machinations of three noble houses are still fighting for the rights, but I was able to squeeze enough Mammon out of all of them so that Betsy now owns her own house now in Chiswell Street, by the artillery ground, and also a little nearby tea shop."

The day was drawing to a close, and I was ready to return home. I knew that Holmes stayed aware of my condition, and if I'd shown indications of excessive weariness beyond what might be expected from such a traipse, he would have immediately insisted upon seeking a more populated street and a hansom cab – although funds for the latter were much more rare for both of us in those early days. At the same time, while I was somewhat sapped, I recognized the therapeutic benefit of pushing myself – even if I would pay for it on the morrow.

As we passed near Baker Street Station, Holmes looked around and, in short order, he spotted an unobtrusive lad of ten or so. He made a subtle and cabalistic gesture with the fingers of his left hand that sent the boy skittering off in the other direction with nary a change of expression, rather like a hare unexpectedly flushed from tall grass.

I laughed. "Did you cast some sort of spell upon him?"

Holmes smiled in return as we neared our door. "I signaled for him to have Wiggins drop by at his earliest convenience."

"All that from a one-second wiggling of your fingers."

"Those boys are sharp," Holmes countered. "You wouldn't be surprised to observe a shepherd direct his dog with such abstruse and miniscule signals."

"Not at all. I have seen such a thing many times, and it is endlessly fascinating and admirable. But surely you aren't comparing your Irregulars to canines – even the most intelligent of them?"

"Not at all. Rather to the contrary: If a smart dog can understand so much from so little, and with such focused intensity, then the Irregulars, who are intelligent but simply do not have the chance to make use of it, are exponentially wiser than the dogs. And now, we have returned. Shall it be tea or whisky?"

I opted for neither, asking Mrs. Hudson to bring up a pot of strong coffee. I suspected that I would sleep well that night, regardless of its stimulating effect so late in the day. Holmes indicated that she should prepare enough for the both of us, and within a few minutes, I was back in my armchair from whence I had departed several hours earlier – my haven from the trials of the world. Meanwhile, Holmes added coal to the fire, knocking back some of the chill that had worked into my bones.

Mrs. Hudson wasn't satisfied to simply bring a hot beverage, and soon after we were enjoying our dinner, consisting of roast beef and various vegetables cleverly prepared with sturdy and tasty herbs. My service in India had opened my appreciation for bolder flavors which Mrs. Hudson was not afraid to provide, and Holmes, indifferent to food, would eat whatever was placed before him – or not, depending upon the day and his mood. That evening, he had a less-than-middling appetite.

We weren't halfway through when the bell rang. There was some conversation down below, and Holmes and I could both imagine its nature: Wiggins had been summoned and wanted to go upstairs immediately, and Mrs. Hudson was leery of the idea. (These were still our first months of residency, but even then her heart was opening to the boys and girls that made up Holmes's unofficial Force. Over the past few months, her innate warmth and goodness had started her slipping them food, or worrying about rips in their tattered garments, holding one or the other back from immediate departure on one of Holmes's errands so that she could sew up some damage or defect. Oh, she would still be stern and gruff, but the Irregulars saw through it, and understood they had more than one friend in that Baker Street house.

Holmes, never one to overeat, hadn't consumed but a portion of his meal, and when Wiggins entered, Holmes gestured him over to finish what was on the plate. I wondered if Mrs. Hudson would realize what had happened, or if she would think that this was one of those days when Holmes was truly hungry. The boy was grateful, and had finished the entirety of the serving before I'd loaded two more bites.

At that time, I'd only known Wiggins for seven or eight months, and in my mind he was more of a curiosity than anything – and I'm sure he thought the same of me. He'd met Holmes in the mid-1870's, when Holmes had first come up to London to pursue his unusual calling. This was still the *first* Wiggins, the original young fellow that was part of Holmes's initial recruits. Over time, he had earned the right of leadership over the Irregulars. There were many other Wiggins-es through the years, all of the same family and spread over several generations, who filled roles in that group. As I would learn many years later, * Holmes had rescued this particular Wiggins' mother from a charge of murder during the time he resided at No. 24 Montague Street, and the family in return seemed to have made some sort of oath or pledge of service to him. And this arrangement went both ways, as Holmes took it upon himself to see that the Irregulars were fed and clothed and educated, even when he could sometimes ill afford it, and when they reached an older age, past their usefulness as his agents, he found them jobs or apprenticeships or scholarships for further education, drawing upon favors owed to him by men and women up and down the social stratum.

This specific Wiggins, the first of his position, was still wary of me, possibly because of the unusual notion that Holmes might include someone else in his investigations. While living in Montague Street, Holmes had lived a rather solitary existence – monastic, as I pictured it – devoting his time to either investigatory work, or educating himself so that he would be better prepared for more investigatory work. He'd held to that pattern for several months after we began sharing lodgings in Baker Street, and it was only by merest chance that one morning in early March he'd unexpectedly and impulsively asked me to join him when summoned by the Yard to the murder investigation that I'd later attempted to chronicle.

When Wiggins has finished eating – the work of just a moment – he stepped back to the center of the room and presented himself for orders, standing at what he thought was attention. Holmes waved him to the basket chair, and I joined them before the comfortable fire, having finished my own satisfying repast. As I settled, Holmes asked the boy, "What do you know of Abel Farris?"

I'm not sure what question Wiggins expected, but this didn't seem to surprise him. He was rarely surprised, having seen so much already. "He's of no account," he replied promptly, twisting his head slightly sideways. I was reminded of the alert sheep dogs to which the Irregulars had been compared but an hour or so earlier. "Oh, he wants to be important, and he's gathered together six or eight little 'bunnies', as we call them – too harmless to make any difference one way or the other – to trail along after him. They try and bluster around the Dials, but it's only their good luck that they haven't gotten themselves cut up before now – but just because they haven't been worth the effort so far."

Holmes nodded. "That was my opinion as well, but I wanted to confirm that Farris hadn't elevated himself to the next level of mischief."

"No. There's a lot of others who are higher on that ladder, and they won't let anyone climb above them."

"What have you heard of the Green Street job?"

"The stolen plate over in Mayfair? Not very much. That kind of thing is rather above my head, you know. Is Abel mixed up in that?"

"We received information that he might be. What about Reuben Huff? Have you ever heard of him?"

Wiggins frowned, considering one after another of the myriad of Londoners that he'd internally indexed. "Possibly," he answered after a moment. "Fourteen or sixteen, maybe. One of the bunnies. If he's the one I think, he's run with Abel for a couple of months. Pretty boy – way too soft for whatever he's wading into."

I had trouble picturing a son of Foxy Huff as a "pretty boy", but life played many tricks. Perhaps Huff only thought Reuben was his son . . . .

"Yes, that's probably him," replied Holmes. He looked around for his pipe, where he'd left it on the side table. Beginning that complicated ritual pipe smokers will understand, he recounted our discussion with Foxy Huff, and the story told to us – the meeting on the following night to deliver some of the stolen plate, and the expected presence there of both Farris and Reuben Huff."

"I know Foxy," scoffed Wiggins. "If his mouth is moving, he's lying. What's his game, then?"

"That's what we intend to find out," Holmes answered. "I want you to learn more about Abel Farris and Reuben Huff. I'll poke into a few places myself and see what I can find. The usual rates."

Wiggins didn't need to receive a more finely drawn plan. He rarely did, which made him a most-effective lieutenant in charge of Holmes's roving eyes and ears. They arranged how to communicate the following day – where to meet or send messages, as Holmes expected to be out – and then the boy was gone, his feet pattering down the stairs. The front door, however, did not immediately slam, which led me to assume that Wiggins had paused to speak with Mrs. Hudson. Likely she had delayed him to provide some further left-overs of her own.

After Wiggins took his leave, Holmes settled deeper into his chair, the first of several pipes that night aiding in his cogitations. While still staring into the fire, he spoke.

"Sir Norman's stolen plate is just the latest in a number of similar thefts. Many of the stolen items used to belong to the Crown – art and coronets and objects and silver plate – that were shifted to various families over the years as collateral for loans, or as outright sales, to bridge some Royal over a financial chasm. Sometimes the Royal personage is able to redeem the pledge, or buy it back. On other occasions, in order to curry favor, the item is returned for free, and the loan forgivin and forgotten. But every once in a while, someone like Sir Norman Devere refuses to return the item for any reason. Sir Norman is of an age where he has no interest in currying Royal favor, and the high-handedness of the recent demands has rubbed him the wrong way.

"Which brings us to Jimmy Farraday. He's the illegitimate son of one of the Queen's coachmen, Cyrus Blair – a relationship that neither publicly claims. On the surface, the coachman is above reproach, although I've been assured by someone within the Government whose information is always reliable that there's a rotten spot in old Cyrus, although it's ignored by that peculiar freemasonry of his profession and position. In fact, he does very little to collect his pay, spending his time lounging about and holding court with his cronies. When certain dark and illicit tasks must be carried out to further the ends of Our Betters, Cyrus is the man they summon – and he in turn counts on his son Jimmy to complete the dirtier aspects of the job.

"Cyrus is able to function in this murky area between the law and the desire of some of the nobility who must have their wishes satisfied, and too many look the other way. Recently there has been a marked surge in the reclamation of items like the Sheffield Plate from people like Sir Norman. The unofficial and secret position within some of the noble lines seems to be that if these items cannot be retrieved legally, then other methods are authorized – for it is their right. All indications are that Cyrus and Jimmy Farraday are responsible for the actual thefts, working under the protection of some minor noble who has taken it upon himself to go after every object that the different houses want back. He's likely taken on this task as a way to win favor from those higher on the hill than him for his own purposes.

"It was my Government contact who arranged to have me called in last Friday following the theft of Sir Norman Devere's treasures."

I had heard Holmes mention this mysterious "contact" on several occasions, but it was obvious from his caginess when describing him that he had no plans to share this person's identity with me – and I could hardly blame him. Holmes obviously felt that information provided by the man was utterly reliable, and I already knew of at least a half-dozen cases where Holmes had been recruited to assist this individual on some discreet and urgent task – after which, he would comment that this person often provided him with some of his most interesting cases.

"In the past," Holmes continued, "Blair and Farraday have carried out several ambitious jobs, and quite a few more just recently, and they've never been caught – although their involvement is without question. The Peck-Memorial Methodist Chalice theft. The destruction of the Morningside *droit de seigneur*. The Lambert Farm deed, in which that cruel and corrupt family finally received their just deserts – showing that all of their thefts weren't necessarily bad, though still illegal. Cyrus has a crafty cunning – he's the planner, and the go-between to his noble clients – while Jimmy has a cruel and violent streak that he uses to control his myrmidons with absolute authority – even rough and broken pieces like Foxy Huff. They each have a specific function – acting as a single cog in the machine – and this division of labor has worked with notable success. Now, by way of my contact, I'm finally been given my own chance to have a crack at him. My contact – rather on his own initiative – feels that this has gone on too long.

"It didn't take me long to get a line on what had happened regarding the theft of Sir Norman's objects. Then, as events are moving toward their conclusion, we were unexpectedly intercepted by Foxy Huff. That's the part that makes no sense – and will need further thought."

He finally glanced away from the fire to where I sat. "I shall see you in the morning, Watson." And then he returned to his ruminations.

I could have remained there, sitting quietly and about my own business, but – in spite of the coffee – I was weary, and adjourned upstairs to my room, and soon to sleep.

Chapter IV

The next day, a cold rain had descended upon the city, giving my room a damp and unpleasant feeling. I dressed quickly and went downstairs to find that Holmes had already departed. Mrs. Hudson reported that he'd left soon after seven, "dressed up in that ostler getup he favors," she lamented as she set down my breakfast tray. "He did want me to make sure you saw his note."

In fact, I hadn't seen it, but only because I hadn't yet looked toward my armchair, where a folded sheet was propped.

Watson,

If you wish to get out and move around, find out about Reuben Huff. The family resides at No. 4 Millman Street, south of the Great Ormond intersection, at the far end from the Foundling Hospital. Discretion is the watchword – perhaps you might present yourself as a doctor consulting at the hospital, and proceed from there . . . ?

Wiggins has already given me a description of the family, and whatever else you provide will be additionally useful.

Acres will collect you in Baker Street at nine p.m. for the conclusions.

SH

I wondered what else Holmes needed about the Huff family that Wiggins hadn't already reported. I didn't think that he would involve me in a pointless task simply to get me out and about, especially on such a rainy and unpleasant autumn day. The note was written as if to give me some choice in the matter – "*If you wish to get out and move around*" – but Holmes knew me well enough by then to understand that with such a specifically suggested task, of course I would go. The only question was how I would present myself. It must be recalled that this was early in our association, and was not nearly as experienced in carrying out certain aspects of investigations independently. I did, however, have the confidence of being a doctor – of walking into situations without any foreknowledge or preconceived notions, and with the presence of occasional danger as well, prepared to ask questions. Armed with my medical bag and service revolver, I departed an hour later, finding a hansom to take me to Bloomsbury.

I had read that Millman Street was named after a famed seventeenth-century landowner, but looking around at the conditions, I wondered what he would think, having his name and legacy tied to an area of this condition. It did not sink to the stink and squalor of many East End domains, but there was an uneasy feel to the place, even in daylight. I would not want to traverse the area at night if it could be avoided.

I began at the end of the street, knocking on the door of Number 1 and spinning a tale about being from the nearby Foundling Hospital and searching for whoever might have left a baby there with an anonymous note pinned to the blanket. This fictitious note was written on the back of a torn receipt showing *Millman Street*, but with the house number missing. Did the lady of the house have any knowledge of the wee abandoned child?

It was not the best story that I might have contrived, but it was quickly cobbled together and seemed to get better when I knocked at No. 2 – the lady at No. 1 being sympathetic but having no knowledge of who might help.

No. 2 was unable to assist me, and the same at No. 3. Then I was at No. 4, the home of Foxy Huff and family. I wasn't sure what Holmes wished for me to determine, but I certainly saw a show.

The front of the house was in good-enough condition, and there were flowerboxes beneath the windows, although they were empty at that time of year. Still, they were cleaned out, with no dead plants left to rot despondently through the coming winter months.

A knock at the door revealed a woman in her sixties, looking at me suspiciously. She was too old to be Foxy Huff's wife. Perhaps his mother? I introduced myself and quickly learned that she was the landlady. Three families, besides that of the landlady, were crammed into the building, similar in shape and design to 221 Baker Street, and the Huffs lived on the top floor. The lady was sympathetic to my tale, and while she had no useful information, she allowed that I might interview her tenants.

"But the Coolidges are out for the day, and the Arlingtons are away visiting family, but I believe that the Huffs are at home. Go on up – third floor." The she muttered, "Poor woman."

"What's that?" I asked, aware that it was probably spoken with the intent for me to respond.

"Oh, you'll see, Doctor. And if you might help her a bit . . . ."

I thanked her as she let me inside, trusting that I would soon understand. As I started up the stairs, I was suddenly icy inside, realizing that I hadn't thought this through very well at all. I had pictured knocking on the front door and Mrs. Huff answering, in the same way that women had answered at the first three houses I visited. Instead, I was moving upstairs, deeper into the house, to where I'd been told that "the Huffs are at home". I should have established whether Foxy was also there. Should I knock, hoping that Mrs. Huff alone would answer, without her husband being curious and coming to see who the visitor was? He would almost certainly recognize me from the day before, no matter now nondescript I pictured myself. I'd done nothing to disguise my appearance in the way that Holmes regularly did, and someone in Huff's line would make a point of recognizing people with whom he came in contact – and whom he considered a threat..

Should I wait a few moments in the upper reaches of the house before descending and departing, having done nothing to engage with the Huffs? I sensed that the landlady was listening below. Perhaps I should have a false two-sided conversation before leaving, one floor below the Huff apartment, to give the impression that I had called. But my steady climb had placed me at the Huff's front door without reaching a decision, and with a sigh, and with the hope that Foxy Huff was already away on his own daily business. I decided to complete my mission while also realizing that I might be causing unnecessary complications to Holmes's investigation, I knocked.

In a moment, the door was opened by a small brown-haired woman in her mid-forties, careworn, and with a suspicious manner about her. Behind her, the rooms were dark, and the woman held herself stiffly, as if she were cold. I took a deep breath, relieved that Foxy Huff hadn't opened the door, but realizing that he might be just inside. I began speaking softly, spinning my tale of the foundling child, while I tried to size up what little I could see of the woman. She had some native shrewdness in her expression, but life and its cares had worn her down. There were deep lines bracketing her thin lips, and her eyes were nested in dark puffy bags, themselves surrounded by radiating frown lines. Her hair was thinning and going white in streaks, and I saw the early stages of painful arthritis on the knuckles of her clenched hands.

I hadn't gone far in my story, my voice still low, when the lady's nostrils flared, and an angry spark flared in her eyes.

"You think that Reuben is the father!" she growled, stepping forward into the light of the window on the landing. I backed up a step. "That's why you're here – that little tramp named him as the father, because she knew he'd be too nice to deny it! Well, let me tell you, Caleb Deets is the father! My Reuben has had nothing to do with that girl, except try to be her friend! I told him not to, and look where it's put him! He has his life ahead of him!I won't let any of you tie him up with someone other boy's b-----d!"

She finished speaking, looking at me with antagonism, while my gaze was drawn from her angry expression to the side of her face, marked by a dark and substantial hematoma, fresh and angry, and the size of a man's hand.

"You're hurt," I said, and she flinched.

"No, no. It's nothing. I fell – against the wall. I was clumsy."

"I'm a doctor. Let me look at that – "

"No!" she shrieked, and I was again fearful that Foxy Huff was waiting inside, ready to charge to her defense – or, as I suspected, to deny that he had been the cause of her injury.

"You're here about that girl!" the lady reiterated. Then she cried, "Reuben! *Reuben!*"

She spun and raced back into the apartment, her body leaning forward as if she were a horse straining to gain speed for a jump. Without thinking I followed, fearful that the boy might also be the victim of violence – from his mother – for a reason that might or might not be true. In my haste, the thought that I might encounter Foxy Huff in his own den vanished from my mind.

But he wasn't there, thank Heavens. If he had been, there's no way he would have kept out of the *brouhaha* that followed.

I followed through the cramped front room, observing in passing a worn sofa and a couple of armchairs – one of them Foxy Huff's, no doubt. Then we passed through a narrow kitchen and dining area to the back of the floor, where there were two doors. The one on the right opened to a small dark bedroom. Mrs. Huff banged into the closed door on the left – not much more than a large closet. I could see the shape of someone still abed, and she stepped up to the figure and began to beat upon it with her closed fist, the way one would hammer dust from a rug.

"I told to stay away from that Yates slut!" she growled. "And now this man is here to pin you as the father! You're fourteen years old, Reuben – too young to throw your life away as I did!"

The young man under the covers howled and tried to force himself upright. Meanwhile, I was making every effort to end the chaos that I had inadvertently wrought.

"Mrs. Huff!" I said, trying to catch her flailing arm and pull her back before she did her son a permanent injury. "Mrs. Huff! You misunderstand – A babe was left at the hospital, and Millman Street was written on the note. We're simply asking if someone on the street might know in which house a child was expected."

Finally she seemed to calm down, looking at me and blinking while her breathing slowed. She really had worked herself into quite a state. Meanwhile, Reuben had extricated himself from the bedclothes and found his footing, standing beside us, but poised as if to flee through the doorway. Only then was I able to get a look at him.

Reuben was a slight fellow, with no muscles to him at all, and there was a cringiness about him too, as if he went much of the time fearing the types of beatings that his mother had just delivered – and from her bruises, received as well. I wondered if a medical examination would reveal bruising on his body – for there was none apparent on his face. There seemed to be a legacy of violence within this little family. He was quite a handsome lad with thick Byronic hair, and I could see that he would attract the attention of the young ladies.

The mother started to work herself up again, so I spoke over here. "Young man, are you aware of any women in the neighborhood who have been expecting? Who would have given birth in the last day or so?" As I spent more time subsumed in my role, the vision of this fictitious woman and baby were becoming more and more real in my mind.

Reuben Huff shook his head. "No," he said softly. "Ain't seen nothing like that." He looked at a pile of clothing on the floor, and then at his mother. "Can I get dressed?"

"You stay away from Amy Dillon!" she said with a growl. "She's a tramp, that one is. How many times . . . ?"

I extricated myself, and I don't think they knew I was leaving. I pulled the door shut and went quickly downstairs, where the landlady waited, an unspoken question upon her lips. I think she wanted to gossip, but I'd had enough, simply my head and passing by. Outside, I considered knocking on Number 5, in case anyone wondered why I didn't continue my quest down the street, but I was weary of it, and surely if the landlady saw that I didn't immediately go to the next house, she might think I needed time to find a pub and recover.

I walked for a bit until I found a hansom in Russell Square. I don't know what Holmes wanted me to see, but at least I had something to report, and I'd fortunately avoided getting caught by Foxy Huff.

Chapter V

The rest of the day was spent in my chair. The rain outside stopped, but it was likely to return, and colder air had followed, with a wind that rattled the windows in their frames. I both dreaded going back out in it that night, and also I looked forward to participating in whatever was arranged to conclude Holmes's case.

Nine o'clock, Holmes's message had said. There were no other instructions, but I understood without being told that I should bring my service revolver. It was a lesson that was becoming more apparent whenever I joined an investigation.

At the appointed time, the cab arrived as planned. It was a driver with whom I was somewhat familiar – Creighton Acres – but I wasn't yet on the friendly terms with him that would be achieved in later years when Holmes and I rescued his sainted mother from a "Ladies Deposit" scheme of the sort popularized by Adele Spitzeder in Germany twenty years earlier – or so Holmes told me at the time, as his encyclopedic knowledge of crime had instantly shown him what we were facing when old Mrs. Acres' dilemma was described.

Holmes was waiting in the hansom, and he was now dressed as himself. Over the past several months, when learning about Holmes's unique profession, I'd heard about his various "hidey-holes", as he called them, squirreled throughout the city. He'd been to one of them to change his clothing.

As we rolled into motion, Holmes asked me about my day.

"I'm not sure what you expected me to find," I said in a few moments by way of concluding my narrative.

"I wanted your opinion of Reuben Huff. I thought that using the cover story, you might find a way to work him into conversation."

"I wouldn't have chosen that route," I responded. "Then I would have implied exactly what his mother quickly assumed: By mentioning him specifically in connection with an abandoned newborn, I would have been spreading the unfounded rumor that he was associated, and likely the fictitious child's father – and his mother's rage would have escalated tenfold."

"What did you think of her?"

"Downtrodden. Hopeless. Surely her injuries were from a beating – almost certainly from her husband."

"Almost certainly, indeed. What you've told me confirms and augments Wiggins' report. Another of many dark spots on Foxy's low-dwelling character. And the boy? What is your opinion of him?"

"From the little I saw, he seemed to be rather timid and introverted – if one can assume that based on a couple of minutes where he was trying to defend himself against his mother's blows and accusations." I shook my head at the sad waste of it all. "She is a harridan."

"A fitting mate for Foxy," Holmes replied. "Many is the time, I've heard, that he's come home drunk and slept in the street because she refused to let him in. Clearly he exercises some vengeance upon her, when he has the chance. It sounds, at least, as if she's trying to raise her son to be decent, even if her methods are rough."

"And what is your interest in the boy?"

"To see if he's worth saving. It sounds as if might be."

At that point, I noticed that we seemed to be going in an unexpected direction. "This isn't the way to the St. Giles Workhouse."

"No, we have a different rendezvous to observe tonight."

I could see that he wasn't in the mood to share information, so I resolved – as was so often my lot – to wait until we arrived at our destination. At one point, we crossed the dark river, and the wind, which had been gusting throughout, rocked the hansom as we were suddenly exposed on the bridge, out of the protection of the various streets along our route. Finally noticing my interest in our route, Holmes explained, "Waterloo Bridge. We'll be observing a meeting in Howley Place, just on the other side."

And in a moment, Acres had stopped the horse in a dark stretch far from any gas lamps. Holmes and I slipped out, leaving the cab to wait for us while we melted into a side street, our eyes adjusting to the black night which denied us even the light of a star.

Holmes pulled my sleeve when I seemed to hesitate where to step, and in a moment we were in an areaway across from a humble dwelling. There was a sole light on the first floor, and I tried not to stare at it, preserving my night vision. A pair of dark shapes greeted us, one a constable, and the other speaking to reveal itself as Inspector Gregson.

"They're inside, as you advised us," he said. "We're cutting it close – we should conduct the raid now."

"Sorry I was late," replied Holmes. "I had to make sure my own agents were informed and in place, and then I'd arranged to swing by Baker Street and bring Watson."

I almost felt like apologizing – hoping that Holmes needn't feel obligated to include me if it meant some aspect of the operation might stumble and fail. But before I could speak, Gregson seemed to take Holmes's comment as agreement and gave a signal – putting a couple of fingers to his lips, he produced a soft but clear whistle which was apparently enough to spread the word to all quarters, for as we moved, I sensed other bodies doing the same to our right and left.

The front door was forced open, the building quickly secured to all sides, and in less than a minute we had gone from our coal-black place of concealment to an upstairs sitting room, where four men were taken without incident, fully shocked at our presence to the point of paralysis. Then one who I recognized began to curse – his tone flat and even and steady, never rising in apparent anger, but with his gaze fixed steadily upon Sherlock Holmes while using terms that I'd rarely heard, even from the roughest of men in the heat of bitter combat.

"I was warned of you," said Mr. Stephen Bedfield, a well-known Society figure who was quite visible about the capital and in the press. About forty and very well dressed, he was one of the more-wealthy minor nobles in the land. "They said you might be called in to investigate." He glanced at a much rougher man sitting across a small round table. "You did this, Farraday – you and your carelessness."

"Me?" was the angry response. "I didn't do anything wrong! Same as before – it's never gone wrong before."

"Perhaps," said the well-dressed fellow to Bedfield's right, "it might be best for no one to say anything."

Bedfield shook his head. "My attorney," he explained.

"Indeed," responded Holmes. "How nice of you to also fall into our net, Mr. Tennison. I had no hope that we'd pin you as well."

"Mr. Holmes," said Tennison, "you would be well advised to keep your slanderous comments to yourself – "

"What he's trying to say," interrupted Bedfield, "is that you've jumped in far over your head this time, Holmes. And you as well, Inspector – Gregson, isn't it? Make a note of that, Tennison. Neither of you have any idea of the support behind me. Some of the most important families want their artifacts returned, and they're tired of waiting through the tedious and fruitless process of offer and rejection, offer and rejection, or of placing their hopes in the courts. I have accumulated some powerful favors by taking care of things quickly and efficiently, and I can call in any one of them and make this incident go away – as will your professional standing, Inspector, and your freedom, Mr. Holmes. Even though my current agent has failed me – " He cast a contemptuous glance toward Farraday. " – you'll find that no charges will be placed against me – "

"Now hold on," growled Jimmy Farraday. "I did nothing wrong!" It seemed important that he made sure to establish that for which he could not be blamed. "I – "

"Ah, but you did," corrected Holmes. "You did do something wrong. You put your trust in a rotten link like Foxy Huff."

Up to that moment, Huff had been sitting quietly beside his master, the fourth member of the group, his face pale and sick as he contemplated the mire in which he was suddenly pitched up to his chin. But now, when things couldn't have seemed worse, he found that they were.

"What do you mean?" snarled Farraday, twisting suddenly to glare at Huff. Seeing how ill his companion suddenly looked shook his confidence. "What did you do, Foxy?"

"I . . . I . . . ." Words failed the shell of a villain.

"He took it upon himself to try and intervene," explained Holmes with a false friendliness to his tone. "Yesterday, he approached Dr. Watson and myself and tried to get us to believe that his son and some of his associates were responsible for the theft of the Sheffield Plate – and that right now, even as we have this interesting discussion, they would be involved in delivering it to a buyer. But as you can see, Foxy's poor efforts didn't distract us from the real delivery." He gestured toward the center of the table, where the silver objects rested. I was surprised that I hadn't noticed them before, but then I realized that when observing the human drama around the table, the dead and dull collection was of little real interest.

"What?" asked Farraday. "What do you mean – tried to convince you that his son . . . ." He looked back at Foxy Huff, whose slack lips were working, but he produced no sound.

"That's right," said Holmes. "Huff is at a level of comtempt far beneath even a thief like you, Farraday – or you, Mr. Bedfield," added Holmes, glancing toward our inadvertent host. "To deflect suspicion from this meeting here tonight, Foxy came up with the notion to tell us a cock-and-bull story that his son would be behind the St. Giles Workhouse right now to get rid of the plate. He stupidly believed that he could sell me on that idea, and that we would be there now while you meet here in Lambeth. In fact, Inspector Lestrade is waiting in concealment there to pick up Reuben Huff and Abel Farris, and whomever else shows up. We'll determine later just how much they know."

A look of true disgust pulled down Farraday's features. "You cretinous little ---!" he snarled at Huff. "You threw over your own *son*?"

Huff again tried to speak, but just made some kind of soft whiny wheeze, like the passing away of an old and dying mosquito.

If it is not yet obvious, I thought very little indeed of Foxy Huff.

"I said that involving Huff was your mistake," said Holmes, continuing to speak to Farraday, "but that's not entirely accurate. Associating with a low type like Foxy is a mistake in any circumstance, but I was already onto you, and I'd known about this meeting here for a long time. Your sources really aren't that secure, and your father, Cyrus Blair, has become far too smug, complacent, and confident of his invulnerability. I've spent a bit of time with him in disguise over several days – including today – as he bragged about his various crimes, and provided details about tonight's meeting. He's under arrest now, too, even as we speak, and," he said, turning to Bedfield, "I can assure you that whatever power and influence you believe you've achieved has been washed away like the day's manure from the stalls where Cyrus Blair holds court. He's the sort that will throw you over for any promise of saving his own skin. You may have been working for some powerful friends, but you've also made a number of powerful enemies, and they were quite glad when I let them know that we had you, and that you are finally done."

The whole party was relocated across the river, less than a mile by road to Scotland Yard – with some of the group traveling in the back of a Black Maria. As soon as Gregson led Holmes and me to his office, we were joined by Lestrade, and both of them, whose rivalry served to sharpen one another as iron versus steel, began to tell of their respective adventures. We'd shared Gregson's night, but Lestrade's was news to us.

"They were all there, Mr. Holmes – Farris' entire little 'gang' – just as you said they'd be, shuffling around in the dark street behind the workhouse with a shabby goblet from the plate collection in their possession, waiting for someone to come and buy it from them. We approached, and they thought we were the men they were to meet. They waited for us just like those baby seals you hear tell of, not moving, and easy targets for the hunters to club."

"How many did you bag?"

"All six – Able Farris, and the Huff lad, and the others. Farris confirmed we have the whole lot."

"That's excellent. Perhaps this will put a rehabilitative scare into them before they get into worse trouble."

"One would hope so. Farris is a little older – he may be beyond salvage, but the others are younger, and only seem to be trailing after Farris because they have nothing better to do."

Holmes nodded. "I have some contacts, and I'm owed some favors. I'll see what I can do about that."

The next morning, we were back at Scotland Yard when the six members of Abel Farris gang were due to be released. Although they had been in possession of one small piece of the stolen plate collection, it was understood that they had been set up by Foxy Huff.

"I didn't know it was him," explained Farris, who was not much older than the boys he led. "I received a box with the cup, a five-pound note, and instructions about where to take it." He glanced at Reuben Huff, who would only stare at the floor. "If we could do this, we'd be trusted with something bigger. I didn't know that it was Reuben's dad that sent it to me . . . ."

Holmes nodded and then explained his idea – that he had positions lined up for all six of them, either in jobs that could grow to something better over time if they earned their employers' trust, or as apprentices in necessary crafts that would provide them a lifetime of gainful and respectable employment. All of the lads took advantage of the offer, even Farris, and, although the way wasn't always smooth, it was a happy ending for six lads whose stories might have ended in a much darker fashion – particularly if Foxy Huff's plan to sacrifice them had succeeded with no one to explain otherwise.

We were there when Mrs. Huff arrived to claim her wayward son. She recognized me, and wanted to rage in my direction – for she had a great deal of rage to express – before turning her attention upon her son.

But she was instrumental in keeping him on the straight and narrow path, and – with the removal of Foxy Huff from their life – her task was made easier.

When Foxy Huff was brought in – for Holmes wanted to orchestrate a reunion, if for no other reason than to see the performance of a human drama – I feared that Mrs. Huff might give away, forgiving him as she must have done so many other times, disappointment after disappointment after disappointment. After all, she had stayed with her husband through many years of such behaviors, and had allowed him to commit physical violence upon her, if my reasoning was correct. But when it was explained what Huff had done – how he had been willing to allow his own son to go to prison so that he could deflect interest away from Farraday's activities, her noted rage knew no limits. She flew at Huff, adding further scars to his scarred head, and no one made any move to pull her off him until she began to tire.

As that played out, it was rather heartbreaking to see Reuben Huff's face as he fully understood his father's treachery. He simply stared at the man who had sired him, expressionless.

"You understand," said Huff to his son, realizing that he'd now finally done something that was unforgiveable. "It was for all of us – to keep me in good with Mr. Farraday so that I could support the family. And I told Mr. Holmes about it beforehand – Didn't I, Mr. Holmes? – so that you would be picked up and given a light sentence. It was really to help *you*, Reuben! To *save* you! You see that, don't you? That's why I did it! You understand! Right? Right . . . ?"

Reuben Huff was able to escape his father's influence that much quicker when the man was shivved in a prison hallway not long after, to be remembered only by his former wife and son as an object lesson, and as a figure of derision in my notes.

The next morning, Holmes walked into the sitting room to see me in in my chair by the fire and staring toward my desk. After greeting me, he said, "So you've decided to let it lie."

"For now," I murmured, thinking of the effort expended so far into crafting my manuscript. Beyond my desk, I could see through the window where the rains from the day before had returned in excess, running in blurring and changing streaks down the panes.

Holmes nodded, poured a cup of coffee, and then chuckled and muttered for the next ten minutes while opening, sorting, and reading his mail.

He seemed satisfied with the idea that he'd deduced my abandonment of the manuscript, but he was wrong. More than ever, after seeing the drama that a malignant force such as Foxy Huff had brought upon his family, I was convinced that a narrative of Holmes's cases must relate the human element to lift them above some dry treatise – certainly informative for some student of crime, but desiccated when ignoring the underlying motivations. I would just need to wait until such time as the middle portion of the book – properly relating Jefferson Hope's incredible life and why he would spend it in pursuit of revenge – could be adequately told, cladding that skeleton with a different kind of meat.

Later that night when the rains ended, Holmes and I went for another long walk, and we returned to find a doctor from Brook Street, Percy Trevelyan by name, anxious to relate his own unusual story. After that matter was concluded, I was even more convinced that if I were ever to share more of Holmes's investigations with the public, the human aspect must not be ignored.

It would take years to confirm it, but my wary suspicions even then were correct: Holmes was not pleased.

NOTE

* For more about how the Wiggins clan came into Holmes's service, and the saving of Mrs. Wiggins from a capital charge, see "The Gower Street Murder" in *Sherlock Holmes – Skeins* and *The Collected Papers of Sherlock Holmes – Volume II: Records*

The Morning Encounter with the Velocipede Racer

We had nearly missed the boat-train back from Calais. Twenty-fours earlier, I hadn't imagined that I would be there at all.

That Saturday had begun as many others, seeing a few morning patients in my Queen Anne Street practice and residence. But like an old dog who longs to hear horns, twitching his feet and giving small whines as he dreams of the hunt, it never took much to distract me – sometimes to my wife's great vexation. A laconic message from Sherlock Holmes changed my plans for the day, and within the hour I had joined him at Victoria, racing toward Dover. Exiting the station, we saw Holmes's prey – Hundridge Boyd, the traitor – climbing into a cab, and in moments we were behind him.

In order to prove his guilt, we had to let him leave the country with the stolen government documents – otherwise, he could have legitimately claimed that carrying them within England's borders was a proper function of his position within a small department of the Foreign Office. But when we crossed into French waters, Holmes, two government agents, and I approached Boyd in the salon and placed him under arrest.

It had been very neat and tidy, as there had been some worry that Boyd might resist arrest, but he complied willingly enough. (It was later determined that he was being manipulated by way of threats to his wife – a mitigating circumstance that later resulted in Holmes working to free the man from the chains that had ensnared him.) The ferry wasn't due to return for a number of hours, and Boyd was placed in custody in a discreet cabin reserved for such purposes. In the meantime, Holmes was prepared to find a corner of the lounge and smoke, but I insisted that we spend our few free hours in the French port city.

It was pleasant enough, though hot for that time of July, and we took a cab to a more hospitable location in town, walking along the Boulevard Jacquard and having a late lunch at Au Calice, a favorite brasserie featuring mussels in garlic cream with a baguette – a feast that was much more difficult to find in England, and rarely as authentic. In fact, I tarried over the large steaming black cauldron for a bit too long, and we realized that we were in danger of missing our ship.

We were fortunate and found a cab. Back in the salon, we settled in with cups of coffee and I began to read a French newspaper that I'd picked up, printed in English.

After commenting on a few of the general stories, I noted that the finish of the great French bicycle race was imminent.

"This 'Tour de France*', as they call it over here, concludes in Paris today," I said. It had been highly promoted in the press, but even as I mentioned it, I remembered that Holmes would have evinced no interest in it. He'd never followed sporting teams, or made any effort to attend a race or match if there was no connection there to his professional interests. I was about to turn the page when, to my surprise, his attention returned from whatever he'd been pondering in our (up to that point) one-sided conversation.*

"Eh?" he said. "Bicycle race?"

Seeing that he was engaged, I nodded. "A staged bicycle race across France: Paris to Lyon, Lyon to Marseilles, and so on, until the return to Paris today. Seven stages total, over fifteen-hundred miles – sometimes in the mountains." I was warming to the topic. "Can you imagine the athleticism? Initially one might think of a leisurely bicycle ride in the country, but these stages have been grueling – only one of them was less than two-hundred-fifty miles in a day, and one was nearer three-hundred! And to take that punishment, all day long, only to get up and do it again the next day. I can only imagine!"

I was about to launch into a complicated explanation of how the winners of stages didn't necessarily mean that a rider was the overall leader in the standings at the end of each day when Holmes interrupted. "You seem quite enthused with this," he said. "Do you wish that you'd been over here to see it?"

I nodded. The thought had crossed my mind when reading about the race all week long. Sixty riders had started, but the grueling pace had weeded that down to just over twenty. That day in Paris, Maurice Garin, who had been racing bicycles since the early nineties and was known affectionately as "The Little Chimney Sweep", was favorited to win.

"You wouldn't enjoy it," continued Holmes. "Seeing the race."

"And why not?" I asked, having pictured it a great deal over the previous week.

"Because having been to a bicycle race, I can tell you that it isn't like a horse race, where you can generally have a view of what's happening from start to finish. No, these bicycle races cover a great deal of ground, and while you may place yourself in one spot to see a minute fraction of it, you only see the approach, the few seconds when they cross your path, and then their departure, around the next curve or over a hill, and then there's nothing for you to do but pack up and go back home."

I had to admit that what he said would be true, although in my imagination, it had been much different, as I envisioned every straight stretch, with riders straining for an advantage or to pull ahead and break away from the pack, or the agonizing slow climbs up steeply graded mountain roads, some little better than footpaths. In my thoughts, I'd been right there with the riders, at their side for every dramatic mile, but I knew that Holmes was right. In truth, going to see a bicycle race, and finding a good vantage point, would only be good for that one vantage, and then the riders would be gone.

"So you've been to a bicycle race?" I asked. "You certainly wouldn't have cared about the athletic contest, so it must have been in relation to some case."

"In those days, I didn't have 'cases'. I simply found myself involved in interesting adventures. And not only did I attend a bicycle race, but I attended the first bicycle race – the first international race, that is – although I had no interest in it, and never meant to see it."

I glanced at the large clock on the salon wall. "We appear to have plenty of time . . . ."

With a smile of feigned weariness, Holmes nodded and began to tell me of his boyhood visit to the Crystal Palace, and how he inadvertently found himself involved in the convoluted affairs of a racing cyclist . . . .

First of all [*Holmes began*], it wasn't a bicycle race. Back then – this was in 1869 – they were still riding velocipedes. Did you have one? No, I didn't either, although I did ride one – once. There's a reason they were called 'boneshakers', and the overly large front wheel was difficult to steer. Additionally, the foot pedals, attached directly to the front wheel's axle, made it quite difficult to develop speed, or to keep pedaling when making wide turns.

I'd seen a few of them during our travels while growing up, but I'd never had any curiosity about them, as the riders seemed to be suffering rather than enjoying themselves. And if that wasn't enough to convince me to stay away, then one only had to see the number of accidents that befell the riders – some quite catastrophic.

I had no thoughts of velocipedes or races that May morning. Instead, I had been sent on a mission of enquiry by my father – not one that I wanted to undertake, you understand, but instead one that was assigned in order to further my diverse and unorthodox education.

At that age, I had no idea what I wanted to be in life, alternating some weeks between scientific studies – perhaps chemistry one day, or studies of nature on another. You smile, Watson, but the natural world has always fascinated me, and I never should have tweaked you as I did when we first met by claiming that I had no notion that the earth went 'round the sun. My interests were wide and varied, and I had the gift – or curse – of retaining what I read and learned. But as much as I *didn't* know what I wanted to be when I reached my maturity, my father was certain of it. My eldest brother would take over running the estate, Mycroft would obtain a government job, and I would become a civil engineer. And with that in mind, I'd been sent to Sydenham to view the structure of the Crystal Palace, as well as some of the educationally rewarding exhibits contained therein.

It was dark and windy day that promised rain, and I'm sure that my thoughts were typical of any fifteen year old as I approached the famed building. As you'll recall learning when we were there in '86, after Löwenbräu strangled that painter, it was first built in London – Hyde Park – in 1851, to house the Great Exhibition, and then, after the event ended six months later, it was dismantled and rebuilt in Sydenham. The place is massive, with a footprint of nearly twenty acres. When one considers the extensive grounds surrounding it – Well, as you know, a great deal can occur there that remains unobserved.

My approach had meandered as I worked my way steadily toward the building, and I was on one of the smaller paths, lost in thought, when suddenly someone came charging out of a side trail. He was looking back over his shoulder and didn't see me, stepping quietly as I was, and he slammed into me as if we were on a rugby field. He was somewhat smaller than me – at first I thought he was several years younger than my fifteen – and typically he would have bounced off, but he was a lean and gristly fellow with layers of dense muscles, and it was impossible for me to retain my balance. I went down, with this chap on top of me. He bounced up like a *gutta percha* ball and, instead of apologizing, immediately reached down a hand, looking behind himself once again, and whispering, "Quickly! Lend me your overcoat!"

Needless to say, I was rather nonplussed as he stood me up, and sadly my reflexes, not as honed to unusual occurrences then as now, left me, having regained my feet, with my jaw slack and agape. After another second passed and with an additional glance behind him, the smaller man – for he was a man, though just five years or so older than me – growled with impatience and began tugging on the collar of my coat, dragging it down one arm and away from me before I could think to resist.

At this point, my senses had returned and I was able to get a better look at him. He was small, not much over five feet and certainly just ten stone, even in his winter wool clothing. He had a lean face, with shadows under his sharp cheekbones and hints of short sandy hair peeking out from beneath his flat woolen cap. His ears and nose were red with the cold – but then, I imagined that mine were too, for there was a marked damp chill in the air. I could see various scars on his knuckles, and when he tugged at my coat and gritted his teeth with the effort, I observed that his upper right lateral incisor was chipped and discolored. His clothing was worn but serviceable, and from hat to shoes, presented various shades of brown with mismatched patterns – herringbone and houndstooth and checkered designs all jarring against one another.

By then he'd divested me of my warm coat and pulled it onto himself. Whereas it had ended comfortably around my knees, for him it was in danger of dragging the ground. I was about to finally utter a protest when he next snarled, "Now the hat!"

Even as he was pulling his own cap off, apparently to offer in trade, I finally mounted some feeble defense. "Here now!" I cried, for wearing another man's hat, as you know, is beyond the pale. Besides, even then I was particular about my headgear, and – I hate to admit it – rather sentimental in that regard. I'd developed a marked fondness for my fore-and-aft hunting cap, and this stranger was reaching up, trying to pluck it from my head!

I became aware of the sound of approaching footsteps, in a hurry, unseen around a curve along the path from which the strange young man had just emerged.

My new companion swore, pulled the hat roughly from my head and, even as he doffed it, he reached up with his other hand and placed his own cap upon me, pulling it down tightly toward my eyes.

He seemed to change before me then, sinking lower so that he took further inches off his height, with the hem of the coat covering his shoes. He turned his head down so that his face wasn't visible, and my hat's rear bill hid the rest of his sandy hair. His left hand was in jammed into the coat's pocket, pulling it across him so that his clothing wasn't visible. And I was surprised when his right hand took mine, gripping it so tightly that I could feel his roughened callosities.

"For pity's sake," he whispered as two men hove into view, "tell them that I'm your little brother!" Then those that had been pursuing him slid to a stop ten or fifteen feet from us, and I straightened to face them.

One was a big fellow, long run to fat and now heaving for breath. He showed all the signs of once having been a boxer – nose broken at least twice, and set in two different directions along the bridge to the tip, and one ear severely flattened and deformed outward like a clay-red lettuce leaf. His lack of wind in the present certainly reflected on his past failures as a fighter. His companion was a ratty little fellow of about forty, dressed not altogether unlike the young man gripping my hand for dear life. I could almost feel my new companion willing me through our contact into going along with his effort to avoid being caught by these two men.

"What's this?" wheezed the larger man, his voice garbled as if he'd also taken punches to the throat. "You two seen a little runt come this way?"

His own little runt didn't seem to appreciate the comment, because instead of spending time looking at either of us, he rounded on the big man and kicked him hard in the shin. He may have been rather down-at-heel, but he'd invested in good shoes, and the sound of his boot soles cracking against bone sounded like a stick breaking. The big man gave a great cry that frightened birds from the trees and set about hopping, trying to massage his injury at the same time. Meanwhile, the smaller man, his attention divided between his victim and me, didn't seem to want to waste much more valuable time in case is quarry was escaping.

"Have you seen a little – Has anyone run by here? Brown cap, brown clothes?"

It must be remembered that this had all occurred across not more than a minute, and I had no time to consider who was in the right or wrong, or to what level I could exercise any attempt to avoid further involvement. But I suddenly felt like I needed to know what else was going to happen in this story – much more than following my father's directed plan to wander through the Crystal Palace with a list of things to ponder, such as the tension and compression forces acting upon the beams holding up the great ceiling, or the curtain wall system that allowed the hanging of the many great glass sheets from cantilevered beams, and their bending moments from the downward forces, or the unique and elegant ridge-and-furrow roofing system that answered the problem of draining the building's vast roof because of the poor tensile strength of the brittle plate glass.

"Haven't seen anybody," I mumbled. "Me and Little Brother – just going on to the Palace yonder." I affected the strong Yorkshire accent of my youth – although my family had traveled so often in those years that my way of speaking had by then become the homogenized expression that I typically use, and the way I spoke when you first met me some years later.

The large man was calming down, and the smaller was looking from one to the other of us, but I made sure to face him straight on, a rather stupid expression set in place on my features. My "Little Brother" seemed likewise afflicted, never looking up, and finally with a raspy sound of disgust, the small man said, "Come along, Beecher. He's getting away." And then they hurried past us, the larger with a noticeable handicap.

"If you see him . . . ." he instructed, but then he was gone.

I started to say something, but the other fellow, still gripping my hand, made a *Hist*-ing noise, and I stayed silent for nearly another minute after the other two had diminished in the distance and then turned in a different direction, vanishing behind a row of bushes.

Finally my hand was freed, and I reached up, ripping the stranger's cap from my head and reaching for my own hat, popping it up and off the other fellow before he could object. Knocking it against my chest and leg and then brushing inside it, I gave a final visual inspection in and out before finally replacing it where it belonged. The day was cold, and being used to wearing a hat makes it much worse when said hat is missing.

"Now my coat," I demanded, and to his credit, my new acquaintance relinquished it without a word, even giving it a shake and handing it to me folded and held up off the ground.

"What was that about?" I asked, and at first the young man wasn't inclined to answer – just shaking his head while he considered something with intensity. When I repeated my question and still no answer, I tried a different one.

"What is your name?"

That seemed to break into his thoughts. "Eh? Littlecott. Carnaby Littlecott." Although there was no time for a comment to cross my mind, or for my expression to change, he immediately became defensive. "No remarks about 'A little cot for Littlecott!' I had enough of that in school!"

I simply shook my head, to agree, or signify that no remarks would be forthcoming. Then, because he was engaging with me, I said again, "What was that about?"

But he had reached a decision. "I'll tell you on the way. You need to come with me."

Now that surprised me. I wanted to know more about what was happening, but not to the point where I'd consider going somewhere with this stranger – in spite of the fact that he'd told me his name. I shook my head, but before I could reply, he continued.

"I need you to confirm something – that Halford and Beeching were after me. That will help to convince Silas – to convince someone that I'm telling the truth. If I tell him on my own, he'll think that I'm just trying to weasel out of it, or that I'm only causing trouble. But if you – a total stranger – tell him too, then he'll at least have to think about it."

I started to protest that this was no explanation at all, but something wavered me. Instead I asked, "And you'll tell me about it on the way?"

He nodded. I thought I saw a flash of happy surprise in his eyes – as if a hook had been set, and I was his hapless fish. "Where are we going?" I asked, wondering just how long this would take, or how far I'd have to go.

"Not far," he responded. "Just over to The Teeford Arms in Penge. Now we'd best hurry. Do you have any money on you?"

I re-thought my position. Was Carnaby Littlecott now, after having conversed with me and even secured my qualified agreement to accompany him, going to rob me? Perhaps he saw my concern, for he shook his head. "For a *cab*," he said. "If we can find one. I have to take you with me to see Halford, and still be back in time for the race. Now come on!"

And with that very-small bit of information to chew upon, I threw over my father's plans to look at the marvelous engineering of the Crystal Palace and instead walked back the way I had come, in the company of a total stranger, and headed toward Penge, a hamlet whose existence had, prior to that moment, escaped my attention entirely.

Perhaps describing Penge as a "hamlet" is a bit incorrect, because by then, it had increased in size considerably past what it must have been over the previous thousand years or so. The coming of the railroad, and the Croydon Canal, had opened up the area, and the draw of the nearby Crystal Palace, and the accessibility to those wishing to visit for the day or live in the area and commute up to London led to a rapid expansion. There were many large and new homes along roads that were also either new or freshly widened, and modernized from the wagon tracks and pathways that had been there for centuries. On the day I was introduced to Penge, it boasted twenty-five pubs to the square mile – and it was to one of these that my new acquaintance was leading me, assuring me several times that my testimony would be crucial to him proving his case.

I had initially arrived that morning by way of the Crystal Palace Station, and hadn't progressed very far northward into the park when accosted by Carnaby, so we didn't have far to walk back to Penge – southeast for just a thousand feet or so before reaching the outskirts. We didn't encounter a cab, and we'd only been walking for a few minutes, the paths mostly deserted at that time of morning, when he asked me, "What's your name?"

I told him, and he shook his head. "Good as any, I suppose. Names don't matter – not on their own. It's what you add to them that matters."

I asked him what he meant. "Your *deeds*. Your *accomplishments*. Whether anyone hears your name and knows who you are, or they remember you when you're gone."

I started to ask what he'd accomplished so far, but I had learned a little tact at that callow age, and knew that it might be a sore question for him. But he wanted to answer anyway, even without me asking it.

"I mean to be a champion racer," he explained. "I'm not much in other ways – average brain, average strength for my size. But I can *race*! That's why it's so important that this morning's race be fair."

"But what is this race?" I asked. "I was just going to see the Palace. I had no notion of a race being held there."

"There was a velocipede race there last Easter, running between Spencer and Mayall, but it was no more than a demonstration. Today is the real race. There's an international derby – first ever, with eight foreigners, and also an Englishman's race with two-dozen riders. I'm to be one of those. It starts in a few hours. The course will be about a mile around, with multiple laps around the basin of the great fountains, and the lower portion of the grounds." He glanced up at the sky, where more dark clouds were building. "It will run, rain or shine, but I would have preferred sun."

"But these two men that were chasing you," I said. "What do they have to do with the race?"

He looked as if he would prefer just to keep walking, having spent enough time on conversation, but perhaps he realized that for me to cooperate, and accompany him to wherever we were going, he had to provide some information.

"Those two men, Halford and Beeching – the little one and the big one – work for my stepfather. He owns the pub where we're going now. My stepfather is a businessman, but he also . . . he's also involved in gambling. He doesn't gamble himself – No, he's too canny for that, and he holds gamblers in great contempt. Instead, he makes book for various races, and . . . and he isn't above applying pressure where he can to give himself an advantage. Halford and Beeching are his agents when this is required."

I was considering what he said. At that innocent age, I was aware of bookmakers, having seen a number of them at horse races with my father, but I'd given no thought to the matter, other than thinking once or twice about how they must have some mathematical edge in terms of the odds so that, no matter the result, they will make money. By then, I had seen much, but you'll have to believe me when I say that I hadn't really reflected upon cheating in sports, and how money could be made from such a thing.

"So these two men," I said, "were doing something to change the odds – to alter the conditions of the race and make some money for your stepfather."

"No, that's exactly wrong!" Carnaby snarled. "They were at the racetrack talking with another bookmaker – when I know that they're supposed to be up in London today. Not only that – I overheard them arranging to fix the race so that the man favored and backed by my stepfather would be lamed at some point, causing him to lose."

"But why would they go against their employer, your stepfather, and arrange to have you injured?"

He was silent for a moment, and then I realized that I had made an erroneous assumption. "I'm not my stepfather's favored racer," he muttered. "In fact, he's given very high odds that I won't even finish the race. He has no confidence in me, and has made that very clear. His favored rider is named Stritter, and it's him that Halford and Beeching were conspiring against this morning."

"Well," I said, "then that just makes your chances better, right?"

He stopped and rounded on me angrily.

"I want to win fair and square!" he snarled. "That's why I'm going to tell my stepfather what I heard – so that Stritter can compete his best race, and so can I. But Halford and Beeching saw me there – and they know I heard them, and that I can tell that they weren't in London, so they're trying to stop me, and that's why I have to get to my stepfather. But they've both been working for him a long time, so I need you as a witness – to confirm that they were at the Crystal Palace this morning, and that they were after me. He . . . he won't want to believe me, but maybe if you tell him . . . ."

I nodded. Then, because that corner of my brain attic was sadly empty, I asked him to elaborate upon the nature of bookmaking, and the mathematical factors of creating *odds*.

Carnaby Littlecott had other things on his mind, and it was obvious that he maintained, as a general rule, a sour disposition, but I was nevertheless starting to like this angry little man, and for whatever reason, he relented and began to explain bookmaking to me.

"Bets were once recorded in a ledger – a *book* – and the person laying the bets is the *bookmaker*. It's his job to accept bets in the right proportion to make a profit, regardless of the outcome. To do that, he adjust the odds, always downward if possible, and always at an amount which is less than what are estimated to be the *true* odds. These are calculated based on which way the betting is going. If a horse is fifty-to-one and someone bets a fortune on that horse, then there's no way the bookmaker could cover the return if the horse won – fifty dollars won for every dollar bet. So immediately the odds will drop to something that would be more easily paid, on the off-chance that the horse does win.

"A good bookmaker can maintain and adjust all of this in his head – and my stepfather has some good bookmakers. He's the money behind it all in these parts, and . . . and that kind of money is attracts crime. My stepfather is a criminal." He added this with sudden emphasis, as if I should understand that fact above all else. "He sits in an office above his pub, but from there he has his eye on a dozen different schemes at any given moment, and Halford and Beeching are his agents. They're wrong 'uns. Wherever you see them, something wrong is going on."

By this time, we had left the grounds of the park surrounding the Palace and were in the outskirts of adjacent Penge. I mentioned that the streets were mostly empty, but we'd occasionally seen people walking, and a few times we were passed by carts driven by farmers or delivery men. I gave no thought to the growler that was coming along behind us until it pulled up suddenly and two men threw open the doors and jumped out – Halford and Beeching!

"Got you!" snarled the little one – Halford, I assumed, from what Carnaby had told me.

Surprised and unprepared as I was, I did nothing to prevent them taking hold of my companion as they bulled past me. Carnaby twisted back and forth, but couldn't get away, and they immediately started dragging him into the growler.

"Go north!" Halford instructed the driver, who was looking on with some surprise. "Out of town! Quick!" But as Beeching pulled Carnaby Littlecott inside the vehicle, the latter cried out, "Harry! Don't do it! I need to tell my stepfather what they've been up to! He needs to know! Take me to him! Drive to the pub! Take me – !"

Then Halford, now on board as well, repeated, "Go north, Harry! Out of town!" He turned and looked back at me. "And you – get away from here now if you know what's good for you." Then he slammed the door.

The driver looked down at me without expression, and then flicked the reins and set the horses into motion. I could hear loud arguing voices coming from within the carriage, and I wondered how the story would end.

And then I decided to find out for myself.

Sprinting into motion, I caught up with the growler, which hadn't yet reached its traveling speed and, with a bold skip and leap, found an uneasy place on the back, out of site of the driver or passengers.

Fortunately, we didn't have far to travel, as we'd already halfway negotiated the limits of Penge, and within five minutes or less, we were stopping on one of the side streets in front of a well-kept pub, with *The Teeford Arms* inscribed tidily across the front. The door to the growler flew open and Halford, seeing where we were, began to passionately curse Harry the driver for being a traitor. There was no response from that quarter, but two burly bruisers came from the pub and took Carnaby Littlecott in hand, and made it clear that Halford and Beeching were to follow. Beeching, as big as the two men from the pub, had the expression of a little child who was about to cry, and any threat he might have presented before had run away like a cup of spilled tea. As the two enforcers were about the usher the other three inside, I hopped from my perch and cried, "Wait for me!"

Carnaby twisted within the grip of one of his captors to see my approach, and a big grin creased his face. I didn't know what I was getting myself into, or how I could help him, but in any case he was pleased that I hadn't abandoned him. Halford began squawking once again, and I'd heard enough to know that some scheme of his was unraveling, and worse – he was about to be revealed to his employer as a treacher.

It was too early for the pub to be open, but I could see that it would be a popular place, as some money had certainly been applied to it. You and I have seen many nasty and run-down establishments over the years, but whoever owned this place had an eye for what was attractive, and was willing to fund it. I only had seconds to look around, however, as we were hustled up a narrow set of stairs beyond the bar. At the first floor, a sharp turn brought us into a wide room, stretching the width of the building, with numerous windows overlooking the street. This, it seemed, was the office of Carnaby's stepfather, and from whence he ran his modest criminal operation.

He was behind a wide desk, empty except for a cup of tea, half-full, and a tidily arranged stack of three ledgers, one atop another, with a big black one on bottom, a smaller brown one in the middle, and pocket-sized green one on top. They were carefully aligned with the left rear corner of the man's desk, and the tea cup was on his left side.

It was a small thing to notice, his being left-handed, but from such initial observations come others. I then noted that he also shaved left-handed, as demonstrated by the poor job along his right jawline. He was expensively dressed, a man of fifty or so, and he wore nothing for decoration except a wedding ring, a watch on a plain chain, and a modest ruby tie pin. But he didn't need any added *accoutrements*, as he radiated power. And danger.

"What is this?" he asked softly. "Carnaby – What have you done now?"

The man holding my recent acquaintance pushed him forward, and Carnaby pointed a finger at Halford and Beeching, standing to one side, unhindered by the other big enforcer, but not exactly free men either.

"I saw them – this morning – at the Palace. They were talking with Wittle, making arrangements for someone to lay down his vehicle in front of Stritter in a turn, crippling him. They were placing bets against your man and trying to handicap him as well. Then they knew that I saw and heard them, and they tried to stop me from telling you. "

"It's a lie!" Halford reupted. "He's lying! We were never at the Palace. We got back from London early, and were here in Penge when we saw Carnaby having some kind of fit. We stopped to help him! He's lying! He's always been a liar! You know that. He – "

"Get Harry up here!" countered Carnaby. "He'll tell you. When they caught up with me, on my way here, they told him to drive north, out of town. Get him – he'll tell you!"

Halford began to squawk once more and the man raised a single finger, stopping the little man as if he'd been rendered unconscious. Meanwhile, the man behind the desk slowly lowered the finger and then remained motionless for a long moment, his eyes never leaving Carnaby, nor making any other motion. Finally he murmured, "Get Harry," and immediately the man holding Carnaby released him and lurched into motion, heading downstairs to retrieve the driver. In just seconds, Harry had returned, shuffling in and turning his cap 'round and 'round in his nervous hands.

"Where did you pick up Halford and Beeching?" asked the man.

"Just coming into Penge," he said. "They was walking along, and I stopped and offered a lift."

"And Carnaby?"

"Not long after. We seen him walking up the road with this other feller – " He nodded toward me. "Halford told me to stop, and then they jumped out and wrestled Carnaby into the carriage."

"And what were their instructions?"

Harry was silent for a few seconds, but then his apparent fear of his master caused him to look apologetically toward the men he was about to doom. "North. They said to go north – out of town."

"And yet you brought them here. Why?"

"Because . . . because something was going on, and I didn't want to do the wrong thing without getting better instructions."

"Very good. You are dismissed."

Harry then fled as if the string suspending him had been severed, and he dropped out of sight instantly. I heard the pub's front door slam shut.

Then, instead of turning to Halford and Beeching as one might expect, he let them stew and looked at me.

"What is your purpose in this?" he wanted to know, and I felt like a mouse who sees that a hawk is perched above him.

I swallowed and straightened up, speaking in a voice that sounded rather thin, not pleasing me at all. "And your name, sir?"

There was no response, except possibly a change in the way the man's eyes beheld me. Was it amusement at my pitiful boldness? Perhaps.

"I am Silas Caine," he said. When I offered no response, he added, "Didn't Carnaby tell you? And your name . . . *sir*?

I cleared my throat. "Sherlock Holmes." Better than I'd hoped – there was no squeak in my response.

"And I repeat," Caine said, something as flat as an old grave in his tone, "what is your purpose here?"

"I was asked to come along to confirm Carnaby's accusation against these two men." And I pointed toward Halford and Beeching. This time, Halford made no response – no sound at all, actually.

"And how can you do that?" Caine asked. "Did you overhear the conversations that Carnaby reported?"

"I did not. I was merely visiting the Palace this morning when Carnaby ran into me while being pursued by these two men. I helped him to hide."

"And why would you do this? Do you know one another?"

"We've never met before today."

"Again, why would you do this? Involve yourself with someone you've never met? Did Carnaby pay you to come along and confirm his story?" He was not calling what he'd heard a lie – not yet. I sensed that wrong or unconvincing answers would be dangerous. Just what sort of criminals were entrenched in seemingly innocent places like Penge?

I could only provide the truth. "I was not paid. I simply saw Carnaby's fear, and that these two men presented a danger. It was the right thing to do."

"And yet, why should I believe you?" With this question, I felt the most danger yet, as if I had now been led right to a precipice. No one knew that I was here, and if I vanished, no explanation would be forthcoming.

I swallowed. "Because I can prove it."

This, then, generated a reaction on Silas Caine's otherwise expressionless face. To that moment, he might as well have been a stone carving upon a tomb door. Now, he raised an eyebrow, and an almost amused look crossed his face, just for an instant, with the implication to proceed.

"Their shoes," I said, again nodding toward Halford and Beeching. "Examine the soil that's still on them. I'm preparing to be a civil engineer," I said, "and as such, I've studied Tewkesbury's British soil maps, and those of Coleford and Aldbourne as well. The soil at the Crystal Palace was brought in from outside this area. It isn't native to London, or to Penge. It's alluvial, from Gravesend, or further east. They must have been in the Palace grounds this morning to have that on their shoes. They're the ones lying to you – not Carnaby."

Then the man smiled. It had no warmth to it. "We don't have time to look at *shoes* or *soils* or send for *maps*, young Mr. . . . *Holmes*, is it?" There was contempt in his voice. "But you'll learn that reading a man's face is a better indicator. I can look at a man's face and know whether he's telling the truth, and know when he's lying, and I knew that these two men were lying before they ever opened their mouths. Now, we'll find out how many more lies they've told . . . and I'll warrant that their faces will reveal every one of them."

"Wait!" cried Halford, while Beecher made a whimpering noise, whispering something that I couldn't make out. The little man tried to protest again, but he and his big companion were shaken like terriers caught by rats until the both shut up.

Meanwhile, I was glad that Silas Caine, despite his ability to read a lie in a man's face, hadn't called my bluff, as I'd been lying to him – but fortunately he didn't realize it. There were no soil maps for me to have studied. I made it up. Only in the last year or so has anyone done any real work toward mapping the different types of soil in various spots around Britain. But it had been the best I could think of in that fraught moment – and it had worked.

I was dismissed then, with orders for Carnaby's guard to escort me downstairs, whereupon Harry would drive me back to the Crystal Palace. My last view of that room was Carnaby looking at me with speculative gratefulness, and the utter fear and despair, duplicated on Halford and Beecher's blanched faces.

"Although I didn't realize it then," Holmes added, "it was my first education in the seamier side of corruption related to gambling. And I suppose that it was valuable as well to get a close look at someone like Silas Caine."

"What happened to Halford and Beecher?"

Holmes shrugged. "At that age, I was simply happy to have skated so close to the thin ice and made my way back to shore. Years later, it occurred to me to make a few discreet inquiries, but they seem to have disappeared from that day forward."

"And Carnaby Littlecott?" I asked. "Did he win the race?" Of course I suspected the answer, and I was correct.

"He lost." Holmes gave a fond smile, apparently at the memory. "By then it was raining heavily, and he was well back in the pack – but he made a valiant effort. I abandoned my engineering homework and instead found a place to watch the contest – which is why I can confirm to you that at a bicycle race, you pick a spot and then wait and wait and wait, and then they approach quickly and pass by quickly – almost too fast to identify specific riders – and then you resume great periods of waiting – and that's assuming there are subsequent laps by that spot. In the case of this French tour, it sounds as if they pass just once, while hurrying from town to town,

and after you've waited for hours to see a few seconds of the race, there's nothing to do but go home. Even managing to jam into the crowd at the finish line boots nothing, for one cannot see anything there at all, jammed together like sheep in a pen.

"Afterwards, I caught up with him and found that unexpectedly, he wasn't upset at losing – because he knew he'd done his best in a fair race. He even convinced me to try out his velocipede."

"Ah – the one time that you said you rode one. How did it go?"

"I immediately turned over and rolled over and over across the muddy track – and had to travel home that way, and then explain to my father how I found myself in that condition."

He smiled ruefully, and I thought he'd stop talking then as he experienced the memory, but I asked, "What of Carnaby? Did you hear of him after that? Did you stay in touch?"

Holmes nodded. "We did, after a fashion. He soon gave up racing, and his misguided notion of obtaining fame. It turned out that everything he was doing was to impress a certain young lady of Penge who was already enamored with him in return, and once they figured this out, they were soon married. Carnaby reached an accord with his stepfather, who provided a loan so that Carnaby could purchase his own pub, separate from his stepfather's questionable business affairs – which you'll still find, doing quite well, should you ever choose to visit Penge. Having abandoned the pursuit of athletics, Carnaby pursued good food instead, and it wasn't long until he took on the shape of a snowman – and apparently he and his wife are fine with that, as she and their eight children adore their father. He gave up his misanthropic tendencies and became quite the jolly barkeep. I stop in and see him when I get the chance, all too rarely, and he's been of great assistance to me once or twice as well."

"You haven't mentioned an epilogue for Silas Caine. He sounds too sinister for you to have ignored forever."

"Ah, yes, the elusive Mr. Caine. I did encounter him a couple of decades later, during the escalating conflict with Professor Moriarty. He made a mistake, one loose thread that he chose to ignore during a murder in Chevening, but it was enough to erode his protections and set his feet toward the gallows."

"I don't recall the case."

"You were newly married then, and establishing your practice. Thus, it was a solitary quest – except for Mycroft, who joined me at the last. Never think that my brother's decision to run along the same tracks day after day is an indicator that he can't move around along different routes and be dangerous if he chooses."

And then Holmes proceeded to relate the fascinating details of what he called "Lennard's Alabaster Tomb", and just how Caine was caught, and the effort that Mycroft Holmes expended to make sure of that outcome. Holmes just had time to finish his narrative when the ship docked in Dover, where the white cliffs were shadowing into blues and grays during the retreat behind them of the setting sun.

The Man with the Stolen Luck

"I'm glad that we get the chance to visit and catch up, before my knighthood ceremony in a couple of weeks."

It was the fourth time since our arrival, just half-an-hour earlier, that Arthur Conan Doyle had worked his upcoming honor into the conversation. I glanced at Sherlock Holmes to see if he was as amused as I, only to find his expression instead indicating that if heard one more reference to the event, he would arise and offer some suddenly remembered excuse before making his way directly back to London.

I glanced out of the south-facing window in Doyle's study, where the afternoon sun was already causing lengthening shadows to stretch from the distant trees. The October sky had been beautifully blue that day, an azure that resembled that shade found on the Scottish flag, land of both Doyle's and my birth, but there were now wisps of high cirrus clouds marring the horizon with increasing frequency, indicating that a change in the weather was coming. This was confirmed by the glass on Doyle's wall, which he'd noted earlier had been falling throughout the day.

This was the first time that I'd seen Doyle since before my wedding, an event which had taken place a few months before. It had been a small affair, just a few London friends, with Holmes standing for me (as he had before) as my Best Man. My wife and I had decided that, both being middle-aged and having been previously married, we had no use for expensive spectacles. A small ceremony suited us both fine.

Of course, making that choice had been bound to offend those who were not notified or invited – someone such as Doyle. He'd heard about it a week or so after and telephoned my Queen Anne Street practice and residence to ask if it was true. I'd confirmed it, explaining the reasons that we'd kept things modest and small and secret, in that way that I'd practiced with others over preceding days, and he'd answered with his seeming complete understanding, also using words that I'd become used to hearing. But I'd also heard in his overly bonhomous booming voice, over the telephone wires, that he was peeved. Thus, I was surprised to receive his invitation to come down for the weekend to Surrey – and to bring Holmes with me.

The latter was particularly unexpected, as Doyle and Holmes had never quite formed a friendship. In fact, the truth was that Holmes had little respect for Doyle. From the time I'd first met Doyle in the early 1880's, nearly twenty years earlier, Holmes had found something off-putting about his overly genial and enthusiastic nature, like some are unresponsive to big, lumbering, and sloppy dogs. Or perhaps it was Doyle's never-very-subtle attempts to promote his own abilities and successes, working them into conversations in ways to remind you that you ought not forget him or take him lightly. And he had certainly made a success of himself, after a number of false starts – as evidenced by the much-mentioned upcoming Royal dubbing ceremony.

And of course, there was Holmes's long-soured attitude toward Doyle's efforts as my literary agent, and the different ways over the years that he had allowed himself to receive a greater share of the credit for my writing than he was due. I had long ago resolved to let that pass, but Holmes, ever my advocate and far more protective of this aspect of my life than I had chosen to be, was not so willing to do so.

Whenever Doyle and Holmes were together, there was a slight tension in the air, as if a storm were somewhere just over the horizon, but I'm not certain that Doyle was ever aware of it. He was always perfectly friendly, keeping the conversation in motion and making sure that refreshments were ever available. On our current visit, he'd met us at the nearby Haslemere Station, and during the drive of just one or two miles back to his Hindhead home, which he'd named "Undershaw" after building it there five years earlier, he'd kept up a running commentary about recent improvements in the village, which local characters had done what (to his great surprise or amusement, although we had no knowledge of whom he spoke), and what he hoped to accomplish in the upcoming year.

"Of course," he'd said when initially mentioning his upcoming honor that day, "when I accept my knighthood, my time will be severely curtailed from what I've been used to – my writing, of course, as well as travel, and participation in sports, and my various investigations."

I noted that he didn't mention his wife's physical concerns, and I wondered if it was an intentional omission, or if she was well enough at present that no comment was necessary. Doyle had chosen this spot upon which to settle and construct the invalid-friendly house in deference to his wife's health, and I wasn't surprised when he thanked me once again for the idea.

"Lovely spot you recommended, Watson," he noted as we'd passed through a short commercial district, including a few small shops and a newly opened tearoom that I didn't call to mind from my last visit. The area had grown somewhat since Holmes and I were first there in late June 1883, nearly two decades earlier. [1] I had never forgotten the beauty and the possibilities of the place, and when Doyle was looking for somewhere to build, I remembered and recommended it, and we'd journeyed there together. He had been charmed down to the ground. Now I could only wonder if the village's new prosperity was in some way related to the famed and energetic doctor-turned-writer (and lest I forget, upcoming knight), or if the growth was simply a natural progression, something to be expected as areas away from the capital continued to become homes for those who wanted simpler lives – unknowingly and gradually bringing the capital's complications down with them.

I turned from the study window to find that Doyle was handing Holmes a whisky, with another for me. Holmes thanked him and strolled around the room, into the corner near the small coal fireplace, and then over to the far wall, looking at some of the framed photographs hanging there. I noticed that most were of various literary and theatrical celebrities – Stoker and Barrie and Shaw and Kipling among them – all inscribed with some personalization for our host. Doyle, settling into the chair behind his desk with a whisky of his own, seemed about to provide commentary about who was represented upon the wall when Holmes turned and spoke.

"I perceive that you've invited us down because there is some incident, perhaps some bit of trouble, that you wish to lay before us. How can we help you?"

I wasn't really surprised that there had been an underlying purpose behind our invitation – and I had no doubts that Holmes was correct in his statement – but I did wonder that Holmes brought up the subject so quickly. Then it occurred to me that if his help was to be requested – as Doyle had done upon several past occasions – then from Holmes's perspective, it might be best to avoid dancing around the subject with social niceties and time-wasting small-talk, possibly prolonging a visit that need not take very long after all. Suddenly I saw that our weekend sojourn might terminate within the hour if Doyle's problem required that Holmes and I surge into motion, following the links of a chain toward a solution.

Doyle took a sip of whisky, looking for all the world like a man who wasn't thirsty, but rather seeking a few seconds to reorient after a sudden and unplanned change in direction. Then he smiled and set down the glass, nodding.

"Dr. Bell used to do those same little tricks. I became rather good at them myself, you know, when I assisted him during his Edinburgh criminal investigations. Later, it helped a great deal in my medical practice, and also when generally dealing with people of all walks." If it had been Doyle's intention to somehow diminish Holmes, or put him in his place, there was no indication that he'd succeeded. Holmes simply stood, as if waiting for Doyle to get it out of his system before coming to the actual subject. Doyle, apparently realizing this, shifted his position and invited us to sit as well. We arranged ourselves in the comfortable chairs facing him, and he again raised his glass, not taking a drink but instead simply holding it at the ready. Finally, shifting his gaze to the glass as if speaking to it instead of the two of us, he began.

"I've always considered myself lucky," he said, picking the glass back up and swirling the liquid, watching it reflect the light from the nearby window. "More than the average man. So much so that – " Here he looked up, at me. "So much so that I've begun to think at times that my good fortune has been at the expense of others – that *my* luck has somehow been *stolen* from them, siphoned from them to me, to their detriment."

He then looked from one of us to the other, as if expecting some comment. To keep him talking, I responded, "In what way?"

"Just . . . Well, that I've managed to find great success, as you know, while those around me seem to have followed less fortunate paths. My poor father, for instance. He had some early achievements, with indications of great possibility, but his fortunes were failing, even as mine were rising. I achieved some of my greatest early successes right around the time that he passed away – after being institutionalized, as you'll recollect, from ever-declining moods and a destructive taste for drink."

He looked back at the whisky in hand and then set it on his desk.

I recalled when his father had passed – and the success to which he referred. It was then that the public's excitement for my stories about Holmes had been reaching a fever pitch. I found it curious that Doyle now defined it as *his* first great success, when it was in fact based upon my work, and at the time, he had already talked me into putting an end to the project and publishing the details of Holmes's supposed death, as he'd become so weary of association with Holmes's adventures, which he felt was distracting people from his own attempts at literary fame. I held my tongue, and did not look toward Holmes, who certainly had his own thoughts upon the matter. [2]

"It was around then, too, that Touie became sick." He looked at me. "You know, Watson – you convinced me to see it when I refused. [3] Just as my star was rising, her illness progressed. In those dark hours when sleep isn't to be caught, the thoughts arise, again and again: *Did my fortunes improve at the expense of Touie's?*"

I harkened back to those months when Doyle had finally acknowledged his wife's illness. I myself had been distracted, for my own Mary had passed earlier that year. Perhaps I'd been less-than-sympathetic as Doyle wallowed in his usual good-tempered denial, but I did feel that I could take some credit for finally making him understand what he had previously refused to see.

"I've been quite lucky," Doyle continued. "I studied and became a professional – a physician – when such a thing was never completely guaranteed or likely for a fellow of my background. As a young man, I traveled and saw things and had adventures that most will never experience. Circumstances were such that I was able to pivot from the profession that might have chained me forever to my true dream of pursuing my literary interests. That has led to wealth and further travel, and now a knighthood. And then, to find love later in life – "

He stopped suddenly and reached hurriedly for the whisky, taking a healthy swallow, and then closing his eyes while the burning sensation from taking too much dissipated. *Finding love*, I thought. *Later in life.* I knew that by then he'd been married for seventeen years, since 1885, to the former Louisa Hawkins, nicknamed *Touie*, and that much of the marriage had been perfunctory, as she had been fighting tuberculosis for more than half of that time. I had to wonder what he meant, as I'd seen no indications of any renewed passion for his tired and ill little wife, the mother of his two children, and the silent supporter of all his endeavors.

Since her illness was discovered in 1893, Doyle had given her the best of care, seeking treatments and easing her responsibilities and building Undershaw as an invalid-accessible haven for her to live comfortably, even if recovery was never going to be possible. *Finding Love – later in life.* I looked at his great square face, his eyes still focused elsewhere. *Oh, Doyle!* I thought to myself. *What have you stepped into?* I'd seen far too many men, particularly of this certain age – he had reached the dangerous milestone of forty-three – lose their sensibilities over younger women. If this was what he'd asked us down to Hindhead to discuss, some seamy situation involving the affairs of an adulterous heart, then I knew with certainty that Holmes would be on the next train north. And even though Doyle was my friend of many years, I'd be traveling that way myself.

"I'm not sure where this is leading," said Holmes, a note of impatience in his voice. "If you feel that you've led a charmed life, and now the shine is fading – which seems unlikely, as I believe you've mentioned receiving a knighthood once or twice – then there is nothing here for a consulting detective to address. Perhaps instead you should approach some of the fortune-tellers and wall-knockers and séance sisters which have lately seemed to capture a too-substantial portion of your attention."

To me, Doyle has always resembled a rather good-natured English bull terrier, with his expression usually settled naturally into a smiling repose. But now, for just a moment, his eyes narrowed and any signs of pleasantness vanished. Then he pinched the bridge of his nose and took a deep breath.

"I'm not asking for some sort of exorcism to restore my stolen luck," he replied. "I've believed in my own personal good fortune all my life.

There was the time that I was nearly killed while on the whaling ship – but by an inch I lived. Another time was when the automobile turned over upon me, just out there on the drive to the house. I should have been crushed." He shook his head. "No, the luck can take care of itself. But I believe that I've acquired an enemy – right here in my own house!"

Now there seemed to be something tangible, an affair related to real-world intentions and actions, motivations and results. This was something, possibly, that might require the involvement of a consulting detective.

Holmes, who had been sitting forward as if intending rise and depart at any moment, now settled back, took a sip, and gestured with his free hand for Doyle to continue.

"I don't say that my luck has left me," explained the future knight. "Or that it's all been stolen beyond recovery. But in the little things, the everyday moments, I seem to be a great deal more . . . *vexed* than I've ever noticed. Small incidents, but they accumulate. My pen goes missing – as does the book I'm reading. Both of them only used by me, and left specifically where I put them. When I find the book, the slip of paper I've used to mark my place is gone – or in a different place. I know – it's insignificant, but still, taking that extra moment to find where I stopped reading, when I know that I took time to identify it, is frustrating.

"There are other things as well. Documents that I've left here on my desk vanish – not necessarily the whole document, but sometimes just the third of five pages, for instance. Or a manuscript has the pages reordered incorrectly, taking extra time to re-sort.

"My clothing suffers the same way. I'm left with one sock, or a jacket lining or pocket is ripped when I know it was fine when I took it off, or I find small tears in my shirts that I know were not there before, and there's no explanation why there would be. The girl who does the laundry swears that she is doing nothing different that would result in this damage, and I believe her."

"And if pixies or fairies or malicious leprechauns aren't causing this reiterated terror," said Holmes, with something of a snide tone, "whom do you blame?"

Doyle hadn't missed Holmes's implied criticism of his too-often tendency to credit otherworldly explanations to mundane events. After all, this was the man who had sought out and joined The Society for Psychical Research in 1893, describing himself then as simply a "novice and inquirer", but over the years his interest – and apparent gullibility – had only increased. After Mary's death, he'd offered several times to arrange a meeting with a table-tipper or spirit-writer in order to communicate with her, but I'd declined – politely, and not giving any indication of how offensive I found his suggestion, as I knew he was only trying with friendly sincerity to help assuage my grief.

At least now he seemed to have both feet on the ground, blaming the recent incidents of minor irritation and time-wasting upon some physical entity, and not a malicious spirit or *poltergeist*.

"Touie is in charge of hiring the servants," Doyle explained. "She manages them as well, and it gives her something to do – some responsibility – so that her days are not spent simply dwelling upon her health. We've lately had a bit of excessive turn-over with the staff – more than normal, but not totally unusual. I suspect that it's one of them – one of the new ones – but I don't know why."

"Have you had call to reprimand any of them?" I asked. "To generate some sort of resentment?"

"Not a bit of it!" Doyle replied. "I tend to ignore them more often than not. If they do their work correctly, I should never be aware of them."

"And you've seen no signs of any intrusions before these incidents are discovered?" I continued, wondering if there was anything here that would interest Holmes. "Returning to a room to find the door open when it should have been closed, for instance, or a rug that's been rucked up, or left with an upturned corner?"

Doyle simply shook his head, and then looked at Holmes.

The detective's mouth was a straight and lipless line, and he looked back at Doyle with eyes wide open – disinterested, and not with the distant gaze of seeing possibilities, or with his eyes shut as he pondered some clue that only he had perceived.

"What advice would you have me provide?" he asked Doyle. "As you pointed out, you've seen Dr. Bell's 'little tricks'. You don't need my help to set small traps, or question the servants that you still trust about what they've seen. Have you spoken to your wife about it?"

Doyle shook his head. "Other than to involuntarily express surprise or irritation when some incident or other presents itself, I have not. I don't want to add to her burden or worries. The only servant that I know well enough to ask – and he isn't really a servant – is Alfred. You know him. He and I have been friends for years, and he's been my secretary for the last five. But he lives in the village, and doesn't involve himself with the running of the household. I haven't mentioned any of this to him. It makes me feel foolish just to be thinking about it. But d----d if I'll let it continue!"

"Again," said Holmes, "I ask: What would you have me do? I'm sure that you're aware of the extended book of *Daniel*, and the three additional chapters that relate the story of Bel and the dragon. Have you tried spreading ashes at the areas of greater incident – perhaps here, around your desk – to determine the size and sex of the footprints that appear when you're absent?"

"I have considered it," said Doyle with tight lips. "As I recollect, you weren't above using such a small trick when you smoked out that murderous Nihilist woman back in '94."

Holmes glanced at me with something between amusement and a frown, and I suddenly felt warm, as if I'd been caught in a lie that I'd never actually uttered. From Doyle's statement, Holmes would immediately realize that I must have related the details of the Yoxley murder to Doyle, and why else would I do that, except as part of a discussion of further stories that he and I might someday share with the reading public?

When I'd believed that Holmes was dead, carried over the ledge of the Reichenbach Falls while ridding the world of Professor Moriarty, Doyle and I had published two-dozen stories in a newly formed monthly periodical, each one appearing to greater and greater interest. When Holmes had returned in April 1894, and had seen how, while he was gone, the public had conceived such a large interest in him – much greater than before he'd vanished, and not in a way that he seemed to prefer – based on these narratives, he'd forbidden that I publish any more of them. In truth, this was not a problem, as Doyle, acting as my literary agent, had already tired of being involved, and we'd brought the venture to a close in December 1893. But several years later, after Doyle took a trip to the West Country, he returned and approached me, having heard while visiting Dartmoor the rumors of when Holmes had laid to rest a family curse involving a devil dog. He'd convinced me to provide him with my manuscript, and after reading it, he became fixated on the idea of publishing it in *The Strand*, and then as a book. I'd finally been tentatively convinced to seek Holmes's permission to share the story with the public. His attitude then – and perhaps it was just that lucky day – had mellowed considerably, and he provided his agreement. Thus, the tale was published between late summer 1901 and April 1902, just half-a-year before that day and our invitation to visit to Hindhead.

Publishing the story of *The Hound* was supposed to be a one-time thing, the truly final public revelation of any of Holmes's adventures. But Doyle and I had, to our surprise – and possibly mine more than his – made a small fortune from it, and it was inevitable that we would eventually discuss releasing a new series of tales, considering the elevated payments we realized that we could now command both from *The Strand* and American magazines. Nothing had yet been said to Holmes in terms of seeking his permission, but Heaven knows that I already had a vast amount of prepared material from which to select, for writing has always come easily and quickly to me, and my association with Holmes had provided an incredible volume of work to record. The Yoxley murder, wherein Holmes used Biblical Daniel's trick of spreading ashes on the floor to see who walked through them, seemed like a good suggestion to me in this case, but Doyle wasn't satisfied.

"Rather than that – a simple trick – I hoped that you might suggest something else."

Holmes shrugged. "I cannot – will not – move here into the house, pretending to be a middle-aged footman for several weeks, trying to catch someone in the act, or even observing someone sneaking into a part of the house in which he or she has no business. It isn't a large household, and I have no wish to stay in the elaborate disguise that would be required, since so many people here know me from this or previous visits. No, what you need – " And he stopped, visualizing a sudden new idea.

"What?" queried Doyle. "What is it?"

"What you need is a servant that *you* have hired – someone new that can insert him or herself into the household and look for indications of unusualness." Holmes sat up a bit straighter. "If you're willing, I have the perfect person in mind. She can be here tomorrow – or the next day if Watson and I stay overnight as planned, and return to London in the morning. You said that your wife manages the servants. Will it look odd for you to suggest one? To hire one and become involved in such a way?"

"Not at all. I can say that this person is the relative of a friend and needs a position. We're fully staffed now, but one more won't be a burden – especially if we're planning for the inevitable additional turn-over if another one leaves as quickly as others have in recent weeks."

Holmes nodded. "Then that is easily settled. I'll speak to the girl tomorrow, and she'll be here on Monday."

I was surprised how suddenly the matter was settled and, having an idea in mind who Holmes was planning on retaining, I also expected that Doyle's questions would be quickly answered.

With that issue tabled, the spirit of the weekend visit seemed to improve immediately, and even Holmes seemed willing to relax and enjoy himself, commenting twice during the rest of the day upon the beauty of the location. We took an afternoon walk about the property, circling around to the village for tea. There was some desultory talk of visiting the Devil's Punchbowl, but Holmes and I had seen it before – although in much grimmer circumstances in which one wicked man lost his sanity and an innocent newlywed couple their lives – and the trip never materialized. After a fine dinner hosted by Touie Doyle, who had roused herself to entertain the visitors from London, we then played billiards with Doyle and his secretary, Alfred Wood, before retiring for the evening.

Upstairs, before Holmes continued on to his own room, I confirmed whose help he planned to seek the next day upon our return. I considered mentioning my concerns with this plan, but decided that already knew whatever issue I might raise. Instead, I simply said good night.

The following morning, rainy as predicted, was no different than many other visits to the country. Breakfast was available in the form of various warmed dishes at whatever time a guest might wander in to obtain it. I learned from one of the maids that Holmes had already risen, eaten a modest amount, and then gone for a walk. There had been no set activity planned, and after I consumed my own meal, sitting alone in the dining room in comfortable silence, I wandered through the house to find Doyle in his study, staring in an almost wistful manner at an object in his right hand, a small framed photo or painting, and his head propped on his left. When I knocked and entered, he gave a small jump and then quickly slipped the frame into his desk, pushing the drawer shut with enough force to make a noise.

"Ah, Watson, you startled me." He sighed. "I was lost in thought." He gestured to his left, where the windows looked out upon the lawn. It was a dark day, with the local drizzle preventing any view beyond a hundred feet or so. "I ought to move my desk to a different spot in the room, or keep these drapes closed, to minimize the distraction, but the view is often so lovely."

He gesture vaguely. "Holmes isn't with you?"

I shook my head. "I'm told he went for a walk – although why, on such an unpleasant day, is beyond me. As you know, he often follows after his own notions."

I heard a noise behind me and turned to see Holmes entering the room.

"Just so," he said. "A strategy that has served me well for quite some time now." He faced Doyle. "Any new problems of the sort you described since last night?"

Doyle's countenance darkened. "As a matter of fact," he said, "if you hadn't asked, I would have told you anyway, before your departure." He reached across the desk and picked up a small book. "I received this in the post just the other day – Thursday. It's a new children's book called *Peter Rabbit* by a lady named Potter. Apparently no relation to some Potters I met once in the West Country while following up certain supernatural speculations – odd folk. This lady – Beatrix, from the Lake District – had it printed privately last year and I bought a copy for the children, and then I did what I could to help get it professionally published. It's quite good – she both wrote the story and did her own watercolor illustrations. She sent me this inscribed copy of the new edition, with her thanks." He handed it to Holmes, having opened it to a certain page. "Look – the inscription page is torn out!"

Holmes took the small book from him and turned it this way and that under what little weak light was coming in through the southern windows. Then, having seen what he wanted, he handed it to me.

It was a dark little volume, published by F. Warne. The cover had a charming painting of a bunny walking upright in carpet slippers and a blue coat. I couldn't tell if it was intentional, but the printing had given him red eyes, and the author had chosen to provide him with something of an encephalitic forehead – perhaps to account for his more-than-the-typical-rabbit intelligence. I could see where the title page had been torn out, with some little force, as the remaining tattered fragments of the sheet were bent and bunched, preventing the book from closing flat. It was ruined, and as much as I hated to see any book damaged or desecrated, this seemed especially upsetting, as it had been signed with the good wishes of the author, probably just days ago.

"I observed this book on your desk last night," said Holmes. "It was in good condition then."

Doyle nodded. "Whoever did this came into the study last night. It *must* be one of the servants! Who else would be able to move about without being observed or caught?"

"You don't know whether this person was observed or not," I pointed out. "Unless you've already questioned the servants this morning."

"I have not," confirmed Doyle. "You're correct – I'm making an assumption with no fact to back it up." He looked at Holmes. "Bricks without clay, as you say. I know that this isn't a murder or theft of a state secret, or anything of great fascination like a family curse or unbreakable cipher, but any help you can provide will be much appreciated."

Holmes nodded. "On my walk this morning, I sent a telegram to London to arrange a meeting this afternoon with a young lady of remarkable skill. If all goes according to plan, she'll be here in the morning, and I expect she'll obtain answers by midweek."

The rest of our visit passed without further event, and after lunch, Doyle returned us to the Haslemere Station, where we entrained for the capital. At one point, Holmes spent a few minutes writing on a sheet of paper torn from his notebooks, and then he asked if I could stop by Baker Street before returning home to Queen Anne Street. I agreed, not having fixed a set time with my wife to appear. Thus, by three o'clock, we were in the sitting room, and I in my old chair, before a pleasant, and conversing with Sally Peake, *née* Wiggins.

It had been something more than a month since we had last seen her, when Holmes and I, along with Inspector Lestrade, had paused to pay our respects following the death of her mother. [4] As she had been on that day, she was holding a tiny babe in her arms, no more than a quarter-year old. I wondered what Holmes thought could be accomplished by this new mother.

After the typical polite conversation in such an instance – the expression once again of our condolences on her recent loss, and questions about her health and that of the new baby – Holmes outlined Doyle's problem.

"It's a small matter," he said, "and shouldn't take more than a day or so. You were ever-quick at making observations, Sally, and drawing the correct conclusions. After initially thinking of you, and then recalling your new duties with young Master Joseph, I considered finding other assistance, but then I remembered that your sister, Vera, also has a child of the same age. Perhaps, for just a day or so, she could act as a baby-sitter and wet-nurse while you go to Surrey?"

Without hesitation, Sally agreed.

"It shouldn't be too hard," she said. "I've played the new servant before, you know. On the first few days, they don't expect you to know too much, and unless the household is beastly, they give you time to settle in, figure out the schedule and where things are, and learn some names. Do you have any ideas of who I should think about first?"

"I do," said Holmes. "I've listed a few points in my notes – but don't let that bias your judgment if you see something else. Present yourself tomorrow morning, and then send word when you have something to report. And in any case, don't stay away from your child more than a day or so."

He then gave her funds for the journey, and the sheet he'd drafted on the train containing his suggestions, the layout of the house, what he'd observed of the makeup of family and servants, and which train she should take so that Doyle could arrange to pick her up. Then, with both of us showing further approval of the baby, now starting to squirm, the young lady departed.

I had mixed emotions about Holmes asking a new mother to separate herself from her child, even for a short period, but Sally Peake had no such qualms. Her willingness spoke to the deeply forged connections between Holmes and the different members of the Wiggins clan.

From what I'd been told over the years, Holmes had apparently formed the idea of using street lads (and lasses) who were otherwise at loose ends to carry out various chores in the mid-1870's, when he'd first come up to London with the intention of becoming a consulting detective.

At that time, he'd had a room at No. 24 Montague Street, alongside the British Museum, and the rarity of cases had given him time to learn a great deal from both study at the Museum and the British Library, and also at the hands of a number of knowledgeable London residents, occupying both sides of that invisible but firm line dividing legal from criminal.

As his activities had made more and more use of the street children, who he took to calling his "Irregulars", one lad named Wiggins had stood out for his intelligence and bravery, and as time went on, for his leadership as well. Time passed, and Wiggins became the *de facto* commander of the small band, its numbers swelling and declining at any given time.

Holmes had once done a great service for the Wiggins family, and by way of this, earned what they considered a debt of loyalty. When the original Wiggins lad had aged-out of practical service, Holmes had recruited a younger and just-as-clever Wiggins to replace him, while providing both an education and an opportunity for a successful future for the original. In all the time since, it had been one of the Wiggins family, under that name or that of some related cousin, who had served as leader of the Irregulars, and Holmes had taken care of all of them as if he were their protector, or some beneficent uncle.

Sally Peake, while never one of the official leaders, had done her share to assist Holmes over the years, most notably during the Winfield kidnapping, when the baby's mother had been killed during the child's abduction. The kidnappers had wanted to use the baby to influence Gable Winfield, a costermonger, into committing an assassination, and the death of his wife had made no difference to them. All of the Irregulars had been tasked with carefully searching a certain East End neighborhood for signs of the baby and, once located, to get word to Holmes. But when Sally located the child, she'd found that the kidnappers were arguing amongst themselves with rapidly escalating violence, and instead of leaving to send word, she'd instead disobeyed Holmes's instructions and cut the tarred rope around the frightened child, and then shielded the tiny body when the shooting began. Then, after the kidnappers had killed one another, the teen-aged girl had carried the child through the bitterly cold night to safety.

Now a young woman in her mid-twenties, she'd received an education, helped in a family fabric business, and was married to a hard-working fellow, also a former Irregular, named Allen Peake. Her life was quite full, and satisfying and promising – and yet, when Holmes needed her help, she did not refuse.

I heard nothing from Holmes on Monday, but Tuesday at mid-day, he wired to ask if I could run down to Undershaw on the three o'clock train. Always happy to re-arrange my schedule, I met him at Victoria, and just an hour or so later, having taken an express, we were met at the station by Doyle, just as we had been four days earlier.

Doyle was upset, saying that he'd endured yet another vandalism of one of his possessions – "A violation!" he thundered. – but he was vague as to what had been damaged. He did comment more than once – along with twice mentioning his upcoming knighthood in the mile or so of our journey to Undershaw – that the escalation of abuse, from missing objects and moved bookmarks that might be taken for absent mindedness to willful destruction, was becoming intolerable.

"This girl you sent," he continued. "She arrived yesterday morning, and set right to work. I wasn't even aware of her comings and goings. Then, this morning, I found . . . I found something else that had been damaged. Ruined! I told her about it, and she said that she'd seen it happen – that she'd been hiding and watching when the damage was done! And yet, she did nothing to stop it! Where could she have been hiding? How? There's no place for her to hide!"

"Where did this occur?" I asked.

"In my study. Something . . . in my desk drawer was taken out and defaced. But you've been in there – there's no place that this girl could have hidden and observed what was done to my . . . what was done."

By then, we'd arrived at the house, and within moments we were walking through the building to Doyle's study. As we passed, Doyle requested that Sally Peake join us, and she did, almost immediately.

As soon as she entered, Holmes asked, "Was it the boy? And the secret room?"

She nodded. "I kept my eyes open, but it soon clear that I didn't need to worry about the staff. They're kept on too-tight a leash."

"Boy?" asked Doyle, looking from Sally to Holmes. "Secret room?" Suddenly he acted very wary. "What are you talking about?"

Upon arrival, we had never sat down, and Holmes took a few steps to the left of the fireplace, gesturing at the wall there. "This secret room – surely you know of it? After all, you designed and built the house. How does it open? Some secret catch, or is it more like a conventional door?"

Doyle, his reaction surprised, started to answer, but Sally stepped forward. "You just push on it, and it clicks open. Then, when you're ready to shut it, you give it a good pull and a swing, and the momentum clicks it shut again. If it doesn't work the first time, you just push it open and try again a little harder."

"Thank you." And Holmes then gave the area just to the left of the mantel a small shove, and a piece of wall opened like a door, revealing a cavity behind it not more than a foot or two deep, with something like a shaft leading straight down. I stepped forward and could see that there was a steep staircase on the study-side of the shaft, acting as a ladder into the dark void below. [5]

Holmes turned to Doyle. "As I said, surely you knew about this. It must have been planned during the building's construction. I doubt that you wanted it as a priest hole, as romantic as you are about certain aspects of history, but when you needed some sort of access to the cellar, you couldn't resist fixing it up in this secret way, as if it were part of some boy's adventure story."

Doyle nodded, rather sheepishly. "There was a space there, and the builders asked about leaving access to it. There's plumbing down there, and I considered keeping it as a wine cellar as well, but I had the devil of a time climbing up and down those vertical cross-pieces carrying a bottle or two."

He took a step toward Holmes and the door. "I didn't mention it because I felt that no one knew about it. How could this girl –" He gestured toward Sally. " – know about it, or hide there, if it was so well hidden?"

"Not so well hidden," Holmes explained, "I saw the indications of a door on Saturday while examining the room. If you want to keep it a secret, you should make sure that the dust along the floor is swept more often – it, like Daniel's ashes, shows both footprints leading to and from the entrance, and random patterns caused by air flowing beneath the hidden door. Additionally, the wall-paper where one pushes to open the door, and here – where one grasps the edge to swing it shut – are showing stains from where it has been touched by your hands when you open and shut it."

Then he pointed lower along the door's edge, about three feet from the floor, and a couple of feet below where Doyle's handprints were accumulating. "You'll notice that there are fainter, smaller stains here – at a height that match the smaller footprints that were in the dust outside the door."

"Smaller footprints?" asked Doyle. "You mentioned a boy. None of the servants has a son . . . ."

Holmes turned and walked to Doyle's desk, picking up the small children's book with the blue-coated rabbit on the front. He opened it to the torn-out page and held it flat in front of him. "Fortunately the sun is out today, and this can be seen with ease. Step closer. What do you observe?"

Doyle leaned in, and then I followed. We each saw that, amongst the many oily finger marks on the glossy pages, were several that were much smaller in size.

"Since the inscribed volume arrived, did you share it with anyone in your family?"

"No," replied Doyle. "There was no need. This copy was for me, signed by the author. The children already have their own copy, purchased last year from the author when she was still selling them privately." He looked at me, a sharpness in his gaze. "A boy – Has all of this been perpetrated by my own son?"

Without answering, Holmes turned back to Sally, who explained. "It didn't take me long to get the layout of the house, and who was where and when. You were gone all day yesterday, Mr. Doyle, so it was easy enough for me to get into your study and look at the door, as suggested by Mr. Holmes. I saw what he meant about the footprints, and the marks and stains where a shorter person – a child – would hold the edge to open or shut it. It only took a minute to climb down into the cellar and see a child's dusty footprints leading from here to another part of the house. There's no ladder there, or even another door, but there were some stacks of loose lumber where this child – a boy – has climbed up and down. I looked and found a trap-door of sorts in the floor above, sawed roughly out of the wood, and with bracing crudely nailed in to support it when closed.

"Later, as the day progressed and I knew that your son was out of the house as well, I examined his room – which was in the right spot to be over the trap door. I found it, hidden underneath some boxes in his closet. For a ten-year-old, he'd done a good job concealing it, but there was really no difficulty."

She reached into her pocket and pulled out a small folded sheet, handing it to Holmes who, after a cursory examination, passed it onto Doyle. "This," Sally added, "was on the floor of the cellar, near the boy's trap door."

I could see that it was the inscribed page torn from the children's book. Doyle's hand gripped the sheet, his knuckles white.

"Last night," Sally continued, "I went back into the cellar and hid myself. It wasn't long after the boy's bedtime that he crept down from his room, crossed underneath the house to the study, and climbed up and in. I quietly followed, and was standing on the steps so that I could just see into the room. He was at your desk, on the far side from the door. He took something from the drawer – a frame – removed a photo, and then started to scratch at it with a letter opener. Then he replaced the photograph into the frame and came back to the secret door. By then I was back in my hiding place, and I saw him return to his room."

Doyle digested all of this in silence. Then he turned, walked from the study, and we could hear him tell a nearby servant to summon his son. He returned immediately, asking us to excuse him and wait elsewhere.

We passed the lad as he entered. Young Kingsley Doyle had always been a pleasant-enough lad, bright and clever, alert and intelligent, and active and healthy. But that day his expression was downcast. Recognizing Holmes and me as he passed, he gave us a look as if we had betrayed him. I wasn't certain that we hadn't somehow.

We found a nearby room with chairs looking out upon a pleasant southern view. In a low voice, Sally added to her story. "I examined the desk and saw the photograph. It's of a dark thin-faced woman, sour-looking and unsmiling. Looks to be in her mid-twenties. It was signed, "*All my love, Jean*". The eyes had been scratched out."

Holmes nodded. "As we might have expected. Boys prowl – it is their nature. I have no doubt that young Kingsley found the photograph, and perhaps a cache of secret letters as well which were foolishly kept, perhaps read over and over again, and he – with his admiration of his father damaged, possibly permanently – decided to torment him a bit, escalating it as time went on."

"I suppose I can understand damaging the photograph," I said, "particularly if the boy was familiar with the woman's name, *Jean*, by way of some indiscreet letters he found and read. But why damage the book?"

"Who knows?" replied Holmes. "Perhaps, knowing of his father's betrayal of his mother with one woman, seeing a grateful message from yet another woman convinced him that his father is a serial adulterer."

"Holmes," I said, "that's rather harsh. We don't know that anything has happened between Doyle and this *Jean*."

"I suppose," said Holmes, "it depends upon where you choose to draw the line. Tell me, Watson: Would your wife – would any of your wives – have appreciated it to learn that you mooned and pined over a photograph of another much-younger woman – particularly during their illnesses? There are more forms of adultery than scratching a persistent physical itch."

"Holmes – " I repeated, a warning tone in my voice as I glanced toward the young lady beside us, but she was nodding in agreement.

"If I found a photograph like that in my Allen's papers," she said with uncharacteristic acid in her tone, "well, I'd do a lot more than just scratch out the eyes on a piece of paper!"

After ten more minutes, in which each of us silently pondered our own private thoughts, the door to Doyle's study opened and father and son stepped outside. Without a word, the boy, head hanging low, turned toward the inner rooms of the house, while Doyle joined us.

"As you have discovered," he explained softly, "last summer Kingsley found a loose board in his closet and realized that it opened into the cellar. Over several weeks, he surreptitiously constructed a removable trap door, and then began his explorations. I suppose that it's only natural

– a bright lad like that, living in a house shadowed by illness, will inevitably seek some sort of distraction.

"In the course of his explorations, he found his way into the study, where he came across some of my personal items which he misunderstood – and which incidentally caused him to feel angry toward me, his father. What began as mere irritations – nothing more than pranks – escalated. But he has now been found out, and measures will be taken."

There was nothing more to be said, and we didn't want to give any indication that we'd guessed more than we'd been told. When Doyle offered to defray any expenses that we'd incurred, and asked in addition about the amount of Holmes's fee, my friend waved his hand. Doyle took it to mean that Holmes had done it all in the name of friendship, but I, knowing better, realized that the incident had left a bad taste in Holmes's mouth, and he would just as soon depart and forget about it.

Although it may have been planned all along, I felt that it was no coincidence that young Kingsley was sent to the Sandroyd School in Oxshott Heath, nearly to London, the next year. Meanwhile, Touie Doyle's health continued to steadily worsen, and in less than four years, in July 1906, she passed away. Half-a-year later, Doyle publicly attended a theatre performance with Miss Jean Leckie, fifteen years his junior. This was not unusual for the two of them. He had first met her in 1897, and several times later that year, she had visited Undershaw, the same year it was built. She and Doyle had maintained a public friendship throughout his wife's illness, and in late December 1907, not quite a year-and-a-half after Touie's death, Doyle and Jean Leckie were married.

I was not invited to the ceremony.

Doyle's reputation continued to grow. Not long after that day in early October 1902 when Holmes, Sally, and I visited Undershaw, Doyle was knighted. [6] He continued to write and travel, and he became a sometime-advocate in legal issues where he identified miscarriages of justice. He and his second wife had three children, and sadly – although he didn't see it that way – he became a missionary for the cause of Spiritualism, not realizing (or caring) that such a stance was undermining the respect he'd earned over many decades.

I remained friends with him, and we continued our literary partnership, to our financial benefit. I'm sure that if I'd asked him, Doyle would recall that the time when he felt that his luck was being stolen as irrelevant, just a short paragraph in the long and successful tale of his entire life.

But I do know that I lost some of the respect that I'd held for him, even if he never realized it, and it's likely that he also lost the same from his oldest son, Kingsley, if our interpretation of the events of those singular incidents were correct. And while Doyle would continue to think himself a lucky man, I could only conclude, to my own way of thinking, that losing the good opinion of his son in exchange for an adulterous relationship, even if it had eventually progressed to him wedding the woman he called the love of his life, made him incredibly unlucky indeed. He'd stolen his own luck in a way that neither success nor recognition nor wealth nor even a knighthood could ever offset or repair.

NOTES

1. For more about the previous history of the site of Doyle's home, Undershaw, see "The Problem of the Hindhead Minister" in *The Collected Papers of Sherlock Holmes – Volume V: Chronicles*, and *The Strand Magazine*, Issue LV (2018).
2. This event is retold in "The Unintended Offenses", winner of the 2022 Arthur Conan Doyle Society Fiction Award, and published in *Steel True, Blade Straight 2022 Annual.*
3. This event is retold in "Fate's Brushes", winner of the 2023 Arthur Conan Doyle Society Fiction Award, and published in *Steel True, Blade Straight 2023 Annual.*
4. See "The Gower Street Murder" in *Sherlock Holmes: Tangled Skeins* and *The Collected Papers of Sherlock Holmes – Volume II: Records.*
5. On 9 September, 2016, I was very fortunate to be invited to visit Undershaw for the Grand Opening ceremony for the Stepping Stones School for special needs children, which had just moved to the site after the building received extensive renovations. This was in recognition of the funds raised for the school by *The MX Book of New Sherlock Holmes Stories.* (As of this writing in September 2025, the books have raised over $165,000 for the school, which has since renamed itself simply *Undershaw.*) On that day, my deerstalker and I were fortunate to be able to spend a great deal of time in Doyle's former study, where he worked with Watson to produce *The Hound of the Baskervilles* and *The Return of Sherlock Holmes.*

   The first photo shows me and my deerstalker at the site of Doyle's desk, working on the opening lines to a new Holmes adventure. Beside it is a photo of Doyle in the same spot, at his original desk.

   The second photo shows the door to the left of the fireplace mantel (with my deerstalker hanging on it). Because of the renovations and new wallpaper, the door isn't quite so hidden anymore. (That's Touie's photo hanging above the mantel.)

   The third photo shows a view looking down into the space below.

   On 17 May, 2025, as part of my fifth Holmes Pilgrimage to England, I was able to return to Undershaw for the celebration concluding *The MX Book of New Sherlock Holmes Stories*, finishing up – after 10 amazing years – at 52 massive volumes and over 1,000 stories from more than 200 worldwide contributors. The fourth photo shows a number of the MX Anthology contributing authors and publisher Steve Emecz in front of the school, following attendance at the party.

6. Doyle was knighted on 24 October, 1902.

The Clue of the Crested Ring

Sofia Allard had always walked a middle path, neither cursed nor charmed.

I first became aware of her sometime in the early 1880's, a few years after I'd settled in Baker Street. When I'd unexpectedly found myself living in Marylebone, sharing rooms with an eccentric fellow a year or so younger than me, I'd had no thoughts that I'd stay there for very long, expecting that I'd either return to the Army as soon as my war wounds were healed or, when those foolish plans fell through, I'd try to save for a medical practice of my own, which might or might not involve remaining in London.

However, by the time I met Sofia, my feelings toward that part of London were that it was now my home for the foreseeable future. I knew my way around quite well, the streets and the shortcut mews and alleys, and I was well-acquainted with many of our neighbors, both close and distant, either as friends, or at least to identify and greet in passing.

And it was in this setting that I initially encountered Sofia.

It was early one morning, and I was walking along Marylebone High Street, aiming to be at a bookstore specializing in travel volumes when they opened, as I was pondering a short holiday to France, should my carefully hoarded finances support it. It was an unusually cool day in June, as I recall, and the sun was out, although the glass was falling and the afternoon promised to be more unpleasant. Very few people were about, and my stride was steady and comfortable when I noticed a girl, walking along the opposite side of the street, noticeably change direction and head specifically my way.

"Excuse me, sir," she said in a thick Russian accent, meeting my gaze for just an instant before looking beyond me. Her tone was flat when she continued. "I am from Cambridge and I have lost my money. Can you spare any that would get me home?"

She looked to be in her early twenties and had thick reddish-gold hair, loose upon her shoulders, and curious cat-like eyes of the same tawny color. Her expression was neutral and her tone flat, almost as if she were speaking rote lines instead of asking sincerely for help. She wore a camel-colored coat belted tight. A tidy-looking blue dress was visible beneath it, and what I could see of her shoes appeared to be sensible and in good condition, and even I – no Sherlock Holmes, but by then learning some of his methods – could tell that she was no common beggar. Still, my instincts told me that she was not a young woman unexpectedly cast adrift in London, needing help to get home to Cambridge.

I was considering how to respond – perhaps to give her a few coins and move on, or take a deeper interest, seeing what help I could provide – when a voice called from across the road, getting closer.

"Sofia! Sofia! Come away and let the doctor be about his business."

I glanced in that direction to observe the harried, heavy-set, and careworn Mrs. Battle, wife of a nearby pub owner. As she reached us, looking as if she'd come outside in a hurry, she apologized.

"I'm so sorry, Doctor! She got away from us. She's a bit soft, but we're taking care of her."

I cocked my head in curiosity, and the lady continued.

"She arrived a few weeks ago, and all she could tell us was her name. Did you ask you for money to get back to Cambridge? She always does. We felt sorry for her and tried to help, taking her in and making a place for her, but she can't tell us anything about it, other than she wants to go back. My husband and I, we made a few inquiries with the police, but turned up nothing. We have a spare room, and we've been letting her stay – until she's better, you know."

A thought occurred to her. "Perhaps Mr. Holmes might see his way to dropping by and looking into where she came from . . . ?" Mrs. Battle nodded agreeably, and I assured her that I'd mention it to him. Telling Sofia that it was nice to meet her, to her obvious indifference, I went upon my errand.

Later that afternoon, I shared the matter to Holmes, and in a day or so, he dropped by The Red Plough, the Battle's pub in Nottingham Street near the workhouse. He decided that the girl was from a good background, and that her Russian accent was real – "St. Petersburg, most likely," he explained. "She speaks French as well." He set some inquiries in motion, particularly in Cambridge where the girl wished to go, but nothing came of it – for Holmes wasn't infallible, and in those early days, when shekels were rare and dear, he couldn't drop everything and go off at his own expense to track down the past of one befuddled girl who, though separated from her earlier life, was doing well in the present. For the Battles had adopted her as the child they'd never had, and like many daughters, she brought them joy, even as she vexed them – a familiar site to those of us in the neighborhood as she continued her local wanderings of the Marylebone Streets, still asking strangers for coins to get back to Cambridge.

So I say she was neither cursed nor charmed, for her situation got no worse, nor any better.

That is, until February 1887, when she was arrested for the murder of Lord Evelyn Daintree, the wayward son of the Duke of Beauchester.

I have been to war, and have seen things in battle that are the epitome of confusion, with noise and smoke and screaming enough to terrify and paralyze a man, leaving him frozen when he ought to jump and get out of the way. And yet there is always some order to it. But I must confess that whenever I have visited a construction site, also filled with noise and smoke and screaming, I can never quite understand how anything is accomplished, and I always have the same underlying sense of nervousness, though much diminished, that I contained on the battlefield, feeling that any direction where I'm not looking is where some unexpected maiming danger will find me.

And yet, in spite of the confusion and seeming aimlessness of the actions of all involved, construction projects regularly achieve completion, making progress in great leaps or scraped forward by inches, one after another, as witnessed by the civilization around us. And so it was that February morning when Holmes and I were standing on the northern end of the newly re-constructed Hammersmith Bridge, not quite finished, but due to re-open in just a few months' time after several years of labor.

"This way, Mr. Holmes," said Inspector Morton, leading us through a gap in the wooden fence, erected to protect the construction site. A constable that I didn't know stood at the informal entrance, his stoic gaze forward. We dropped down toward the Thames onto an ancient and worn footpath that ran along the bank. Crossing it, we stepped carefully around various piles of construction materials to approach the great northern bridge pier jutting upward from the earth.

"How long ago was the body discovered?" Holmes asked, as we had immediately been taken from our cab to the scene without pausing for discussion. It was fortuitous that Holmes had been at home to receive Morton's wire, as his initial plans that morning had involved a visit to Chandos Street, where he irregularly sought advice from a Scandinavian exile on what was currently being smuggled into London from that region.

"Not more than an hour," was the inspector's reply. "When the tide dropped, the workers went out to probe the new concrete affixed onto the pier – something to do with ensuring the quality as part of an inspection for the bridge reopening in a few months – when they retrieved this."

Morton was a healthy-enough looking specimen, but he often ran cold, wearing heavier tweeds even in warm weather. That day he seemed to especially protected, in a heavy wool coat atop his regular wool suit. His color was typically rather pale, but then he seemed more so than usual, as if he'd arrived at that state from something that had made him queasy, rather than having a true illness. He stopped before us, his feet crunching on the shingle, turned, and fished something from his pocket, wrapped in a handkerchief. Handing it to Holmes, he said, "Careful. It isn't very clean. And don't drop it."

Holmes, who would not have dropped it, instead unwrapped it, and I could see that it was a ring – a thick heavy man's ring, gold with dark insets marked by a few small jewels, both clear and with red or green highlights, and with some sort of crest or signet upon the front. I immediately sensed that to which Morton referred. There was a faint but foul scent clinging to the ring – an odor of rotted meat – that wafted toward me in the littlest of breeze generated by the unfolding cloth. Leaning closer, I confirmed that the stench was emanating from the ring.

Morton glanced at it, and then looked away. "They knew something was up when the hole opened and the smelled rolled out. When they fished out the ring, they had sense enough to call the police, instead of digging further. For the body, I mean. I waited until you arrived in order to let that proceed."

"Dig it out?" I asked. "From the bridge?"

"You'll see in a moment, Doctor. Over there." He gestured vaguely toward the great pier, while Holmes completed his examination of the ring with his glass.

"Do you know whose crest this is?" Holmes asked, and Morton nodded.

"The Duke of Beauchester."

"Then," I said, with a flash of inspiration, "this must be the ring that belongs to his son, missing this past year."

Morton nodded again. "It seems likely. As you'll recall, the search was extensive when he vanished – but no one ever thought to look inside the Hammersmith Bridge."

"Then we'd best get the body out of its makeshift tomb and make sure it's him," said Holmes. "Lead on, Morton."

The difference between the river water and the morning air was enough to create a small bank of fog clinging to the Thames' surface, wide enough to spread around us and along the shore. We stepped carefully, completing the short journey to the pier, and then along one face to the next, where a small cluster of figures lingered by the far side. Another pair of constables stood with five other men, clearly laborers. One was a heavy-set bald man of sixty, their apparent leader. Morton introduced him as Barnabas Sledge, the foreman of the construction crew doing the work that morning when the body was discovered. He silently shook our hands, and I was impressed at the strength and grip in his large and very-calloused hand.

At Morton's prompting, Sledge told us what happened. He rolled his shoulders, as if shifting a load.

"The main part of the bridge repair was the decking and suspension cables," he growled in a strong northern accent. "There's others that were hired for that, but we are subbed to do these tasks. The original piers only needed some mild work done. This one here required a bit more, and part of it was removed – this side taken right down so that it could be rebuilt. The old face was removed, and then some of the internal stonework was shifted out and then re-laid."

"And all of that work would have been done about a year ago," interrupted Holmes.

Sledge nodded his head. "Almost. It was last April. After it was replaced, the new outer facing was constructed. Now, with a few months to go before the bridgework is declared complete, we're doing our final tests – and that includes confirming that the concrete here isn't rotten, and that it's up to required strength, and not honeycombed. Petey here – " He indicated a small but wiry lad with shorn darkish hair on a knobby skull, standing forward on his toes like a ratter dog, bouncing on inner springs and tensioned cables as if ready to jump into motion in an instant. The young man's face had a sickly hew – likely not his normal aspect. "Petey was using a probe – a metal rod about three feet long with a cross-handle at one end – to press against various points on the concrete. It's routine work, and rarely reveals anything, but we still do it to make sure. This morning . . . Well, you tell them, Petey."

The young man stepped forward and began to garble out what had occurred in a thick Yorkshire accent, which I won't attempt to duplicate here. Essentially, his story was that after checking a number of other random spots, he'd been most surprised when the probe rod punched through the concrete into a *void* – and an odor of purification had blown forth, as if the air in the dark pocket had been under pressure for too long from the accumulating gases of the rotting body.

Petey had called for Sledge, and upon the foreman's direction, he'd widened the hole somewhat before forcing a metal hook through the gap. This had caught on something, and with a slight tug against very little resistance – Holmes was careful to confirm this point – the older man pulled out the ring, apparently wrenched from the hidden corpse.

"I got a light and held it to the hole," Sledge continued. "I could see crumpled clothes – likely a body – about six inches in, so I sent one of the lads for the police. A constable was soon here, and he notified this inspector. Once he arrived and took one look, he hied off – I suppose to collect you, Mr. Holmes."

My friend took a minute to glance around, taking a few steps here and there before asking, "Mr. Sledge, how long do you suppose the body has been here?"

"It's coming up on a year, or near it. I can confirm in my records, but we excavated that segment last April, and it wasn't but a day or so to make the repairs and then set up the forms and pour the concrete. Whoever did this would have had just one night to accomplish it. We poured in the afternoon and then left it to set up. By morning, it would have been too hard to push in a body and still smooth out the disturbance. We let it sit for a week after that with the forms in place, to cure, and then another month before we came back to do any other work here. That one night was the only time the concrete would have been soft enough to disturb to such an extent, and then repair so that we didn't notice."

All around us, hidden by the rolling mist, I could hear the mysterious sounds of construction – banging and yelling, and the grinding of great steam-powered behemoths, excavating and moving mountains of earth as the landscape around the construction, torn up and shifted for several years, was now being reshaped to something resembling how it had looked for the previous six decades when the bridge was initially constructed. Those workers were as invisible to us as we were to them, and they were unaware when the order was given to widen the hole into the *lacuna* and bring forth the body.

Sledge's men were efficient, and it didn't take long. He stood to one side, offering direction without specifics. "A man might want to use that long pry bar on the left," he would say, or "A man might want to throw down a tarp over there to lay it on," with generality, and one of his crew would jump to grab this or that before instinctively using it in the most efficient way to expose a bit more of the cavity. Soon it was an opening about two feet in diameter – no more damage done than necessary, while still enough for two of Sledge's men to reach in and grab the clothing, pulling forth the corpse.

All of the men, constables included, stepped back. Only Morton, Holmes, and I held our ground. The two men who had touched the body dropped it and then went to the river, quickly, to wash their hands and quietly be sick.

The smell was strong, but not as bad as it would have been an hour before, when the concavity was first opened. Now, the breeze from the river did much to carry away the strong fetor of decay. I had encountered much worse. Early in my medical career, when studying the forensic disciplines, one of our teachers had walked us one morning down to the Thames, without explanation, where a body had just been retrieved. The odor was staggering, and many of my fellows lost their breakfasts there along the shore. "This is how we weed out the chaff," said the teacher with a rather cruel smile. "If you can't tolerate the smell of a floater, you cannot work in the field of forensic medicine." I retained the contents of my stomach, earning a faint word of praise from my teacher, but he could probably see from my face just how close I came to joining the others, bent over at the tideline. Years later, when that teacher was a professional colleague and we were standing over another body, he recalled the incident and said, "Do you know what that smells like to me? *Employment*."

Still, even with the morning breeze, it wasn't very long before the sickening odor became unavoidably present, and I could even taste it. I knew from previous experience that it would cling insidiously to my clothing, although it would have been much worse if the day were hot and muggy.

The constables had led Sledge and his workers away to the other side of the pier. Meanwhile, Holmes was the first to step forward, kneeling upon the damp scree and rolling the dead man face up. The filtered foggy light showed that the corpse had progressed through many of the stages of decomposition, although some typical features – the presence of insects, for instance, grown from eggs deposited on the body by their flying mothers – were absent, since the corpse had been sealed off from the outside world.

The clothing, though rumpled and much stained, had once been of good quality, and indicated wealth. The shoes were well made and looked new, except for one bright fresh scratch on the left that had apparently just occurred when the body was pulled out of the hole and across the rough concrete. The dead man appeared to have been in his early twenties, and had blondish hair of a length typical to his class.

Holmes was busy examining the body, and it appeared to make Morton a bit nervous. "Perhaps . . . we should wait for the Police Surgeon . . . ?" he asked timidly. Holmes shook his head.

"Dr. Fernard is on call this week, I believe. I would rather have an ape . . . That is to say, I'd rather rely my own conclusions – and Watson's – than the curiously over-esteemed Fernard." He glanced up, apparently finished. "Watson? Your turn."

With an inward sigh, I joined him, feeling the damp soak up through the small stones, wetting the knees of my trousers. Though sure that Holmes had seen more than me, I was soon able to offer my own thoughts.

"One might say that this man has been murdered thrice," I said. "Four times, if by some chance he was still alive when sealed in the bridge, whereupon he would have suffocated, although any of his other injuries would have killed him. The autopsy might confirm whether he suffocated, but it's irrelevant when considered with his overall condition."

I stood and stepped back from the body, as it was just as easy to point and discuss from that position as continuing to kneel upon the wet river bottom, temporarily exposed by the retreated tide.

"Although the stains are difficult to see amongst the others, the middle left side of his torso has bled considerably from two wounds – up-thrust, and received from a knife about one inch in width. It was a brutal weapon – no silly little Continental stiletto, for instance. Although depth will need to be determined, I estimate about four inches. Both wounds pierced his waistcoat and shirt, and likely penetrated the pericardium, if not the heart. Removal of the knife caused blood to gush forth. Whoever killed him would have likely also been covered in blood."

Taking a step to one side, and noticing from the corner of my eye that Holmes was nodding, I continued. "The back of his head has been damaged. Although the skin hasn't split, the skull is crunched like a broken eggshell – possibly from a hard fall, but more likely from having his head violently hit against something like a stone wall."

"Or with a stone," interrupted Holmes.

"Yes. But the break is flattened, not concave, so if it was a stone, it was a flat one.

"Finally, he has been strangled – violently. It's difficult to see due to the decomposition whether there are any finger or ligature marks on the throat, but it's apparent that his hyoid bone has been shattered, and likely his larynx crushed as well, probably by the killer's thumbs."

"I concur," Holmes said simply, and I had a small sense of enjoyment. His praise was rare, but it was always sincere when offered. "Someone truly wanted this man dead." He turned to wash his own hands in the river – not the cleanest option by far, but instinctively preferable to retaining traces of the dead man's dried juices on our skin. I went over to join him.

We then returned to Morton, who had pivoted away from the body and was smoking a cigar. I was a bit surprised that an Inspector of the Yard was squeamish around bodies at that point in his career, but such notions took different people in different ways at different times. He offered cigars to each of us, which were gratefully accepted.

"I'd say it's enough to be going on with that this is Evelyn Daintree," he said. "Wouldn't you?"

Holmes nodded. "The quality of his clothing, the good condition of his teeth and nails – all show his class, and the ring is a clear indicator of identity, pending identification by the family. It won't be pleasant."

"It never is," muttered the inspector."

"There is nothing about his clothing to provide any information – no tailor's labels, for instance. Even his shoes are featureless. The clothing is well made, but it's been purchased ready-made, not bespoke. Perhaps, during the autopsy, something else might be found. I wonder why . . . ." He trailed off for a few seconds, and then continued. "And there is no wallet or papers of any sort on the body. The decomposition of the features make identification rather difficult. If not for the ring, we might not have had an idea who he was."

Morton nodded. "It seems to be a complicated one. If you could see your way to make one of your investigations . . ." he added, a hopeful tone in his voice that seemed to have hidden implications.

Holmes nodded. "You must wait here for the corpse to be collected?"

When Morton confirmed it, Holmes added, "Then you won't mind if I speak to a few people who might be able to tell us something."

"No, no, not at all." He nodded with exaggerated agreement. "Just keep me informed, of course."

"Certainly. Watson?"

And with that, he led me across the shingle and up onto the river bank, where our cab was waiting not far away. Glancing back, I hoped that the wagon to remove the body arrived soon, as there seemed to be less space around it and the living men who kept vigil there as the tide was starting to return.

To my surprise, Holmes instructed the cabbie to take us to an address in Mayfair. Seeing my expression, he explained, "The Duke of Beauchester's residence when in town."

"I had thought we might return to Baker Street, where you would refresh your mind about the case."

He shook his head. "I recall enough from when it was related in last year's press reports."

"Morton may not appreciate it you get a jump on him by notifying the family before the body is officially identified, or before he can speak to them himself."

Holmes smiled and slipped finger and thumb into his waistcoat pocket, retrieving Morton's handkerchief and, within it, the crest-bearing ring.

"While you were examining the body, he took me aside, gave me this, and asked if I would unofficially take charge of the investigation."

I was shocked, as so many of the Yarders – even those who by then appreciated Holmes's talents like Lestrade and Bradstreet and Gregson – were still very guarded against the possibility of releasing any of their authority. For Morton to so overtly cede his to Holmes was unheard of.

Reading my thoughts, Holmes replied, "It has to do with the Atterson killing. You recall it last year? Ah, perhaps not, for that is when you were traveling. Particularly gruesome – a veritable slaughter in the East End – and Morton muffed it. The violence of the crime, and the shocking innocence of one of the young victims, caused him to miss the moment when valuable evidence was spirited away under his nose, not long after the bodies were discovered. All was officially forgiven, especially after I was able to point the Yard in the killer's correct direction, but privately Morton was sternly warned. Instead of having the desired outcome, however, it has left him rather skittish and hesitant, like a dog that has been beaten. I suspect that whatever caused him to summon us this morning was due more to his newfound nervous indecision than the unusualness of the case."

"But it *is* unusual," I added. "Somewhat *outrè*, as a matter of fact. A body buried in the pier of a bridge? A ring fished forth, purely by accident, from the rotted corpse. It's rather like something out Poe."

"I shall take your word for that," replied Holmes. "Writer, wasn't he?" Then he fell into silence as we continued the four-mile ride to Mayfair.

I knew that he was aware of Poe, but it was one of his curious eccentricities that he liked to maintain the fiction that he remembered only what was needed, as useless facts crowded out those of greater importance. I had gullibly believed his statement, very early in our friendship, that he was unaware of the motions of the planets around the sun. Only later did I understand his sometimes-peculiar sense of humor.

Glancing at him now, I saw that, whatever his purpose at pretending ignorance of Poe, his thoughts had moved on, likely considering our upcoming errand to speak with the dead man's father.

The Duke of Beauchester's town home was in Upper Brook Street, just west of where it touched Grosvenor Square. The Duke – Gerald Daintree – had made a name for himself in his younger days – specifically those years around the time when I was learning to walk – by demonstrating his fierce resolve while presenting Her Majesty's official demand that Russia withdraw from two Ottoman provinces, just a few months before our involvement in the Crimean War. From what I'd read over the years, in various histories chronicling the events prior to and during the conflict, the young Gerald Daintree was most effective as a diplomat – until he suddenly wasn't, his attentions instead abruptly required to govern his own domestic affairs upon the early death of his father, the previous duke. Publicly, he had rather coasted on his reputation ever since – although I'd heard that he was still much more involved behind the scenes than was casually realized – and he was now sometimes seen about the city, ill-tempered and rather settled-looking, in his sixties and going from here to there about his business. He had two sons – this I knew from the press reporting at the time of the elder's disappearance the year before – both considerably more useless than their father had been at that age. The Duke had been in his forties before either was born, and his wife, never a strong woman, had passed several years before her older son, Evelyn, disappeared.

The Duke's door was opened by a crippled old man in butler's togs, his curved back thrusting his head forward while robbing him of a foot or more of his original height. His bare speckled scalp was framed by the wispiest of white tufts, too feathery to stay lying down as they ought. He had along beak of a nose that seemed to draw his lips back, leaving him with a perpetual vulpine grin. This was augmented by his squinty cataract-filmed eyes, with whites to either side of his irises that were stained faintly brown, as if dyed by a lifetime of peering through tobacco smoke. This was confirmed by the fingertips of his right hand, darkened by frequent cigarette use. His voice was a rough as one would expect, asking us our business.

Holmes presented his card, identifying us and wondering if the Duke was at home regarding an urgent matter. After peering at us for a moment, the old man croaked, "I'll see," and shut the door in our faces.

This situation wasn't as unusual or as rude as some might think, for to knock did not automatically mean to enter, even at the most gracious of homes, and we waited patiently for a moment until the door was re-opened and we were let inside. The old man, introducing himself as Tibbles, took our hats and coats, hung them, and then led us toward the back of the ground floor and into a small and tidy study. A high window was behind a great desk, looking out on what would be a beautiful garden come spring, and the other walls were made up of high shelves filled with books that looked as if they were for reading and study, and not simply decoration.

The Duke was seated at the desk, the top of which was covered by a number of official-looking documents. Seeing the number of governmental seals on many of them, I wondered just how much work he still did for The Crown, in addition to managing his own affairs. He looked as if he was undecided whether to stand or remain seated, but finally, with a small heaving noise, he pushed himself upright, stating, "You told Tibbles that it was urgent."

Seated beside the Duke, his chair pulled around behind the desk as if he had also been consulting upon the paperwork, was a callow-looking fellow in his early twenties. This was, no doubt, the Duke's younger son, Christopher Daintree. He looked at us – and Holmes particularly – with undisguised curiosity, and perhaps just the hint of an amused sneer.

Holmes faced the older man. "May we sit?"

The Duke raised his eyebrows. "Oh? Of course." When we'd all settled ourselves, the Duke thought to introduce his son, who simply nodded, once, still focused on Holmes.

"I'm afraid that we bear bad news," Holmes stated. Then, without pausing to soften it, he continued. "Although your identification is still pending, the body of your older son, Evelyn, was discovered this morning in Hammersmith."

The Duke's body tensed, and his fingers, where his hands had been resting placidly on his desk, suddenly curled into talons, wrinkling several of the official-looking documents. Beside him, Christopher Daintree dramatically paled, and his mouth dropped open like a landed fish.

"What . . . What . . . *Where?*" The Duke had now half-risen, leaning with his propped arms upon the desktop. Only then did his son look away from Holmes, briefly glancing at his father before returning his now-haunted gaze to the detective.

"At a construction site," Holmes replied, apparently choosing to be vague rather than immediately stress the unusual location of the body. "A worker was checking some of the work and uncovered him, where he'd been hidden away – likely since he vanished last April.

The older man sat back down, collapsing into his chair and raising a shaky hand to his brow. His son was now staring at the desk, his gaze unfocused, as he thought about Holmes's surprise announcement.

After a moment, the Duke seemed to rally himself, sitting up a bit straighter and clearing his throat. Not once did he glance toward his other son. Instead, with a tight mouth, he rasped, "Tell me."

Holmes nodded, and then began with a recitation of what had occurred: How our presence was requested by a Scotland Yard inspector once the body was tentatively identified, and how it had been found in the bridge pier, apparently placed there when the concrete was wet last spring during bridge repairs.

"A workman was testing the concrete this morning, exposing the cavity where your son's body was placed."

The Duke nodded. "I see. And how was he identified? Some letter or document he was carrying, I suppose."

"No," Holmes replied. "His pockets were empty, and there was no wallet. His clothing was of good quality, but could have been purchased from any number of shops. I was curious about that. Why wouldn't he be wearing tailor-made items?"

"Because he had foolish ideas about making his own way, and turning his back on his family!" the older man snapped angrily, apparently giving vent to something long suppressed, and now free to burst forth when Holmes ripped away the scab of the man's control by revealing his son's death. "The little hypocrite – still willing to take my allowance, but then rejecting his own family and choosing to live in near-squalor while spending all his time with his rough crowd and Socialist friends. And then he – "

The Duke stopped abruptly, apparently aware that he was washing his dirty laundry in public. Meanwhile, the rant had focused Christopher Daintree's attention back on the present, and he was watching his father with something like a poorly kept secret shine in his eyes. Whatever the loss of his brother meant otherwise, it also seemed to please him in some just-barely revealed way.

Regaining his composure, the Duke asked, "If he had no papers, and his clothing was unremarkable, how did you identify him?"

Only someone who knew Holmes well would recognize that he was slightly vexed. Apparently he'd held onto this fact, but now that it was requested, he had to share it. Pulling out Morton's wrapped handkerchief from his pocket, he replied, "This was found with the body." And he half-rose to lay the ring upon the Duke's desk.

Both father and son looked at it with shock, a few long seconds at the ring, and then simultaneously raising their eyes to stare at one another. I glanced at Holmes, who was watching this silent exchange with keen interest. *What had he seen?* I wondered. Whatever it was now interested him greatly, and I could see that his observational powers were focused to the highest degree.

Then the moment passed, and the Duke reached and picked up the ring. I saw his nostrils twitch at the lingering smell of dead body and, after a moment, he moved to slide open the top middle desk drawer, as if to place the ring inside. Holmes raised a hand.

"I'm sorry, sir, but that is evidence, and will need to be returned to Scotland Yard."

The Duke, still lost in thought, was startled. "What? Nonsense! This is my son's ring – Look here: His initials, *E.D.* are there, cleverly woven into the crest. – but now it returns to his family."

"Not yet," said Holmes. "I really must insist." And he stood, his height imposing over the peer until the older man shook his head in disgust. With pursed lips he rewrapped it and handed it to Holmes, who thanked him and tucked it back into his waistcoat pocket.

Holmes glanced my way, signaling that it was time to leave. "Inspector Morton will be in touch," he explained. "To see about identifying the body. In the meantime, we will take your leave, and will be in touch soon."

The Duke nodded, his eyes drifting up and to the left, where he was no doubt visualizing some aspect of his lost son's life. Meanwhile, the younger son was staring at Holmes intently, and I wondered what he could be thinking. I glanced back at the two of them as we walked out, pulling the door shut behind us, and the young man was now staring at his father, chewing his lower lip.

We'd taken a dozen steps or so toward the front of the house when Tibbles, the old butler, stepped out from a side passage, blocking our way. Beside him was a woman of similar age, but meaty where he was withered, her posture straight as a weathered fence post. Her hand was resting upon the old man's shoulder in a possessive manner. She was a great slab of a woman, with a sharp chin like the prow of a whaler and canny eyes peeping from underneath heavy weathered lids.

"Is it true?" whispered the man, an emotional catch in his voice. "That young Mr. Evelyn is – that you found him this morning? Dead?"

"It is," said Holmes, while I added, "I'm afraid so."

A tear quickly formed on the reddish lower lid of Tibble's right eye. He started to say something, but his voice choked, and he turned and quickly shuffled away. The woman let her hand drop and shook her head. "I'm Mrs. Tibbles, the housekeeper," she explained. "Master Evelyn has always been a special favorite of ours. After the boys' mother died, we – In some ways, it felt like Master Evelyn was our own." She said it as if speaking to herself, and then she looked up suddenly, perhaps feeling she'd revealed too much. "Not that we place ourselves too highly, you understand. No, sirs. But we cared for him. When he and his father began to have their differences, and then when the young man moved out – Well, it hurt his father, the Duke, but it broke our hearts too, it did. He still kept in touch, but we missed him. And now . . . he was missing for a year, and we knew nothing, and now . . . ." Finally her craggy façade broke, and she turned to follow her husband.

We let ourselves out.

It wasn't too far to Baker Street, perhaps a twenty-minute walk, but Holmes was too impatient for that. He had seen something that he wanted to pursue. I had my own ideas as well, but he clearly wished to think instead of talk.

I considered strolling back to our rooms, but as Holmes indicated he was going to find a hansom and head in that same direction, I joined him. When we arrived, he dashed ahead and was already in his room, hurrying into some disguise while I more leisurely settled myself. In just a few moments he returned in one of his favorite get-ups: An idle laborer.

"Back to Mayfair?" I asked from my chair.

He nodded. "I want to find out what the Tibbles know regarding the disagreement between the father and his dead son. You noticed the reaction when I revealed the ring."

"Surprise. I didn't ascribe any special significance to it."

"Ah, Watson, how many times – ? But you've heard me preach enough about *observing.* Think back. Put yourself once again at the bridge. Reexamine the body in your mind. Consider our visit with the Daintrees *per* and *fils.*"

"And should I do anything else?"

"Hold yourself in readiness. I hope to know more in a few hours. Until then, *adieu*!"

With his departure, I idled the next hour or so while awaiting lunch searching through our combined collection of reference materials to learn more about the Duke of Beauchester. There wasn't much in the official volumes. *Debrett's* and *Who's Who* had the same dry details of the man's pedigree. Holmes's scrapbooks weren't much better, containing a few cuttings from the press of a year before when Evelyn Daintree had disappeared. As Holmes had mentioned, I was away during that time, while I knew that Holmes had been quite busy with a number of other cases, including one service for Otto von Bismarck to investigate a plot against the "Mad King", Ludwig II, who had died a couple of months later. While not personally involved, I have full access to Holmes's notes, and perhaps one day I can see a way toward presenting this important manner to a curious public.

The newspaper reports were sparse, and I wondered if the Duke, while interested in locating his lost son, had also suppressed the coverage to avoid any undue embarrassment. The reports simply requested information that would help locate Evelyn Daintree, unseen since departing from his father's Mayfair home on the night of 17 April, 1886.

After lunch, I settled in to revise some notes related to a case that Holmes and I had shared the previous week regarding some curious mendicants. I was unaware of how much time had passed when I became aware of an urgent ringing of the downstairs bell. Within moments of hearing Mrs. Hudson open the front door, quick and frantic steps were climbing the stairs to our sitting room.

The door flew open to reveal young Abel Sykes, not more than nine or ten. He was one of Holmes's Irregulars, that band of street Arabs who carried out various investigatory tasks, ran mysterious errands, and watched and sometimes followed men and women as directed. Just now, Abel's mission seemed to be delivering a message to me.

"Dr. Watson!" he blurted breathlessly. "Mr. Holmes needs you – now! You're to go to The Red Plough in Nottingham Street. The police have arrested that poor simple girl, Sofia, what lives with the Battles, for the murder of some toff. Hurry!"

I glanced at the clock – nearly six, and later than I'd supposed – when Mrs. Hudson joined us, having chased the lad upstairs at a more leisurely pace. She tried to hold a scowl upon her features, but looking at the boy caused it to be softened and replaced by a fond expression.

"Thank you, Abel," I said. "Mrs. Hudson, can you reward Abel's well-done job with something to eat? He appears to have once again run off without his coat."

The boy grinned and nodded, and then turned toward Mrs. Hudson with the trust that she would lead him back downstairs to an unexpected feast. He could believe in this with confidence, as such a thing had happened before, and more than once.

Within minutes I was on foot, moving through the now-dark streets. Long gone were the days when my various war wounds had impeded me too dramatically, although I did still feel a twinge during colder weather. I considered a hansom for such a short journey, but the idea was irrelevant, as none presented themselves. That portion of London – particularly Baker Street, which had a sizable commercial element – became much more quiet and deserted at night when the businesses were closed.

The Red Plough was one of those tidy corner pubs, well established before the current Mr. Battle took it over from his father, long before I ever moved to Marylebone. I had some sense that his grandfather, and perhaps even great-grandfather, had also run it, back in the hazy mists of time. I supposed that one of the Battles might have been the first owner, when the pub and the building around it was constructed.

I walked in, expecting to find the usual evening crowds, but the place was emptied out, except for Mr. and Mrs. Battle, their unofficial ward Sofia Allard, Inspector Morton, two constables . . . and a half-disguised Sherlock Holmes.

I tried to remember more about young Sofia as took off my coat and hat, and then walked to join the group. It was an odd *tableaux*, a twisted *Last Supper* with the girl as the central focus, seated on a chair in the middle of the bar, the most well-lit part of the room, and looking down at the floor with her long blonde hair hanging limply. On her right side was her unofficial adopted family, the Battles, the publican tense with balled fists and the older lady resting a hand on the girl's shoulder. To her left was the inspector, his hand raised as if he also wanted to place it on the girl, but to restrain instead of comfort. His two big-framed myrmidons stood slightly behind him, expressionless while awaiting instructions. And past them, standing on his own in half-shadow, and half-slouched on a stool and looking like The Jester, was Holmes – resembling himself, but also not, with much of his disguise still in place.

"Doctor," said the inspector. "The girl here has confessed."

I glanced at Holmes, who shook his head and rolled his eyes. Clearly in his estimation, Morton had not shined in this investigation.

"Tell him, Prior."

One of the constables stepped forward – one step, as if to recite a hard-learned poem in school. His face was tight with emotion, glancing toward the Battles with a look of remorse. In return, they glared at him as if he was a treacher.

"I was in here an hour ago – stopped in after my shift," he added hastily for the inspector's benefit, "and was talking with Mr. Battle when the girl started screaming."

"Apparently while you and I have been about our business, Watson," Holmes interrupted, "the story was discovered by the press – no doubt leaked by one of Sledge's construction workers."

"She's not a stupid girl!" blurted Mrs. Battle. "When she arrived here, she was like a starved cat – didn't know anything but her name. But she can read, she can, and looks at the newspapers every day. When she saw the story about that young man's body being found – "

"She started screaming," continued Constable Prior. "There was no way I could ignore it. My duty – " he added, again looking toward the Battles as if to somehow make them understand that he'd had no choice. "She was crying and going on about how she killed him – how she'd killed her 'beautiful Evelyn', and it was her fault."

If the girl had been crying before, there was no sign, other than her eyes being reddened. She not sat without betraying any emotion.

"I had no choice," Prior went on. "My duty, you see – I had to report it. I whistled for Niery here, and he sent word to the Yard, where the inspector heard about it. He came straight over, but Sofia – the girl – hasn't said a word since. It's like she's gone way back in her head and won't speak to anyone. Then Mr. Holmes came in and told the inspector he was a fool – " He looked abruptly at his superior, realizing he'd perhaps gone too far, and fell silent, his report as complete as he was willing to make it.

Morton frowned, glared at Prior, and then at Holmes, who slid forward off the stool and walked toward the group. From my position across from all of them, me in the dark while they were centered in the light, I felt as if I were watching a play, hurtling toward some climax.

"I've spent the afternoon ingratiating myself around the Duke's household," he said. "It was from them that I learned of Evelyn Daintree's connection with this pub – and with Miss Allard – during that period between when he angrily moved out of his father's home and when he was killed last April."

Both Battles' faces expressed sudden surprise, and the husband growled, "Evy? A duke's son? I thought he was some kind of clerk. Hung around her for months – interested in Silvia he was. And we didn't mind. She may be simple, but he didn't care, and it looked as if they might be headed toward marriage. Then he disappeared without a word last spring. Broke her heart, it did. She hasn't been the same since."

"And we know why," said Morton. "She confessed. She killed him."

"Don't be ridiculous," snapped Holmes. "How could this slight girl strangle a big man like Daintree to the point where his hyoid bone was broken? Watson – did you happen to notice which way the bone was damaged?"

"From the left," I replied. Then, seeing where he was going. "Likely from someone who is left-hand dominant."

"And the knife wounds were from a left-hander as well. If you'd had a chance to observe this girl, Inspector, as we in this neighborhood have done over the last few years, you'd know that she is *right*-handed. And in any case, even if she had stabbed Daintree and crushed in the back of his head, she wouldn't have been able to push him down into the bridge pier and repair the fresh concrete to the point that Sledge's workers didn't notice."

Morton was growing excited. "Then it was Mr. Battle." He turned toward the pub's owner. "*He* killed Daintree for some offense done against the girl. You can't argue that he has the strength to strangle a man to death, and to carry the body out to Hammersmith and place it in the bridge." He turned, as if to declare that Battle was under arrest, but Battle spoke first, holding up his right fist.

"Aren't you listening? I'm right-handed too – and so is my wife, as you'll likely accuse her next!"

"You didn't *observe* this morning, Morton," interrupted Holmes. "The curious fact about the ring that Watson also missed. Granted you didn't have the benefit of subsequently interviewing the Duke and his son, which gave extra emphasis to that fact, and during your afternoon at the Yard you didn't interview any witnesses – such as the butler and housekeeper at the Duke's residence – to find out additional pertinent information. But I'm disappointed that you didn't notice the fact about the ring." He turned to me. "Watson?"

Suddenly I wasn't in the audience any longer, but now also part of the play. I was the sole performer as everyone but the girl turned to stare at me. And I didn't know my lines.

I turned inward for a moment, seeing the ring when it was first revealed to us that morning by Morton, unfolded from Morton's handkerchief. The smell clung to it, rising immediately so that we all knew the ring had been associated with a dead and decaying body. I focused on that memory of the ring, thinking. Thinking . . . .

"The handkerchief," I said, suddenly looking up to see Holmes smiling at me. He nodded for me to continue. "It was *clean*. The ring had left no stain on it. There was no desiccated flesh or fluid clinging to it, because . . . because it wasn't on the body!" I took a step forward, joining the other actors in the drama. "Holmes, when we examined the body, *there was no wound on the any of the fingers.* When the ring was hooked out of the bridge, it wasn't torn loose from a finger. It must have been lying loose somewhere on the body. Loose, on the clothing . . . ."

"Exactly, Watson. And why wouldn't young Evelyn Daintree have been wearing his family ring?"

Without waiting for an answer, he turned back to Morton. "I suggest we adjourn to the Duke's residence and question Tibbles, the butler, and his wife the housekeeper. They have some interesting information that will lead to the answer, I think."

Morton rocked on his feet for a moment with indecision, still firm in his belief that the girl and the Battles were somehow involved, and unwilling to let it go entirely. Finally he said, "Niery, stay here and watch them – especially the girl. Prior, come with us."

"Begging pardon, sir," said Prior, stepping forward with a nervous gulp. "Might I be the one to say behind? I . . . I know the Battles, you see. Perhaps I can be a comfort."

"Your job isn't to comfort!" Morton snapped, but then, seeing that he'd already ceded control of the situation to Holmes (after he'd already asked him to run the investigation that morning), he relented, nodding for Constable Niery to join us instead.

We walked for just a moment before hailing a passing growler. Morton asked Holmes a few questions, but he was pointedly ignored, and soon he was quiet.

The streets were mostly deserted, and Upper Brook Street was a quick trip from Nottingham Street, though worlds apart in prosperity. Holmes had the cab stop several houses away from the Duke's, and when we'd paid the cabbie, he led us not to the front door, but around to the rear entrance by way of Lees Mews. A soft knock upon the door was answered by Mrs. Tibbles, who let us inside and through to a large table, where her husband was hunched over an empty teacup. Beside it was a bottle of brandy, apparently used to fortify his strength.

Holmes introduced the policemen and then got right to it, explaining that he'd spent the afternoon in disguise, questioning the servants of the Duke's house, as well as the those of the neighbors, as the opportunity arose. He'd heard enough to paint a picture of life in the Daintree residence. By then, hearing about the father and his two sons and their various characteristics, he'd been confident enough to approach the Tibbles, revealing his identity and asking some pointed questions.

"When Watson and I interviewed the Duke and his son," Holmes explained to Morton, leaning forward expectantly, "they had a marked reaction to hearing that the body had been identified by the ring – much more of a reaction than should have been expected. Knowing already that the son wasn't wearing the ring when he died, as there was no damage to his fingers such as would have been expected if the ring had been yanked off by the construction hook, I recognized that there was something curious going on that needed explanation.

"The Tibbles have always felt like young Evelyn was the child they never had – and apparently that was reciprocated." The older couple nodded. "They knew of his growing socialist beliefs and interest in the lower classes – a fact that outraged his father. They were also aware that he had a growing interest in a young lady he'd met after he moved out."

Tibbles nodded. "He said she was named Sofia. She was simple-minded, but very sweet and pretty. She was an orphan, cared for by a barkeeper and his wife. He was planning to marry her."

Morton looked surprised, and also as if he wanted to speak – perhaps to claim that this was evidence that his theory about the girl was correct – but Holmes silenced him with a frown and small shake of his head.

"Tell us about the last night Evelyn was here," he instructed.

"It was last April. We – my wife and me – were listening at the door, as we were today. Evy was here to tell his father about his plan to marry the girl. There was a bitter argument. Many things were said on both sides, but it ended when the Duke told Evy that he was disinherited."

"And what happened then?"

"Evy stormed out. That's the last we ever saw of him."

"And what night was that?"

"April 12th – Evy's birthday."

Holmes glanced at Morton. "And in the press reports, it's noted that when Evelyn Daintree was reported missing, that was also the date that the family last claimed to see him." Looking back at the Tibbles, he asked, "And the ring – what you told me this afternoon."

The butler started to speak, but his wife interrupted. "Why, he pulled it off and threw it at his father just before he walked out."

Holmes leaned back satisfied. "Do you see?" he asked, gazing intently at the inspector, but sparing the occasional glance my way as well. I nodded, immediately understanding the implications. Morton pieced it together a bit more slowly.

"So when he left, he didn't have the ring," he said slowly, "having thrown it at his father. Later, it was with the body when it was buried, but he wasn't wearing it – so somehow it had managed to get from his father here to the Hammersmith Bridge." He was nodding slightly. "Clearly we have to question the Duke now."

Holmes agreed. "We do."

He stood and led us unerringly through the bowels of the house to the showier places where the Daintrees maintained their domain. I noticed that the Tibbles were following us, apparently planning to eavesdrop once more to learn the next piece of the story.

The Duke's study door was partway open, leaving a slash of light extending along the dark hall floor. Holmes led the way, giving a small knock and then pushing his way inside.

The Duke was sitting behind the great desk, his eyes fixed on some distant spot, indifferent to our arrival. The four of us – Holmes, Morton, Constable Niery, and me – crowded in, while the Tibbles remained in the dark hallway, where I could hear them getting into position to listen, their shuffling reminding me of the sound of mice in the walls.

Holmes stepped forward, waiting silently until the Duke's eyes refocused on him. There was no surprise there, really no emotion at all. He looked weary and blanched and defeated.

"We've come about your son – " began Holmes, but the Duke interrupted him with a tired wave of his hand.

"You'll find him upstairs," he rasped. I saw that there was an empty whisky bottle to one side of the desk, with a nearby glass containing only dregs of amber liquid at the bottom. The Duke had been drinking, although how much was unclear.

"No," corrected Holmes. "We've come about your older son's murder."

Now the Duke frowned, seeming to tighten up and become something like his normal self. "I understood what you meant," he said, more force in his voice. "My son's murder, and my son upstairs – it's connected, you see." He tapped a sheet on his desk with a blunt forefinger. I recalled the masses of documents that had filled that surface earlier in the day. Now the desk was clear except for the whisky detritus and this one solitary page – seemingly a handwritten letter with a signature at the bottom.

"This is his confession – for the police, you know. But I can tell you what it says."

Holmes glanced at me, and then Morton. The latter started to speak, but again Holmes frowned and shook his head. Possibly one day Morton would be enough of a good policeman to know when to be quiet and simply listen.

"Go ahead," replied Holmes softly.

"I knew," explained the Duke after a long moment of silence and a wistful glance at the empty bottle. "I think I knew that Evelyn was dead. I sensed his absence, if you understand. But I had no idea until today, during your visit, that Christopher had killed him."

He drifted into introspection, but Holmes prodded him. "Go on . . . ."

"Hmm?" The Duke cleared his throat then and pulled himself straighter in the chair. "The ring. I knew that Evelyn had thrown it at me when he left . . . for the last time. Later I couldn't find it. But I still thought . . . that it was here in the room, fallen down behind something. I didn't know that Christopher had picked it up. That he had it with him when he followed after Evelyn that night."

He closed his eyes, found further strength, and then told the rest of it.

"Evelyn came here to tell me he was going to marry some girl – a trollop he'd met in a bar. That was the last straw. I told him that I was disinheriting him. That I'd paid for him to dally in this wastrel common life for too long, and that if he persisted, he was cut off. I . . . never thought . . . I never thought that he'd choose that life over me, not if I gave him a final ultimatum. He took off the ring, threw it at me, and said he was never coming back.

"I wanted to be alone. I ordered Christopher out of the room. I didn't know that he picked up the ring, or that he went after Evelyn. When I heard that the ring was found with the body, in a place where it must have been left at the time the body was hidden, I knew. I knew what Christopher had done, and that he'd left the ring with his brother while concealing his . . . his corpse.

"I assumed that Christopher did it on purpose, but he said it was an accident. He followed Evelyn – all the way to the pub where the girl he wanted to marry lived. Christopher arrived just as the girl came out to meet Evelyn in the mews. They argued while the girl was watching, and when Evelyn turned away, Christopher picked up a brick and struck him from behind. His brother was dead."

The Duke made it seem like an impulse, almost an accident. Apparently the version told to him by Christopher had left out the stabbing and the strangling – as if the make absolutely sure that the elder brother was dead.

"Christopher panicked. He saw the girl, still watching, but she was speechless – horrified, no doubt. He – Christopher told me that he considered killing her, too, but he couldn't. He later found that there was no need. Her mind is somehow damaged, and apparently she didn't understand what had happened, for she told no one.

"Christopher then loaded the body into a carriage that he found in the mews, and he then drove around London for hours, considering what to do. In his wanderings, he came across a construction site at the Hammersmith Bridge. Originally, he thought to throw the body from the bridge, or perhaps to arrange it to look like an accident – as if Evelyn had wandered onto the site and been injured. But then he saw the forms for the concrete and, understanding what they represented and that the concrete was still wet, he created a space in which to hide the body. Then he spread around the material that he'd removed to create the cavity, found some more concrete and mixed it up, and covered the hole before replacing the forms.

"But he made a mistake.

"When leaning and pushing to push Evelyn into the cavity, the ring, which he'd carried with him from this room after retrieving it, fell into the hole, where it was sealed up until this morning. He didn't know he'd lost it – he said he never knew it was with his brother's body. He thought that it had fallen somewhere else in his travels that night, lost forever. When he heard that . . . when I heard that, he understood that I knew. That he'd killed his brother last year. And he knew what he had to do."

He squared his shoulders and laced his fingers before him. His voice was stronger.

"As my son – as the surviving son of the Duke of Beauchester – Christopher had a responsibility. All of his life, he inevitably disappointed me, but at the last, he knew what he had to do." He cleared his throat. "And he did it. He understood what was expected, and he carried through as I expected."

He again tapped the sheet on the desk. "This is his confession. You'll find him upstairs . . . ."

And we did.

I've never understood what drives a man to suicide, and hopefully never will. I've seen so many victims of circumstances that forced men and women to that lonely desperate place, and for each one, I cannot help but imagine the final moment when he or she makes the quick slice or pulls the trigger or steps from the high place. With an opened vein or artery, there's still a moment when help might be sought. Sometimes the gun doesn't aim where the desperate man or woman hopes, leaving them alive but horribly mutilated. And what of those who hang themselves? If their neck isn't immediately broken – and it rarely is during the home-made hangings – then there are moments of what must be excruciating pain as the rope cuts into the throat and the body, an animal desperate to live and separate from the brain and having no concept of suicidal intent, immediately fights to survive.

Christopher Daintree's hanging was messy. He had thrown a rope over a high ceiling hook, stood on a chair and adjusted the amateur noose around his neck, and then stepped off. There were claw marks upon his neck and flesh under his nails where he'd fought to get under the tight rope, to release the awful constriction as his instinct to survive immediately recanted his decision to die. But it hadn't mattered, because as shabby a job as it was, it was effective. When we found him, his feet were hanging down, pointed a foot above the floor. He had been dead for hours – most likely not long after Holmes and I left, when his father confronted him. The *post-mortem* lividity had left his distorted face as white as the walls of the marble tomb where he and his brother would soon be interred, each on biers to the right and left of their mother's coffin. Their father, a broken man, would join them in just a few months, having commenced to waste away due to grief from the moment he learned of his son Evelyn's fratricidal murder.

Although Morton received praise for his quick solution, it was no secret that Holmes was the man who had actually uncovered the truth. I suspected that this came about by way of Constable Prior, who left the force not long after, taking a job at the Battles' pub. It turns out that he grown up in that neighborhood, had known them for years, and had felt a special interest in poor Sofia Allard from the time she'd arrived. Within a month, he and the girl had married.

In spite of this good news, the case left a bitter taste in both Holmes and my mouth. Morton had tried to thank him, but Holmes waved him away.

Some weeks after Prior married Sofia, we went 'round to the pub. The former constable told us that he'd managed to get a bit of the story from his new wife.

"She's not as simple as some would think," he said. "She met Evelyn Daintree when he was playing at living his poor man's life. There was talk of them marrying, although I don't think she was especially keen on it. He had the idea in his head, and that was that. She remembers seeing the two brothers fighting, but I don't think she understood what happened – until the day the body was found, and she read about it in the newspaper. Then she remembered and, thinking the fight was about her, she believed that Evelyn Daintree was killed because of her. I was here the night the body was found, to see her, and that's when she started screaming – confessing to something she hadn't done. I had no choice. Too many people had heard. I . . . I had to notify the Yard, and the inspector. But it worked out. You found the truth, Mr. Holmes, and now Sofia and I are married, and with our child on the way . . . ."

It was a happy ending, but Holmes wasn't satisfied, and he dived in on something he hadn't been able to do several years before: Looking for information about Sofia's origins.

By then, it was no challenge, and he castigated himself for not doing so earlier. She was the daughter of a Russian emigrant, a widower who was one of the lesser instructors at Cambridge. He had taken care of his daughter for all her life, as she couldn't adequately take care of herself, and when he passed unexpectedly from heart failure, an unscrupulous college student had taken charge of her. Holmes didn't share with me what sort of abuse had inflicted on the poor girl, but she had escaped and somehow made her way to London, and into the warm care of the Battles.

Holmes passed on this information to former-Constable Prior, including the name of the girl's abuser, and the girl's new husband and a few of his former associates took a holiday from work in order to visit Cambridge. I'm uncertain as to what occurred there, except that justice was privately and fully served, and after that, Holmes looked back on the entire affair with a much cheerier disposition.

The Bishop's Painful Path

"But why '*A Study in Scarlet*'?" asked Sherlock Holmes in a contentious tone, his teeth clenched around the stem of his cherry-wood pipe.

Throughout the morning, I had done my best to ignore him, as he was in an ill-tempered and quarrelsome mood. I had recognized the signs of disputatiousness when I'd descended to breakfast, and realized that I should have seen it coming the night before, with the delivery of the day's last post.

Up to that moment, Holmes had been in a good mood, almost jolly, having just completed a neat piece of work related to an East End murder the previous April, in which a streetwalker named Smith was assaulted by a group of unidentified men. Holmes was able to privately prove to the authorities who was responsible – a trio of young noble scions attached to one of the Continental Embassies. As they were all protected under diplomatic immunity, there was nothing that could be officially be done – but privately, Holmes assured me, there would be retribution.

With that cryptic assurance of forthcoming justice, Holmes and I had to be satisfied, and we had been discussing the matter at length when the postman brought an official-looking letter. Thinking it further related to the Smith investigation, Holmes opened it with enthusiasm. Then, having read it, he made a noise of disgust that sounded like *Pfui!* before tossing it my way, and then proceeded to rise and pace the sitting room.

I was surprised to see that the document was unexpectedly related to events from the previous year, when Holmes's Herculean efforts had cleaved asunder the tangled financial schemes of Baron Maupertuis. The convoluted and extended affair had left his health shattered for a brief time, but he had since recovered and had been in fine form ever since. Now, however, I worried, as the letter, from a Whitehall official who had been most useful during the investigation of the Baron's Netherland-Sumatra Company, wrote to state that certain aspects of the case were not quite as finished as we had supposed.

A careful second reading on my part gave me to understand that there was simply some question about the interpretation of the Baron's coded ledgers, and Holmes – who had initially found and translated them – was requested to offer additional assistance as some of the cases progressed to trial. But the memory of his association with the investigation was apparently still sensitive, and I soon understood that he feared those involved in carrying out the prosecution, through their inability to completely comprehend the Baron's schemes, would – even at this late date – somehow give the villain a tiny hole through which to escape.

I had him re-read the letter, and upon reflection he seemed to agree with me and return to his previous equilibrium, if not jollily, but his captious mood was in evidence once again the following morning.

I had chosen to mostly ignore him as I ate my breakfast and worked my way through the morning newspapers. (Fortunately, in his present mood, Holmes had thus far neglected to read them, so I was able to peruse them in their undamaged entirety, without finding them pulled apart and left as a mare's nest on the sitting room floor, or already scissored-up as interesting pieces were culled out for his scrapbooks.) But then he randomly and unexpectedly asked the reason for the specific title of my first chronicle of his adventures, published the previous November and now (I noticed) lying on the small octagonal table beside his chair, and when I let that pass, he continued.

"You really should have called it something more accurate," he said, his tone demanding a response like a bored child who would not be ignored. "Perhaps '*An Investigation into the American* Idée Fixe *to Carry Out Extended Revenge Mania upon British Shores*'. While the Hope case was an excellent example, you wrote it as if it were a penny dreadful. I could have offered you a half-dozen others just as interesting to bolster your thesis – had you chosen to present it in the proper scientific manner. There was the Coulter killing in '82 – you'll remember our merry chase up and down the West Country. And Mitchell, that great bearded bear-like schemer who stole all the hospital money and fled to Surrey. If ever a man deserved his fate – . And if you'd waited just a bit to publish, until this year, you could have included last January's murder at Birlstone, when that shabby American killer sought Moriarty's help in tracking down his victim. But really, Watson, I cannot congratulate on that sensational yellow-back title. As I've said before – "

"Yes, Holmes," I said, finally rising to the bait and from my chair. "As you've said before – many times in the last six or seven months. And as I've said in response, my purpose was not to write a scientific treatise! If that's what you want, you'll have to do it yourself. When the Jefferson Hope case concluded in '81, I promised that I'd write it up so that the public would know the truth of your efforts, and so your light wouldn't be occluded under Scotland Yard's basket. The idea was for the pubic to read it, and not for it to be ignored in the back of some technical journal, or to be some pamphlet of only one-hundred printed copies – ninety-eight of which sadly remain in the possession of the author – rather like that dry chapbook of yours that takes up dusty space on the bottom shelf there. For all your concerted effort, how many people are beating down our door to read *An Examination of the Influences of Trade upon the Form of the Hand*?"

"Scotland Yard would certainly benefit – "

I was becoming heated. "'*A Study in Scarlet*' was chosen as the title because *you* said it – *Twice!* – during the course of the investigation."

"I never did!"

I stepped over to his table, retrieving the volume in question and flipping through it. I had worked on the thing for almost seven years, revising and tweaking *ad nauseum*, and I knew exactly where to look.

"Here – in Chapter Four," I read. "You said, '*I might not have gone but for you, and so have missed the finest study I ever came across: a study in scarlet, eh? Why shouldn't we use a little art jargon. There's the scarlet thread of murder running through the colourless skein of life, and our duty is to unravel it, and isolate it, and expose every inch of it.*' And again at the very end." I flipped through the pages. "'"*Didn't I tell you so when we started?" cried Sherlock Holmes with a laugh. "That's the result of all our Study in Scarlet: To get them a testimonial!*"' Are you questioning my memory?" I took a deep breath as I shut the book, gently as it was my only copy, and he didn't respond – as he knew that my account was accurate.

I replaced the cheap volume upon its shelf, thinking as I always did that for all my efforts, I wished every time I saw it that my literary agent had done better when placing it for publication. In fact, it was a rather dingy little book, to be purchased cheaply at a newsstand for quick and impermanent reading and then tossed away. Due to his carelessness at confirming details with the publisher, my agent's name, instead of my own, was on the cover as the listed author. The book always made me a bit despondent, and perhaps that sudden familiar feeling took some of the heat out of my argument with Holmes. He had a complete right, after all, to express his dissatisfaction with it – especially since he was the subject, and the narrative recounted one of his investigations. I knew how unhappy the book made me, with the authorial credit so blatantly misdirected, but I worked to keep that to myself. Holmes was certainly allowed to be interested in how he was presented to the public, and – I admitted to myself – to express his opinion. *Perhaps,* I thought– and not for the first time – *it was a mistake to waste all of that effort. Holmes's reputation certainly needs no assistance from me.*

Of course, he read all of these thoughts as they passed across my face, as if they were printed black-on-yellow on a news sheet. He took a deep breath, as did I, and we both stood down for the moment from an argument we'd had before, and would certainly have many times afterwards.

It was at this juncture the front doorbell rang and, considering our moods, that may be an explanation why Holmes initially didn't initially seem to give the proper interest that he should have to his new client.

Edward King was not a large man and, passing him on the street, one would have been tempted to nod and move along, retaining no memory of the encounter. He was dressed in a plain suit that had seen better days, and his shoes clearly showed evidence of much use, as if he walked a great deal. Having been taught to look at shirt cuffs, I saw that he wrote a great deal, although when he offered his hand, I couldn't identify any spots of residual ink upon his fingers. His hand was soft – *Not a laborer* my thoughts continued. Noting his pleasant and rather unforceful expression, I decided that, in spite of his well-used footwear, he was not a salesman, but perhaps a clerk in some small shop or legal office. Certainly not a bank, I concluded, as better-looking attire would have been acquired and required.

As our visitor walked toward Holmes, I turned to request fresh coffee from Mrs. Hudson. Then, having hung up the man's hat, I was startled to hear Holmes state, "Please have a seat here, Bishop. I think you'll find this chair most comfortable."

Spinning around, I saw the same small man I'd just negated to a clerk being addressed as *Bishop.* Holmes saw my surprise and smiled. "Doctor Watson, when glancing at your apparel a moment ago, observed your right hand when our landlady brought you and you shook it, but he neglected to observe the left hand, where you wear a most-distinctive ring identifying your faith, and that you hold a position of importance." He then held up a card with a small grin. "He also didn't observe that you handed me your card, declaring your title, as he was turned away to hang your hat."

The man, about sixty, with close-cropped dark hair on top of his head and longer graying whiskers down the side of his face, past his ears. His eyes had a weariness to them, but one sensed, the longer that he spoke, that there was no sadness or bitterness to it, but rather because there was still good work left to do, though time and energy were both waning. He wasn't a large man and, even sitting down, his back retained the slight forward slump that, if not already too late, would continue to collapse and exaggerate as he aged.

I noted that he had a few crumbs upon his waistcoat, and took this to mean that he was somewhat absent-minded as to his own care. Not knowing if he'd eaten early or recent, or from whence he'd traveled, I asked, "Would you like me to have something to eat served with the coffee?"

"No, no," he said with a tired smile. "I purchased a little something when I departed this morning, and ate it on the train." His gaze sharpened.

"I must apologize, Mr. Holmes, for not sending a message, warning of my arrival, or to make an appointment. I have been most upset, you see, and when I decided last night to seek your advice, I didn't sleep, and never thought to send a wire. I was on the first train this morning."

"First train?" I asked. "From where?"

"Why, Lincoln," he said, as if I should have known.

"I don't believe that I've retained any record of you, Bishop," said Holmes, handing me the man's card. "You must have kept yourself out of trouble so far."

It was plain and unostentatious, simply identifying him as *Edward King, Bishop of Lincoln*, and giving his residence as *The Bishop's Palace – Lincoln Cathedral.*

Holmes's mention of the possible trouble in the older man's past seemed to cause him some worry, as his expression darkened. "There has been no trouble," he said, a hint of stress entering his voice. "Until recently, that is. But I fear that someone is trying to destroy my reputation."

I handed the card back to Holmes, who dropped it upon his chair-side table. At that moment, Mrs. Hudson returned with the coffee, and after everyone was served and she'd departed, Holmes asked King to share his story.

"I am the son of the Archdeacon of Rochester, and the grandson of the Bishop of Rochester, so I suppose that a life in the Church was my destiny – and not that I mind. From my earliest days, I've found kinship and comfort in the church.

"I graduated from Oxford in 1850, and was ordained four years later. After serving in a variety of posts, Prime Minister Gladstone appointed me as Canon of Christ Church at Oxford in 1873. I was always somewhat a favorite of his, although some of my ideas have rubbed people the wrong way. At Oxford, I was somewhat known as an 'Anglo-Catholic', and at times, some of my writings have been criticized as 'Romish'. Actually, there were a number of us – referred to as the 'Oxford Movement' – who have attempted to nudge the ship a bit in that direction. There was push-back, of course, particularly when Disraeli was in office, and it was always something of a surprise to me that Gladstone, with his initial anti-Roman zeal, would later be supportive of what we were doing. I believe that as he aged, he became more interested in the evangelical instead of the ritual. In any case, when he regained the Premiership in 1885, he placed me as Bishop of Lincoln – which was once the diocese of John Wesley, I'm pleased to note.

"All has been well since then – until one week ago, when a friend of mine brought me this. He had received it in the first post last Monday." He reached into a pocket and pulled forth several folded packets of sheets. Sorting them, he handed one to Holmes, who then studied it intently for several moments, including a close perusal with his glass before handing it across to me.

It was a series of seven octavo sheets of cheap manufacture, yellowish from the inclusion of too much wood pulp. I held it up to see that there was no watermark – which was no surprise. The message, written with a narrow-nibbed pen in bluish-black ink and using anonymous square letters, had bled and smeared along the thin woody paper, and the lines were narrow, close, and cramped, filling the pages, but still legible. It was a rage-filled attack on King, and specifically against various Catholic-type rituals that were creeping into his ministry. A number of lines were underscored, including *Edward King's Satanic Roman rituals will be punished!*

Holmes was looking at me with an amused expression, but one so subtle that only one who had known him for quite a while would spot it.

"There is nothing in which deadly anger can be so easily generated as in religion," said he, leaning back against in his chair. "It can be built up as an excuse to commit almost any crime by either the zealot or the politician who influences or controls it. I see that there are other letters," he added to the Bishop. "All along the same theme?"

King nodded. "That was only the first – last Monday. These three others were sent to other friends, who also brought them to me, knowing that I would be concerned. They are indeed written along the same lines as the first."

He handed the other letters to Holmes who, after the same examination, reached over and placed them in my hand as well. They were on identical paper, and written in the same anonymous manner, with emphasized declarations like *Satan will have his payment!* and *Edward King is a Sinner and the Devil will have him!* and *It is too late for Edward King!*

"You were right to bring these to my attention," said Holmes. "While the author may simply be venting his anger at you, there is the distinct progression towards preparing himself to carry out physical violence."

King waved his hand. "I don't care about that," he said, surprisingly. "God's plan will proceed as it will. If he wishes for me to die, then that will be my time. What does worry me is that this will taint the *work* – that what we're accomplishing will have this smeared on it, so that it cannot be ignored. So that – should these diatribes become public knowledge, it will always cross someone's mind and stain their thoughts. We cannot have that. Suppose the next letter goes to someone who is not a friend – someone who does not let me know that he received it. What about if a subsequent letter is sent to a reporter, who inflates the matter like throwing coal oil upon a fire, simply to generate a scandalous story?"

Holmes nodded. "I understand your fears. Have you given any thought as to who might have written and sent these screeds?"

King shook his head. "Tait, the former Archbishop of Canterbury, was down on a number of us that he called the 'Oxford Movement', but he died in 1882. A couple of years ago, a fellow named Hanchard published a critical little volume, purportedly about my life, but really just an attack on what he feared were my Romish tendencies. There has been criticism of the fact that I've remained unmarried, but I think that St. Paul puts before us the unmarried life as the higher state. But then, you must remember, Paul added '*for those who are called to it*'. I am single myself, but simply because I never felt called to anything else. I have the highest view of married life."

As he spoke, he slipped a bit into what must have been his "preaching voice", for there was a strength that he took on that was missing in his typical conversation – even when he was discussing the threat that the letters represented. I found myself curious enough that I wanted to hear and see him conduct a real service. This rather surprised me, considering my own hit-or-miss religious upbringing, chiefly influenced by the dour Church of Scotland, which didn't even celebrate Christmas, as it was also considered too "Romish", being a contraction of "Christ's Mass".

Holmes was silent for several minutes, and King seemed content to let him think, staring placidly into the cold fireplace while sipping his cooling coffee. After a moment, my friend roused himself. "I am afraid, Watson, that we shall have to go," he said.

"Go! Where to? Lincoln?" In truth, I had suspected that would be our plan.

"Yes. As a start, in any case." His head turned to King. "Do you plan to return today?"

The Bishop nodded, and Holmes added, "Then we will plan to join you in Lincoln later this afternoon. If you could arrange to have the four friends who received these letters on hand to meet with us – Shall we say four o'clock? – it would be most appreciated."

"I shall do so," said the minister enthusiastically while rising to his feet. Nothing had been done to advance toward a solution to his problem – nothing, that is, except to involve Sherlock Holmes – but he already seemed ten years younger, and I thought that I could see, underneath his six decades, something of the chipper boy that he had once been.

"The Bishop's Palace," he said at the door, after shaking both our hands and making no effort to retrieve the letters. "Every cabbie at the station knows it. We shall see you both this afternoon." And then he was gone.

Holmes turned to me. "Watson, do you suppose the Archbishop of Canterbury is on the telephone?"

Three hours later, we were on a train for the relatively short journey to Lincolnshire, in a first-class compartment where Holmes recounted some of what he had learned between the time of King's departure from Baker Street and our embarkation north. He had departed from our rooms almost immediately after our visitor left, vaguely instructing me to check with my friend, Lomax, at the London Library for anything that might be relevant. My own subsequent journey to St. James's Square had been mostly pointless. Lomax had helped me sort through the various official biographical entries in a varied accumulation of reference books, but I saw nothing that was useful. King had been born in December 1829, making him now fifty-eight – an age when he might be expected to provide another twenty years of service to his church. He had come from a long line of ministers, all serving with distinction. As stated, he had never married, and his mother had served as his housekeeper until 1883, when she had passed away.

Since the mid-seventies, King had been an active opponent of prosecutions made under the 1874 Public Worship Regulation Act, established by Disraeli and Tait (whom King had previously mentioned), the former Archbishop of Canterbury until 1882. The Act, introduced in Parliament by Tait as a Private Member's Bill, had attempted to limit what he fearfully called the "ritualism" of Anglo-Catholicism, and the "Oxford Movement", of which King was a noted supporter. The bill was strongly endorsed by Disraeli, so it was a foregone conclusion that it was likewise condemned by Gladstone – who had subsequently endorsed King for the position of Bishop of Lincoln when he regained his position as Prime Minister.

The Oxford Movement had been more active and influential in the middle of the century, and while it had somewhat diminished by Edward King's time, it was still a favorite bugaboo of Disraeli and his cronies, who called it a "Mass in disguise", leading to the Queen's support of the Public Worship Regulation Act, as she saw the Act as a support of Protestantism.

I reported this to Holmes, who then provided a *précis* of his own mid-day activities. As he'd implied, he'd visited the telephone exchange in Lombard Street to place a call to Canterbury and the Archbishop, Edward White Benson. From there, he'd walked quickly to nearby St. Paul's, fortunately finding the Bishop of London, Frederick Temple, available for a quick discussion. "I was able to be of service to him in the late seventies, when some of his clergy were murmuring against him about his harsh control. They were the last hold-outs of the group that had protested his appointment as Bishop of Exeter in the middle-sixties." He shook his head in disgust. "So much misplaced passion and anger and ill-will in a structure supposedly dedicated to love and goodwill."

He wasn't specific in what either of these conversations advanced, and he concluded by stating that he'd also visited a couple of knowledgeable folk within the government, asking their opinion regarding this internal squabble within the Anglican Church. "One remarkable fellow whose fat hands hold every strand in the web told me that while to us this might seem like small potatoes, as the Americans say, just a collection of fractious clerics, such disagreements have the ability to fester and spread if not treated. The internal divisions over whether or not to include certain ritualistic usages in the services are deadly serious to some – and if there's a chance that this is the true reason that King has received these letters, then this might be an opportunity to make a course correction and also let the air out of some of the opponents' sails at the same time, to somewhat mix a metaphor."

I was really uncertain as to what he was implying, but he'd conveyed all that he intended, so I had to make due by sitting back and opening a book that I'd brought along. I must have soon dropped it when I fell asleep, for when I awoke, Holmes had placed it on the empty seat beside me.

King had been correct when he'd stated that the cabbie would know how to find King's home, nearly adjacent to Lincoln Cathedral. It was a most impressive structure, a great stone three-story edifice, roughly *L*-shaped, and joining another similar structure. We were met at the door by a fellow in his late twenties who introduced himself as Edwin Streeter, King's secretary. He led us through a great hall and up some stairs, around and about until I was turned quite around. Seeing my expression, Streeter smiled, and I stated, "The house seems far too large for one man."

"The house sits on the same site as the former Bishop's Palace from medieval times," Streeter explained. "This structure was built in 1727, and then remodeled just over twenty years ago. When Bishop King came to Lincoln three years ago, he chose it to be his residence and office."

By then, we had reached the open door of a well-appointed study, where we found our persecuted client and four other men of similar mien and age. They all rose and we were introduced as Streeter backed into the hallway, pulling the door shut behind him.

All four were ministers of varying levels of responsibility within the Anglican Church, and what they had in common was that they had been friends with Edward King since he was a young man. Thomas Madge was a stout fellow with a Friar Tuck-like bearing. Milton Hennessy was tall and pale, and from various signs that I perceived, he was quite ill, and not long for this world. Isa Longden had an athletic look to him, with his silvery hair coiffed just so. I noticed that he wore no ring, and wondered if he set ladies' hearts beating in his particular circle. Franklin Weaver was the most forgettable of the four, a short fellow with wheaten hair and round glasses that obscured his eyes by being refracted just so that in whichever direction he turned, the light seemed to be reflected.

The order that I've introduced them was also the order in which they had received the objectionable letters, and they all stressed that they had no knowledge of who might have sent them. Holmes was silently disgusted that, in each case, none of the envelopes, which had come through the public post, had been retained. He explained that he might have learned something useful, had he been able to examine them.

"There was nothing to see," said Madge, his voice rather high and wheezy. "I was the same kind of paper – cheap stationery, I would guess. The writing was the same – though a bit bigger because it had to be read by the postman. Same squared-off letters and runny ink."

"And when you observed this," countered Holmes, "did you note from whence it was mailed?"

"Lincoln," Madge replied promptly. "Marked by the post office the same day as it was delivered, and likely sent from the main post office so as to arrive the same day."

"And was it the same for all of your letters as well?" Holmes asked the other gentlemen. They simply nodded in agreement, although I had my doubts that every one of them had made the examination or retained the information.

"Who would do this?" asked Milton Hennessy in a rough voice. Of the four, he seemed the most aggrieved that his friend was being persecuted in this way.

Weaver replied in a rather wry tone. "That's what Mr. Holmes is here to find out." He look at Holmes. "Do you have any ideas so far?"

"About who sent the letters? Not yet, for we just arrived. As to what to do about them – Well, that will be decided tomorrow morning at ten o'clock." He turned to Bishop King. "That is, with your permission. I've taken the liberty of scheduling a meeting, and if you have something else taking place then, I beg of you to make the necessary adjustments. Both the Archbishop of Canterbury and the Bishop of London will be traveling here tomorrow to explain how to go forward."

Three of the friends started to squawk in astonishment and protest, but the voice of the fourth, Isa Longden, rose over them with something that sounded rather like amusement. "I'll be here as well, Mr. Holmes. After you spoke with the Archbishop this morning, he next called me. I think you'll be surprised about how far your little suggestion has progressed since then." Then his expression changed, darkened with sadness and pity. "You have a bit of rough road ahead, old friend," he said to King. "This will be your *Via Dolorosa*, I'm afraid. But your friends – those who know and love you – will be there with you. Throughout, you won't be alone."

King looked confused, and as if he'd aged five years in a moment. "The Archbishop? And Bishop Temple? He certainly has little use for me. How can he help?" He seemed to slump downward and he looked at Holmes. "What has happened, Mr. Holmes? Who did this? What is happening?"

Holmes frowned, and for a moment I thought he would go ahead and explain to all of us what he had arranged. But then, with a small shake of his head, he instead stated, "All will be clear tomorrow, Bishop. Now, Doctor Watson and I will depart. I'm sorry that I must leave you in temporary ignorance." Then he looked at Isa Longden. "I understand the feeling, since I don't yet know what Reverend Longden has arranged." With a nod and "Until tomorrow, Bishop," he turned, and I followed.

Outside in the hallway, I had the unsettled feeling of wanting to question my friend, but I didn't know what to ask, and it seemed as if I did, Holmes wouldn't know how to respond. He was concentrating intently, pinching his lip with his brows drawn down over staring eyes that were looking beyond where we stood. Finally he looked up. "Let's find that secretary."

It wasn't difficult, as he was behind a desk in a small room two doors away.

"How many people are permanently in this building – residents and staff?" Holmes asked.

"Eleven," answered Streeter, simply supplying the fact without any apparent curiosity. "For the household, the butler, the housekeeper, a cook, her assistant, a footman, two maids, and two fellows who work outside. On the church staff, there's just me and Mr. Fellows, an older fellow who retired from one of the parish churches, and is now is something of a jack-of-all trades – running errands, and so on."

"May we speak with the butler?" Holmes asked, and Streeter rose and led us further and deeper into the building, down several sets of stairs to the lower levels, where the smells of cooking became more apparent as we approached the warmth of the kitchen.

We were led along the periphery of the activity, where dinner was being prepared for the Bishop and his guests. A heavy-set woman, apparently the cook, was haranguing a pale wisp of a girl about something she'd done wrong. Several other staff were taking their early dinner at a nearby table. They all watched us with bovine and expressionless curiosity, and then we were past them, and Streeter was knocking on the butler's office door.

Being bade to enter, we found a big fellow who, rising to meet us, introduced himself as Mr. Blevins, and asking us how might be of assistance.

Holmes turned, thanked Streeter with the clear implication that he was no longer needed, and then shut the door. Blevins, who had apparently been working on the house's books, shut them and pushed them to one side as Holmes indicated that he had a few questions to ask.

We all sat and then, identifying himself and me as his associate, Holmes proceeded to explain that letters threatening Bishop King's position had been received by several people, and that we were there to investigate. Blevins nodded.

"I suspected as much," he rumbled. "I've heard of you, Mr. Holmes – when you were up here two years ago, about that little girl who went missing. Her mother is my cousin, and we can never do enough to repay what you did. I saw then that you're a canny fellow, so it's no surprise to you how much the servants hear and see and know about the Master's business. He and his guests – the fellow reverends – were talking about it today. Rather indiscreetly, I might add. Bishop King is a fine man, but somewhat . . . *innocent* I suppose is the best way to say it. As soon as his guests arrived, he button-holed them in the entryway, in front of the other servants, and started talking about the letters – '*Who sent them?*' he asked, and '*Are you sure you don't have any ideas?*' No one ever takes any mind of the servants."

Holmes nodded. He had said much the same himself, upon many occasions.

"Blevins," he said, leaning forward, "I'm afraid that I must ask a favor. I hate to trade upon locating your missing first-cousin-once-removed, but I have a question that must be settled, and quickly." And he then explained what he needed.

The butler nodded halfway through, understanding the implications. Then, turning his head, he said, "But based on your request, how do you know that I'm not the very person you're looking for?"

"I've eliminated you as very unlikely. Before traveling here today, I telephoned Inspector Burkhart of the Lincolnshire Constabulary, with whom I worked closely two years ago, and on several other matters as well. Having reason to suspect that the letters were generated by someone close to the Bishop – surely you observed that – and possibly within this house, I asked him to get me a quick report on the various occupants. He had the information within an hour. Seeing your former military experience, Mr. Blevins, it was then a mere formality to query your background. You have a sterling reputation, sir, and it seemed as if you would be a strong ally for what I propose."

In spite of being seated, Blevins seemed to gain three inches in height as he straightened his back, his mouth tightening with pride. "My pleasure, Mr. Holmes," he said softly.

"Watson," Holmes said, turning my way, "do you go and get us rooms at the hotel in Moor Street. It was good enough when I was up here two years ago – you were traveling then. I'll be along later tonight. With Mr. Blevins' help, I only have a few rooms to search, and I'm sure he can help provide the distraction that I need."

Holmes glanced at the butler.

"Indeed I can, Mr. Holmes. Indeed I can."

I was able to secure a sitting room with two bedrooms, and I sat up late waiting for Holmes's return. When he finally arrived, he was uncommunicative, but gave some indication that his efforts had been successful.

"It's an ugly business, Watson," he said.

"Are any of King's four friends that we met today involved?" I asked, saddened if they were, but fortunately Holmes shook his head.

"No, which is well, as he'll need them for what he's going to be asked to do. Every report is that he's a good man, but he's going to be required to make a sacrifice."

"Longden said it will be his *Via Dolorosa*. Is that correct?"

Holmes gave a small shrug. "For some, it would be insignificant. We'll just have to see how Bishop King holds up." Then he shook his head, as if annoyed by something. "Good night, Watson. I intend to smoke for a while. Sleep well."

But I did not, my sleep prevented from ever deepening by vague worries about what the following day would reveal.

"This is a serious business, and we've ignored it for far too long."

Archbishop of Canterbury Edward White Benson was just half-a-year older than Edward King, but he looked ten years younger. He carried himself with more vigor, and he gazed upon the world as if he owned it – or if asked, as if he were its caretaker. His longish silvery hair was brushed back on the top and sides, framing his ears, and he was fortunately born to have one of those faces that seems to be on the point of a perpetual friendly smile, even when his thoughts are going in the opposite direction.

Benson had arrived promptly the next morning in the company of Frederick Temple, the Bishop of London. He was then approaching his sixty-seventh year, and he wore it comfortably. A solid fellow, he had apparently thickened instead of thinned as he aged. He had a pleasant expression, framed by a solid set of mutton-chop whiskers, but one could see that his eyes were always watching, calculating, and that the fixed smile upon his lips never quite lit his eyes.

The meeting was scheduled in a small but ornate room in the Cathedral, apparently in recognition of the gathering's gravity. I was uncertain as to what to expect, as this seemed to involve the type of rarefied matters that typically swirled above the average man's head. I was reminded about the old debates of how many angels could dance on the head of a pin, and wondered if this would devolve into opinionated arguments over points of the same debatable importance.

Holmes and I had met King and Longden at the door to the Bishop's Palace walked over with them. It was clear that King hadn't slept, and Longden shook his head at my tacit evaluation, although I wasn't sure what information he was trying to convey. We arrived at the Cathedral just as Benson and White's cab from the station stopped in front, whereupon greetings and introductions were exchanged. We then went inside, Longden leading us through back hallways to our location. We were just about to go inside when a small dark figure detached himself from the shadows. The Archbishop frowned but nodded. Holmes turned to me to explain.

"This is Guthrie. He represents the government, and will be making notes for his superior."

The man, a fellow in his twenties nodded and joined us inside. As we settled around a large table, Guthrie found a spot along a wall, pulled out a notebook, and settled in like some court reporter. He never said a word throughout the entire proceedings, and kept his place until they were finished, when he rose, nodded, and departed.

With a sigh, the Archbishop looked around the table, and I had to wonder why I was there. At least, I thought, I could take notes like Guthrie to accomplish some useful task, and I surreptitiously pulled my notebook from my coat pocket. The Archbishop noticed it, but made no move to prevent it, and I felt relieved, as if I were a schoolboy who had broken a rule but was excused . . . this time.

"This is a serious business," the Archbishop began, looking from King on his right and Temple on his left. Longden was beside King, slouching back but watching the proceedings with a hawk's gaze. Holmes and I were farther down the table, and I expected that we were both to be nothing more than simple observers. However, after referring to a number of rather esoteric topics that made Temple nod and King stare at his knuckles, Benson suddenly reclaimed my attention by saying, ". . . and

Mr. Sherlock Holmes's intervention has brought about this important meeting. In fact, it was his telephone call yesterday, and his suggestion as to a way forward, that led to this gathering."

Benson shifted, his attention now focused on Bishop King. His face took on an expression of sadness and pity.

"Edward." King raised his eyes. "You, better than anyone, understand the differences between the Anglican and the Catholic Churches, and also the passions that religion can bring about in men's hearts. Initially something that seems insignificant can suddenly take on incredible importance – flaming into dangerous importance. One side favors a red flag, and the other likes the blue, and they rub along fine for years – and suddenly someone takes offense, and past grievances are recalled, and then groups are going to war, new transgressions adding fuel to the fire. If we don't diffuse it, I fear that differences like this within our church – simple questions of ritual – will escalate into something far worse."

He tapped a folder he'd brought with him, lying closed on the table. "These are past complaints against you for performing rituals during the service that are perceived to be of Roman Catholic intent." He opened the folder and began to read, with Temple nodding as each "charge" was listed.

"You have lighted candles on the altar. You have faced eastward during most prayers – turning your back upon the congregation. You have used the *Agnus Dei* as a hymn before Holy Communion – "

"This," interrupted Temple, his fixed smile clenched, "in spite of the fact that it was removed from *The Book of Common Prayer* in 1549!" Benson frowned, and the London Bishop subsided.

"You have made the sign of the Cross when blessing the congregation," the Archbishop continued. "You have mixed water with the wine in the chalice – "

This time Longden interrupted. "The ancients regularly did that. It's now taken as a symbol: Uniting with Christ through the Sacrament."

" – and then," Benson continued, as if Longden hadn't spoken, "you have made a great deal of ceremonially cleaning the Communion vessels – again, not an Anglican practice." He closed the folder. "None of these do any harm in and of themselves, but in today's atmosphere, the realm of men is a fragile place. People look for ways to be insular, and ways to identify enemies hiding among their brethren, and ways to find offense and immediately ignite to anger. We may be in the 'modern' and 'civilized' year of 1888, but it's no less dangerous than the Dark Ages. There are forces at work out there – sinister forces – attempting to foment revolution and war, and to turn brother against brother. Something as simple as this – unfamiliar and uncomfortable rituals within the Holy

Service – are raising the temperature. We need to drag this question into the open and settle it – and the incident of your threatening letters, Edward, has given us that opportunity."

Edward King nodded, wearily. I wondered what he was thinking. He was the Bishop of Lincoln, and had spent his life doing good work, when unexpectedly darkness had dropped into his life in the form of crude threatening letters. And now, simply trying to address that problem had led to another issue that cut to the heart of who he was as a minister, for he had long been on the side of the Anglo-Catholic movement, and here he'd seemingly reached the end of that rope and come up short.

"Edward," said the Archbishop, regaining King's focus. "Edward," he said again, more softly, "we're going to address this question publicly, once and for all." His voice lowered even further. "I'm going to hold a trial, Edward, to address these issues."

He reopened the folder and pulled forth a sheet and held it close to his face. I realized from the indentions on either side of the bridge of his nose that he used reading glasses, but he apparently hadn't brought them.

"The other day – the second of June – I received a petition from Ernest de Lacy Read – he's a churchwarden from Cleethorpes. Do you know of him?" King shook his head. "He, along with several other Lincolnshire men – William Brown, Felix Thomas Wilson, and John Marshall – ask that a citation be issued to the Bishop of Lincoln to answer upon certain ritualistic charges. Specifically, these offenses were committed during Holy Communion at the Church of St. Peter at Gowts in early December of last year – the fourth – and again on the tenth here at the Cathedral. It's the same sort of things that I mentioned, Edward – the actions that are perceived to be Catholic."

He set aside the sheet and laced his fingers, his voice soft and warm, and filled with compassion and a trace of pity.

"I'm going to decline to issue the citation, but this will proceed beyond the Church. That's the Government's interest – The Public Worship Regulation Act – and that's what Mr. Holmes perceived yesterday when he read the letters referencing the rituals and telephoned me. The process will be a long one – these things grind slowly and exceedingly small, and I foresee this occurring over the next several years – and it will be a weary tribulation for you, Edward. But I want you to understand – " He unlaced his fingers, and placed one hand upon King's wrist. "This will settle the question, and I'm not doing this so that you will lose the fight, but rather have a chance to *fight the fight.* Do you understand?"

And then he turned his head to Frederick Temple, who had been nodding with a not-so-secret smile – which had vanished upon Benson's last statement. "I do not see the harm in many of these so-called 'rituals'," Benson continued. "They aren't exclusive to the Catholic Church, like some secret handshake. There are true issues to worry about, rather than squabbling and bickering within our own denomination. Frederick, you have been fanning these flames, and the world is becoming too dangerous for that. Perhaps if you got out of the shiny parts of London once in a while and took a walk a mile or so east among your sheep, you would understand. Visit Limehouse or Whitechapel or Spitalfields. Find some feet to wash, instead of worrying about whose fancy table will host you at your next meal."

His tone was level, but there was steel in his gaze.

Frederick Temple dropped his eyes, his face suddenly pale and apparently abashed. But he didn't simply roll over. After that day, he fought for his position as well, although in a more subtle way. When Benson declined to issue a citation on 26 June, 1888, the instigators from Cleesthorpe appealed for "lack of justice", as had been expected, setting in motion the entire litigatory process. Little did they realize their moves had been foreseen, one after another as if on a chess board, and that they were doing what had been planned. On 4 January, 1889, after much debate, Benson went ahead and issued the citation against Bishop Edward King regarding his ritualistic practices. The following February, Benson – along with the Bishops of London, Winchester, Oxford, and Salisbury – met at Lambeth Palace to hear Bishop King's official protest response. The matter went back and forth for two years until the case was finally heard in February 1890. To avoid King being prosecuted in a lay court under the Public Worship Regulation Act, Benson cleverly revived his own Archiepiscopal Court, which had been inactive since 1699, allowing him to manage the entire trial within the Church.

In November 1890, the Archbishop issued his opinion, allowing most of White's "rituals" to continue, but that he had to position himself in such a way as his actions were visible by the congregation, and that he was prevented from making the sign of the Cross during the service. The counts held against King were touted by some as a repudiation of ritualism, but ironically, over the years most of King's added practices, including the sign of the Cross, became commonplace in Anglican services.

Of course, the matter was appealed, and in 1892, this appeal failed on all counts. And Frederick Temple didn't rest. In 1896, he became the Archbishop of Canterbury and proceeded to prosecute two priests for daring to use incense and candles in a service, implying that there was great danger in such insignificant acts.

The entire experience aged King terribly, but the matter was held to be important for several reasons, including settlement of some of the questions related to ritualistic practice, and also establishing that the Archbishop of Canterbury had the judicial power and right to try bishops for ecclesiastical offenses, rather than allowing the Government to do so. And even though in later years Benson felt the entire matter to have been an embarrassment, it was also a necessary one in order to better define church authority, and also to somewhat diffuse some of the growing divisions amongst the congregants.

But all that was in the future on that morning in June 1888 when the plan was explained to Bishop Edward King. His visit to Sherlock Holmes had taken a most unexpected turn, and I worried for him just then as his friend Longden led him back to his rooms in the Bishop's Palace.

The Archbishop and the Bishop of London stood to one side. Then they nodded, neither offering to shake hands, and departed quickly in their carriage.

Guthrie, the Government man, had vanished like smoke.

I turned to Holmes. "I don't think that this is what King wanted or expected when he came to you about those poisonous letters."

"No, it wasn't. It took a turn when I telephoned the Archbishop to see whether any of this could be related to King's past difficulties and connections with the Oxford Movement. From that point, it was rather quickly taken out of my hands, as Reverend Benson saw an opportunity to address the greater problem. Apparently it's been on his mind for a while – the rituals, the divisions, and the 1874 law, which he finds most objectionable. This is a way to tangentially challenge it – by making poor Bishop King his test case. And it didn't take long for the Government to become involved as well."

I shook my head. "Not your typical sort of case – messing about with this type of politics."

His lips pursed in distaste. "Indeed. But there is one matter that does lie more in my area of expertise. Let us also return to the Palace."

He led me unerringly back through the maze we'd first traversed the previous afternoon, and up to the Bishop's offices. The rooms were empty – except for Edwin Streeter, who looked up in surprise.

"The Bishop isn't here right now," he said. "I believe that he's still in the meeting over in the Cathedral."

Holmes shut the door. "That meeting has ended, and Reverend Longden has taken the Bishop to rest. He's at the beginning of a long trial – and he doesn't need to have any of the type of distractions that will certainly arise from nourishing a viper to his bosom."

Streeter stood abruptly, some response on his lips, but Holmes was having none of it.

"This entire matter has been distasteful to me," he said, "and I will not tarry any longer than I have to, worming forth your confession. Yesterday, the Bishop brought several of the offensive letters to me. There were certain parts that drew our attention – underlined threatening segments referencing Satan and the Devil – but the other parts were telling as well: Various references to the Bishop's daily activities, and even vagaries implying knowledge of the functions of this household. It was worth investigating.

"Fortunately, enough people are now connected to the telephone service that I was able to obtain the information I needed with relative ease. I confirmed that, in addition to the letters shown to us by the Bishop, others were sent as well – to other Bishops and similar figures who, while having no love for Edward King, fortunately had enough honor to simply disregard them as something written by a malicious crank. One told me that in his daily duties, he'd had cause to have one or two similar letters written about himself, and he gave it no value.

"The subtle references to the household functions led me to seek information about the various residents here – including you, Mr. Streeter. Your mother is the widowed housekeeper who took over those duties when the Bishop's mother died three years ago. She immediately sought to win the Bishop's recommendation toward finding you an accelerated path within the church – but the Bishop did not see you in that role, and instead kindly offered you a job as his secretary. Instead of being grateful, however, you apparently chose to brood on your failure, and to attack the man who offered you a helping hand. Someone who came up with the letter-writing scheme has no business serving within the church."

Holmes, impatient to get this matter behind him and shake the dust of Lincoln from his shoes, made his statement with no allowance for response, and with each sentence hitting like a blow. At first, Streeter would open his mouth to reply, but Holmes simply rolled over him, and as it became clear that Holmes had a clear understanding of the situation, the young man collapsed back in his chair, a variety of expressions chasing across his face – anger to denial to sadness, and back to anger – but eventually he simply went slack with shock.

"Last night, with my eye already upon you as the likely inside culprit, I arranged with Mr. Blevins to stay behind and search your room while you were out. Your hiding place was expectedly childish, and not only did I find the matching stationery, ink, and pen, but also the additional letters that you've prepared for your next wave of venomous mayhem.

"As Bishop King is temporarily distracted just now, I will advise Reverend Longden to arrange for your departure immediately. Sadly, your mother must go as well. She may be a fine woman, and I'm certain she'll receive excellent references, but just in case she knew about your scheme – "

"She did not," Streeter whispered, shaking his head.

" – Just in case," Holmes continued, "she cannot be allowed to be another viper in this household. Bishop King will need his strength in the coming months. His friends will see that he is protected."

Holmes turned to go, and I moved to follow. Then he stopped. "Watch him, Watson, while I get someone up here. This cur doesn't need to be sneaking out with any documents, or destroying them." Then he walked out, leaving me with the young man whose life had changed so abruptly in just a moment – but due to his own actions, leaving me without pity.

Neither of us said a word until Longden came to personally supervise the young man's departure.

We returned to the hotel and retrieved our luggage. We didn't discuss the matter until the train for London had departed from the station.

"So much froth and bubble," I finally said. Holmes looked up, puzzled.

"All of this froth and bubble about which way to stand, or whether to make the sign of the cross. It's from a poem by a fellow named Graham who died twenty years or so ago. Doyle is a great admirer of his.

> "*Life is mostly froth and bubble,*
> *Two things stand like stone.*
> *Kindness in another's trouble,*
> *Courage in your own.*"

Holmes nodded. "I agree, and it would make a fine pithy epitaph – but many people are very serious about what others consider their 'mostly froth and bubble'. They get angry about it. You've seen that. They're willing to die for it. The first spark of wars ignite because of it."

"And are things really that bad right now – under the surface?"

"Some think so. My heavy-set associate within the Government with all the threads in his hand believes that fuses are already burning, and it will only take a few random events to set things in motion. Something causes a reaction, which leads to an escalation, and before you know it there are deaths, and riots – and some fear revolution."

We were silent for a moment as the train left the small city, gaining speed through the spring-covered countryside.

"And addressing this little affair – about whether or not a minister faces east, or if he blesses the congregation with the sign of the cross – has some cause-and-effect relationship with the overall health of society?"

"So I'm told. Even releasing the tiniest bit of pressure here will perhaps bring ease another place. One can only hope."

"This friend of yours – who holds the threads. He sounds like an interesting person."

Holmes was silent for a moment, and then a slight smile tugged at the corner of his mouth and he nodded.

"'Interesting' is certainly one way to describe him. Perhaps I should introduce you to him."

"I would enjoy that."

We then retreated to our own thoughts. I don't know about Holmes, but I spent the rest of the journey trying to pierce the veil of the future, and wondering what the second half of 1888 might bring us. Little did I know that, like Bishop Edward King, Holmes and I were also at the beginning of our own *Via Dolorosa.*

But sometimes it's better not to know, so one doesn't have the chance to turn away from what must be done.

NOTES

Bishop Edward King was accused of using Roman-Catholic-leaning rituals in his Anglican services, and proceedings against him commenced in June 1888, extending over several years. The precipitating incidents of the threatening letters and Holmes and Watson's related investigation is revealed here for the first time.

Bishop Edward King
1889

For more about Holmes's later posthumous service to Frederick Temple in December 1902, see "The Canterbury Manifesto" in *The Collected Papers of Sherlock Holmes – Volume VI: Muniments* and *The MX Book of New Sherlock Holmes Stories – Part XXX: More Christmas Adventures (1897-1928)*

The Crofter's Curious Demise

6 March, 1867

Sherrinford,

I trust that this letter finds you safe and well, and that you have been able to avoid the usual Continental temptations that affect so many other young men of our age. The fact that you are two years older than me does not preclude that some base impulse will lead you down a dark alley. And congratulations upon your early completion at Oxford. Having also completed my studies ahead of schedule, I understand the value of being able to get on with one's life.

I understand that you're currently in Spa, visiting our old family friends, and that you will soon relocate to Brussels before traveling on to Paris. Allow me a bit of advice: The French are withdrawing from their latest Mexican intervention, and the mood in their capital is likely to be fractious. I know that you possess a great deal of common sense, but you may not be aware of certain political undercurrents. Be wary of associating with strangers (like that time outside the hotel door in Barcelona).

I apologize for missing your birthday gathering last November. I had planned to arrive on the 28th, giving me two days to visit before the celebration, but I unexpectedly found myself rather more deeply involved than I'd expected in preparing for the London Conference, which began on 4 December. As you may have read in the newspapers, various Canadian provinces were in London to continue the questions raised at the Quebec Conference two years ago, while I was still attending Oxford. Perhaps if I'd been there, the more recent conference would have been unnecessary. A major issue of contention for the six delegates who recently traveled to London involved the efforts by the Roman Catholic bishops to lobby for guarantees protecting the separate school system. This was initially opposed by the Maritime delegates, but I was able to suggest a compromise guaranteeing separate school systems in Quebec and Ontario but not in Nova Scotia or New Brunswick. It was not intended that I be involved at all, but there was an issue at the Westminster Palace Hotel, where the conference occurred – one of the aides to a Canadian delegate had gotten up to some mischief, stealing a boot from another of the attendees. Sir Rodney asked me to look into it, and after that affair was settled, I was asked to advise the rest of the conference, that I might be of some additional use.

I also apologize for the state of my handwriting. You will have perceived that I'm composing this letter on the train – the handwriting is best where we are stopped in a station, less-clear where the line runs smooth, and the most illegible when we cross the points – thankfully fewer now that we're on the final stretch between Leeds and York. I had meant to begin writing earlier in the journey, but my attention was diverted by the study of certain documents related to Fenian rising – and also by taking time to address Sherlock's incessant questions.

He was, for instance, fascinated by this morning's partial solar eclipse, which we were able to observe successfully and safely from the train. Having known of it ahead of time, I constructed a couple of reverse viewing boxes that allowed us to see the reflection without staring directly at the sun. It amazed me how many on the train chose to risk blindness by looking straight at the event. I warned a mother and her children who were seated near us, but they paid me no heed.

Our journey north took most of the night, and after being awake for a few hours this morning and watching the eclipse, Sherlock is once again asleep, curled upon the seat, his lean form wound in upon itself like some starved cur trying to keep warm. I cannot convince the boy that a layer of self-applied insulation in the form of extra meals and subsequent personal poundage will serve as an effective protection against much of the world's cold – both literal and figurative. Perhaps when he's a bit older, he will settle down and apply himself, instead of racing so fast after his current philosophy of filling his brain with every fact he can find, regardless of its value, that he forgets to eat. Sometimes I believe that I shall never understand him.

He'll have to settle down soon. The reason I'm taking him back to Yorkshire is that he's been ejected from yet another school and, as I was already scheduled to travel North, I was elected as the boy's shepherd. I'm unclear upon the details, but Sherlock appeared at the door of my new rooms in Montague Street two days ago with all of his belongings and a sealed letter addressed to *Siger Holmes, North Riding, Yorkshire.* As it was meant for Father, and none of my business, I didn't read it, and when I sent a telegram home to explain, I received no further instructions regarding the letter one way or another. Instead, as they were aware of my upcoming reason for traveling to York, and my intention to visit home while there, I was asked to bring the wayward child with me.

Sherlock attempted to give me some sort of disjointed explanation about what happened – the school's legendary ghost, and a missing boy lost in forgotten Elizabethan passages under the cellar, and how Sherlock and some hastily assembled friends had intrepidly gone underground to find the lost lad, only to expose a respected teacher's chicanery – but I found the tale rather tedious and frankly lost interest, as my mind was absorbed in my newest assignment – to accompany the recently quarried foundation stone for the upcoming exhibition hall in Kensington on the rest of its journey to London.

Sir Rodney says it's a massive thing – a block of the famous red Aberdeen rock. They're finally building the hall, after all these years. You may have read that Prince Albert first proposed such a structure in 1851, when you and I were six and four respectively, but he died before it ever came to fruition. Then, six years ago, a memorial for the Prince was proposed in Hyde Park, with a great hall opposite, and construction has finally begun.

Initially, I was to journey to the border near Berwick-upon-Tweed and accompany both the stone and the Scottish officials accompanying it onward from there, but there is now to be some sort of ceremony along the way, a pause of several days, as some minister with ancestral ties to Robert the Bruce feels that arranging the event in York will satisfy an obscure symbolic "Covenant of Unity". I have no idea what he means, but rearranging the schedule in this fashion suited me quite well for my own personal reasons.

Sherlock is starting to stir, so I will conclude for now and continue later this evening.

6 March – Continued

Consider yourself lucky that you're far across the *Oceanus Germanicus*. Sherlock and I returned to find a mare's nest.

The arrival in York passed without incident and, as the foundation stone isn't due until tomorrow, there was nothing to do but go home. With each passing mile, Sherlock became more agitated, asking me repetitive questions about his situation as if my uninformed responses might somehow negate whatever Father has planned for him. As you know, this is the third school that he has attended – and left – in the last three years, for various reasons. Father seemed to respect Sherlock's opinion about the first school in Kensington, from 1864 to '65, when Sherlock communicated that it wasn't preparing him for anything useful. But then, after the incident at the second school, when he was sent home in '66, Father was less interested in the reasons why. (Between the two of us, however, I did rather admire Sherlock's little scheme to get back everything that the young bully, Wisham, had acquired from Sherlock's little friends – even if the unpleasant lad turned out to be Lord Wisham's grandson, and the young thug had foolishly signed away his expected inheritance. If we had chosen to pursue the matter, I have no doubt that the document Sherlock wrote up to defeat the tormentor would have been so legally airtight that we'd all now be living in Wisham's manor house and enjoying his famed whisky collection!)

"What will he do?" was Sherlock's most-oft-repeated question, meaning of course what would Father's reaction be, now that Sherlock had been separated from yet another school with the doors shut firmly behind him. I could only imagine what was in the sealed letter that I'd been entrusted to convey – far more than the story Sherlock had told me about the ghost and tunnels under the school. Of that I was certain. I could only advise Sherlock to stiffen his spine, speak the truth, and manfully accept the consequences, whatever they might be.

After the tedious journey from the station to the manor, the initial homecoming was as expected. Mother hugged and kissed us both, while Father sternly watched beside her. One never forgets his great height, his bear-like stature, or his great black beard, but still, after not seeing him for a number of months, and living among lesser men, it's always something of a surprise. After greeting us both, I handed him the sealed letter. He took it, tore open the envelope, read it in silence, and then put it away in his pocket. He turned his full gaze upon Sherlock who, after a moment where it seemed as if he would dart behind me and hide, took my advice, stood up straight, and nodded. "Shall we have our discussion now or later, Father?"

"Later," Father replied, his voice rumbling. "I have something else to attend to first. I've just received a message from the local constable. A body has been discovered in the North Pasture." Father looked at me. "Your opinion would be most welcome."

I nodded, even as a carriage and horse was brought around by one of the stable-hands. Father and I climbed aboard and he took the reins, sending us immediately into a steady trot out of the yard and along the road to the north, through ground that was increasingly rocky and rugged, only good for keeping sheep.

As we progressed, I heard a slight scraping sound in the flat bed of the carriage behind our seat. Thinking some loose object had shifted from side to side, I glanced over my shoulder to discover Sherlock, squatting low to maintain his place without sliding off the back. Even as I started to say something, he raised a finger to his lips, imploring me to maintain my silence. Inwardly cursing my own complicit foolishness, I turned to face front, deciding that I would plead ignorance and let Sherlock take his punishment when we arrived. That wasn't necessary, however, as Father spoke immediately.

"You'd best climb up front, Sherlock, and find a proper seat. Staying aboard will become treacherous when we reach the steep turn."

When the lad had settled between us, Father added, "I felt the slight dip when you boarded the carriage – something to consider when planning such a campaign."

Father never ceases to surprise me. Just when I'd thought he'd be angry, or order Sherlock to climb down and walk back to the manor, he'd not only allowed him to stay, but given him practical advice for how to do something guileful in a better way the next time. One tends to forget that Father, now living the life of Lord of the Manor, was once a noted military officer, beloved by his men, before being invalided home from India.

Looking over the top of Sherlock's head, I asked Father, "What do you know of the body?"

For a moment, Father said nothing, although his dark brows dropped as he frowned. Then he said, his voice low, "Constable Tanner sent one of the lads with a message. It seems that Witt Kendall burned to death." He glanced over at me, and then down at Sherlock. "It appears to be one of those affairs where he erupted into flame of his own volition."

Sherlock turned his head quickly in my direction. It will not surprise you, of course, that his eyes were wide with excitement, and not with the horror for which one might have hoped. I despair where this lad's fascinations will lead him.

"He burned to death in his own fat?" Sherlock said, his voice breaking. "Like Mr. Krook in *Bleak House*?"

Father was silent for a few seconds, as if pondering whether a response would be the wrong sort of encouragement. Then he nodded. "Witt was quite fat – well over twenty stones, I would guess – and it's been difficult for him to get around for quite a while."

Sherlock nodded. "It's often fat people who burn alive in such a manner, but not always. There was an Italian countess who self-erupted into flame in 1731, and from what I've read, she wasn't fat. Instead, she bathed in brandy every day to improve her skin. One morning the maid entered the bedroom to find the air filled with oily soot, and beside the bed was the countess's charred skull and her two legs, standing there with a pile of ashes between them!"

Father's eyes widened when Sherlock paused for a breath. "Dear God, Sherlock! Don't let your mother hear such a tale! Where did you read that?"

"It was something that Mr. Dickens wrote, after Mr. Krook's death in *Bleak House* was criticized. He documented several cases where men and women died in such a horrible manner. It's often the same – they're found in a closed room, filled with oily smoke. There is a film of it on the walls and furniture, and there are always reports of a terrible odor. The heat produced by the body burning away from inside-out must be terribly hot, for there is usually almost nothing left, but it must also be very self-contained, because there is usually no fire-related damage to the room, except sometimes the floor is scorched, or the bed or chair where the body is found might be smoldering a bit." He frowned, and then spoke more softly, as if to himself. "But if Mr. Kendall burned in the North Pasture, there won't be any oily residue – except, perhaps, upon the grass around him."

Father raised a hand. "You're racing ahead of yourself, Sherlock. Wait until we get there before you start constructing theoretical edifices. All that you know now – all that any of us know until we get there – is what the lad told me: Kendall was found burned, and the constable suspects that he burned from within."

We rode for another minute or so in silence, and then Father, looking forward as we neared our destination, asked, "You felt the need to further research this type of death?"

Sherlock nodded, suddenly a bit more subdued.

"Why?" Father asked.

I expected Sherlock's enthusiasm to immediately reignite, telling us of other cases where humans had died while burning in their own grease, but instead he gave a reasoned answer.

"When I read *Bleak House*, the edition I used had a supplemental paragraph in the *Preface*, written by Mr. Dickens, defending the idea of spontaneous combustion. Apparently, when the book was initially printed as monthly installments, a friend of his had attacked the notion. The paragraph had several examples of this type of death, including that of the Countess, so I set out to research them for myself – deciding that if someone is willing to publicly question Mr. Dickens, then the matter of whether someone can burn to death in such a manner isn't quite cut-and-dried."

"And what did you determine?" I asked, intrigued.

"That there really are a certain number of cases that have been reported over the years, but that there are conflicting aspects, depending on where the accounts are recorded, and that one would need to go and see for one's self, and speak to those involved, to determine what is truth and what is gossip or legend."

Father nodded and glanced my way. I nodded in return. I could see that he was impressed, although he didn't express it verbally, and I don't believe that Sherlock saw our silent exchange.

And then we had arrived at Witt Kendall's blackened corpse.

The scene as we approached was desolate and grim. You've known the North Pasture in both the lush green of summer and when it is covered by the unbroken sweep of new-fallen snow, but today, the dry and brittle grayness of early March was almost too bleak to bear. You know that I am no poet, but climbing down from the carriage and walking to the cluster of figures silently watching our approach put me in mind of the last stanza of a poem I had copied in school, although the victim commemorated in that verse had died from falling down a well, and not from being incinerated:

They got him out and emptied him;
Alas it was too late;
His spirit was gone for to sport aloft
In the realms of the good and great. [1]

I glanced to see if Sherlock was also so affected, but he was alert, walking forward softly and carefully as if not to disturb anything upon the ground, and his gaze fixed intently on the men awaiting us.

I recognized Constable Tanner, now several years older than when I'd last seen him, and clearly benefiting from his wife's excellent cooking. He really ought to be provided with funds for a newer and looser uniform. Beside him were a couple of local lads, Timson and Wagner Jamison, both now in their mid-twenties. And with them was Witt Kendall's son, Oswald.

He's always been a big fellow, taller than his father, but I hadn't realized quite how much he's grown. Of course, you'll have seen him much more often and recently that I have, but I was thoroughly surprised. His mien, however, has not altered in the slightest: He's still surly and unfriendly, answering questions with short replies and hints of hostility and resentment. Nevertheless, Father and I both spoke our condolences and nodded in his direction, although he provided no response.

Tanner stepped forward, nodding and touching a finger to his helmet. Fifty years ago, he'd have pulled a deferential forelock. As I've told you before, it's always awkward when the local folk are so unctuous to Father when he makes no demand for it. He would much rather simply get on with whatever labor is at hand, and such was the case this afternoon.

"It's a bad business, sir," explained Tanner. "Oswald here appeared at the Jamison's door, stating that he'd found his father, self-immolated on his cart, here in the pasture." He glanced over his shoulder to where, twenty feet or so away, the blackened lump was slumped upon the cart's seat. An old horse, still in harness and tied to a nearby tree, stood patiently, head down, seemingly indifferent to the hideous burden just behind him. He neither flicked his tail nor gave a whicker of apathy.

"Oswald said that – " Tanner continued, but Father raised a hand.

"Let's hear from Oswald," he said. "First evidence is best evidence." He turned to the dead man's son. "We're sorry for your loss, Oswald, and to have to meet under these circumstances. Can you tell us what happened?"

Father's typical rumble was quiet and subdued, in deference to the young man's situation, but Oswald seemed quite unconcerned, and he responded in his typical sour way.

"The Old Man lost his temper again this morning," he said. "The usual way – he'd been drinking, and he was angry. He's always angry. He left, slamming the door behind him. My mother, God love her, still has feelings for him, and she was worried. He's been feeling much more poorly of late, and after an hour or so, she sent me after him.

"When he leaves that way, he always goes to the same place – the spot on the other side of the North Pasture near that great pit in the ground." He vaguely pointed in that direction. "We don't have a second horse or cart, so I set off on foot. Today is the first time it's been above freezing in weeks, so it was almost enjoyable – until I spotted the cart here, not even halfway to the pit. As I got closer, I could smell that something had been burned – and then I saw him. There's no mistake – it's him – and he's been burned just like one hears about, from the inside to the outside. The cart seat is barely blackened. I went and found help at the Jamison house. It would do no good to return home and tell Mother."

Father nodded and then indicated he wanted to see the body. Tanner turned that way, asking the others to wait. I assumed that he meant Sherlock as well, but he walked with us, and Father did nothing to send him back.

It has always amazed me how Tanner and some of the others defer to Father's leadership. While we have land, it isn't any great estate of the size owned by many of the neighbors. We traveled so often while growing up that Father never made any attempts to claim a leadership role within the government, local or otherwise, but when he's around, men like Tanner seek his counsel and relinquish their own authority to him. He inspires and expects their confidence, and he receives it. It has been a great lesson for me as I observe it and try to lead in my own life.

Witt Kendall's body was a hideous thing, but then, he was never a great beauty in life. Heavy-set and unhealthy in his ways, he'd been even bigger and heavier than his son. Now, collapsed upon the carriage seat, he seemed to be sagging and spreading like some great blackened bag. I heard Sherlock clear his throat and glanced to see if he was sickened or ill, but he still showed the same alert curiosity as he kept pace with us upon our approach.

It was Witt Kendall. Of that there was no doubt. His eyes were closed, but his face was frozen in the bitter scowl he'd held in life. His skin was very white, as if *livor mortis* had already set in. The back of his head was covered in longish white hair, and a great curly beard, grayish-white like some filthy fleece, was clinging to his flaccid jowls.

He walked with us, and Father did nothing to send him back.
(Illustration by Thaddeus Tuffentsamer)

His clothing was burned, and in particular his legs and feet seemed to have taken a great deal of damage. His arms and right hand were blackened as well, but curiously the left hand was untouched. As reported, the seat was scorched around him, but otherwise there wasn't any observable damage to the cart. Should one wish to do so, it could be reused immediately.

Glancing over to make sure that Oswald Kendall and the Jamison brothers weren't close enough to overhear us, Father said softly, "This doesn't fit the pattern for a person who dies from spontaneous combustion."

Tanner raised his brows. "It doesn't? From what I've heard, they burn from inside, and don't even damage the chairs they're sitting on."

"As Sherlock recently informed us," replied Father, causing Sherlock's head to turn with pleased surprise, "there is usually nothing left but ashes and a few bones – and perhaps an article of clothing. There is also greasy miasma – a film that covers everything. Granted, we're outside, so one wouldn't necessarily expect to find such a cloud lingering around the body, but there is no wind to speak of, and there doesn't seem to be any residual grease of that sort upon the seat, or the parts of the body left unburned. And quite a bit of it remains unburned, as you can see."

Sherlock turned his head this way and that, sniffing. "There is some sort of smell, however," he said, without any hesitancy to assert himself in a group of grown men who know much more about life than he does.

Father nodded, a look of sadness upon his face. "It's coal oil. One encounters it more and more these days. It's quite recognizable, if you've smelled it before." He lowered his voice even more. "It seems as if we're being led by the nose to the wrong conclusion. Tanner, where did you get the idea that Witt had spontaneously combusted?"

"Why, from Oswald. That's what he told the Jamisons, and that's what Timson told me when I was fetched."

"And that's what Wagner told me," added Father. "Perhaps he thought we'd simply believe it without question."

"What?" Tanner's expression darkened. "Trying to make a fool of me, is he – !"

Father put a hand upon his arm. "Calm yourself, Tanner," he urged softly. "There's more to this than we understand right now. Let's ask Oswald some more questions, and try to determine what he hoped – "

He was interrupted by the sound of a snap, followed by a gasp from Sherlock. We all turned our heads to see that the boy had wandered over to the body while we weren't looking. We had turned quickly enough to observe him stepping back a few feet, gazing oddly at something in his hand. He had a sickly look upon his face, and I wondered what he had discovered.

Moving closer, and looking over to see that Oswald and the Jamison brothers were still ignoring us, we gathered around Sherlock, who held out his hand, showing us something without offering any explanation.

It was a human thumb.

As one, our heads jerked to look at the body. There, we could see the unburned left hand, still resting where we'd last seen it – but the dead man's thumb had been broken cleanly away, as if cleaved away by a knife.

Sherlock looked from one of us to the other before settling his gaze upon Father. "I . . . I reached to move his arm," he said. "I wanted to see if *rigor mortis* had set in yet. I knew it was probably too soon, but some people start sooner than others. I . . . the sleeve was burned, so I took his hand, but when I pulled . . . when I pulled, *the thumb came off in my hand*!"

Father, with a small motion, reached for it, and Sherlock gladly tipped it into his palm. Father immediately reacted with surprise, as if it wasn't what he expected. Then he held it out to me, turning his body so that the others across the way couldn't see.

"Touch it," he commanded.

Warily, I did so – and was immediately surprised to see that not only was it curiously solid, but it was damned cold!

Father held it to Tanner, who reached out a timid finger. He was a surprised as I was, and jerked back his hand.

Father glanced at the body and started to speak, but Sherlock interrupted him. "He's *frozen*!" he whispered. "Frozen solid! That's why his arm couldn't move!"

"And yet," I added, "he's supposed to have burst into flames, causing his death." I shook my head. "There is much more yet to be determined here."

"I agree," said Father, "and we shouldn't give Oswald any indication that we haven't fully accepted his story – not until we find out more information. Tanner – hitch up this horse to the back of your cart, and bring it – and the body – back to Kendall's croft. Oswald can ride with the Jamison's. We'll see what Mrs. Kendall has to say.

While Tanner set about his task of moving the old horse, Father and I approached the dead man, Sherlock not far behind us, and each pushed upon the body's torso. Kendall radiated cold, as if he were a three-hundred-pound block of ice, and except for a bit of give at the surface, he seemed to be as solid as a rock. Glancing toward Tanner, I asked Father, beyond the constable's hearing, "Can Tanner be trusted not to let on that we suspect something is amiss?"

"I expect so," replied Father. "He is a man of little imagination. In any case, we only have to keep our knowledge hidden for a couple of miles."

When we'd gone a few hundred feet, some distance opened up between the carts, and Sherlock felt that it was now safe enough to share an additional fact.

"Before I grabbed the thumb," he said, speaking precisely, as if not to recall the sensation, "I looked around the body as best as I could, from all sides. It looked as if there was blood on the back of his head. It showed clearly on what little white hair is there."

"Why didn't you mention it before?" asked Father.

"The Constable, sir," said Sherlock. "I didn't know if he could be trusted with any more than he already knew."

Father nodded. "That's perceptive of you. He did seem ready to burst with the one secret he's already keeping. Well, we'll know more soon enough."

I hadn't seen Kendall's croft in quite a while, but it surprised me that it was in such poor shape. The stonework needs repair, and the thatch is in sorry shape. If it was one under our responsibility, it wouldn't have ever been allowed to get into such poor condition.

The carts all stopped in the yard, and from within I could hear a woman calling, asking who was there. Only then did I recall that Mrs. Kendall has been in poor health for some months. I realized that it was unlikely she could rise to come to the door.

After climbing down, I contrived to pass behind Kendall's cart and take a look at the back of his head. It would need a closer examination, but from where I stood, it appeared that Sherlock's observation was correct: There was a stain of old darkened blood.

Inside, the house was dark and cold, lit only by one lantern hanging from a central rafter. Sniffing, I realized that it was fueled by coal oil. Glancing at Father and Sherlock, I saw that they had noticed as well.

I'll skip over the details of informing Mrs. Kendall of her husband's peculiar death, except to comment that her reaction was also somewhat peculiar, in that the expected wailing and gnashing of teeth did not occur. She shed tears and shook her head, but there was no hysteria, and no wish to go outside and see the dead man, still perched upon the cart where he'd been discovered, under the watchful guardianship of the Jamison brothers.

Oswald leaned toward his mother, towering over her, patting her shoulder just a bit and telling her that Witt Kendall had caught fire and burned to death atop the cart on the way to his favorite spot. She simply nodded, as if it was a perfectly normal explanation, no different than if the great heap of a man had slipped and broken his neck.

I looked at Tanner, and he seemed to accept the scene as presented. Father gave a slight shake of his head, and I turned to see Sherlock's reaction.

But he wasn't there.

Asking Tanner to stay with the "grieving" family, I motioned for Father to accompany me outside. By then, he'd also realized that Sherlock was missing. I stepped closer to the Jamisons and asked if they had seen them. They motioned toward the rear of the house, down a small slope, where a barn and a couple of out-buildings were located.

We found him in the spring house. He didn't seem surprised to see us, and he motioned us closer.

"If Mr. Kendall is frozen solid," he started with preamble, "then it must have taken a while – several days at least. He couldn't have achieved that condition overnight. The weather has been cold in Yorkshire for several weeks – very cold – so he could have frozen at any time during that period, and have remained frozen. I asked myself where he could have been kept all that time."

He motioned around the spring house. It's like so many others, dug out below ground around the spring, with stone shelves along the walls. The various shelves were full of various sacks and containers, every one frozen solid after the bitter conditions of the previous few weeks – all except for one low stone bench, rising two or three feet from the ground. There, a space of about six feet in width had been cleared. It was obvious that it wasn't a spot where the stored supplies had been used up, as the shelves on either side were double-stacked with items that had been moved from the empty place.

Sherlock stepped closer and pointed to one end of the empty shelf. We leaned closer and saw what he meant: Blood. A pool of it, the size of a man's hand, and frozen to the bench.

"It might have been from a joint of meat," I said, but I didn't really mean it, and Father shook his head.

"Look closer. There are white hairs frozen into the blood from where Witt Kendall's body was placed here. The wound was touching the shelf, and froze to it. When he was removed, some of the hair was left behind."

"One has to wonder – " I began, but Sherlock finished, a look of horror upon his face.

" – If he was already dead when he was brought here, or if he froze to death on this spot."

The answer, according to Mrs. Kendall when confronted, was the former, although I had my doubts. When confronted with what we'd found – that her husband had not spontaneously combusted, but was rather superficially burned by the use of coal oil, and that the evidence was compelling that he'd been frozen solid in the spring house – she broke down. Her initial story was that Witt Kendall had lost his temper, and then had some sort of attack, falling and hitting his head before expiring. She and her son had feared some sort of accusation would be made against them, so they had come up with the idea of concealing his body until they figured out what to do with him. Oswald, who clearly was not happy with his mother's confession, had moved his equally sizable father to the spring house, for his mother was too small and weak to help. Then, when the weather had warmed just a bit, they became concerned that he might thaw and decided to arrange a story whereupon he would be discovered in the pasture.

Oswald, who had heard of spontaneous human combustion, had decided that the body could be burned, thus hiding the fact that the corpse was frozen into a solid block of ice. He had realized that he couldn't simply say his father had left that morning and had fallen and died, as that was no explanation as to why they had hidden him, frozen, for several weeks. He hadn't taken into account that the body wouldn't thaw naturally in the time he'd allotted, and that the flames wouldn't accomplish that either. He'd also left the scene before making sure that the fire was truly burning. The coal oil he'd poured upon the corpse had quickly consumed itself, and had apparently gone out almost immediately, after only burning the dead man's clothing and some of his limbs. [2]

Constable Tanner seemed inclined to accept this story, putting down the temporary hiding of the corpse and the following attempt to sew confusion as simply a poor choice upon the part of the dead man's wife and son. Father, Sherlock, and I all shared glances that indicated we were willing to be culpable with Tanner's decision, as we had all seen the bruises upon Mrs. Kendall. It was our suspicion that they had been caused by the dead man, but I could only hope that they weren't in fact caused by ill-tempered Oswald.

We were agreeable to accepting the story as presented on the assumption that the lady, and likely her son, had put up with abuse from Witt Kendall, but there were still some unresolved issues that remain unexplored – for instance, the amount of blood from the dead man's head wound. If he was already dead when placed in the spring house, then his heart had stopped pumping, and no blood should have flowed from the wound. It was more likely, as Sherlock feared, that Witt Kendall was still breathing when left on the shelf to freeze.

But we are giving the surviving Kendalls the benefit of the doubt.

It is late, and I've written far into the night. I'll continue this letter, updating throughout my visit, and mail it when I return to London.

9 March, 1867

We have had a tempestuous few days since the small affair of the dead crofter.

If you'll recall, there was to be a small ceremony related to the foundation stone, as planned by a descendant of Robert the Bruce. In fact, this minister had contrived to have the stone stopped in York so that he could destroy it in a public fit of Scottish zealotry. But Sherlock noticed him conferring with a couple of suspicious ruffians shortly before the ceremony, contrived to overhear their plans, and informed me in time to prevent the minister's mischief. I'll have to share the story with you in person someday, for it is too sensitive to commit to a letter.

I do want to relate a conversation that I had with Father last night. In his study, he shared with me the letter from the school. After describing the specifics of the incident involving the arrest of the corrupt teacher, the headmaster concluded:

> *It is with heavy heart that I must dismiss Master Sherlock, and I do so only at the insistence of the teacher's uncle, who has been a substantial financial benefactor to the school for many years. While there is no denying the criminality of what has occurred here, the school's funding is in jeopardy if our benefactor doesn't have his petty revenge on Sherlock.*
>
> *But having your son as a student has been a joy and a privilege, and an asset to the school, and I would keep him here if I could. He is intelligent and inquisitive, and his advocacy for and protection of the smaller weaker boys from the usual abuse and injustice heaped upon them by the older lads marks him as someone who will do a great deal of good in the world.*
>
> *Mr. Holmes, I urge you – I implore you! – not to punish Sherlock for what has happened here, for he did the right thing. There aren't so many people like that in the world. I wish that I were one of them, willing to stand up and defend him better, instead of cowardly giving in to the wrong sort of pressure. Please find him another school – a better school than ours, beholden as we are to the wrong ways of thinking. With the right opportunities, Sherlock – one way or another – is going to be a great success.*

"He's a bright lad," Father stated when I finished reading. "He has impressed me with these recent events, but he is unfocussed. Instead of keeping his eyes on the target at these various schools, he allows himself to be distracted by other things – favors for friends, and explorations of old tunnels and other places that aren't any of his business. He has potential – I feel that he will be a fine engineer one day – but he needs guidance."

At this, I sensed the first hint of how the wind was blowing. I nodded for him to continue.

"I'll find him another school," Father said. "In London. But someone with such a bright mind needs extra attention – *your* attention, Mycroft." He raised a placatory hand. "I know, I know. You've recently started your own new career, and that is where your attention is focused – and rightly so. But spending time nurturing your brother is a worthy focus as well.

"I want him to go back to London with you tomorrow, and to stay with you until I locate a new school. I'm sure that Mrs. Holmes won't mind . . . ."

He knows better, but I could only agree. As you'll recall, Mrs. Holmes, the sour widow of Cousin Wendall, was none-too-pleasant about Father's request that she rent a room to me in her Montague Street house – and I didn't want to live there either, as finding someplace more fitting in Charles Street or King Street or Pall Mall would be much better for my career. But for now I'm in Montague Street, as it's what I can afford, and apparently Sherlock will be there with me too. At least for a little while.

While he's there, I'll attempt to lay some sort of groundwork for him – a systematic method of thinking, rather than the scatter-shot way he's been careening through life up to now.

I hope that when you return to England from your Continental tour, you'll pass through London and arrange a visit. Possibly Sherlock will still be there, and you can give me your opinion as to whether my training has had any good effect.

In the meantime, I wish you the safest of travels.

Very best,

Mycroft

NOTES:

1 The full poem is "Ode to Stephen Dowling Bots, Dec'd", found in Chapter XVII of Mark Twain's *Huckleberry Finn* (1884).

2. The discovery of Witt Kendall's body somewhat parallels an experience that I had while growing up.

My father was a special investigator with the Tennessee Bureau of Investigation, covering several counties, and often called in by local police and sheriff's departments for complex cases. He had a number of notable and commended successes in his long career.

As I was growing up, my dad had his office in our house, so he let me read his case files – and there were some vividly crazy cases. One time he followed a murderer who had fled north to Covington, KY, where he threw the murder weapon, a revolver, off the bridge over the Ohio River. My dad arranged to have an industrial magnet brought and placed over that spot – and he retrieved the gun from the river. Another time he had a whole yard dug up to successfully recover a single shell casing which was the damning evidence in a murder case. One of his most difficult cases was when he tracked a group of killers who had used a shotgun one night to blow off a doctor's head when they invaded his home to rob him. Seeing those photos meant that when I read *The Valley of Fear*, I knew exactly how the dead body looked – and my dad made sure that every one of them was convicted and punished to the full extent of the law.

In addition to letting me read about these cases, he taught me how to take and lift fingerprints, and to make plaster casts of footprints, and later, when he became the State's first polygraph operator, he taught me how to do that too – all before I turned eighteen. On one occasion, when I was around thirteen, he received a call one evening from our local sheriff about a body that had found under suspicious circumstances, burned in a car that was discovered in a state park about a hundred miles north of where we lived. The local authorities were going to search the victim's house, and did my dad want to go along?

And when that call came, he invited me along too. I was thrilled. I was going on a murder investigation!

This case was somewhat different from the Witt Kendall affair. The dead man had been found in a burned parked car, and the wife and grown son's story was that the car had inexplicably caught fire and they couldn't pull him out in time to save him. But that didn't make sense, and they had no good reason why they had driven so far from home just to park and let the car burn. When searching the house that night, a few facts became apparent: The neighbors agreed that the dead man had been very abusive to his wife and son. A few weeks before the body was found, the wife had tearfully given away a lot of frozen food to various neighbors, explaining that the family freezer had broken – but it wasn't. When examined, it was running fine – and there was frozen blood in the bottom. The subsequent autopsy revealed that while the body had been superficially burned, it had previously been frozen.

It was uncertain whether the mother or son had killed the father, but as the woman was in poor health and too small to move the body, it was clear that the big-framed son had at least been involved to the point of putting the dead man in and out of the freezer, and then moving him into the car.

I can't claim to have helped the investigation in any way that night. I had no profound Ellery Queen moments, helping my father, Inspector Queen, brilliantly solve the case. My one contribution was laughable: The entire freezing and moving of the body had taken place in the garage of the house, where the freezer was located, and which allowed for all of this activity to remain hidden. However, as I looked around the house and grounds, I found what looked like blood stains on the front steps and – even though that spot was in full view of the street – I became convinced that the body had been carried out the front door and around to the car for some unknown yet criminally clever reason. I went and found my dad, confidently asking him, "Where's your blood expert?" The Blood Expert tolerantly followed me over to look at the "blood stain", and then informed me that it was, in fact, the droppings of a bird who had been eating red berries.

Thus ended my own investigatory efforts – until a decade later, when I became a United States Federal Investigator, and had some of my own adventures.

But those are different stories . . . .

The Curse Business at the Princess's Theatre

I had stopped by that afternoon to see how Sherlock Holmes was adjusting to once more being alive.

"Have a look at that letter on the table by my chair," he advised from where he was bent over an experiment in his chemical corner. He spoke when I entered with any greeting or preamble, as if I'd been there all day, and we were continuing a conversation of the previous hour's duration. "Of all the correspondence I've received in the last few days, that is the only one of any passing interest."

It had only been two weeks since the day that Holmes had dramatically reappeared from his three-year absence, settling back into his preserved rooms as if he'd been abroad no more than a month. Since then, having little interest in my own responsibilities when compared with this sensational event, and no longer having any meaningful ties to my Kensington home and practice since my sad bereavement the year before, I found myself returning more and more to Baker Street each day. And yet, I knew that I must remain vigilant not to fall into the temptation of visiting Holmes and joining him upon his investigations too often, for the medical practice was my main source of income, other than some royalties for stories written during the previous couple of years, and without it, I'd soon be in an unfortunate situation.

Spring was making its way into London, and just two weeks earlier, the temperatures had been hovering in the forties, but on this day, they had climbed to nearly seventy, and I felt greatly overdressed in my tweed overcoat. However, it was easier to wear than carry it as I went upon my rounds, and I hadn't had a chance to return home and leave it since departing that morning.

"Don't stand there like a gawper in a museum," said Holmes, with a good-natured tone, still facing his beakers and test tubes. "Come in and make yourself at home."

I cautiously sniffed and found that even though there was a faintly sweet odor hanging in the air, the sitting room was apparently safe to enter. Like one entering a deep mine shaft and seeing a canary upright and singing upon its perch, observing Holmes across the room in a similar position, conscious and alert and humming softly to himself, meant that the air was still breathable.

On several past occasions, I'd arrived to observe that Holmes had concocted various chemical combinations of greater or lesser degrees of lethality. In the bitterly January of 1884, when temperatures had bitterly dropped below freezing, he'd deftly proven Foster Chandler Cross innocent of the hydrogen sulfide murders, but he'd also given us both a raw cough for a week by experimenting with the deadly gas in his corner without thinking to ventilate the area by way of the nearby window. (He'd felt it was too much trouble, as it was frozen shut.) And upon another occasion, while proving that Shenley Beckett had killed his wife, he'd accidentally re-created the same unholy mustard-colored gas that Beckett knocked up from common materials found in his own tool shed and kitchen, and it was only my quick action in tossing of the fuming vial out the open window to shatter on the pavement below that both of us were saved. Fortunately, this incident took place late at night and the street was empty, or my action might have accidentally killed an innocent passer-by. Holmes was fascinated with the idea of an unknown gas of such dangerous potential stirred up from easily obtained household liquids, but he quickly realized that its wider existence was better left unknown. "Can you imagine what an enemy might do with such a substance in warfare?" he asked, destroying his notes.

On that particular afternoon of my visit, the nineteenth of April, his experiment seemed less likely to kill us. As I walked over and picked up the letter from the odd eight-sided table beside his chair, one of his sentimental keepsakes from some former case, he remarked, with seeming randomness, "There are great possibilities with the coal-tar derivatives."

Leaving off the immediate examination of the letter, I looked closer to see what he was doing. Clamped over the small blue flame from his Bunsen burner was a single test-tube, its base filled with some black and tarry substance. A thin string of smoke drifted upward, and I was glad to see that Holmes was keeping his face drawn back from any possibility of inhalation. In fact, the window was thankfully open, and the vapor seemed to be lazily pulled out the window, accounting for the smell in the room being less than it might have been.

With a pair of tongs, he was holding a sheet of paper in the rising thread of smoke, turning it carefully this way and that, his gaze fixated as if waiting for some result. Surely, I thought, the full-sized sheet wasn't some massive piece of litmus paper, for it was white and appeared to be no different than what would be found in any writing desk. After a few more seconds, Holmes turned off the burner and leaned toward the window, picking up his magnifying glass to make a careful examination off the sheet in the afternoon light. Then, with frustration, he tossed both upon the table and turned my way.

"You're aware of some of my research upon the identification of finger marks," he said. When I nodded, he continued. "While easily seen upon glass and certain other polished locations, as created by the oils on the skin and the ridge-and-valley patterns upon one's finger-tips, it is less visible on other surfaces. However, at times you will have seen various papers – documents or pages in books – where a finger mark is visible – from a smudge of dirt or soot. I'm becoming more certain that these marks can be used to identify specific individuals, with the right methods of categorization, and have corresponded with several individuals on this topic. It's no great difficulty to find the marks on smooth surfaces, such as glass or a polished tabletop, but I'm convinced that with the right method, these marks made by the oils of the skin can also be highlighted upon paper.

"While in Montpellier a few months ago, I did a number of experiments with coal-tars – from medicants to paints and dyes to poisons – and I found that some seemed to react with skin oils." He held up the sheet of paper, turning it so that I could see that both sides were blank. "Earlier today, I covered this with my own finger marks, as well as those of Mrs. Hudson and Billy. I've sketched my own thumb print, and theirs too, and could identify them in a trice if found on a window glass, but I had high hopes that reacting the oils from the fumes of this heated tar would make them show up just as plainly upon the paper." When a sigh he tossed the sheet aside. Then he suddenly frowned, looking off into the distance. "But possibly, if I were to put the paper into a sealed box, vented with the fumes in a much-more concentrated dose . . . ." He glanced upward, as if viewing something in the future. And if the marks could be identified from paper, might we also be able to find them on the skin of a dead body . . . ." [1]

Fearing that he was going to follow that thread and leave me pondering the letter he'd directed me to examine upon my arrival, I said, "Perhaps, someday when you crack this problem, you will be able to see who handled a letter such as this. The author, of course, and then whomever carries it through the postal system – the sorters and the postman. Mrs. Hudson, with baking flour on her fingers, or even the page, whose finger marks will be soiled from touching the rug when he lifts the corner to sweep the dust underneath . . . ."

Holmes shook his head, his gaze returning to me. "What's the use?" he asked, suddenly skirting the edge of a brown study. "The author of the letter signed her name – there's no mystery there – and she will be here in – " He turned his gaze to the mantel clock, suddenly standing up, now alert with his souring mood averted. " – in five minutes! Your arrival is well-timed, Watson! Do straighten up a bit – and throw open the other window. It's become a bit stuffy in here."

He strode toward his bedroom to improve his appearance while I raised the other window as my first priority and then rebuilt a few collapsed stacks of documents, heartened to see several already added from recent days on top of piles that hadn't been improved since April 1891, when we'd left London, not knowing that only one of us would return.

A glance at the basket chair showed that it was clean enough for the soon-to-arrive visitor. Only then did I examine the letter. Both the envelope and the small half-folded quarto-sized cream-colored sheet were of heavy stock. The ink was a dark black, and the handwriting was that of a woman – specifically Mrs. Ignatius Grossman – indicating that she was staying at Claridge's and, if acceptable, she would call upon Holmes at three o'clock. I glanced at the clock, even as the bell rang. She was on time.

"The paper is American," said Holmes, rejoining me, now much more presentable to greet his caller, "and I suspect that the lady might be as well – should she turn out to be the same Mrs. Grossman that I read about upon the occasion of her marriage. I wonder what she's doing in England . . . ."

Curious as to who the lady might be, and with no indication that I should depart, I stepped to my old chair, comfortably settling ever more into the tempting old Baker Street life when I should have been out and about, pursuing my own medical duties.

The two sets of footsteps climbing the stairs indicated that Mrs. Hudson had chosen to accompany Holmes's guest. That they were climbing slowly either meant that Mrs. Grossman was elderly – which seemed unlikely as there were no pauses for her to catch her breath – or that Mrs. Hudson, who was used to climbing those steps many times a day without pause, was steadily carrying up refreshments.

It was the latter that proved to be true, and I realized that Holmes, when aware of the appointment, had made arrangements with his landlady to provide a light tea. I recalled that he thought he might know of Mrs. Grossman, and I looked his way when she entered to see if he displayed any signs of recognition.

She was a dark-haired woman of middle height, in her early thirties. She was pretty, although not what one would call beautiful, and she was dressed in the American style. Her long but curly hair was left loose, but rather flattened to her head, bring emphasis to her deep-set eyes and rather stern mouth. But there were laugh lines around this same mouth, and a light of clever intelligence in her eyes. And there was something familiar about her . . . .

"Mr. Holmes!" she cried. "It's wonderful to meet you after all these years – particularly after we were all so devastated upon reading of your death!" She looked my way. "And Dr. Watson too! I had no hope at all of finding you here as well! Your account last December of how Mr. Holmes apparently died at the Reichenbach Falls was masterful – simply too masterful. I wept! After hearing from my father so much about both of you, it simply broke my heart to read it!" She looked back at Holmes. "And it turns out that you survived after all! Father was so upset three years ago when we learned of your supposed passing."

"I'm sorry," I interrupted. "Your father is – ?"

"Edwin Booth," answered Holmes with a smile.

I looked at the woman, now understanding why I seemed to recognize her. There was much about her features that favored her father, the famed actor who had passed away nearly a year earlier.

I immediately recalled the events of mid-1881, when I had only known Sherlock Holmes for a few months – our unexpected journey to the United States and the dramatic events related to Edwin Booth and his family – a story for which the world might never be prepared. [2]

Holmes and I had kept in touch with Booth for some time afterwards, but I was sad to recall that that during the last few years of the man's life, when so much turmoil was occurring in my own, my communications with him had flickered and faded, and it had been with great regret when I read of his death from a stroke, the last of several, in June of 1893. I knew that he'd had a daughter, but it had never occurred to me to write to her and express my condolences. And now she was in Holmes's Baker Street sitting room. I could only wonder if her visit had something to do with the explosive events of 1881, when the truth of the Booth family tragedy had been discovered – and then hidden away again almost immediately.

Holmes's smile had faded. "I was sorry to read about your father's passing," he said. Apparently, during his travels, he'd seen some mention of it in the press.

Mrs. Grossman nodded, the smile at seeing the two of us also dropping slowly from her expression. "It was a mercy, I suppose, but still, it happened far too soon. He had a melancholy nature, but still so much to live for, in spite of being retired. He was only fifty-nine . . . ." Her thoughts drifted for a moment, and we waited for her. Then she looked up. "I wish that Father could have known that you'd survived, Mr. Holmes. It would have cheered him greatly. He thought the world of you – of both of you. He once told me that if I was ever in London and needed help, you would be the men to ask." She looked from one of us to the other. "I'm afraid that I need that help now, even if I'm calling in the favor for something rather insignificant, and not for myself."

Holmes waved her to the basket chair. "Your father was correct, Mrs. Grossman – you have but to ask."

Edwin Booth and Edwina Booth (later Mrs. Ignatius Grossman)

As we'd been speaking, Mrs. Hudson was laying out the tea and cake, and within a moment we were settled and making polite conversation before addressing the real reason for the lady's visit.

"I'm here," she explained around small bites and sips, "because I'm preparing a book honoring my father. It's nearly done, and will consist of three parts – my own reminiscences of him, letters that he wrote to me when I was a child, and letters exchanged with others – not necessarily famous individuals, but instead with friends and admirers. All of them help to paint a picture of the man and his character. [3]

"The book is essentially complete, and will be published later this year, but I decided – rather spontaneously – that I might be able to include a bit more, if only I could obtain some additional information from a few of my father's friends here in England. He had a great affection for this country, as you both may know, and visited here several times. He was on tour here in 1861, when I was born. The family was staying in Fulham then, not five miles from here, I suppose. He returned here in 1880 through early the next year, and then back again in 1882. But it was during his first trip that he met one of his dearest friends, Telford Nevill Corby – or 'Tel', as my father called him. I have always called him 'Uncle Tel', although there is no actual family connection.

"I have a number of their letters – both my father's, as he always made a copy of whatever letter he sent – and replies from Uncle Tel. They offer a great deal of insight as to my father's philosophy, but I cannot print them as written, in the manner of all the other letters I'm using, because Uncle Tel's language is rather . . . shall we say 'salty'? He has long been associated with the theatre, functioning behind the scenes in a number of positions, and it's simply part of his personality. I hoped to get his permission to used edited pieces of his letters, but when I wrote to him, he didn't reply.

"There were several others that I also wanted to visit. If I'd known you were alive, Mr. Holmes, I would have written to arrange an appointment with you before I departed – "

She stopped abruptly and darted a glance my way, as if realizing she'd admitted to wanting an appointment with Holmes but not me. I was not offended, and I nodded with understanding. She smiled, rather sheepishly, and continued.

"Almost on a whim, I decided to journey here – with an amazement that one can accomplish the trip in a week or less in relative luxury. When I think about how it would have been when Father and Mother came over in '61, on a sailing ship that had to depart in the early days of the Civil War . . . .

"But I digress. After my arrival, I visited several of Father's old friends, and then yesterday afternoon, I went to the Princess's Theatre in Oxford Street, where Uncle Tel has been ensconced for some time. Do you both know of it? Well, then I hope I'm not being too critical of one of your sentimental favorites when I mention that it has apparently seen better days. [4] I know something about it, as it's where Father first played when he arrived in 1880 – without much success – before Sir Henry Irving extended the hand of friendship and asked if Father would join him at the Lyceum. Perhaps you had a chance to see them?"

Holmes nodded, but I shook my head. In those days, I was either overseas, or back in London living on eleven shillings and sixpence a day while trying to regain my shattered health. Attending the theatre, no matter how much I'd enjoyed it during my carefree student days, was not on my list of affordable distractions.

"Edwin and Sir Henry played Othello and Iago," Holmes explained to me, "alternating performances each night. I was lucky enough to attend on two different sequential nights, seeing both men in the two roles." He looked back at Mrs. Grossman. "Your father had written to me at one point with another idea he'd had – adapting Mary Shelley's *Frankenstein* into a play, with he and Sir Henry playing the doctor and the monster in alternating performances. Did that ever come to fruition?"

Mrs. Grossman's lips tightened. "Sir Henry was rather . . . *direct* about his disdain for the idea. Although their friendship remained, it did put something of a shadow on it – at least from Father's perspective." Then her mien brightened. "But it was no great loss, I suppose. Father had a wonderful career – even if he did become rather tired of being identified as the perfect Hamlet."

She took a sip of tea. "Father remained close to all of his friends, up to the day he died. That was why it surprised me so much not to hear back from Uncle Tel when I wrote to ask about using his edited letters. When I went to see him . . . when I went to see him at the theatre, I understood why. It seems that recently, he's been under a great deal of stress – Initially trying to mount a new show, and then more recently, there have been threats of some sort. And that," she said, looking from one of us to the other, "is why I came to you for help – to see if anything can be done to assist dear old Uncle Tel."

She sat back as if all had been explained and now it was just a matter of Holmes offering a solution from his armchair. I knew that, as skilled as he was, too much was still left unknown.

I thought that Holmes would question her more, but he seemed to realize, as did I, that getting the details second-hand from Mrs. Grossman would not be nearly as effective as speaking directly with Telford Nevill Corby – should he be inclined to speak with us.

"It would be best, I suppose," Holmes explained, "to see Mr. Corby and ask him a few questions. Is he at the theatre now?" He glanced my way to see if I could fall in with his plans, and I nodded. I had nothing further scheduled for the day, except to return to Kensington and my empty house.

"I expect so," replied Mrs. Grossman. "He practically lives there – especially now, as he's so involved with the new play."

"Dr. Watson and I can go there now. Can you accompany us?"

"I was hoping that you would do so," she replied. "Of course I want to go along."

And so, five minutes later, we were in a four-wheeler headed south along Baker Street, the streets becoming steadily more crowded as we progressed.

A few careful questions from Holmes determined that Mrs. Grossman had no knowledge of how we'd come to meet her father in 1881, and I agreed with Holmes without speaking that there was no reason she should learn any of it now. Before she could raise questions of her own, Holmes diverted the conversation, explaining that he'd actually been in New York the previous year in early June, when Edwin Booth had passed. "I attended the funeral," he admitted, "but I was in disguise then, working on a number of different affairs, and couldn't offer my condolences in person." He went on to casually mention a few of those cases, and I committed the references to memory, so that I could follow up with him later to get more extensive details. [5]

Holmes then briefly explained how he'd survived his near-death at the Reichenbach Falls before pivoting to Mrs. Grossman's family. For the rest of the journey, along Baker Street and then down Oxford Street to the theatre, they discussed Mrs. Grossman's paternal grandmother, Mary Ann Booth, *née* Holmes. Famed actor Junius Booth, Mrs. Grossman's grandfather, had abandoned his wife for young Mary Ann in 1821, and they'd had eleven children together before finally marrying in 1851, just a year before Junius's death. I had first learned of Mary Ann Holmes Booth in '81, when Holmes and I met Edwin Booth, and learned more of her during Holmes's discussion with Mrs. Grossman.

The Princess's Theatre
73 Oxford Street, London

The Princess's Theatre at 73 Oxford Street was a rather run-down affair by 1894, and it would permanently close just eight years later, becoming a warehouse. I had been by it, one way or another, upon countless occasions, but had never been tempted to cross its sill. Like so many theatres, its street face failed to give any indication of what lay inside. It was a rather narrow building in front, only three stories high, with a small shop on the right, and the entrance and ticket office on the left. Having been in many such theatres before, both in London and elsewhere, I had a sense of how it would be laid out – once inside, the building would widen toward the back, so that the narrow lobby – rather laid out like an omnibus – would spread into a theater with seats arranged directly in front of the stage, as well as angled toward it on both the right and left.

This proved to be the case. We disembarked and went to the door, where the man in the ticket window recognized Mrs. Grossman and waved us inside. We traversed the small lobby, past a rather neglected-looking bar on one side, and made for the doors to the theatre itself.

When a performance is not underway, a theatre is a sad and shabby thing. There are people meandering about, relaxing in the audience seats, or in the aisles having conversations. Others are upon stage carrying on technical discussions, or perhaps rehearsing some more complicated bits of business. That day at the Princess's Theatre, an out-of-tune and metallically toned upright piano was standing to one side – stage left as theatre companies refer to it. A man was hesitantly playing one of the tunes from Gilbert and Sullivan's *Utopia*, which had premiered the previous fall.

When rehearsing, a theatre's lighting is usually raised, highlighting the areas – most of them – that are run-down and worn. Richard D'Oyly Carte's Savoy, just half-a-mile to the southeast, had installed electric lighting in 1881, but the Princess's Theatre still had no such amenities, and the yellow light of various lamps around the hall gave everything a dingy aspect that could only leave everyone involved in a foul temper. It made me wonder if Telford Nevill Corby's problems were simply a manifestation of the mood of this theatre itself.

It was difficult to tell just what play was currently being rehearsed. The stage was bare, with only a few plain wooden chairs scattered about. All backdrops and screens were raised into the rafters above the stage, so no clue was to be found there, and the men and women standing around on the bare boards, presumably actors facing the director, wore plain everyday clothes.

The only concession to the upcoming production was a sloping wooden platform that was being built to the left, as one faced the stage. Over ten or twelve feet in length, it rose about one foot toward the back of the stage. A couple of carpenters were crawling around behind it, hammering some unseen bracing.

Mrs. Grossman looked around until she spotted a man sitting alone in a chair toward the front, in the right-hand section. He was slumped with a dejected and weary attitude, but he perked up with surprise as Mrs.

Grossman approached him. He stood, hugged her, and then looked our way. They spoke for another moment, he looked at us again, and then waved us forward. As we approached, he turned and walked away, leading us backstage and into the bowels the theatre.

Following Corby – for I assumed that it was he – I could see that he was about sixty, heavy-set, and wearing loose dark clothing. His white hair was shaggy, indicating that he was somewhat indifferent to his appearance, but when we passed under a lamp, I could see that he was also clean-shaven, and unlike a number of theatre-folk, he didn't display any signs of excessive use of alcohol – or other worse substances.

He took us into a small office and shut the door. Then, turning to face us, he gave a tired but sincere smile and shook our hands.

"Edwina says that you're Sherlock Holmes," Corby said, "but I've seen you before, years ago, and I'd have sworn that you were William Escott, the Shakespearian actor." He cocked his head. "I never forget a face, sir. Yes, you're Escott – no question. Or at least, you *were* Escott, of Sasanoff's troupe. [6] Before he took everyone off to America in 1880, I saw you at Drury Lane – finest Horatio I've encountered. I'll swear to it." He took a step back. "After I never heard of you again, I assumed that you stayed in the United States. But you're really Sherlock Holmes? Well, that's quite interesting. Quite interesting indeed."

We found chairs and sat down.

"Mr. Holmes. Doctor," continued Corby. "It's a pleasure – one I thought I'd never have. I just heard a few days ago that you were back in London, Mr. Holmes. I suppose you'll hear it a thousand times over the next few months, but I was most grieved when we thought you had died. Most grieved, sir." He looked toward me. "You wrote a most gripping account of it, Doctor. 'The Last Problem', I believe you called it? Perhaps one day – when I've finished with this current project – we might discuss dramatizing it – " He looked back at Holmes. " – along with the revelation of just how you survived, Mr. Holmes . . . ?"

He clearly wanted to know the rest of the story, beyond where it had been left in the previous December's *Strand Magazine*, but Holmes simply nodded and stayed on the path that had brought us here.

"Mrs. Grossman is concerned," he began, "about you, and she asked us, as old friends of her father, and in the name of your friendship with him, if there was anything that we could do to help."

We were seated rather closely together in the small space, and Corby leaned back and rubbed his face tiredly with both hands. It was so quiet backstage that I could hear the rasp of his palms on his unseen whiskers.

"I wish that you could," he said. "I suppose you might ask a few questions, but I'm not sure if anything can help at this point." He looked fondly at Mrs. Grossman. "Your father was one of my dearest friends," he said, "and I know that he'd be proud that you're trying to look after me."

Then he resettled himself in the chair, sighed, and told Holmes, "I'm currently producing and directing a new play – it's one that I wrote – and I hope it will premiere in a month, but we keep having setbacks. Things going wrong here in the theatre, and now anonymous notes promising accidents. Investors are getting nervous. And all of it is making the owner of the theatre nervous too."

He sat forward, warming to his subject, cupping a fist in his other hand, and sometimes shaking them slightly for emphasis. "I know that this play will be a success!" he said softly. "The idea came to me in a dream, and it's unlike anything seen before. It's something of a sequel to the Scottish Play."

He looked from one to the other of us, and at me the most. I suspect that he was waiting for me to blurt out, "*MacBeth*?", but I well knew the old theatre superstition of carefully not saying the name of that play within the theatre when not a part of the actual performance, and I simply nodded and held my tongue.

Seemingly satisfied that I comprehended proper theatre etiquette, Corby continued. "You're all aware of the three witches in the play – the *Wyrd* Sisters, as they're sometimes called, representing fate as they do – and how they cryptically explain the main character's path, even as he misinterprets their prophecies on the road to his hubristic failure and defeat. Well, I conceived of a new and unique idea – a play based around these characters – a new story where one of the witches falls in love with a mortal – a young man – and tries to become human herself, to live out her life with him. Of course, her sisters, the other two foretellers of fate and destiny, are working against it, and the other humans – the young man's family and friends and his church – have only hostility for her. The story ends in the only way it can – as a tragedy – with the young man dead and the prodigal sister returning to her own only possibly fate, alone and loveless forever. There are some aspects of the old *Barbara Allen* song twined within it, and taken from that, I've named the boy *John*.

"I'm not sure anyone has ever before staged a sequel to a Shakespeare play, and certainly nothing to add to the story in the Scottish Play. The producers were interested, and the play is good – it almost seemed to write itself – but since we've been in rehearsal, things have started going wrong. Accidents, as I mentioned, and a general uneasiness that grows by the day. If it continues, the play will die before ever being staged, and I'll lose all that I have – for it was my own personal investment that, in the end, helped get the play produced."

"The accidents," Holmes asked. "Have any of them related to someone saying the name of the Scottish Play?"

I glanced at him, equally curious and amused. Holmes is the most scientific of men, and he has no use for superstition – but I also know that he held his short time as an actor – primarily in Shakespearian roles – with great fondness and affection, and he also has a massive respect for the theatre and its traditions. Clearly, in spite of his lack of fear concerning curses, and his contempt for those who fall under superstitious delusions, he was not going to say "*MacBeth*" while inside the theatre. If nothing else, this served as a comfort to Corby, who would have been most upset and certain uncooperative had one of us uttered the word aloud.

"Thankfully, none of that," Corby answered. "According to legend, Shakespeare's play has been cursed from the beginning, as actual witches objected to his inclusion of their incantations within the play. Some may scoff, but I've known of too many instances over the years where the curse is true. Someone forgets and says the wrong word, and then they – or someone else – pays the price. A trip or fall. Something dropped on a head from the heavens – " Corby looked at me, in case I wasn't familiar with the term. I was, but nodded anyway when he explained, "That's the area above the stage – the fly loft and the catwalks. We've been fortunate that, whatever has occurred here, has – so far – been unrelated to any accidental or deliberate flaunting of the curse. But the notes that followed have made people quite nervous, nevertheless."

"The notes *followed* the accidents?" Holmes asked. "Be more specific."

"There have been three accidents so far in the three weeks since we've started rehearsal – two in the first week, none during the second, and then the third two days ago. On the second day, one of the carpenters was using a chisel that slipped and badly cut the ball of his thumb. Then, a couple of days later, one of the trap doors in center stage was partly raised – just an inch or two for now reason – and one of the actresses playing a witch tripped and twisted her ankle. She's still with us, but she's limping badly. And the third accident took place day before yesterday, on the 17th, when a counterweight – a sandbag – for one of the hanging flats came untied and nearly dropped on Agnes Leeds – she plays the lead female, Katrina – the witch who falls in love with the mortal boy, John. Agnes was quite upset, and went home for the rest of the day, although fortunately she's back today."

"And the notes," pressed Holmes. "They were found after the accidents?"

Corby nodded. "In each case, a few hours after the accident, they were found in the center of the stage. Although no one is certain how they could have been placed there without being seen, in truth there are always moments when no one is actually in the theatre itself, and it would be only a few seconds to leave the note and slip away."

"So you don't believe these to be some sort of manifestation of a curse? Or something left by a theatre ghost?"

Corby shook his head. "I don't discount the existence of theatre ghosts, Mr. Holmes. I've seen too many of them in my day. There's the Gray Man at the Drury Lane, and the time Helen Terry saw a severed head watching her from the balcony at the Lyceum. Many is the time that I myself have seen John Baldwin Buckstone at the Haymarket, and he died decades ago. But I don't know of any ghost who leaves warnings written on paper *after* something has happened."

"Where are the notes? Do you have them?"

Corby nodded and reached behind him to a credenza piled with papers. Pushing a few aside, he took hold of three sheets, pivoted back to face us, and handed them to Holmes. My friend studied each with great care before passing them to me, and I in turn gave them to Mrs. Grossman.

Each was on a new-looking unfolded quarto-sized sheet – standard blank paper that could be purchased in any stationery shop. The text was the same in each message, written in black ink, centered in the sheets, and in strictly shaped block letters which would prevent any easy identification of the author's sex, age, or left- or right-handedness.

Open, Locks, Whoever Knocks!
Share what's owed or it's the Dead Man's Box!

"'*Open, Locks, Whoever Knocks!*' is the name of my play," explained Corby. "From the second witch's speech at the opening of the Scottish Play:

> *"By the pricking of my thumbs,*
> *Something wicked this way comes.*
> *Open, locks,*
> *Whoever knocks!"*

Holmes nodded absently, again studying the sheets which had been returned to him. Then he looked up, about the speak when a scream from the direction of the stage penetrated the silence we'd enjoyed in Corby's backstage office. Within seconds, we were all dashing toward the stage.

We arrived to discover a group of people, likely the same ones we'd seen upon our arrival, standing together at one side of the stage, facing toward the recently constructed upward-sloping platform. At first I couldn't see what they were looking at, but then it became apparent that someone was lying on the stage floor behind the platform, partially hidden where it dropped off.

A man was kneeling there, and the sounds of a woman whimpering in distress were obvious. I raced around the platform to find her lying there, her ankle bent at an unnatural angle.

I knelt down, pushing aside the young man who was attempting to provide some sort of comfort. I peripherally observed that the injured woman seemed to be in her late twenties, but might appear older due to some undefined coarseness about her appearance. If standing, she would have been not much over five feet, and she had thick black hair, rather wild and unkempt. I wasn't surprised to later learn that she was cast as one of the three witch sisters.

"My ankle!" she gasped, her hand clutching my sleeve. "I fell off the back of the platform – I thought that I was farther down. Is it – ?"

I nodded. "Broken. Yes, and unfortunately a small compound fracture. You must be taken to hospital immediately." I looked up and spotted Corby, standing ten or so feet away with Holmes and Mrs. Grossman. "Is there a telephone?"

When Corby shook his head, I turned to the young man still kneeling beside me, a burly lad in his mid-twenties. "You – summon a constable, outside on the street, and have him send for an ambulance. He'll know what to do. *Go!*"

Without requiring further instructions, the young man leapt up and sped across the stage apron, down the side steps, and up through the auditorium. He was in such a reckless hurry that I feared my urgency might be the cause of another accident, but he successfully navigated the aisle and was soon out the door.

Meanwhile, I tried to calm the young woman, asking her name.

"What is your name?" I asked.

"Diana. Diana Bonfardin."

"And what part do you play?"

"I'm . . . I'm one of the witch sisters – the second witch. Betsy and I – we don't get names. Only Agnes does – she plays Katrina." She winced and bit her lip as a wave of pain washed across her. Then she gave a short bitter laugh.

"There's no getting away from the curse!" She cried, struggling to prop herself up on one elbow so that she could see over the raised platform. Her gaze went left and right until it settled on Corby. Then she shakily raised a hand and pointed it in his direction. "The curse!" she said in a much louder voice. "You didn't heed the warnings, and now look at what is happened!" She sobbed. "This is your fault – all yours!" Then, weeping, she settled back to the floor. I held her hand and offered what comfort I could until the ambulance arrived. I oversaw the immobilization of her ankle and advised that she be taken to Charing Cross Hospital.

As she was being carried away, Corby stepped forward, weakly saying, "Diana – ?" but she didn't acknowledge him. Then he took a few more steps, telling the ambulance men that he'd be along soon, and that all of her expenses would be covered. They nodded and kept walking, going about their business until they had passed through the doors to the lobby, leaving the rest standing in stunned silence. Then, grumbling and whispering began, everyone's worried or angry gazes gradually turned toward Corby.

He stepped forward in their direction, meeting them halfway. "What happened?"

At first, there was no answer, and then someone, a tall lanky fellow, handsome in his way, I suppose, said in a deep baritone, "I don't suppose any of us are sure. Everyone was rehearsing, or going about his or her business, and suddenly Diana screamed. We looked around to see that she'd fallen. It happened very quickly."

They heavy-set young man who had run for the constable spoke up. "She said it was the curse! Somehow this play is cursed!"

The group began to mutter, and I could imagine that soon they would work themselves up into something quite possibly dangerous, there in a building along one of London's main thoroughfares. There was tangible fear in the air, and when mixed with anger, it was a dangerous combination.

Holmes, who I hadn't noticed drawing closer, whispered, "Pacify them for a moment, Watson."

I turned to see that he and Mrs. Grossman were already turning Corby away and leading him quickly from the stage and back toward his office. I faced forward again to gaze upon the two-dozen members of the theatre company.

"You," I said, pointing to the young man. "What's your name?"

"Melvin Sledge."

"And your function?"

"My *function*," he snarled, "is playing one of the towns-folk – John's best friend." He nodded toward the tall handsome fellow. "John is played by Eric – Eric Grazier."

I looked toward him, hoping to diffuse the situation through questions. "Mr. Grazier told what he saw – looking around to see where the young lady had fallen. Did anyone else see anything?"

There were murmurs and the shaking of heads, but nothing was forthcoming. However, they seemed to have calmed somewhat for the moment, and before they could again become agitated, and uncertain just how much pacifying Holmes required of me, I thanked them, turned, and walked with purpose from the stage and back to Corby's office.

The older man was sitting in his chair, a shaking hand covering his eyes, and Mrs. Grossman leaning over him and whispering words of comfort. Holmes immediately turned my way, saying, "Did you tell them who you were?"

I raised my eyebrows questioningly but shook my head. "I just asked a couple of their names, and whether anyone had seen anything. None had. I – "

"Good. A plan occurred to me as we returned to the office, but I realized that if you identified yourself, it wouldn't work. You see, no one out there knows that you and I are here – We are just strangers to them."

I smiled and nodded at his hat and coat. "As has always suited you, wearing an Inverness and fore-and-aft hunting cap as your regular outdoor attire serves to identify you quite well – particularly after Mr. Paget started drawing you in them more often after I corrected some of his earlier mistakes."

"True, but as you also know, many people – if they knew who I was at all – still believe me to have perished three years ago. And I'm not the only one who wears this type of hat in the City. We learned that while pursuing the Rippers in '88. No, I think that we can count on the fact that we weren't recognized. With a suitable disguise, my plan should work."

"And that would be – ?"

"I'm going to obtain employment at the Princess's Theatre – specifically in the company of *Open, Locks, Whoever Knocks!* – and determine what's at the bottom of this supposed curse."

A smile turned up the corner of his mouth, and there was a glint of merriment in his eyes. "Following a long international tour – well over a dozen years – William Escott, the noted thespian, has returned to London!"

Things moved quickly for a few minutes. Holmes explained his plan to Corby, who was still somewhat bewildered by what had occurred, but apparently willing to cooperate. Holmes planned to slip away from the theatre, and then return later that day as William Escott, who Corby would welcome with great enthusiasm, hiring him to a yet-unwritten part that he would amend to the play, while telling everyone just how fortunate the company was to have secured the participation of the famed player. Holmes hoped that he would determine what was going on in just a few days.

Mrs. Grossman elected to stay with Corby, and Holmes and I let ourselves out of the rear door of the theatre, winding through several alleys until we were walking north along Rathbone Place. Our pace was rather fast, as Holmes's adrenalin was rampant due to the excitement of a new case and, I suspected, the chance to return to the boards, if only for a few days.

I wanted to ask questions as we walked, but in truth, I was hard pressed to match his pace. It was only when we neared his rooms in Baker Street that he slowed, as if realizing my effort to keep up.

"I apologize, Watson," he said as we paused on Paddington Street between the park and the workhouse. "I'm so looking forward to returning to the theatre that my mind was racing ahead of my body, and my body was racing to catch up – with you racing along after both of us!" He gave one of his peculiar silent laughs at his joke. Then his expression became more serious.

"Thank you for accompanying me today. I know that you took valuable time away from your practice, and it's much appreciated. I'll go my own way for now, and be in touch." He nodded again before I had a chance to speak and continued on in the direction of Baker Street, leaving me wondering which way I should walk to find a cab that would carry me back to the empty house in Kensington.

The next three days were a return to the tedium of life before Sherlock Holmes's return from the dead, but in some ways, it was worse, because I now knew that he was back and carrying out an investigation, while I had been offered no invitation to join him.

Not that he should have invited me to help, of course. In previous years, when my marriages and practices and separate residences had kept me quite busy, I had only been aware of a fraction of his activities, and he had managed just fine without me. I'd only learned much later and after the fact about his dangerous trip to Odessa, and the curious affair of three blood feasters in the Harlesden High Street, and the encounter with the four-fingered mime which so nearly cost him his life.

Intellectually, I could appreciate both the facts that Holmes was thoughtfully allowing me to carry on the work of maintaining my practice – my livelihood – and also that whatever he was doing at the theatre was best carried out on his own, and that there would have been no apparent place for me to assist without raising suspicions. Still, I thought with a bit of pettiness, I could have been given some task to assist – asking questions about the cast members and crew, for instance, or possibly carrying messages from Holmes to the police or his Irregulars.

I shook my head. Wishing for such pitiful and menial chores was rather pathetic. I was a professional – a physician – and that was my role in life. It was best to accept that. I was more grateful than words could tell that Holmes was alive and back in London, and he'd picked up his life from where he'd left it, and my own duty was to carry on with the life that I had crafted, empty though it was.

Still, I did find my steps taking me through Baker Street more than once with the intention of stopping in to ask how his investigation was progressing. Once I went of an evening, but the sitting room was dark, and on another occasion, I met Mrs. Hudson walking along the street, and she informed me that Holmes was out, and that there was no indication of when he would return.

On the twenty-first of April, I found myself in Oxford Street, not far from the Princess's Theatre, and could not resist the urge to slip inside in the hopes of seeing something that might assuage my curiosity. I was in luck, for a rehearsal was underway, indicating that the play had not been shut down after the latest manifestation of the curse.

Standing in the back of the auditorium, in shadows and pressed against a long drape hung to cover the plain walls underneath, I watched the stage. Although I was sure that no one could see me, or would care if they did, I tried to stand slumped in a way that didn't look like myself – although I knew that if anyone could notice and identify me, it would be Holmes.

At first I didn't see him. There was some sort of business on stage where the tall young man, Eric Grazier in the role of John, had his back to an attractive young woman whose long blonde hair was hanging down over her shapely form, obvious even from the back of the theatre. From their still-somewhat stilted performance, I could tell that they were working "off book" – that is, without reference to their scripts – possibly for the first time, and that the lines were not yet completely memorized. John appeared to be defending the witch, Katrina, from a group of townspeople, all standing on the rising platform. As he moved, he looked down at the stage, and I knew that he was studying marks placed upon the floor to determine his "blocking". To one side stood the heavy-set actor, Melvin Sledge, and in front of the large group was a tall man carrying some sort of book, likely a Bible – held out and up in front of him as if it were a talisman and he was invoking its power. When he spoke, although he looked to be a stranger to me, I recognized Holmes's voice, in full theatrical mode.

"Avaunt, ye demon!" he thundered, and the girl playing Katrina cringed and seemed to diminish. Then she shook as if recovering from a blow and resumed her full height – diminutive as it was – throwing back her shoulders defiantly.

"Avaunt yourself, hypocrite!" she cried, and Holmes in turn was rocked back as if slapped. Katrina took a step forward, her own arm outstretched. "Long have I known of you, Garrison Stephens!" she cried. "*Sinner! Adulterer! Adder's fork and blind-worm's sting!* Your sins cry out to Heaven, and yet you would deny this true love – something which you will never know! Wouldst thou care to know your own true fate, Garrison Stephens?"

Then, she waved a hand toward him, as if brushing away a buzzing insect, and Holmes, in the part of the minister, was swept backwards off his feet! He seemed to jump away from the witch as if he'd been struck before landing flat on his back at the feet of the townspeople. I started to rush forward, uncertain as to what had happened, and fearful that he'd done permanent damage to the back of his skull upon the wood of the platform, but I stayed myself when the townspeople didn't seem to be concerned, instead stepping forward and helping him to his feet. He then faced Katrina, now diminished and cowering before her.

She stepped forward, her hand still raised. "I've seen the fates of a thousand men – A thousand *thousand!* – and you are no different than the least of them, Garrison Stephens. The difference between you and the others is that they were strangers – mere threads in the great tapestry – without meaning or interest. But you have *crossed me*, sir! *Crossed me!* And you will pay – as did foolish Mac – "

She stopped abruptly, as if paused into the form of a statue, before turning toward the auditorium seats. "I can't say it, Tel," she whined in a completely different voice. "I can't say . . . the Scottish name. It's the curse . . . ."

A heavy fellow with white hair, sitting in one of the front seats, stood. It was Telford Nevill Corby. "Agnes, you know how the curse works – you can't say the name of the play in the theatre, but during a performance, it's all right."

"But that's during a performance of *The Scottish Play* – not as part of a *different* play. This is no different than if I said it while sitting out there next to you. Can't you change the line, or leave it out?"

"No. We've talked about this. Without the reference to . . . the Scotsman, the segment at the end where Katrina returns to her sisters makes no sense. It gets to the meat of *her destiny* – Don't you see?"

"I don't – and even you're scared to say it!" She took step toward him. "Go ahead – it's your play. *You* say the line!"

I thought for a minute that Corby would, but in the end he sagged in defeat, also too fearful to speak the name.

I slipped out before I heard how he intended to resolve this dilemma.

Having heard nothing from Holmes for several more days, I had resolved myself to occasional visits and intermittent involvement in his cases as he got on with the resumption of his life and me with the continuation of mine. Therefore, it was with some surprise that I received a note on the night of the twenty-fourth, asking that I be at the Princess's Theatre at ten o'clock the next morning – "*if your schedule permits.*"

My schedule could be rearranged, and the next morning, I was standing out front along Oxford Street at the appointed time, about to enter when a cab approached, delivering Mrs. Grossman.

"Has he solved it?" she asked immediately.

I could only explain that I'd heard nothing for several days, except for the invitation to be present that morning. "Holmes," I added rather lamely, "likes to present a theatrical solution, if you'll forgive the reference, standing here in front of just-such an establishment." I didn't add that, in this case, I couldn't even be sure if we were there to see a solution, or instead that our presence was part of some mid-case ruse, constructed to advance the investigation.

I held the door for the lady to precede me, and we crossed into the auditorium to see the cast and crew assembled and seated upon the stage, now brightly lit, as if it was the night of a performance. The limelights were harsh at that time of morning, and unforgiving to the group seated upon the stage, all staring at us as we approached.

At one side, in another grouping of chairs, sat Corby, and near him, reclining on a low-backed settee, was Diana Bonfardin, her legs stretched before her and one ankle encased in a plaster cast.

At the front of the stage, facing them and with his back to us, was the unmistakable figure of Sherlock Holmes. Seeing the others watch our approach, he turned and smiled.

"Ah, Watson! And Mrs. Grossman! Hail and well met! You're just in time – I've only just now revealed my identity."

"You're a liar is what you are!" rumbled Melvin Sledge, not quite rising from his perch upon the edge of his chair.

Holmes glanced back toward him. "A rather ironic statement, Mr. Sledge, considering that I was playing a part, the same as you do, as part of my profession. In this case, I was asked by Mr. Corby – and Mrs. Grossman, now joining us – to look into this trifling little curse business. How better than from inside your company – and how to do that if I was known to be a detective? Better to put my skills as an actor to use and spend time with all of you."

"You certainly have skill, and there's no denying it," said Eric Grazier with a smile. "I would have bet my last dollar you were this Escott chap, returned to England after a long spell in the Colonies. Your British accent was just bent enough to account for a long period away."

"Thank you," Holmes nodded, and then turned to see that Mrs. Grossman and I had found chairs near Corby. "Now to continue.

"As I believe everyone here knows, there has been a series of minor accidents, followed by notes which everyone understood to imply some sort of curse – which was easily accepted, as this drama has roots in The Scottish Play. However, the actual wording of all three notes – '*Open, Locks, Whoever Knocks! Share what's owed or it's the Dead Man's Box!*' – are clearly more of a threat to do something, or else, than an execration. *Share what's owed or it's the Dead Man's Box* is fairly clear – share something owed, or it's a coffin – a *dead man's box.*

"I've recently been working on using the fumes of coal-tar derivatives to highlight finger marks upon paper – and I wish that my work had progressed to the point where I could simply identify who wrote the notes in that manner, but instead I had to rely on old-fashioned investigation methods – seeing who might have a motive for causing accidents, making threats, and allowing the idea of a curse to take hold.

"With that in mind, I joined the troupe and simply had conversations, many of them, keeping my ears open and trying not to theorize before I had any data. And I soon learned an interesting fact."

He took a step toward where Corby sat, not too far from Diana Bonfardin's settee. "The two of you were recently involved in a passionate, though quick-burning, relationship that terminated just a month or so before the script of *Open, Locks, Whoever Knocks!* was shared with the owner of the theatre and the producers who would provide some of the funding."

Corby, who had been staring down in a dejected way, now looked up, his eyes in shadow under his shaggy white hair. "That's true. What difference does it make?"

"How long did it take to write the script?" Holmes countered. I noticed that while the entire group was watching the performance with interest, Diana Bonfardin seemed to have a special focus, her face tense and her mouth pursed with pinched acidic bitterness.

"Oh, a month or so. I write quickly, and as I told you, it seemed to write itself."

Holmes turned, pivoting on a foot toward Diana Bonfardin, who looked at him with surprise. "Speaking of writing," he said, "I noticed something else. That was nothing brilliant on my part – everyone else noticed it too. We've all been waiting with baited breath to see when the next warning note would be placed in the center of the stage, referencing your accident, Miss Bonfardin. But that note was never placed. Curiously, after the most serious and injurious of the four accidents – much worse than the other three – no note appeared. Were you aware of that?"

Agnes Leeds, who had been sitting quietly between Eric Grazier and Melvin Sledge, now sat forward with great energy. "There was no fourth note," she said with enthusiastic realization, "because Diana couldn't leave it! She hasn't been back to the theatre until this morning – not since she fell and broke her ankle!"

"Precisely, Miss Leeds," said Holmes, glancing at her with a nod before looking back at Diana Bonfardin. The dark-haired young woman had propped herself up, swinging her legs to the floor as if she meant to rise and fight – or flee. But the latter was impossible, and she seemed to realize that there was no hope for the former as well. With a vulgar curse, she turned toward Corby.

"Tell them!" she hissed. "Tell them what you did, you old fraud! Tell them how you stole my idea!"

Corby sighed, and I thought he would respond softly, but then he jerked upright and faced the younger woman, his face now masked with rage.

"You hideous shrew! What does it matter if you gave me the germ of an idea? Did you take it and develop it? Did you provide anything more than a suggestion to tell the witches' story? Not at all. It was *my* idea to marry what you said while drifting to sleep with elements from *The Ballad of Barbara Allen.* It was *me* who wrote it, *me* who birthed the idea and secured funding, and it was *me* – Curse the day! – that allowed a serpent's tooth like you to be part of the cast. You should be thanking *me* – but *no*! Instead, you tried your best to poison what could be my masterpiece! My *legacy!*"

"Did you realize that it was her?" asked Holmes. "That she was the one leaving the notes?"

Corby took a deep breath. "I suspected. But I thought it best to ignore her. She's never been able to hold onto a thought for very long, and I knew that if I just waited, she'd lose interest. But then Mrs. Grossman stopped to visit, and I let my irritation show through – she took it as worry or concern – and before I knew it, she'd brought you along as well. Then a real accident occurred, and I feared even more what Diana might do – or say. It was easier to let you hang around for a few days. I knew you'd find no curse, and hoped you'd say so and lose interest and go away."

Holmes nodded and turned back to Diana Bonfardin. "The first accident with the chisel – it was nothing more than a typical incident that occurs in any theatre during rehearsal. But the other two – those might have been more than accidents.

"I happened to notice," he continued, "when we first visited the theatre on the nineteenth, that you, Miss Bonfardin, were limping. I learned that it was you that tripped on the trap door, setting up the belief that a second accident was part of the curse."

"That's right," Agnes Leeds confirmed. "She was."

"And then," said Holmes, "a few days later, a sandbag dropped from the fly loft, nearly hitting Miss Leeds, the leading lady. If it had struck her on the head, such a blow might have fractured her skull or snapped her neck. Was that an accident, I wonder – or by that point, had you, Miss Bonfardin, started directing events instead of simply characterizing them?"

The dark-haired girl's eyes widened, and she opened her mouth in denial, but Holmes held up a hand.

"I'll give you the benefit of the doubt. The notes only appeared after all three accidents. If you decided to cause the third accident –which might be categorized as attempted murder – then you would have left notes beforehand to heighten tension and enhance the idea of a curse. So we'll let that go with the assumption that you're innocent of that action, and instead simply guilty of leaving the notes.

"In any case, it seems that any curse that might have been awakened by your actions has bounced back upon you. Your ankle is broken, and it's certain that your work as part of this company is finished. Working out whatever credit for authorship of the play that you deserve can take place between you and Mr. Corby in the now-bright light of discovery and disclosure."

It is immaterial what the bitter former lovers decided, as the play was never performed. Two days later, not long before her scheduled return to America, Mrs. Grossman stopped by Holmes's rooms, where I was visiting at the end of a busy but unvaried day.

"Mr. Corby's investors have disassociated themselves with the project," she explained, rather sadly. She looked from one of us to the other. "I know that I asked you to look into this, but now I can't help but regret it. If I hadn't meddled and asked you to involve yourself, Mr. Holmes, it might have worked out better, and Uncle Tel's play would have been performed. Luckily, he didn't lose a great deal of his money, but he'd counted on this play as his masterpiece – a work that would leave him remembered long after his passing." [7]

Holmes shook his head. "I was part of the cast for several days," he said. "I can assure you that, while the idea is original, the play itself isn't very good. A safe bet is that he wrote it too hurriedly, and it wasn't much better than a hackneyed music hall production. Better to have no legacy at all than one to be ridiculed."

After she departed, Holmes and I sat in silence for a while, sipping whisky and smoking our pipes. Finally, I stated, "I cannot believe that three years away has dulled your perceptions as much as you might wish to imply," I said, a smile upon my face to take the sting from my words.

Evidently Holmes understood my meaning. "You mean that my solution took the better part of a week?"

I nodded. "You would have noticed by the next day that no new note was forthcoming, and you probably knew just as quickly about Corby's relationship with Diana Bonfardin." I took a drink. "What I suspect is that you enjoyed, even just for a few days, slipping back into your long-ago acting role of William Escott."

Holmes turned his head as if considering. "Perhaps, instead, I was resisting slipping back into my long-ago role of *Sherlock Holmes.*"

He was silent for a moment, and I could see that he had more to say. Then, "It's a curious thing, Watson, to have been away for such a long time, living under another name, and behaving under a different set of rules. For three years, I haven't been *Sherlock Holmes, the Consulting Detective.* Rather, I've been the blunt instrument of the British Government, under the direction of Brother Mycroft. Make no mistake: I am thrilled to be home, and to pick up the reins just as I'd left them, but since returning I've also felt a bit . . . *untethered.* It was therefore something of a relief to once again spend each of the last few days as someone else, as I've done for so much of my travels."

I was uncertain if I should offer some understanding comment, but he raised a hand and smiled. "Not to worry, Watson. After a fortnight back in London, I already feel much more like myself, with a great satisfaction that things are returning to normal.

Then, as if perceiving my thoughts as he often did, Holmes stated, "I apologize for leaving you out of this matter. I know how you enjoy these little investigations, and I hope you'll join me in more of them, as your time allows. Now, however, I have a visitor arriving in just a few minutes – No, not it isn't about a case, I'm afraid. Rather, it's a bit of other necessary personal business, and I'm afraid that I'll have to ask you to leave – but can you find a way to be here tomorrow morning? About nine o'clock? I'm expecting a visitor, and I perceive that your involvement may be crucial."

He tossed a note my way, wherein a certain Dr. Aberfeldy of Scunthorpe requested an appointment to discuss the confidential affairs of one of his patients. I looked up in surprise.

"He thinks that this lady of his acquaintance is a *kelpie*?" I asked. "In Lincolnshire? That's a long way from Scotland."

"A *murderous kelpie*," Holmes clarified. "The doctor is convinced that she has killed four children already, and must be stopped. If he's right – "

"Surely you don't think she's a *kelpie*?" I asked, convinced that he surely hadn't changed that much during the three years he'd been gone.

"Not at all. But she may be a killer. Conversely, she may be innocent, but Dr. Aberfeldy – likely a Scottish name – finding himself convinced of her guilt, might take it upon himself to stop her by taking *her* life. In any case, I believe that by tomorrow evening, we'll be traveling to Scunthorpe – if you can get away."

I simply nodded, and at that moment, the doorbell rang.

"Ah," said Holmes, "that is my caller. If you will excuse me now, Watson, I'll see you back here in the morning."

Then he stepped over to the door, threw it open, and called down, "Come on up, Henry."

I stepped aside as Dr. Henry Verner, a long-time acquaintance of Holmes's, walked into the room. [8] He and I had met years before, but I knew little about him, having found him rather surly and stand-offish. We nodded to one another, and I wondered what business he and Holmes had to discuss as I went downstairs and out into Baker Street.

But I didn't worry about it for very long. I found that I was walking along toward my Kensington home in Vicarage Gate with a spring in my step that had been missing for quite some time. I needed to pack, uncertain as to how long we would be in Scunthorpe. I knew that it was likely to be colder up there than in London, and I considered which clothing to bring. I would have time to do some research about the local countryside, and to clean my service revolver, which I had long-ago learned never to leave home without.

And with any luck, I'd be leaving home quite a bit more often, for reasons of much greater interest than those of recent months.

NOTES:

1. While Holmes didn't perfect the lifting of fingerprints from dead bodies by the use of petro-chemical fumes, Arthur Bohanan, a famed Knoxville, TN criminologist and friend of my late father, did discover the process.
2.. For more about Holmes and Watson's initial encounter with Edwin Booth in 1881, see Christopher Leppek's brilliant *The Surrogate Assassin* (1998).
3. Edwina Booth Grossman's book about her father, *Edwin Booth: Recollections by His Daughter, Edwina Booth Grossman, and Letters to Her and to His Friends*, was published in late 1894.
4. For more about a later adventure at the Princess's Theatre, and how Holmes returned there, see "The Subversive Drama" in *The Singular Papers of Solar Pons.*
5. Holmes's travels during The Great Hiatus took him around the world, and to New York for much of Spring 1893. My own Holmes Chronology documents more than a dozen narratives of Holmes's New York adventures during this period. He was specifically in New York on June 7th, 1893, the date of Edwin Booth's death, during *The Case of the Etruscan Treasure* (as recounted by Robert Newman, 1983) and *Sherlock Holmes in New York: The Adventure of the New York Ripper* (revealed by Philip J. Carraher, 2012), although attending Booth's funeral a few days later isn't specifically mentioned in either volume.
6. More about Holmes's time as actor *William Escott* and his tour of America with the Sasanoff Company in 1879 and 1880 can be found in William S. Baring-Gould's brilliant biography, *Sherlock Holmes of Baker Street*, Chapter 5 (1962).
7. While a sequel to The Scottish Play entitled *Dunsinane* was first performed in 2010, there has not yet – to my knowledge – been a story examining the *Wyrd* Sisters. However, some of the concept of *Open, Locks, Whoever Knocks!* by Telford Nevill Corby (and Diana Bonfardin) seems to have anticipated the 1945 stage play *Dark of the Moon*, in which a supernatural Appalachian witch boy, John, falls in love with a human girl, Barbara Allen. As one would expect, the relationship is tragically doomed, and at the end, John the Witch Boy returns to live as a spirit upon the mountain. The play has been immensely popular since its premiere, and I was fortunate – in my stage debut – to play Barbara Allen's unfortunate bullying suitor, Marvin Hudgens, during my freshman year in college. (Like Holmes, I had to pretend to be thrown backwards by magic, blindly leaping without looking and landing on my back, night after night, hoping that I wouldn't break my head.)
8. Dr. Henry Verner: Very little is told to us about Dr. Verner in the Canon. In "The Norwood Builder", it states:

> *At the time of which I speak, Holmes had been back for some months, and I at his request had sold my practice and returned to share the old quarters in Baker Street. A young doctor, named Verner, had*

purchased my small Kensington practice, and given with astonishingly little demur the highest price that I ventured to ask– an incident which only explained itself some years later, when I found that Verner was a distant relation of Holmes, and that it was my friend who had really found the money.

In a series of tales brought to the public by Sam Siciliano, it's been established that Dr. Verner is actually Dr. Henry Vernier. In these various adventures, narrated by Vernier, Holmes's cousin, we see the Great Detective from a different perspective. Sadly, Vernier is a rather petty and unlikeable fellow, constantly and irrationally jealous of Watson, and inaccurately portraying himself as Holmes's best friend. But aside from Vernier himself, the adventures are quite good.

I've determined that Dr. Henry Vernier is actually the young Watson-like fellow that accompanies Holmes in the filmed and novelized adventure *Young Sherlock Holmes* (1985). Since Holmes and Watson first met on January 1st, 1881, the events of *Young Sherlock Holmes*, set in December 1870, cannot also be their first meeting, and if Holmes didn't meet Watson in 1870, who did he meet? *Dr. Henry Vernier*, of course.

It wouldn't have been unusual in those days, especially considering Holmes's many boyhood travels, if the two cousins hadn't previously encountered one another. When the script and associated novel for *Young Sherlock Holmes* were written from Vernier's old notes and diaries, the filmmakers correctly perceived that there would be less commercial interest in a Holmes and *Vernier* film as compared to a Holmes and *Watson* film, so Vernier's name was changed. If Vernier was still alive when the film was made, this would no doubt be yet another one of his unfounded grievances against Watson – even if this, like the others, wasn't Watson's fault.

Much more about Dr. Verner being identified as Dr. Henry Vernier, and also his participation in *Young Sherlock Holmes*, can be found in my essay, "Actually, That Wasn't Watson: Some Notes Eventually Circling In Upon the Major Obfuscation in '*Young Sherlock Holmes*'", which originally appeared in *The Watsonian*, Fall 2016, Vol.4, No. II, and then in a slightly different form as an entry in my online blog, *A Seventeen Step Program*:

https://17stepprogram.blogspot.com/2017/03/actually-that-wasnt-watson-some-notes.html

A Travel-Worn and Battered Tin Dispatch Box

The cold wind rattled one of the two tall windows overlooking Baker Street. Glancing that way from where I stood at my desk while retrieving some notes, I paused in my task, took a moment to fold a piece of waste paper, walk over, and wedge it between the window and the frame – silencing the distraction, if only for a little while.

Outside, what little sunlight that we'd seen on that bleak autumn day was fading, and the dark shapes hurrying along the pavement beneath the window were huddled as they passed in each direction – some on the way to evening shelter, and others upon errands that would allow for no rest this night. I wondered how many were doing good work, and which others were about on bad business. I liked to think that the majority of them, those shadowed and anonymous figures scurrying below me, faces invisible as their heads were turned down to hide from the wind and cold, tended toward the former, but I had long-ago learned what Sherlock Holmes had been at pains to teach me – about things I might never have suspected otherwise.

"Do you remember," I asked without looking around at him, "when you once told me that life is infinitely stranger than anything which the mind of man could invent?"

Holmes, who had spent the day updating his commonplace books with stacks of butchered newspapers, shears, and a glue pot, grunted something to acknowledge that I'd spoken.

"You said something along the lines of being unable to truly conceive what's going on out there," I continued. "Things that might seem so unusual to us, but to the people passing back and forth, they are mere commonplaces of existence."

I turned then to see that Holmes had paused in his self-imposed labor, his gaze distant as he recalled the conversation. I suspected that, if he truly turned his mind to it, he could tell what specific day it had taken place, and what I'd been wearing.

"I said something along the lines of us flying out of the window and removing the roofs, looking in at all the odd and connected things going on all around us, year after year and generation after generation. Coincidences and connections and accidental assistances and cross-purposes – chains of events that sometimes stretch for decades before culminating in the most curious and *outrè* results."

"You said it would make all fiction stale."

He nodded. "In the years since we had that conversation, have you seen anything to contradict the thought?"

"Not at all. In fact, if I was still somewhat surprised at the notion then – having known you for the better part of a decade when you said it – I've certainly seen and experienced enough by now to recognize that you were correct in every sense."

I returned to my desk, retrieved another bundle of papers, and then settled back in my chair by the fire, my old tin dispatch box open at my feet. It wasn't so different than the tin box that Holmes kept underneath his bed, and it was put to the same purpose: Holding records of past cases.

I recalled those first days of early January 1881, when Holmes and I had taken possession of these comfortable but humble Baker Street rooms. I had relocated on the evening of the very day when we first inspected the place, moving from a small private hotel in the Strand and transporting what little I owned in a single hansom cab. I had returned to London the previous November, a wretched shell of the man who had departed so confidently just a few years before. I had abandoned the British shores with neither kith nor kin left in my homeland, and quite frankly I hadn't expected to return – at least not for many years, if not decades. The Army life for me – or so I thought.

But my road took a sharp and nearly fatal turn at Maiwand. I would have died there but for my orderly, Murray, who threw me across the pack-horse carrying our medical supplies, already loaded for the retreat, and transported me to safety. I awoke in the Peshawar base hospital, destroyed, limp with terrible pain. For a few terrible moments, that was the limit of my awareness. I somehow lurched to my feet, unable to comprehend where I was or how I'd arrived there. If pressed, I could not have even stated my name, so great was my confusion. Then, as the staff rushed to lay me back down, I saw, pushed under the foot of my cot, my old tin dispatch box. Painted across it were the words *John H. Watson, M.D. Late Indian Army.* It had already been tied to the pack-horse when Murray slung me across and fled to relative safety. Somehow, he had contrived to see that it stayed with me at the hospital. Seeing that small piece of my old life was enough to calm me.

I'm not sure why Murray went to the effort. When we'd prepared for the retreat, the box was quickly emptied of all the useless detritus I'd accumulated since my arrival in Bombay some months before – meaningless souvenirs collected across India and Afghanistan – and filled with necessary medical supplies. Now, lying before my cot, it was empty, the supplies long-since having been put to good use elsewhere.

Even as I started to recover, I was soon laid low once again with that deadly scourge, enteric fever, and I was told afterwards that I came as close to death then as I have at any other point in my life. In my feverish dreams, my thoughts returned again and again to that tin dispatch box – as if it were an anchor to pin me to that spot where my body fought so that my soul couldn't not entirely drift away, or a rock to which I clung while the boiling waves tried to rip me from my perch.

One's mind is a funny thing. I have no sense whether the times I leaned up to check and see if the box was still there actually occurred, or if that was all part of the tangled pattern of dreams which assailed me. Those occasions certainly seemed real enough – but then so did the bedside visits from my revered grandfather, who had passed away before I ever joined the army. He stood silently, offering no encouragement or instruction – Nothing at all. I couldn't tell if he meant for me to stay or go on.

When I recovered enough, I was returned to England, setting foot on the Portsmouth dock in November. I had very little with me – the clothes on my back, and a spare set tucked into the dispatch box. And my journals – those records that I'd begun to make during my recovery. I have always been a writer, from my youngest age, and I found that when I could not sleep – or would not, to avoid the terrible nightmares that stalked me in that horrific place of dreams, *la petite mort* – I would write. Daily sketches, or memories of my travels across the frontier, or of little incidents that I'd seen. Writing came easily, and it eased my mind so that eventually, sleep was not always the enemy.

I'd moved into our Baker Street rooms on the second night of January, and Holmes brought 'round his belongings from Montague Street the next morning – and it took far more drayage for him than a simple single hansom cab. We spent several days arranging our possessions to their best display, but in truth, I had very little to present. Holmes, of course, noticed immediately, and considering that we were essentially strangers then, it's a wonder he commented at all.

But he did.

"That is a singularly sad and abused piece of kit," he said, nodding toward the dispatch box – by way of starting a conversation, I think. I found myself defensive.

"It's been with me since – "

I stopped, not wanting to explain, even a little. I didn't know this proud young man, seeming so callow and untested when compared to what I had just been through. Though less than two years older than him, I felt that I'd lived more than a lifetime in the last half-year, and now I was an old and feeble man who wanted nothing better, having found a warm and quite place, than to hide and be left alone. Upon our very first meeting, Holmes had somehow rather rudely read my past as easily as if I'd handed him a sheet with the important highlights of my life recorded upon it. Why be forced into sharing anything further?

If nothing else, he was aware that he'd crossed some line and dropped the subject. And I moved my dispatch upstairs, to my own room.

There it remained for a long time. It was something of an object of simple veneration to me, and at first it stood empty, doing nothing but taking up a spot on the floor where it would regularly catch my gaze. Then, I had an idea. I would use it to store items that were precious to me.

I had very little that would meet such a qualification. A few family documents and photographs. Some papers that marked events or achievements in my life that, by someone's reckoning, might be considered important. (I did not choose to give very much honor to my Afghanistan Medal. It was tossed into a desk drawer, subject to my ambivalence when, after several months of recovery, the Army chose not to continue the association that I had fully expected. I would not, I had been informed, be returning to military service after all. Rather, I was left to reside in Baker Street and continue my convalescence and try to decide what I would do with the rest of my life, as my initial plan was burst asunder.)

What finally went into the tin dispatch box was what mattered to me most – *my writings*. For those recordings of life as I saw it felt to me like my most valuable possessions. I had poured my time and thought into each document, and it was only natural that, as more and more of my writing began to be filled with records of Holmes's cases, the box became, by default, primarily dedicated to that purpose.

After an incident or two where we learned that our lodgings weren't as secure as we'd believed, and attempts were made to get at our papers, I came to the conclusion that I would need to relocate my dispatch box to a more secure site. No better place, I thought, than Cox and Company of Charing Cross, a fine institution in general, with that specific branch (at No. 16) long-devoted to addressing the needs of soldiers.

But I had recently retrieved the box, as I regularly did, to add further records to the tightly packed notebooks and tied bundles already contained therein. Having deposited what I needed to, along with sorting and reminiscing about what was already there, I closed the lid, turned the key, and sat back with a sigh.

"It's filling up," Holmes said quietly, a smile in his tone.

I nodded. "Still plenty of room, though," I countered. "If I continue to pack it carefully – it will hold many more narratives of your investigations." I shifted in my seat. "And what about your tin box?" I asked. "How does it fare?"

He glued another clipping into a commonplace book. "There is still room as well. I'm not quite ready to start sorting it and writing my *Whole Art of Detection*. It continues to reside under my bed. I feel that its more esoteric and unexplained contents – as compared to your notes and narratives which specifically describe certain people and events with scalpel-like precision, despite the occasional changed name or place or date – make it somewhat less dangerous if intruded upon."

"Quite. I expect that, should someone once again burgle these rooms, and locate and open the box, they would simply cast aside much of what resides there in frustration. After all, without the stories associated the peg and the ball of string and the rusty discs, or the oversized dried rat paw, those items are meaningless."

"Exactly." He seemed then to be finished, closing the fat and misshapen book before setting it aside and putting the lid on his glue pot. He glanced at the window, and then sniffed.

"From the lack of appetizing aromas drifting up from the kitchen, I suspect that Mrs. Hudson will be serving what remains of the shepherd's pie. I'm rather flush after Colonel Blevins sent a check for that sordid business in Little Venice. What do you say to dinner at Simpson's?"

I leaned forward in my chair, preparatory to standing as my way of answering the question. It was then that doorbell rang, and in a moment, Mrs. Hudson showed in a young lady in her early twenties. *A governess*, I thought. *Not from London. Near-sighted. Recently engaged.* Holmes had taught me well, but I was still the pupil. I would see if his questioning confirmed my initial assumptions.

The young lady sat in the basket chair and began to tell her story, holding out an ancient brass key and a scooping of ash that was found after the most recent visitation of the ghostly founder of the estate where she had been employed for the past quarter. "He's been dead these four-hundred years," she breathlessly explained, "and yet, he appears at my door every night – since I first found the key. He never speaks, but seems to be begging for my help."

Holmes looked at the ash with great interest, pleased to see something new – a surprise that he had not yet encountered or categorized.

My eyes drifted down to the dispatch box beside my chair. The young lady had ignored it – it was just more of the overall clutter that filled the sitting room. It all must be overwhelming to a new visitor – so much of it unique that nothing stood out.

I considered Holmes to be my oldest friend – "*a brother in bond if not in blood*" as we had once been told – but I realized that perhaps the box was perhaps an older friend still. It had been beside me when I set off upon my military career – first to Netley for training, and then sailing to India. Like me, it had been rescued from Maiwand and then sent home. I was no longer an army surgeon, and it was no longer meant for the military. But both of us had found new purposes, and ways that we could serve. That travel-worn tin dispatch box, my old and faithful friend, continued to be the repository of nearly all my most treasured possessions. As I'd told Holmes, the battered box still had room – quite a bit – to hold many more adventures before filling up.

And I felt the same way about myself . . . .

About the Author

David Marcum plays *The Game* with deadly seriousness. He first discovered Sherlock Holmes in 1975 at the age of ten, and since that time, he has collected, read, and chronologicized literally thousands of traditional Holmes pastiches in the form of novels, short stories, radio and television episodes, movies and scripts, comics, fan-fiction, and unpublished manuscripts. He is the author of over 140 Sherlockian pastiches, some published in anthologies and magazines such as *The Best Mystery Stories of the Year 2021* and *The Strand*, and others collected in his own books, *The Papers of Sherlock Holmes*, *Sherlock Holmes and A Quantity of Debt*, *Sherlock Holmes – Tangled Skeins*, *Sherlock Holmes and The Eye of Heka*, and *The Collected Papers of Sherlock Holmes* – now eight volumes and more to come.

He has won back-to-back first place fiction awards from *The Arthur Conan Doyle Society* (2023 and 2024) and the Nero Wolfe *Wolfe Pack*. He has edited over 1,200 Holmes adventures and over 100 books, including dozens of traditional Sherlockian anthologies, such as *The MX Book of New Sherlock Holmes Stories*, which he created in 2015 to promote traditional Canonical Holmes. The collection ended in 2025 after ten years at 52 volumes and over 1,000 stories from over 200 worldwide contributors. Royalties from the series has raised (so far) over $165,000 for the Undershaw school for special needs children, located at one of Sir Arthur Conan Doyle's former homes.

He was responsible for bringing back August Derleth's Solar Pons for a new generation with his collections of new authorized Pons stories, *The Papers of Solar Pons*, *The Further Papers of Solar Pons*, and *The Singular Papers of Solar Pons*. Pons's return was further assisted by his editing of the reissued authorized versions of the original Pons books, and then several volumes of new Pons adventures. He has done the same for the adventures of Dr. Thorndyke and Max Carrados, and has plans for similar projects in the future.

He has contributed numerous essays to various publications, and is a member of a number of Sherlockian groups and Scions, as well as *The Mystery Writers of America*. His irregular Sherlockian blog, *A Seventeen Step Program*, addresses various topics related to his favorite book friends (as his son used to call them when he was small), and can be found at *http://17stepprogram.blogspot.com/*

He is a licensed Civil Engineer, living in Tennessee with his wife and son. Since the age of nineteen, he has worn a deerstalker as his regular-and-only hat. In 2013, he and his deerstalker were finally able make his first trip-of-a-lifetime Holmes Pilgrimage to England, with return Pilgrimages in 2015, 2016, 2024, and 2025, where you may have spotted him. Another is planned in the future. If you ever run into him and his deerstalker out and about, feel free to say hello!

Also by David Marcum
from MX Publishing

Traditional Canonical Holmes Adventures

Hardcover, Paperback, E-editions, and Audio

The Papers of Sherlock Holmes

"The Papers of Sherlock Holmes *by David Marcum contains nine intriguing mysteries . . . very much in the classic tradition . . . He writes well, too."* – Roger Johnson, Editor, *The Sherlock Holmes Journal,* The Sherlock Holmes Society of London

"Marcum offers nine clever pastiches."
– Steven Rothman, Editor, *The Baker Street Journal*

Sherlock Holmes and A Quantity of Debt

"This is a welcome addendum to Sherlock lore that respectfully fleshes out Doyle's legendary crime-solving couple in the context of new escapades . . . ." – Peter Roche, Examiner.com

"David Marcum is known to Sherlockians as the author of two short story collections . . . In Sherlock Holmes and A Quantity of Debt, *he demonstrates mastery of the longer form as well."*
– Dan Andriacco, Sherlockian and Author of the Cody and McCabe Series

Sherlock Holmes – Tangled Skeins

(Included in Randall Stock's, 2015 Top Five Sherlock Holmes Books – Fiction)

"Marcum's collection will appeal to those who like the traditional elements of the Holmes tales."– Randall Stock, BSI

"There are good pastiche writers, there are great ones, and then there is David Marcum who ranks among the very best . . . I cannot recommend this book enough."
– Derrick Belanger, Author and Publisher of Belanger Books

Also by David Marcum
from MX Publishing

Traditional Canonical Holmes Adventures

Sherlock Holmes and The Eye of Heka

"Marcum could be today's greatest Sherlockian writer, and Conan Doyle himself would be proud of this story."
– Lee Child - New York Times *Bestselling Author*

"David Marcum is the reigning monarch of all things Sherlockian, and his latest long-form work, Sherlock Holmes and The eye of Heka, *showcases his utter mastery of Watson's narrative voice, while at the same time entertains and enthralls with his spot on descriptions of the characters and themes which animate the world of the Great Detective himself. No mere pastiche,* The Eye of Heka *is a robust and creative novel in its own right, not to be missed!"*
– John Lescroart - New York Times Bestselling Author

"Marcum assuredly handles multiple intriguing plots while plausibly adding emotional depth to Dr. Watson . . . Marcum expertly balances deduction and action as he more than meets the challenge of recreating the spirit and tone of Conan Doyle's originals. Sherlockians will clamor for a sequel"
– Publishers Weekly Starred Review

Also by David Marcum
from MX Publishing

Traditional Canonical Holmes Adventures

The Collected Papers of Sherlock Holmes

Volume I: Tales
Volume II: Records
Volume III: Accounts
Volume IV: Narratives
Volume V: Chronicles
Volume VI: Muniments
Volume VII: Annals
Volume VIII: Documents

"Among the best I must number David Marcum, who, by this point has written more Holmes stories than Doyle himself. Characterized by unflagging imagination and ceaseless ingenuity, along with felicitous prose, these tales continue to provide what we all crave: more Sherlock."
– Nicholas Meyer - *New York Times* Bestselling Author

Also by David Marcum
from Belanger Books

The Papers of Solar Pons
The Further Papers of Solar Pons
The Singular Papers of Solar Pons

"*As a long-time admirer of the Praed Street sleuth,*
I know no one better to chronicle his further exploits."
– Roger Johnson, Editor, *The Sherlock Holmes Journal* (Summer 2018),
The Sherlock Holmes Society of London

The MX Book of New Sherlock Holmes Stories

Edited by David Marcum
(MX Publishing, 2015-2025)

"*This is the finest volume of Sherlockian fiction I have ever read, and I have read, literally, thousands.*" – Philip K. Jones

"*Beyond Impressive . . . This is a splendid venture for a great cause!*"
– Roger Johnson, Editor, *The Sherlock Holmes Journal*,
The Sherlock Holmes Society of London

Part I: 1881-1889; Part II: 1890-1895; Part III: 1896-1929

Part IV: 2016 Annual

Part V: Christmas Adventures

Part VI: 2017 Annual

Eliminate the Impossible
Part VII: (1880-1891); Part VIII: (1892-1905)

2018 Annual
Part IX: (1879-1895); Part X: (1896-1916)

Some Untold Cases
Part XI: (1880-1891); Part XII: (1894-1902)

2019 Annual
Part XIII: (1881-1890); Part XIV: (1891-1897); Part XV: (1898-1917)

Whatever Remains . . . Must be the Truth
Part XVI: (1881-1890); Part XVII: (1891-1898); Part XVIII: (1898-1925)

2020 Annual
Part XIX: (1882-1890); Part XX: (1891-1897); Part XXI: (1898-1923).

Some More Untold Cases
Part XXII: (1877-1887); Part XXIII: (1888-1894); Part XXIV: (1895-1903)

2021 Annual
Part XXV: (1881-1888); Part XXVI: (1889-1897); Part XXVII: (1898-1928)

More Christmas Adventures
Part XXVIII: (1869-1888); Part XXIX: (1889-1896); Part XXX: (1897-1928)

2022 Annual
Part XXXI: (1875-1887); Part XXXII: (1888-1895); Part XXXIII: (1896-1919)

"However Improbable . . . ."
Part XXXIV: (1878-1888); Part XXXV: (1889-1896); Part XXXVI: (1897-1919)

2023 Annual
Parts XXXVII (1875-1889), XXXVIII (1889-1896), and *XXXIX (1897-1923)*

Further Untold Cases
Part XL: (1879-1886), Part XLI: (1887-1892) and *Part XLII: (1894-1922)*

2024 Annual
Parts XLIII (1874-1888), XLIV (1889-1897), and *XLV (1898-1917)*

Occupants of the Canonical Realm
Parts XLVI (1861-1889), XLVII (1890-1898), and *XLVIII (1899-1924)*

The True Mr. Holmes: England's Greatest Hero
Parts XLIX (1880-1888), L (1889--18XX96), LI (1897-1901), and LII (1902-1923)

The MX Book of New Sherlock Holmes Stories

Edited by David Marcum

(MX Publishing, 2015-2025)

Publishers Weekly says:

Part VI: *The traditional pastiche is alive and well . . . .*

Part VII: *Sherlockians eager for faithful-to-the-canon plots and characters will be delighted.*

Part VIII: *The imagination of the contributors in coming up with variations on the volume's theme is matched by their ingenious resolutions.*

Part IX: *The 18 stories . . . will satisfy fans of Conan Doyle's originals. Sherlockians will rejoice that more volumes are on the way.*

Part X: *. . . new Sherlock Holmes adventures of consistently high quality.*

Part XI: *. . . an essential volume for Sherlock Holmes fans.*

Part XII: *. . . continues to amaze with the number of high-quality pastiches.*

Part XIII: *. . . Amazingly, Marcum has found 22 superb pastiches . . . his is more catnip for fans of stories faithful to Conan Doyle's original*

Part XIV: *. . . this standout anthology of 21 short stories written in the spirit of Conan Doyle's originals.*

Part XV: *Stories pitting Sherlock Holmes against seemingly supernatural phenomena highlight Marcum's 15th anthology of superior short pastiches.*

Part XVI: *Marcum has once again done fans of Conan Doyle's originals a service.*

Part XVII: *This is yet another impressive array of new but traditional Holmes stories.*

Part XVIII: *Sherlockians will again be grateful to Marcum and MX for high-quality new Holmes tales.*

Part XIX: *Inventive plots and intriguing explorations of aspects of Dr. Watson's life and beliefs lift the 24 pastiches in Marcum's impressive 19th Sherlock Holmes anthology*

Part XX: *Marcum's reserve of high-quality new Holmes exploits seems endless.*

Part XXI: *This is another must-have for Sherlockians.*

Part XXII: *Marcum's superlative 22nd Sherlock Holmes pastiche anthology features 21 short stories that successfully emulate the spirit of Conan Doyle's originals while expanding on the canon's tantalizing references to mysteries Dr. Watson never got around to chronicling.*

Part XXIII: *Marcum's well of talented authors able to mimic the feel of The Canon seems bottomless.*

Part XXIV: *Marcum's expertise at selecting high-quality pastiches remains impressive.*

Part XXVIII: *All entries adhere to the spirit, language, and characterizations of Conan Doyle's originals, evincing the deep pool of talent Marcum has access to. Against the odds, this series remains strong, hundreds of stories in.*

Part XXXI: *. . . yet another stellar anthology of 21 short pastiches that effectively mimic the originals . . . Marcum's diligent searches for high-quality stories has again paid off for Sherlockians.*

Part XXXIV: *Mind-bending puzzles are the highlight of Marcum's fully satisfying 34th anthology, which again demonstrates that multiple authors are capable of giving Sherlock Holmes and Watson innovative mysteries to tackle while staying in character. Marcum's inventory of canonical pastiches shows no signs of being exhausted any time soon.*

The MX Book of New Sherlock Holmes Stories
Part I: 1881 – 1889
Edited by David Marcum

An Investees' Anthology

Edited by David Marcum

(MX Publishing, 2022)

Selected Contributions to

The MX Book of New Sherlock Holmes Stories

by Members of

The Baker Street Irregulars

Edited by David Marcum
from MX Publishing

Imagination Theatre's Sherlock Holmes

The Further Adventures of Sherlock Holmes:
The Complete Jim French Imagination Theatre Scripts

Edited by David Marcum
from Belanger Books

Holmes Away From Home:
Adventures from The Great Hiatus
Volumes I and II

Sherlock Holmes:
Adventures Beyond the Canon
Volumes I, II, and III

Edited by David Marcum
from Belanger Books

Sherlock Holmes: Before Baker Street

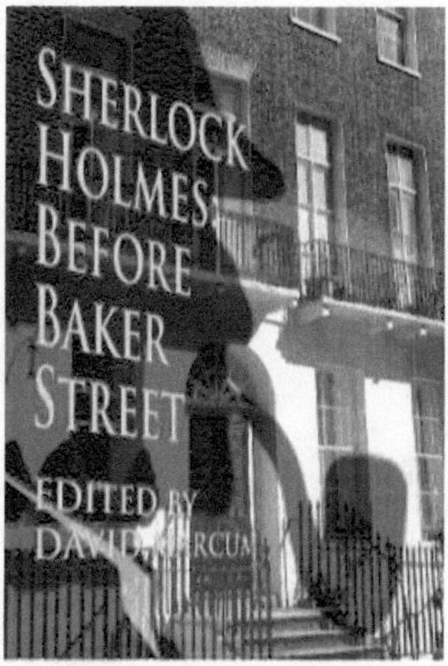

Sherlock Holmes and Doctor Watson:
The Early Adventures
Volumes I, II, and III

Edited by David Marcum
from Belanger Books

**After the East Wind Blows:
WWI and Roaring Twenties Adventures
of Sherlock Holmes
Volumes I, II, and III**

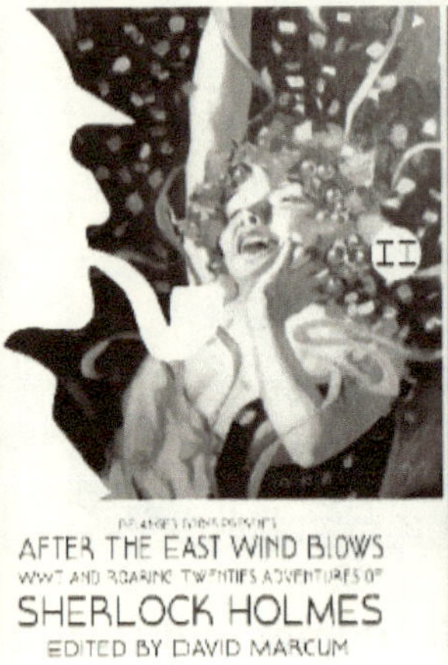

**The Nefarious Villains
of Sherlock Holmes
Volumes I and II**

Edited by David Marcum
from Belanger Books

The Detective and the Clergyman
The Adventures of Sherlock Holmes and Father Brown

Edited by David Marcum
from Belanger Books

The Complete Solar Pons
by August Derleth

8-volume Paperback Edition

4-volume Hardcover Edition

Edited by David Marcum
from Belanger Books

The New Adventures of Solar Pons

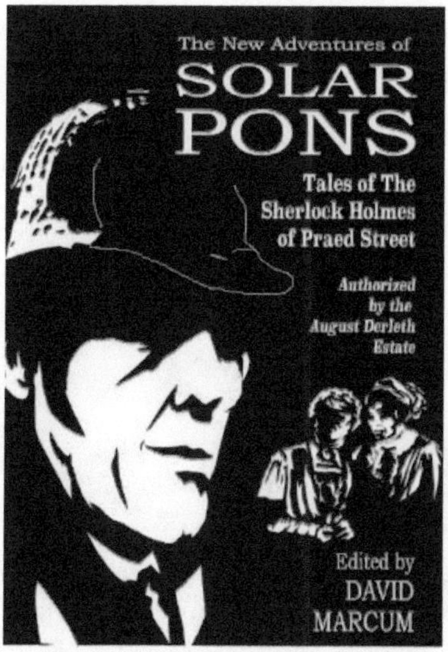

The Meeting of the Minds: The Cases of Sherlock Holmes and Solar Pons

Edited by David Marcum
from Belanger Books

The American Adventures of Solar Pons

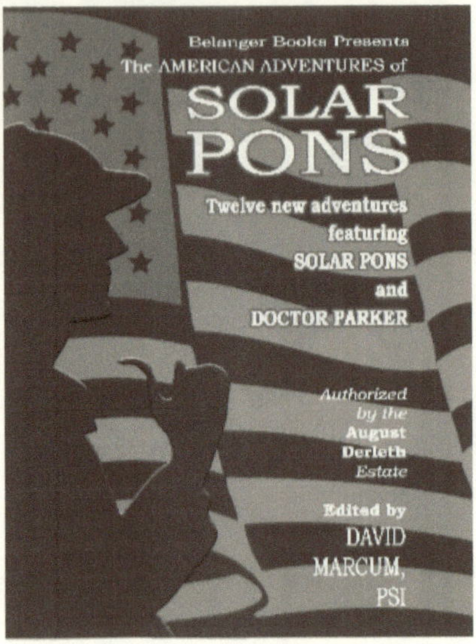

Edited by David Marcum
from MX Publishing

Sherlock Holmes in Montague Street
by Arthur Morrison
Sherlock Holmes's Early Investigations
Originally published as Martin Hewitt Adventures

Reimagined, Edited, Holmes-ed, and with Original Material
by David Marcum

Separate Paperback Editions

Combined Hardcover Edition

"It's been suggested that Hewitt was the young Mycroft Holmes,
but David Marcum has a more plausible and attractive theory
– that he was Sherlock, early in his career as an investigator
. . . these are remarkably convincing in their new guise."
– Roger Johnson, Editor, *The Sherlock Holmes Journal,*
The Sherlock Holmes Society of London

Edited by David Marcum
from MX Publishing

The Complete Dr. Thorndyke
by R. Austin Freeman
Volumes I-IX

Edited by David Marcum
from MX Publishing

The Complete Max Carrados
by Ernest Bramah
Volumes I-III
Edited by David Marcum
from MX Publishing

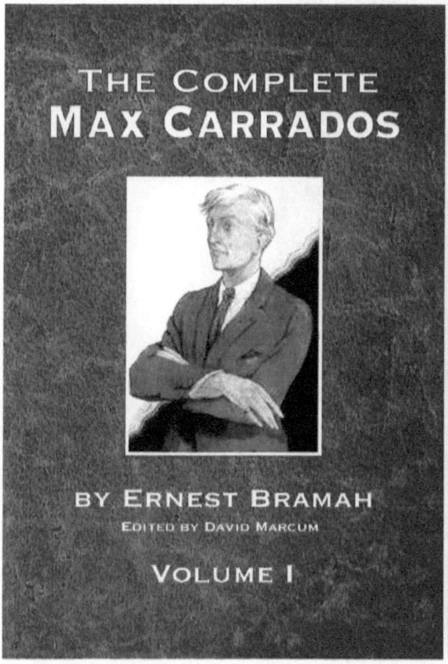

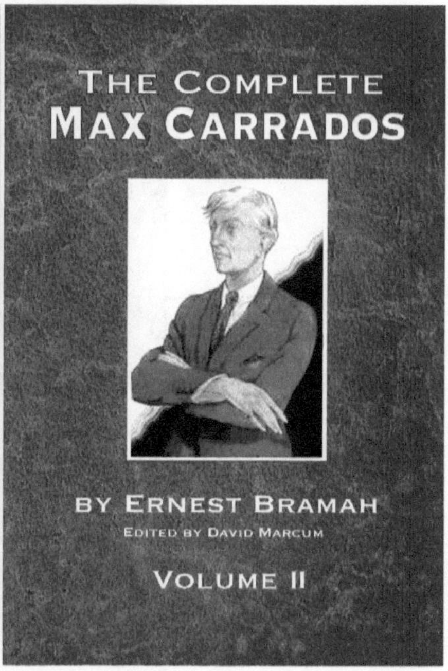

Edited by David Marcum
from MX Publishing

A Proof Reader's Adventures of Sherlock Holmes
by Nick Dunn-Meynell

The Rediscovered Annals of Sherlock Holmes
Written by Terry Golledge
Curated by Niel Golledge

Edited by David Marcum
from MX Publishing

Tales of Light, Shadow, and Darkness
by Tracy J. Revels

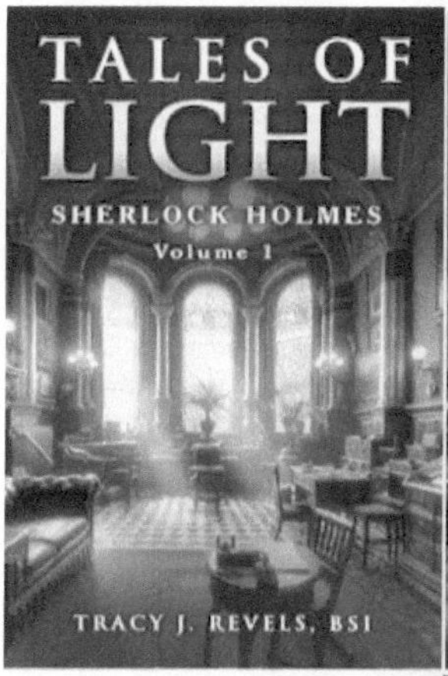

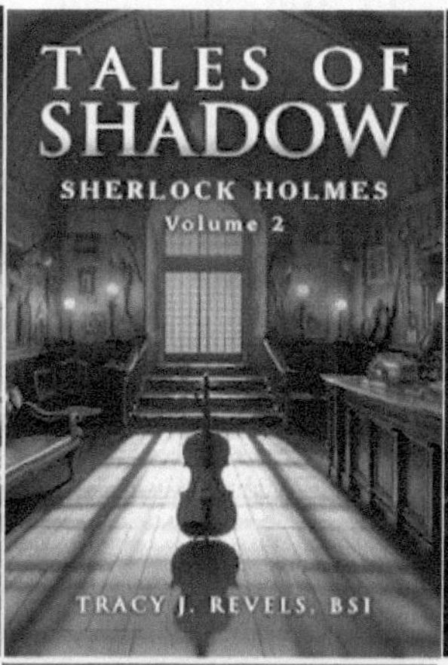

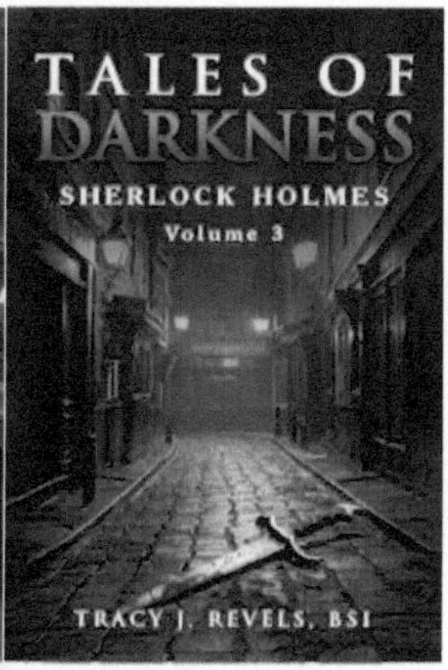

Edited by David Marcum,
Derrick Belanger, and Sonia Fetherston
from Belanger Books

Sherlock Holmes and the Scotland Yarders
by Marcia Wilson

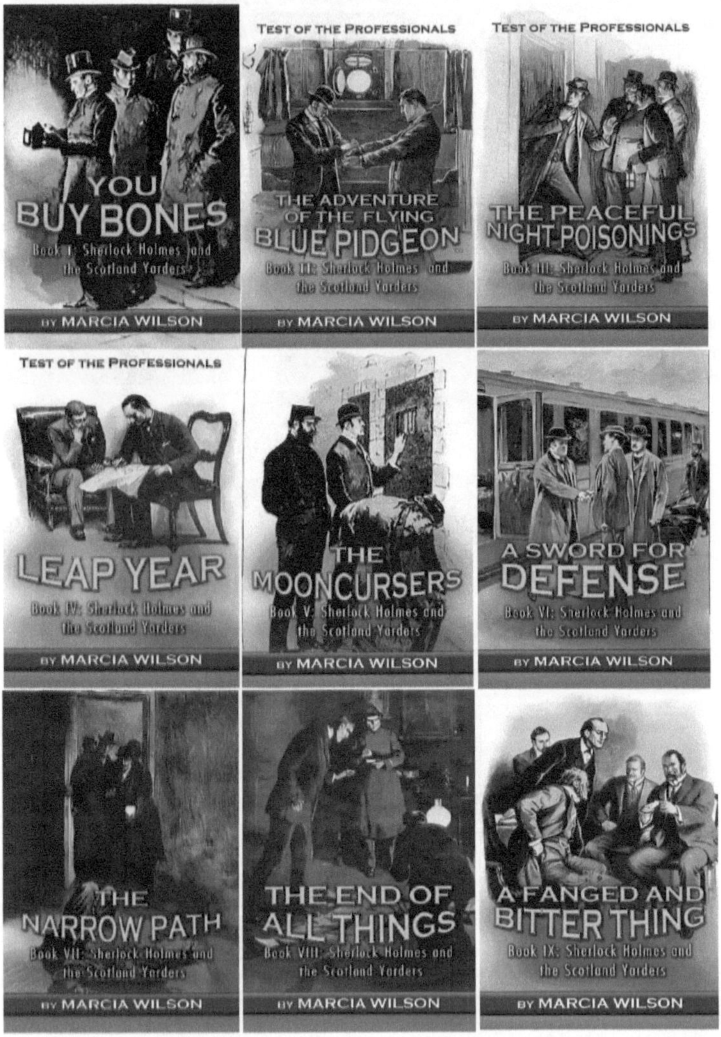

MX Publishing

MX Publishing is the world's largest specialist Sherlock Holmes publisher, with over six-hundred titles and over two-hundred authors creating the latest in Sherlock Holmes fiction and non-fiction

The catalogue includes several award winning books, and over four-hundred-and-fifty have been converted into audio.

MX Publishing also has one of the largest communities of Holmes fans on Facebook, with regular contributions from dozens of authors.

www.mxpublishing.com

@mxpublishing on Facebook, Twitter, and Instagram

www.ingramcontent.com/pod-product-compliance
Lightning Source LLC
Chambersburg PA
CBHW020925020726
47495CB00002B/353